SERVANT OF THE DEAD

Ashland Brown

ASHLAND BROWN

Vista
publishing, Inc.

Edited by Carolyn Zagury

Cover design by Thomas Taylor of Thomcatt Graphics

Vista Publishing, Inc.
473 Broadway
Long Branch, NJ 07740
(908) 229-6500

This publication is designed for the reading pleasure of the general public. All characters, places and situations are fictional and are in no way intended to depict actual people, places or situations.

Printed and bound in the United States of America

First Edition

ISBN: 1-880254-40-9

Library of Congress Catalog Card Number: 96-61493

U.S.A. Price $15.95
Canada Price $19.95

DEDICATION

To my father.

MEET THE AUTHOR

Dr. Ashland Brown lives and practices in a small town in the South. He is a member of several professional organizations and the Mensa Society.

Dr. Brown's spare time is spent between writing his second novel and helping his son with his little league pitching.

DIENER

Diener (dee'nər) n. 1. manservant, footman, lackey. 2. (U.S. colloquial) the person responsible for the care and upkeep of cadavers at a medical school, a caretaker for the dead. [‹ German].

Chapter One

On the night of December 22nd, shortly before he was murdered, Sylvester Derricks, a.k.a. The Jamaican, congratulated himself on his criminal success. In the three years since Derricks had seized control of the street gangs in Chicago's Jamaican community, he had shaped the various, loosely knit groups into one cohesive force that was now on the verge of competing head-to-head with the larger, established gangs. His success was based on a combination of two simple principles. One was the time-honored American tradition of supplying the consumer with the best product at the lowest cost; the marijuana The Jamaican poured onto the streets of South Chicago, straight from the mountains of his homeland, had the highest potency at a price that was unbeatable. The other principle was also an American custom; he simply eliminated anyone that stood in his way.

But now his growing trade was faced with serious problems. The Jamaican had used the safety of his insular neighborhood as a refuge while expanding his influence into the adjacent neighborhoods, border areas that had traditionally been considered the turf of other gangs. One of these, the EL AZIWA, was one of the city's largest, strongest, and best organized gangs. The resulting conflict between the two had seen bloodshed that threatened to escalate far beyond the usual level of gang warfare.

Derricks, who was known as The Jamaican by both the gang-crimes division of the police department as well as the people on the street, knew his position was not yet powerful enough to go head to head with the EL AZIWA. The extreme violence that was the trademark of his Jamaican posses would be no match against the sheer numbers that the EL AZIWA could throw against him if full scale war erupted. Derricks desperately needed more time to build the cash, muscle, and guns that would be required if his plans for expansion were to succeed, so he readily agreed when the first hints came through neutral channels that the head of the EL AZIWA requested a meeting in order to discuss a truce. He had tested his enemies and now knew their weaknesses, knew where to strike, and how to craft the fatal blow. All he needed was a little time.

Negotiations were held in a private room in the back of a small bar in the center of Little Jamaica. Derricks would not venture outside the safety of his territory. Jefferson Pack, leader of the EL AZIWA, would not agree to personally meet in the enemy's backyard; he had sent a top subordinate, a tall African with corn-rowed hair who wore three small gold crosses dangling from his left ear. The Jamaican was flanked by two of his top men--"Familyman" Marvins and Rickey Smithey. The EL AZIWA representative was called Stone. He came to the meeting alone. Dressed in monochrome, Stone wore a black turtleneck sweater underneath a black leather vest that matched his leather boots. The smell of sweat and musk cologne filled the room when he removed his overcoat to allow the frisk, his eyes impassive as he was searched for weapons. The Jamaican gestured to the opposite side of the narrow table where he sat. Stone pulled the chair back and took his seat.

The meeting went well for The Jamaican. After some initial posturing, the delegate from EL AZIWA had presented his chief's demands. The conditions were not as painful as Derricks had expected. Jefferson Pack was not interested in humiliating the Jamaican, Stone explained, he just wanted his territory to be left alone. Continue the encroachment, Stone warned, and full scale war would ensue; the resulting violence would draw too much heat down on both sides from the mayor's office and the police department. It would be a situation that would benefit neither of the gang's goals.

Derricks, with his lean, mottled face and dreadlocks pulled up beneath his tri-colored knit cap, studied his adversary from across the table. He scratched his scraggly whisk of a beard with a long, untrimmed fingernail, then pushed for a few token concessions but Stone would not yield. The effort made, Derricks conceded and, as the EL AZIWA representative rose to leave, they shook hands on an agreement that would allow both factions to save face and permit them to concentrate on other business.

Stone lowered his head as he exited the back room, fastened the buttons to his long coat, and casually glanced in the direction of the bar. He quickly made eye contact with the bartender, then just as quickly averted his gaze and strode on past the crowded tables and out the door. The bartender, a small elderly man with yellow-brown skin, made no sign of recognition. He turned his back to the bar and glanced at the departing figure in the mirror that hung behind the rows of dark green, amber, and crystal-white bottles. He then placed a bottle of red wine on a tray with three glasses and carried it to the back room where the Jamaican, Familyman, and Rickey were smoking a celebratory joint.

2

"Mr. Derricks?"

"Yea, mon?" he said as he studied the bartender through the thick haze of the marijuana.

"Mr. Grant left a message for you, said he needed to see you tonight. He's at his store." Grant, working out of a liquor store two blocks away, handled the liquor trade, legal and illegal, for the Jamaican.

Derricks acknowledged the message with a nod as the bartender filled the glasses, spilling some of the red liquid, his hands trembling as he poured. He quickly wiped up the spill with the small towel he kept tucked to one side in his belt and fled the room before the gang lord sensed his fear and read the betrayal in his eyes.

Half an hour later, happy and flushed, the trio donned their long overcoats, wrapped their Kente cloth scarves around their necks, and walked through the bar to the front door. As the Jamaican bellowed his Christmas greetings to a group of young ladies celebrating at a table near the corner window, the bartender nervously untied the strings to his apron, picked his coat off of a peg near the door to the kitchen, and stumbled over an empty cardboard box in his haste to reach the back exit. He checked his pockets for the tenth time that evening, found the roll of money and the airline ticket still there, then disappeared out the back door into the dark alley.

Plumes of frosted breath streamed from his nostrils as the Jamaican stepped out into the cold air. He glanced right and left, surveying the neighborhood until he was satisfied that the streets were safe, then gazed up toward the streetlights. Only an occasional snowflake swirled past. Light-headed from the buzz, his foot slipped on the ice at the bottom step but he caught himself before he fell. The three men laughed and turned north against the wind.

Halfway up the block, two figures emerged from the shadows of an alley on the opposite side of the street. One was tall and thin with stooped shoulders. He was called Six. It was a name given to him as a youth when his grandmother had chastised the rail-thin boy for not eating ("You so skinny you look like the hands of a clock when it strikes six."). Over the years he had kept the name but changed the meaning. The members of his gang now knew that the name stood for the depth at which his enemies could be found. The name, however, was the only vestige of his childhood that remained. Six-foot-two inches of spine and appendages, he had hardened over the years into an emotionless shell, as if his tight, shallow ribcage had not allowed sufficient room for a heart to grow. The flicker of his heavy-lidded eyes as he scanned the street was the only sign of life on his hard, inflexible face.

The other man was short with a thick scar that ran down his forehead and the bridge of his nose before it turned across the left cheek of a broad, square face that, together with his thick, muscular neck, gave him the appearance of a cinder block with ears. He called himself K.L., short for Key Lord, another childhood name that was his misunderstanding of a term a physician had used to describe the scar tissue on his face that had resulted from a knife fight when he was thirteen. He did not know what the doctor had meant, but he had liked the sound of it.

Both wore hairpieces of shoulder length dreadlocks. Both carried pistols concealed beneath their coats. Both were lieutenants in the EL AZIWA hierarchy.

The two men waited for a car to pass before they crossed the street where they turned north and slowly walked ahead of the Jamaican. On cue, the two men stopped at the front stoop to one of the apartment buildings that lined the block. Six took a piece of paper with an address out of his coat pocket, unfolded it, and looked from the paper to the number above the door. K.L. began an argument, pointing first to the street sign at the corner, then back to the paper and the street numbers.

The snow crunched beneath the feet of the approaching men. When the Jamaican, flanked by his partners, drew even with the two, Six tapped his companion on the shoulder. K.L. immediately turned, pushed a snub-nosed .38 revolver toward the face of the big Jamaican, and pulled the trigger. Derricks's mind briefly registered a brilliant flash of light that rivaled the fierce Caribbean sun of his childhood memories before all went dark.

Familyman and Rickey jumped at the shock of the sound. Sylvester Derricks's body jerked backwards and slammed into the pavement, sliding several feet across a patch of ice before it came to a stop. Before they could react, the dead man's companions each found themselves staring into the barrel of a gun. K.L. and Six swiftly dragged them down the street to the corner where a car, its driver alerted by the sound of the gunfire, pulled to the curb. Six opened the rear door, entered, and the short killer pushed the two shocked captives into the back seat. Before he entered the car, K.L. reached up to remove his wig of false Rasta locks and turned to check the street behind him.

In the window on the second floor of the corner building a light appeared. K.L. looked up into the scared eyes of a young black girl holding an infant. She

4

cradled the baby's head with one hand and turned it away from the window as if to shield it. A wicked grin broke across K.L.'s face, the light flashing off the enamel of his teeth. He wagged the pistol in the air, flashed a gang sign just to let her know who ruled, his mouth open in a defiant taunt, and jumped into the car. As the car sped away she reached across the window and slowly pulled the curtain shut.

Several miles away from Little Jamaica the car containing the hostages finally slowed and turned. The driver dimmed the headlights as the car coasted to a stop at a brick wall at the end of the alley. During their journey the captors had kept the two Jamaicans' heads forced down between their knees by twisting their fingers deep into the braided dreadlocks. The other hand of each kept the cold barrel of a pistol pressed into an ear. Familyman heard the click of a door being opened and began to shake, at first mistaking the sound of the door for the mechanism of a gun. Then the hands that held them by the hair jerked their heads to an upright position.

A man now sat in the passenger side of the front seat with his back to them. He adjusted the rear view mirror so that he could see into the back seat without revealing his face. The cold dark eyes of Jefferson Pack, head of the El AZIWA, studied the features of the two Jamaicans.

"Which one of you is Rickey?" a deep voice asked.

When neither one of the captives answered, Six slammed Rickey's head against the other Jamaican's with skull-splitting force.

"I .... I am."

"Good," the man in the front seat gave a slight nod. "Now, your boss wasn't very smart, expecting me to negotiate with him. He wanted me to compromise, and I don't like to compromise, especially when something of mine has been taken away from me. So I decided not to talk with him anymore. Do you think I can talk with you?"

When there was no answer he continued. "This is the offer, plain and simple. You two now work for me. Understood?"

Rickey erupted, "There's no way in hell we gonna work for a ..."

K.L. slammed the butt of the revolver into Rickey's face. Rickey slumped to one side but K.L. straightened him. Rickey cupped his hand to his face as blood began to pour from his nose.

"Take him out and kill him," the man in the front seat directed.

K.L. grunted, a guttural expression of satisfaction. He slid out of the car dragging the Jamaican by the hair and slammed the door shut. From inside the

5

car Familyman could hear the muffled blows as K.L. savagely beat his victim, could see only vague shadows of movement through the smoke-tinted window.

"Your friend will be dead before our conversation ends," Pack paused. "... and you may be too if you don't listen very carefully. Do you understand?"

Familyman stared at the two eyes in the mirror, felt the dark flame that burned behind their obsidian centers. The tall gangster beside him pulled the hammer back on his pistol. Barely audible from outside the car was the crunch and snap of heel on rib.

"Ya! Ya mon! I understand!"

"Good. Now listen. You are now the highest ranking member of the Jamaicans. You are now THE Jamaican. You understand?"

Familyman Marvins nodded.

"And you work for me." The eyes stared, unblinking, through the mirror at the Jamaican. Familyman nodded again.

"Here is the deal. Everything in Little Jamaica is yours except the drugs. Anything you want to do -- gambling, liquor, protection, prostitutes -- anything except the drugs, I leave you on your own with a free hand to run things as you would like to run them, except for the drugs. Understood?"

He grunted his agreement.

"The drugs, all drugs, you buy from me. You no longer buy the stuff yourself, O.K.? You connect me with your source, but buy it from me. For a reasonable price. A very fair price. Fair enough for you to make it worth your while. You will make money. I'll make money. And you get to run the Jamaicans. I will back you on that. If you have any problem you can't take care of, we'll take care of it for you." He paused. "If anybody fucks with you ..."

Their eyes were locked through the reflection of the mirror. Pack's voice grew softer. "You've seen what I do to people who don't cooperate."

Familyman tried to swallow but his mouth was dry, so dry that he found it difficult to speak. He nodded and whispered in a raspy voice, "I understand, mon."

Outside the car the sounds of the beating had ceased. As Familyman waited in silence for some sign that he would be allowed to live, a bead of sweat rolled down his forehead, around the side of his nose, and hung on his upper lip. The salt from the perspiration stung his dried, cracked lips.

Finally the head of the EL AZIWA reached up and shifted the rear view mirror away from his face.

"Take him back," he said as he stepped out of the car.

It was only after the door slammed shut that Familyman Marvins, new head of the Jamaican criminal organization, realized that he had lost control of his bladder.

At 3:40 a.m. on the last Thursday in January a young man in a blue parka walked into a donut shop on the corner of an intersection opposite the University Medical Center in Jackson, Mississippi. A baseball cap, black with a golden New Orleans Saints fleur-de-lis, covered most of his short, yellow-bronze hair. He took a corner booth by a window, sat where he could face the street, and ordered two frosted donuts and a cup of coffee from the thin waitress with the straight, stringy hair. He held a newspaper in his hands but did not unfold it. Instead, his gaze was fixed out the window at the intersection.

The waitress, pale and flat-chested, had worked the graveyard shift at the donut shop since she had run away from home at the age of fifteen, but six years of all the donuts she could steal had still not put any flesh on her tiny frame. She had seen the young man before, and many others like him. He had the look of a student from the medical school just one block down the street. His skin had that washed-out lack of color that comes from chronic fatigue. There was a dark swollen quality to the eyes. His face spoke of too much stress and not enough sleep. When no one was looking, she popped a donut hole into her mouth, smashed it against the roof of her mouth twice with her tongue, and swallowed.

"The poor guy," she thought, "so out of it he can't even read his paper. He's just sitting there staring out the window."

At four o'clock, across the street from the donut shop, a late model burgundy Cadillac pulled up to the gasoline pump at the corner convenience store at the same time that the patrol car parked near the door of the donut shop. As the two policemen walked in and took a seat at the counter, the young man in the blue parka rose, pulled his cap down over his eyes, placed some money on top of his bill, and left.

When the clerk at the convenience store saw the two black men in the Cadillac pull into the parking lot and stop by the gasoline pump, he lowered his hunting magazine and inspected the occupants of the car. When neither one of the men emerged from the car after a few minutes, the clerk scratched his beard, then reached under the counter for his Smith and Wesson .45 semi-automatic pistol. He tucked it between his enormous waist and the big silver belt buckle

7

which had his name, Kyle, embossed on it. He settled back on his stool, snatched a bag of cheese puffs from a clip display, and returned to his magazine.

Inside the car Six and K.L. were arguing.

"You don't need the damn gun, man. Just pay for the gas."

"Don't go nowhere without my gun," K.L. said as he fumbled under the dashboard where he had taped his revolver earlier that night. He slipped the gun into the pocket of his jacket.

"Pay for the gas," Six said as he pointed at a finger at his partner.

"Back off, man! This is the last time I'm warning you. You been giving too many orders lately." K.L. emphasized the point by folding his arms and slumping down in his seat.

When he refused to move, Six jumped out of the car and slammed the door shut. Since their arrival in Mississippi over a month ago the two had grown increasingly edgy. Six hated the South. He especially hated the weather. One day it would be hot, the next day cold. And, unlike the dry cold of Chicago, it was a damp cold; a wet cold that soaked through the clothes and into the skin. He especially hated the boredom of the small town in the Mississippi delta where Pack had sent them to hide since K.L. had been identified in the murder of the Jamaican. No wonder Pack had left Mississippi as a young man and headed for Chicago; there was nothing happening in Elgin, Mississippi. Six hated K.L., too. This was all his fault. After they had done the Jamaican, K.L. had showed off, let the young girl see him on the street. The bad luck of it was that the girl was a relative of Sylvester Derricks and she had done the unexpected by telling the police what she had seen. Rather than lose two of his best men, Pack had slipped them out of Chicago for a short period of time until the girl could be reached and silenced.

Born and raised in Chicago, Six felt lost outside the city. After killing the Jamaican he thought he should have been rewarded. Instead, he felt they were being punished, sent into exile, even if it was for their own good.

Sent to stay at a club owned by Pack but managed for him by one of his relatives, Six chafed at the lack of activity. In Chicago, Pack relied on them to do the gang's most difficult work. In Chicago, Six and K.L. were always moving, always in action. Now they spent their days around the club. Under orders not to attract attention, they didn't venture out, sleeping in a back room at the club. They drank beer, played cards, then drank more beer. After closing hours the two played the video games at the club until they no longer presented a challenge, then watched what little television could be received on an old black-and-white set with rabbit-ear antennae. Elgin was so backwards they did not even have cable.

So Six blamed K.L. for his exile to hicksville. K.L. was rash and unlucky -- a bad combination.

Tonight they had been sent on an errand by Antonio, Pack's cousin who ran the club. An errand! Six and K.L. were insulted but did not argue. They would do anything to get out of that back room at the club for a while.

When Six walked into the convenience store, the man behind the counter immediately rose from the stool behind the cash register, wiped the orange residue from his fingers onto the side of his jeans, and tucked his thumbs into his belt. Six noticed the gun. Did everyone carry a gun down here, he wondered. It was worse than Chicago, he thought, especially the pickup trucks everywhere with gun racks in the back window.

"Can you change this?" He flashed a hundred dollar bill.

"Nope." Kyle tapped a slot in the counter. "Anything over a twenty goes in here and I don't have the key."

Six grunted, flipped a twenty out of his roll, threw it on the counter and left.

As he walked back another car pulled up to the gasoline pumps. A young white man in a blue parka stepped out, pulled out his wallet, and counted his money as he stood beside the open door of his car.

Six was surprised to hear the man speak as he drew near.

"Did Tony send you?"

Six stopped. The man talking to him had not looked up from his wallet, and Six couldn't see his face for the brim of the baseball cap the man was wearing.

"Did Antonio send you?" the stranger said a little louder as he finally looked up to stare directly at Six.

He thought for a moment. "Yea, but I didn't think we were supposed to meet here."

"Too crowded."

Six turned to look across the street and noticed the police car at the donut shop. He nodded to show he understood.

"You have something for me?" he asked Six.

"If you have something for us."

The man in the parka looked into the car. K.L. sat motionless, staring straight ahead through a pair of wrap-around sunglasses.

"I'll be back," he said as he walked past Six toward the store.

9

Inside the store the man in the blue parka bought a can of soda and a pack of chewing gum.

"Any trouble out there?" the clerk asked, looking out the window toward the Cadillac as he dropped the merchandise into a brown paper bag.

"No. No problem." He gave a warm smile. "They were asking directions. Out-of-towners," he explained.

As he walked back to the car he removed a plastic bottle from his parka and exchanged it for the soda can that was in the brown paper bag. Back at the pumps he glanced around, then positioned himself so that the clerk inside the store could not see him as he handed the bag to Six.

"1000 tablets."

In return Six handed him a plain envelope. He opened the flap and counted ten groups of ten one hundred dollar bills, each separated by paper clips.

"Ten thousand," he confirmed as he stuffed the envelope into his pocket.

The gasoline pump clicked to a stop on the Cadillac. Six removed the nozzle and slipped it back into the slot on the pump.

"Give Tony a message. Tell him the next shipment will be ten thousand tablets. And tell him the price is going up to twelve dollars a tablet. Ten thousand tablets at twelve dollars apiece. Got it?"

Six scowled as he entered the Cadillac. He shut the door and spoke through the window. "Antonio will have to talk to Chicago about that."

The man looked up from under the brim of his baseball cap. "I don't care who you have to talk to. I want one hundred and twenty thousand. In one week." He turned to leave but paused. "Oh," he added, "tell your friend that it's the middle of the night. He doesn't need his shades." He snorted a laugh as he walked to his car.

Six grabbed K.L. by the left wrist before the pistol was halfway out of his jacket.

"Not here. Not now," he warned.

Six turned to stare at the license plate of the departing car. He waited a moment before he pulled out of the parking lot, then followed the other car from a safe distance, thinking that it might be useful to know where this smartass lived.

10

Chapter Two

In his dream Duncan Russthorne knew he was in trouble. He was on one of his favorite climbs, a rock face just north of Chattanooga called the Hose. The first eighty feet were not too difficult, mostly a crack climb where he could wedge his feet or hands into small fissures in the rock with only one or two areas that required the more difficult small hold moves. It was here, near the end of climb, where the really difficult part began. An overhang loomed directly above him. From the overhang came the steady splash of water that had collected from the cliffs above. Hanging only by his hands, he slowly worked his way out to the edge of the overhang. As he reached the edge, his hand reached up and over to search for a small ridge, less than an inch deep, that he knew would be there. The water, chilled by the wind and the frigid stone, hit his hand and he immediately felt his fingers begin to stiffen. Slowly he began to swing his legs from side to side, building momentum until the voice in his head told him the time was right. With a grunt he swung his body up into the Hose with a twisting motion. At the dead point where his upward momentum stopped, he jammed both feet against the opposite wall while wedging his shoulders back against the cliff face directly above the overhang and froze, hoping that he would hold.

For a taller person this would have been a lot easier. A shorter person would not have tried it. For Duncan it was just barely possible.

He was now in the Hose -- two opposing faces that could only be climbed by slowly wedging oneself upward the final ten feet to the top. There were no cracks and no holds in the slick rock. Progress was made by inching his shoulders up slightly, then slowly moving his feet while he kept his body wedged against both surfaces. This was difficult enough by itself but the water made the rock surface treacherous. Worse yet, the cold water numbed his hands and cooled his body. If he didn't reach the top soon, his legs could cramp and he would fall the ten feet down the tube. If his rope held, he would then be slammed beneath the rock face down below the overhang.

Although he moved as quickly as he dared, the final few feet seemed to take longer than the rest of the climb. Just as he neared the top, he heard the sound of footsteps on loose stones. Startled, he looked up to see Dr. Goza, Dean of Student Affairs at the medical school, standing at the edge of the rock above him. His long white clinic coat stood out in stark contrast to the charcoal-colored wall of wet granite behind him.

"How are you, Duncan?" he asked.

"Fine, sir," he said. His shoulders and arms had begun to ache. His fingers could no longer sense the texture of the rock or the degree of pressure he exerted with them.

"Good. Good." He pushed his glasses back up his nose with his thumb. "Can we talk for a minute?"

"Yes, sir. If you'll just let me finish this climb -"

Dr. Goza held out his hand, not to help Duncan over the edge, but more like the gesture that traffic policemen use to stop cars.

"That is what I want to talk to you about, Duncan." He clasped his hands in front of his full figure. "You know, Duncan, you are one of our best interns. The teaching staff here at the medical center feel that you have great potential."

"Thank you, sir." He felt his right leg begin to quiver.

"That's why we feel like we need to challenge you more."

"What?" He snapped his head up toward the Dean.

"Challenge you. Make things a little more difficult for you. Help you to see what you are really capable of doing."

Duncan was dumbfounded; his mouth fell open in confusion.

"I wanted to explain. I wanted you to understand why I am doing this."

He stared in shock as Dr. Goza waved his hands and the rock face magically grew higher. Duncan looked down and then up. The Hose was now five feet taller. Instead of being almost at the top, he was only two-thirds of the way up the Hose! His arms were completely numb and now both legs were shaking from fatigue.

"I know you can do it, Duncan." Dr. Goza said from his newly elevated position.

Duncan had no time to reflect on his predicament. He had to act immediately. He moved his right leg and slipped. He tried to compensate by increasing the pressure on his left leg but it was too late. As he started to tumble, a sick feeling squeezed his stomach as he waited for his rope to jerk him to a halt with a force that would leave him sore, stiff, and bruised for weeks.

12

If his rope held.

Duncan's head jerked up from the pillow, his heart pounding in his chest as the instinctual fear of falling sent a shower of sparks cascading through his nervous system. He shook his head. Another strange dream. There had been too many strange and vivid dreams lately. He shrugged it off and blamed it on sleep deprivation. He tried to remember an article he had read concerning psychosis brought on by lack of sleep. Weren't violent dreams one of the initial symptoms?

Stiffly he sat up on the side of the narrow bunk. He rubbed his eyes and kneaded his forehead with his thumb and forefinger as a question crossed his mind. Which would be better, he wondered, the gradual, self-inflicted death of medical school or the violent but quick death of a rock-climbing accident?

Before he could ponder the question further, his thoughts were interrupted by a tiny muffled beeping sound in the background. Duncan reached up and locked his fingers into the bed-springs of the bunk above him. He leaned forward, allowing his arms and shoulders to stretch, then rolled his head to his left, then to the right, until a distinct bony click could be heard on each side.

A faint glow from the streetlight outside filtered through the venetian blinds as Duncan surveyed the on-call room. A small table with a reading lamp sat between two worn recliners. A low coffee table held a tumbled stack of magazines that were torn and for the most part without covers. The bare walls were a light, supposedly soothing, pastel green. The floor was worn tile of a neutral color with what appeared to be small metallic flakes in it. In one corner someone had scribbled "Perchance to dream" with a felt marking pen. In the other corner was a television that had not worked since he had become an intern at UMC six months earlier. Duncan had never heard anyone comment on the broken television; no one seemed to care. The importance of the on-call room rested in other things -- the coffee machine that sat on top of the useless television and the two sets of bunk beds that rested against the wall opposite the window. The bathroom was equipped with a shower but it was rarely used. The two principal concerns of an intern were coffee and sleep. Although sparsely furnished, the on-call room was a cell of tranquillity in the vast honeycomb of the University Medical Center.

The faint beeping noise continued. It was an alarm, Duncan decided. He checked the clock radio next to his bunk. The digits read five forty-five a.m., but it wasn't the source of the sound. He turned and focused on the other bunk. The soft outline of a body dressed in a green surgical scrubsuit lay face down on the bunk. One foot hung over the edge of the bed still in the static-free cloth foot covering that was required in the operating room. A beam of light from the slats in the window blind highlighted a golden red wave of hair that curled out from under the woman's surgical cap. The alarm seemed to be coming from a wristwatch on the arm that was tucked under her stomach.

Duncan smiled. The sleeper was Deena. She had obviously come straight from a long stretch of surgery to crash askew on the bunk.

Duncan stood and stretched again. He stiffly moved to the other bunk and sat down by the sleeper.

Deena was in her first year of a coveted surgery residency at the medical center. To be selected to join the surgery program at UMC was the medical school equivalent of an anointing from heaven. The fact that only the top students in the nation were admitted stamped Deena as one of the best of the best.

She was also beautiful, with a light reddish head of hair that framed her fair complexion. It was a face that did not need makeup to enhance its natural, simple beauty. At this moment, however, her head was cocked to one side on the pillow and her mouth was open, her jaw off-center. A small circle of drool had collected on the pillow.

"Deena, wake up." Duncan gently rocked her shoulder with his hand. "Deena?"

"Uh?" She woke with a start. She squinted at Duncan as she rolled over, trying to orient herself to her surroundings.

"Your watch," he said.

"What?"

"Your watch," he repeated and pointed to her wrist.

She stared at her watch as if she had never seen it before. When her eyes focused she pushed a button on it to stop the noise, then she dropped her arms and closed her eyes again.

"I got two hours in. You?"

"Three. Maybe three and a half," he answered.

"It's been two weeks since I had more than four," she mumbled.

"Don't go back to sleep, Sleeping Beauty." He reached over and wiped a strand of saliva from her chin with the ball of his thumb.

She scrunched up her face in disgust as she looked first at her scrubtop, then at the wet pillow.

14

"Sleeping Ugly would be more appropriate, or maybe Sleep At All Cost," she said. She smiled as she tried to sit up but stopped and grabbed her neck.

"I slept the wrong way," she groaned.

"I didn't know there was a wrong way. Here, let me help."

When she turned her back to him, he massaged both sides of her neck and shoulders, slowly working his fingers into her stiff muscles as she tried to stretch her head from side to side.

"If I'm Sleeping Beauty, then you must be my Prince Charming," she spoke as she hung her head down against her chest.

"Nothing personal, Deena. I would love to be your Prince Charming, but right now I would much rather be Rip Van Winkle."

"What?"

"Go to sleep for about thirty or forty years, then wake up when this is all over."

She nodded in agreement. "You've had a bad week?"

"A tough one," he answered as he continued to knead her shoulders. "And you?"

"A bad week but a worse weekend. There were three MVA's in a two hour period and some assorted gunshot wounds on Saturday night. One had been hit with buckshot; the left side of his chest cavity looked like a colander. We worked on him for four hours but he had lost too much blood and didn't make it off the table." She paused to gather her strength before continuing. "And the last patient we worked on was a nine-year-old girl whose stepfather had raped her. We had to sew her up, front and back." As her voice trailed off, she pointed to a spot on the right side of her neck for Duncan to massage.

"You know what the worst part of it was?"

Duncan knew but didn't respond as he worked the knot out of the muscle with his thumb.

She paused for a moment before she answered her own question. With a soft voice full of fatigue and disappointment she said, "I didn't feel anything for her. No sympathy, no anger, nothing. I tried. I really tried, but I couldn't. I just felt detached. Detached and numb." After a moment she snorted in derision. "I've become just like a garage mechanic, Duncan. Lift the hood, check the oil, put in a new fan belt, slam the hood down and go on to the next one."

Duncan carefully chose his words before he spoke. "I guess this is where I should tell you that your clinical detachment allows you to perform your duties efficiently and without emotion affecting your performance."

15

"Pretty neat speech. Did you make that up yourself?"

"No. I heard one of the staff say that during rounds one day." He then added in a more serious tone, "I know what you are feeling, Dee."

She reached over her shoulder and gave his hand a quick firm squeeze of thanks. She stood up, stretched, and crossed the room to sit in one of the recliners.

"What we need is another weekend in Florida!"

Duncan laughed and dropped back onto the bunk.

"Dee, I still haven't recovered from the last time."

"The last time? The only time! And that was eight months ago."

Duncan thought back to the first year of medical school when Dee and Duncan had entered the classroom for the first time, both full of excitement and confidence. Although they had sat in the same classrooms for four years, shared the same laboratory exercises, and occasionally even sat next to each other in lecture, it wasn't until their last year in medical school that they had struck up a friendship. That friendship had exploded into something more than a casual relationship just prior to their graduation from medical school. On a whim, she had invited him to join her for a weekend at the beach. To the surprise of both, he had accepted.

That weekend had been a release, a purging of the backlog of tension that the previous four years had accumulated. Long after they had returned to the medical center, Duncan had refused to let the memories of that weekend dim. He had stored them carefully in his mind and called them up when the days on the wards of the hospital were dark and endless and it seemed as if the sun no longer tracked across the sky above the hospital.

But the relationship that started that weekend had never progressed much further. The week of their return was filled with preparation for graduation. After the graduation ceremony both had returned to their respective homes to visit family prior to the start of their internships. Then, on July 1st, they again surrendered their lives to the medical center and immersed themselves in the waters of suffering and death.

"That's the only time I have ever been to the beach and spent more time indoors than I spent outside," Dee laughed, still reminiscing.

"Oh, we managed to get a little sun, didn't we?" He cut his eyes at her and grinned.

16

"That only took twenty minutes. Neither one of us had seen any sunshine for four years."

She leaned forward and rested her elbows on her knees.

"So what happened? We had such a promising start."

"We can't have a relationship, Deena. We're both married to this hospital."

She gave a short grunt of disgust, then began to pull and twist a strand of hair that dangled out of her surgical cap as she gazed at the coffee table. "I tried to call you," she said.

Duncan sat up. "And I tried to call you. I even went to your apartment and left a note."

She smiled as she remembered the note she had found wedged under her door one Friday evening. She had kept the note for two days, folding the paper to prop it up on the table where she studied. She read and reread its message, each time thinking of Duncan as he worked his weekend shift at the hospital. It was a guilty schoolgirl pleasure she allowed herself to enjoy until early the following Monday morning when, prior to leaving her apartment for rounds, she had calmly dropped the note into the garbage without a second glance, determined in her sense of purpose not to allow any distraction in her life that might interfere with her surgical training.

"Yeah," she said as her lips turned up at one corner in a whimsical half-smile. Her train of thought was broken when a muffled intercom announcement filtered through the door from the hallway. She picked up a magazine and showed it to Duncan. On the cover was a picture of John Lennon.

"He's been dead for over a month but I just heard about it this week," she said in disbelief. She dropped the magazine and cradled her face in her hands, struggling with the words as she slowly forced a muffled sentence from her mouth. "I'm ready to have a life. I just want a life."

Duncan hesitated. The honesty and vulnerability in her voice required a delicate response. He rose and walked over to the coffee machine, fumbled with a styrofoam cup, and checked the glass bowl of the coffee maker to see if it was warm.

Deena sensed his hesitation and quickly pulled her defenses back up. She took a deep breath and forced a smile to appear on her tired face, then glanced at her watch. "I think I'll run home for a shower and a change of clothes before rounds. What about you?"

"I'll stick around here. Shave. Grab a bite to eat, maybe."

She stood and turned to the door.

17

"Dee ..." he said.

She stopped as she was opening the door.

"I'll call you. I promise," he said.

She tried to force another smile but failed, then quietly shut the door behind her as she left.

Chapter Three

Duncan flipped the coffee cup into the trash can in disgust.

"Duncan, you jackass. She needed some encouragement and all you can say is 'I'll call you. I promise?'"

He brought his hands to his face and rubbed his swollen eyes. The adrenaline surge from the dream had faded and his body's systems had quickly returned to their normal state of borderline exhaustion. Parts of his body were numb; other parts ached from a bone-deep weariness. He had been fatigued before but never to the point of collapse. He had reached this point, not from one day or one week of hard work, but from month upon month of twenty-plus hour a day stress.

He walked into the bathroom and flipped the light switch. When the small fluorescent light over the sink flickered on, he examined himself in the mirror and was surprised at the strange, haggard face that greeted him. The silver light made his skin even more pale than usual and accentuated the bags around his eyes.

He did not consider himself handsome. He had a face that a friend had once described as "cute." Duncan thought this translated as "not ugly." From his clinic coat he pulled a prep razor that he had swiped earlier from the nurses desk, turned on the hot water, pulled off his scrub shirt, and surveyed himself in the mirror again. At one time lanky, years of rock climbing had filled out his frame with a moderate amount of muscle. An average face on an average body that exercise had hardened and toned.

He thought back on his college days when he had been just a little too average for most of the girls he had wanted to date. Too average, that is, until word got around his senior year that he had been accepted into medical school, then they were eager to accept his invitations. For Duncan, though, it was too late to believe they were sincere. He put the thought from his mind and began to splash handfuls of hot water onto his face.

The door to the on-call room silently opened and closed as a small figure crept past the empty beds and eased toward the bathroom. He watched Duncan a moment through the partially open door, then moved around the beam of light cast from above the sink so that he could move closer to the door without being seen.

Duncan pulled the razor over his chin as the stranger slapped the door open with his palm. Duncan jerked in surprise as a hand with small delicate fingers caught the edge of the door before it hit Duncan.

"Dunc!" A narrow face with metal-framed glasses grinned up at Duncan.

"Damn, Wild Bill. Give me an MI this early in the morning." He inspected the cut on his chin in the mirror. "And ruin my good looks, too."

Bill Wammack was still grinning as he pointed to the cut. "So that's why you turned down a surgery residency. You're NO DAMN GOOD with your HANDS!" He leaned closer to inspect, then in a softer voice said, "Sorry 'bout that. Hope it didn't hurt."

"No. I'm numb."

"I know what it's like when the fatigue factor sets in." He held up both hands and massaged his fingertips with his thumbs.

Wild Bill Wammack, a general medicine intern like Duncan, was small and wiry. His black hair was thin in front and receded into a widow's peak. His nose and chin were sharp angles that framed a pair of lips that seemed to be permanently locked into a smile. It was an infectious grin that he backed up with a kinetic sense of humor.

Duncan finished shaving and wiped his face.

"How do I look?" he asked as he surveyed his face in the mirror.

"Almost lifelike."

Duncan studied his friend's reflection in the mirror. If Deena was Sleeping Beauty and he was Rip Van Winkle, then Bill Wammack had to be the Cheshire Cat.

"Damn, Wild Bill. How can you always be so cheerful? You've reached your caffeine tolerance level, haven't you?"

"No such thing. I'm just high on life," he grinned. "Let's get some coffee and then I've GOT to show you something." His grin assumed even larger proportions. "You WON'T believe this!" He shook his head as he finished and again punctuated the sentence with a smile.

Duncan followed him out of the on-call room to the nurses desk where Bill found a stack of styrofoam cups and poured them both some coffee.

After a few minutes of conversation with the nurses, Bill nodded toward the elevator. Duncan picked up his cup of coffee and followed.

20

"Where are we going?"

"The E.R."

"Oh, no." Duncan stopped short.

"What's wrong? I thought you had a special friend in the E.R."

"Too special."

Bill grabbed Duncan by the sleeve, pulled him into the elevator, and held him by the arm as he pushed the button to the basement. Duncan, resigned to his fate, dropped his head to his chest as the elevator doors closed.

"She's pretty," Bill said between sips of coffee. "Kate, isn't it? E.R. nurse?"

"Yes, Kate." Duncan grimaced.

"So what's wrong? Why too special?"

Duncan leaned his head back against the elevator wall.

"Do you remember the young boy I treated a couple of months ago who had broken his pelvis and right femur in a three-wheeler accident?"

"The kid that was all freckles and ears?"

"That's the one. Kate was the nurse that brought him up from the E.R. the day he was admitted. She was friendly, but business-like. A few days later I saw her in the cafeteria. She was seated at the next table, and she asked about the boy's progress. We talked for a while, she seemed nice, so I asked her to dinner. She agreed. Since that time we've had a few dates. I haven't had a whole lot of time for dating," he said as an aside. Bill nodded in understanding.

"Anyway, we have a good time together, she's a great girl, but the next thing I know she's talking about moving in with me."

"That was fast."

"Too fast"

"Is that a problem?"

Duncan didn't speak; he just shook his head.

"What do you expect? You shouldn't have led her on like that," Bill said.

Duncan brought his hands up in a gesture of bewilderment. "But I didn't! I really did not."

Bill gave Duncan a hard look of disbelief.

"It's true, Wild Bill." He held up his hand as if to take an oath. "The only time we were in bed together, nothing happened. I had just come off a seventy two-hour shift with no sleep. I cooked dinner for her at my house. We had a few glasses of wine. We went back to my bedroom and while she was in the bathroom I ... well, ah, I passed out."

Bill rolled his eyes. "Before or after?"

21

"Before. She left a note pinned to my shirt when she left. It said, '*You really know how to make a girl feel special.*'"

"I don't believe it."

"Do you think I would make up a story like this?"

Bill thought for a second. "Are you sure you can still function?"

"What?"

"Can you still function? You know what I mean. Function, perform?"

Duncan let out a deep laugh. "Yes, except when I am in a deep coma. Non-vital functions tend to shut down under those circumstances."

Bill nodded, then asked, "So what's the problem. She's a great girl. Attractive. Smart. She adores you. Wants to take care of you. It's not like you couldn't use a little attention, you know."

"I don't know what the problem is, Bill, I just don't know," Duncan answered with a shrug of his shoulders.

After a moments pause, he punched Bill on the arm, "So tell me, what's the big secret?"

Bill looked up at Duncan and flashed him his biggest grin yet.

"Two words." He held up two digits for emphasis as he moved face to face with Duncan.

"Boner lock!"

Before Duncan could ask, the elevator stopped at the basement. Bill exited to the right into a maze of corridors. Exposed pipes coded in a spectrum of colors ran along the length of both walls and the ceiling. The pipes, added over the years, had constricted the hallway into a dim narrow tunnel.

"Here?" Bill asked himself as he slowed his pace, stopped and swiveled his head to check his location, then started again. "No ... here!" He turned to Duncan and shook his head. "I still get confused, even after five years."

One side of the hallway opened into a brightly lit area with a high ceiling. Green curtains, hung from metal tubing set in the walls and ceilings, delineated a half-dozen treatment areas where patients with medical problems of a less urgent nature were treated.

"We've seen a lot of strange things, haven't we?" Bill asked as he led Duncan to one of the green curtains.

"Yes," Duncan agreed.

"The man who had swallowed, inch by inch, almost one hundred yards of fishing monofilament?"

"Yes."

"The construction worker who had fallen from a scaffold and impaled himself on an iron rod? He walked in here as if nothing was wrong, but three feet of a concrete reinforcing rod stuck out of his chest and back."

"Yes." Duncan was relieved when Bill failed to include the Land Whale.

"Well, this patient gets top honors in the weird and strange category."

As Bill stepped forward, the curtain drew back and a white-clad figure stepped from the cubicle. The physician facing them was shorter than Bill, with short wavy blond hair and chubby cheeks scrubbed shiny pink.

"Dr. Norton!" Bill greeted him like a long lost friend.

"Wild Bill ... and Duncan." Dr. Norton had a voice that always carried a hint of sarcasm that belied his innocent face, a cherub with a Humphrey Bogart snarl. "I should have known you two would have gotten wind of this."

Unlike most of the emergency room physicians, Norton always managed to appear immaculate. Even after hours of frantic work, his long, white clinic coat would be spotless and unrumpled. This was a minor miracle considering the wide variety of brown, green, red, and yellow body fluids that were usually splattered about the E.R. during a twelve-hour shift.

Dr. Norton had the nervous habit of continuously rocking back and forth on the balls of his feet when he was talking. As he spoke, he punctuated his sentences with a cocky tilt of the head that signified the absolute infallibility of his words while he kept his hands tucked in the sides of his clinic coat in a manner probably inspired by Napoleon. His fingers always rested in the pockets, thumbs hooked out, as he used his elbows to point. All of these combined to give Norton an air of smugness unmatched at the medical center.

Bill, usually the first of the interns to size up each member of the staff, knew that Norton's sense of humor was stuck at an adolescent level and used it to his advantage. Dr. Norton seemed to favor Bill and kept a looser rein on him than he did most other interns.

Bill pointed a thumb up at Duncan.

"Can I show him?"

Norton looked at Duncan. "I don't know. We don't need to turn this into a circus." He cocked his head to one side as the left corner of his lip turned up in a combination of smile and sneer.

"C'mon, Doc. This could be a valuable educational experience for Duncan."

As Bill talked with Norton, Duncan eased to one side and pushed a hand through a slit in the curtain. From where he stood he could not see the treatment table, but a nurse stepped into view as she picked up an instrument from a cart. When he saw Kate, Duncan began to edge away from them.

"Duncan."

"Yes, sir?"

Norton nodded toward the curtain and somehow managed to pull it open slightly with his elbow.

"Tell me what you see."

From the hallway Duncan looked at the patient seated on the treatment table. He frowned, tried to speak, then his frown grew deeper.

"The wrong way to take a patient's blood pressure?" Bill interjected.

Norton exchanged grins with Bill.

"Duncan?"

"I ... uh ... I see what appears to be a half-naked cowboy with a blood pressure cuff wrapped around his ..." Duncan said before his voice trailed off.

Norton snorted. "Not a very accurate assessment. A hotshot intern like you can do better than that. Try again."

Duncan stared at the patient. "Is that really his ...?"

Bill was acting like a third grade student who knew the answer when no one else did. He waved his hand and begged, "Teacher, teacher! I know the answer!"

"OK, Bill. Give him a hint."

Bill put on his most serious face and with great relish pronounced, "Boner lock!"

Norton choked back a laugh. "A totally inadequate clinical assessment."

Duncan continued to stare and frown at the patient.

"I'll give you a hint, then -- priapism."

When Duncan failed to respond, Norton repeated the word to him.

"Priapism. Can you expound on that subject for us, please."

Duncan blinked a couple of times before he turned back to Norton. "Priapism is a persistent erection."

"Yes," Norton nodded. "And the causes?"

"Usually a hormonal imbalance, probably excessive androgens."

Norton nodded again, pleased. He motioned for them to follow him. "Let's go take a look."

Duncan hesitated. He had hoped to avoid Kate but Dr. Norton turned to motion him forward as they approached the patient. Duncan was obligated to follow.

24

On the cushioned treatment table sat a young man with his head pressed back against the wall as he arched his body in pain. His handsome face was twisted in a tight grimace, his eyes were shut, and his cheeks were drained of color. He was naked except for a pair of leather cowboy chaps on his legs, a red bandanna around his neck, and a blood pressure cuff wrapped around his penis.

Norton addressed the patient. "Mr. Phipps, this is Dr. Wammack and Dr. Russthorne. They are here to consult with me concerning your problem. Do you mind?"

The cowboy gave a slight grunt without opening his eyes.

Norton nodded to Kate. Kate glanced at Duncan as she handed Norton the patient's chart. She adjusted her stethoscope, slipped the round end of it under the pressure cuff and started pumping the rubber bulb. An immediate groan came from the cowboy as Norton began to read the chart.

"Mr. Phipps is a twenty five-year-old white male who was presented to the emergency room at 4:20 a.m. today with the chief complaint of severe pain in his groin area. No history of disease. No sign of trauma. The patient is not on any regular medication."

He then switched from his professional voice to a more casual tone.

"Mr. Phipps was going to a party. A costume party."

Duncan had noticed the chair beside the exam table. On it sat a pair of cowboy boots. Draped over the boots was a holster and toy pistol set. A brown felt cowboy hat lay on the floor. Duncan noticed that there was no evidence of any pants or shirt in the pile of clothes. What kind of party, he wondered?

Norton continued. "I guess the best way to say this is that he wanted to really impress everyone at the party so he stole some medication from his father's medicine cabinet."

"A prescription medication?" Duncan asked.

Norton nodded. "Probably papaverine. The U-G people sometimes allow its use for the treatment of impotence. It's injected directly into the organ."

"Which causes smooth muscle relaxation. Lack of vascular tone causes the organ to fill with blood."

"Exactly. But this has now developed into a serious problem in Mr. Phipps's case. In healthy people the effect of the medication is too pronounced; it allows too much blood to engorge the spongy erectile tissue. Normally this would drain by itself, but now the drug is preventing that from happening."

Norton turned to Kate. "Anything?"

She shook her head. The patient squirmed as a wave of pain moved up through his abdomen.

"Two reasons for the pressure cuff?" Norton demanded of Bill.

"Pulse and blood pressure. To see if he is getting any oxygenated blood flow to the tissue," Bill offered.

Duncan supplied another reason. "To try to force some of the venous blood out."

"Good. Good." Norton smiled. "Exactly. In this patient's case his blood supply is slowly choking his own tissue and leading to necrosis. Notice the purplish black discoloration."

Duncan had already noticed. He chose not to look again.

The patient had opened his eyes to stare at the ceiling, his blank face drained of emotion. "Please," he mumbled. "Please." Duncan could not tell if the patient was talking to them or offering up a prayer.

"Pretty painful, huh?" Bill observed.

"Very," Norton confirmed. "The tissue is slowly dying for lack of arterial blood."

Duncan scratched his temple. "So how do you treat him? Can you counteract the medication?"

Norton shook his head. "There isn't enough blood flow into the tissue to allow the medication to reach the area where it is needed," he said as he looked over the patient's progress on the chart.

"At first the pressure cuff helped. We could force some of the pooled blood out and hear a faint pulse. I had hoped we could provide enough relief until the drug's effect could dissipate. But now the patient is losing ground. We are going to have to try something new."

"New?"

Norton smiled. "You, gentlemen, are about to witness medical history. As far as I know this has never been tried before."

He walked over to the counter where a large glass jar sat. The label read, "Sterile Medicinal Leeches."

"No. Not leeches," Bill shook his head.

"I've seen these used in the surgery wards," Duncan said, "after severed fingers have been reattached."

"Exactly," Norton said. "I borrowed the idea from the orthopedic surgeons. Leeches are now routinely used post-operatively after severed fingers are reattached. They act to siphon the congested blood in the traumatized areas and allow the blood supply to flow in a normal fashion."

Bill gave a look of disgust. "You're not going to use them on his ..." He finished the sentence by pointing to the blood pressure cuff.

Norton grinned. "We are going to attach about half a dozen of the leeches up and down the shaft."

Bill looked down below his belt and shuddered at the thought.

"Isn't there another way?"

"Well, yes, there is. But it is considerably more drastic."

Bill stepped closer to Dr. Norton and cut his eyes in a conspiratorial fashion. "What do you mean by drastic?"

Norton rocked up and down on his feet. "Duncan?"

Duncan was afraid he knew the answer. "I and D?"

"Yes." Norton was pleased. "Incision and drainage."

Bill reacted with mock horror. "You mean ... cut?"

Norton nodded again. "A series of incisions to allow drainage of the congested blood."

"Won't that screw up the erectile tissue?" Duncan asked.

"Almost certainly. He may lose that function, but at least we won't have to amputate."

"Incisions. Amputation," Wammack whispered as he shook his head in amazement. He turned to Dr. Norton. "Does this mean Cowboy Bob won't be able to shoot the old six-gun anymore?"

Norton gave his biggest grin yet. "I knew I could trust you to say something completely tasteless."

In the background the Cowboy whispered, "Please ... please ..."

A nurse stuck her head inside the cubicle. "Dr. Norton," she motioned with her hand.

Norton turned to Kate. "Get the rest of his costume off of him and get him a gown. You can help me with the leeches when I return," he snickered to the interns as he left.

Kate made an effort to ignore the two interns as she used a pair of scissors to cut the leather strips holding the chaps. Duncan signaled for Bill to leave while her back was turned, then stepped closer to her. When he touched her arm, she turned to face him.

There was an awkward silence as both of them tried to measure the other. Finally Kate broke the stalemate.

"You look terrible."

Duncan gave a nervous laugh. "Thanks, but I feel a lot worse than I look."

"I hope that isn't true because you really, emphasis on really, look bad. You've got to take better care of yourself, Duncan. You know, you should ..."

Duncan raised his hands to cut her off.

"Sorry," she said sheepishly. "I can't help it." Kate tugged on a thin gold bracelet she wore on her left wrist. She began to pull the strand around and around, fidgeting with it as she looked at the floor. Without looking up she said, "You'll be relieved to know that I've moved my clothes out of your house."

Moved out? When had she moved in? Duncan tried not to show his surprise. Did she have a key? Had he given her one and forgotten about it? Then he realized that Barrett must have had a hand in this. Barrett, that asshole. He had to get him out of his house.

"Well, I hadn't seen you in two weeks. I thought that was a pretty strong hint."

He took her by the elbow and moved away from the cowboy who was now staring at Duncan, his soft blue eyes begging for relief.

"Kate, I'm sorry. It's not you."

She pulled her arm out of his grip and shook her head in disbelief.

"Honest, Kate. I haven't been home in two weeks. I didn't have a clue that you had moved in, much less moved in and then moved out."

She finally looked at him, searching his eyes for the truth.

"I know you don't want to hear this, Kate, but I don't have time for a relationship. It's not fair to you." In desperation he added, "I don't even have time for myself."

Kate reached up and put a hand on his chest. "Duncan, I want you to listen to me. I've been working the E.R. for eight years. I've seen hundreds of medical students come and go. I've seen them change from bright and enthusiastic to tired and uncaring. The nature of what we do carries a high emotional price due to all the death and suffering that we see, the pain that people inflict on others and themselves. It eats away at you. In order to defend yourself you build a wall to block out those emotions."

When he found it difficult to look her in the eye, she clenched the collar of his clinic coat and gave it a slight tug to get his attention.

"Don't cauterize your soul, Duncan. The cost is too high."

Suddenly Bill's head popped through the opening in the curtains. "Duncan, you're being paged," he said, then just as quickly disappeared.

Kate stopped him with a shake of her head when Duncan started to speak. "You had better go," she said as she returned to her patient. With her back to Duncan, she began to inflate the blood pressure cuff. Duncan slipped quietly from the room as the sound of cowboy's groans increased.

In the hallway Bill met him with two styrofoam cups full of coffee.

"Here's breakfast," he said as he handed one to Duncan. "I added extra sugar. You look like you need it."

Duncan swallowed a mouthful of hot coffee. It tasted like syrup.

"Caffeine and sugar are the two essential food groups," Bill said. "In case you haven't guessed, there was no page for you. I just thought you might need an exit excuse."

"Thanks. I needed both."

"You need the roof, too, don't you?"

"The roof," Duncan agreed as they strode off down the hall.

Chapter Four

Duncan scanned the layers of notes and announcements that covered the bulletin board as they waited for the elevator to arrive. Oncology rounds had been moved to the new auditorium complex next to the walkway to the Dental school. Thursday at seven P.M. there would be a banquet honoring the Great Kidney Doctor, discoverer of the body's mechanism for blood pressure control, upon his retirement. He looked without seeing, lost in thought, as Bill chattered in the background.

"He's hanging up his holster, taking off his spurs, 'cause Cowboy Bob won't be getting back in the saddle ever again."

"Bill."

"His lariat's gone limp. He's a cowpuncher who's lost his punch. A cowpoke . . ."

"Bill."

". . . who can't poke. He's . . ."

"Bill!"

"What?"

"Enough with the cowboy metaphors. I've got a real problem here."

"Kate?"

"Yes. I'm going to kill him."

"Him? Kate is a him? Boy, I'd like to meet the surgeon who did that!"

"No, not Kate. I'm going to kill Barrett Jeter."

"Good. I'll help. Any particular reason this time?"

"He gave Kate a key to the house, let her move in."

"You're kidding. Gee, I sound surprised but I'm not. Nothing he does would surprise me."

"I've got to get him out of my house. I've got to think of a way to get him to move without a full-scale war breaking out. This is your fault, you know. You shouldn't have let him move into your room."

"My fault?" Bill countered. "You didn't protest too much when I suggested the idea to you."

"I knew you needed the money." Duncan stared into his coffee cup. "I still don't understand why you had to be the one to move out. I rented the room to you, not him. I don't understand why you let him share a room with you in the first place."

"Like you said, I needed the money. You know that my finances are zero." He made a circle with his finger touching the tip of his thumb for emphasis. "Medical school is tough enough without working odd jobs on the side to earn grocery money. My father isn't a doctor. My aunt didn't bequeath me a house to live in while I was in medical school."

Duncan held up a hand in surrender.

"Sorry. I'm sorry," he quickly apologized. After an awkward pause he said, "I just don't understand why you let him move in."

"I knew he was a bastard, I just didn't know how big a bastard. Besides, he was really helping me at the time. He offered to pay most of the rent and helped me with some of my autopsies when I got in a bind. He really poured on the charm." The elevator finally arrived with an ominous mechanical thud from deep within the elevator shaft as the door slowly jerked open.

"A snow job," Duncan bluntly stated. "Barrett wanted that research assistant's position on Dr. Chew's staff. He knew that since you were the other research assistant, you could convince Dr. Chew to hire him. Since Dr. Chew is on the committee to select interns for our residency program, he knew if he presented a good image ..."

"Brown-nosed," Bill interjected.

Duncan grinned. "Brown-nosed -- and he is a master at that -- brown-nosed Dr. Chew, he would get one of the slots in the general medicine residency program here."

"Because with his grades he sure as hell wouldn't be offered a slot at any other medical school," Bill finished.

"You're right, Dunc. As always. As soon as he knew he had a slot here, he reverted to his old obnoxious self. And I moved out soon after."

The elevator bumped to a halt. "You could have come to me, Bill. I would have helped you get him out of the house."

"No, it was best that I go without causing a squabble. He's a mean and vicious thug, Duncan. Things would have gotten ugly, and I don't have the time or the energy to keep watch over my shoulder for Barrett."

31

A strange and eerie calm greeted Duncan and Bill as they stepped from the elevator onto the seventh floor, a conspicuous lack of activity that made them tread softly as they entered the ward. The hallway looked more like the lobby of a quality hotel than a hospital ward. A deep red oriental carpet covered the floor. Elegant gilt-framed paintings were highlighted by slim brass portrait lights. Upholstered furniture was clustered in groups as opposed to the plastic and chrome chairs found on the other floors.

"Have you ever seen any of the psychiatric patients out here in the lounge area?" Duncan asked.

"No, never a soul. This place always makes the hair on the back of my neck stand up. It's too quiet."

They turned and stopped at a door marked "Housekeeping." Bill started to force a credit card through the door when he stopped and turned to Duncan.

"It's unlocked." He frowned.

Bill slowly opened the door and they cautiously looked inside. A single incandescent bulb revealed a small room lined with shelves stacked full of neatly folded sheets and towels.

"Is it standard policy on the psychiatric ward to leave a doorway to the roof unlocked?"

Bill shook his head. "It's a radical new treatment called gravity therapy. Very controversial because it is so drastic."

They shut the door behind them and walked past the linen. The door at the opposite end of the supply room had the words "No Admittance" painted in faded red letters. On the other side was a maintenance stairwell to the roof. They bounded up the stairwell two steps at a time.

The exit to the roof was the closely guarded secret of only a handful of students. The few who knew of it did not speak openly of it for fear that the medical center administration would hear of it and install better locks on the door. Other than the on-call room, the roof was the only place of refuge for students at the medical center.

In the summer, Duncan had used the roof during the few short breaks he could squeeze from his duties. Once up top, he would peel off his scrubtop and soak in the sun's rays whenever time allowed. In the winter, Duncan slipped up to the roof in the early mornings before rounds. He used the cold air as a type of shock therapy to refreshen his dulled senses. He had learned to time his visits so that he usually arrived just before sunrise and stayed until the chill forced him to return indoors. Lately, this was the only time during the day that he would see the sun.

Duncan looked forward to this ritual to the degree that he felt cheated when the weather or his schedule prevented his morning trip to the roof. The few moments spent there each morning was often the only time he had to collect and organize his thoughts.

The metal door to the roof swung open to reveal a sky still dark. The eastern horizon had just begun to show a slight change of shade. Duncan walked across the roof to the parapet surrounding the edge of the building and looked over the city.

The early French explorers that founded the settlement which would eventually become Jackson had chosen the site along the banks of the Pearl River because of the cluster of hills that provided a defense against the numerous Indians and also provided relief from the insects and miasma associated with the lower marsh areas.

The medical center covered one of these hills overlooking the river. Situated on a quarter section of wooded land, the hospital was the tallest building in the medical center complex. From his vantage point Duncan looked down on the various buildings -- the nursing school, the Veterans Administration Hospital, the library. The dental school, the newest addition to the medical center complex, was the farthest building from the hospital and sat at the edge of the dark area of trees that covered the eastern half of the property. The woods dropped away from the complex down the hill toward the highway.

A chain of headlights streamed into the city along the interstate from the suburbs to the north. A dark void in that direction was ringed by lights and indicated the large reservoir named for a former governor. Another area devoid of light, a dark ribbon that snaked from the reservoir toward them, was the Pearl River. Duncan knew the dark path of the river would join the lighted highway just out of sight at the base of the bluffs below the medical center.

"Hey!" A voice broke from the darkness behind them. Startled, they turned to see a dim figure in a white clinic coat approaching. As he stepped closer Duncan recognized the swagger. Another step brought the face into view. Duncan could see his short blond hair, the sharp, upturned nose and the permanent sneer for a smile.

"Barrett," Duncan acknowledged his presence. Bill simply turned his gaze back to the east.

"Roomie! Wild Bill! How's it going?" When no one answered, Barrett continued, "Hey, Roomie, where you living now? You didn't sell the house, did you?"

Duncan wanted to ask Barrett why he had allowed Kate to move into his house but hesitated. Now wasn't the time. Besides, Barrett wouldn't admit to any wrongdoing. It wasn't his nature to accept blame.

"I've had a hectic schedule, Barrett. What little free time I've had has been spent in the on-call room."

Barrett stepped up and slapped Bill on the back.

"How's it going, Barrett?" Bill asked without a trace of sincerity.

Barrett stretched his arms high over his head and yelped out a yawn.

"Great! Just great! I'm outta here after rounds. My first weekend off in a month. Jenny and I are going to New Orleans."

"Oh, no," Duncan thought. "Here we go again."

To Barrett Jeter, New Orleans the greatest city on earth, mainly because it was the only city he had ever visited in his life. Duncan waited for Barrett to tell his story about how he had tried out for the New Orleans Saints. Barrett seldom missed an opportunity to repeat it.

"I'm going to pack a bag and hit the road. Jenny is going to drive while I take a nap." Barrett's anticipation grew and his voice rose as he talked. "As soon as we hit the Quarter we are going to eat a lot of Cajun food and drink a lot of beer."

"Wait a minute, Barrett," Bill stopped him. "Today is a sacrifice day. We've got two dozen rats scheduled."

"No," he groaned and pressed the palm of his hands to his temples. "I forgot. No, no, no! Not today! Can't we wait until next week?" he pleaded.

Bill answered in a short harsh tone of voice, "You know how strict the timetable is on the project. We have to collect all the data today."

Barrett thought for a moment. "Bill, ole buddy, if you could handle my part of the work today I promise I would ..."

"Don't even think about it, Barrett. I had to sacrifices the rats AND run the tissue samples by myself when you didn't show up last time. It took me the whole damn day and I still haven't finished graphing the results. Chew has asked me for the data twice this week. If he asks me what the problem is, I'll have to tell him."

"Damn," Barrett muttered, resigned to his fate.

Duncan noticed a solitary light coursing the dark area to the north that was the reservoir. A fishing boat heading in after an all-nighter? Or someone getting an early start?

"Damn," Barrett repeated. "I'm sick and tired of these damn rats, Bill. I have too little time as it is to have my schedule dictated by a bunch of damn rodents."

"In case you don't remember, Barrett, you came to me begging to be added to the research team. There are a lot of other people that would love to take your place. Any time you want to quit, you just let me know."

"OK, OK," he conceded. "What time?"

Duncan turned to look at Barrett, surprised at his sudden change of attitude. He had expected more of a fight.

"Let's start as soon as rounds are finished. If we work hard we could wrap it up by two or three o'clock," Bill said.

"Yea," he grunted. "That blows the weekend all to hell. No gumbo and crayfish. No tall drinks. No strip joints."

"You weren't going to drag Jenny into those dives, were you?"

"Aw, Jenny doesn't care. She knows I need a little R & R."

Duncan started to comment but checked himself. The sun was just below the horizon and the eastern sky was empty of all but a few faint wisps of clouds that glowed magenta and orange. A warm front had passed through the previous day and the morning air, though still crisp, held the first, faint promise of spring. He took in a deep breath. The cold air stung his nostrils as he inhaled. He closed his eyes and tried to clear his mind, but Barrett did not give Duncan the opportunity.

"I heard you lost the Land Whale, Duncan. Boy, is Shukowsky going to tear you to pieces at rounds this morning."

"You should know how that feels," Bill shot back at him.

"Hey, everyone loses patients," Barrett defended himself.

"Some more than others."

Barrett glared at Bill as he took a menacing step toward him. Bill turned his back to Barrett, shut his eyes, and braced himself for the blow to come.

There was a long moment of expectation. Finally Barrett backed away and shivered. "I'm cold. Let's get some breakfast before rounds."

"Not hungry," Bill said.

"I'll just stick with my coffee," Duncan said as he raised the cup to his lips.

Barrett shrugged off their refusal and started to walk back to the stairwell door.

35

"Eight o'clock. At the lab," Bill reminded him.

"Yea, I hear you," Barrett snarled over his shoulder as he stalked away.

As soon as the heavy metal door slammed shut behind them, the two interns looked at each other and shook their heads.

"You should have let him go to New Orleans."

"Why's that?"

"There are some bad neighborhoods down there where a lot of muggings occur. New Orleans is also the per-capita murder capital of the United States."

"We couldn't be that lucky. Man! What kind of guy takes his girlfriend to a T & A joint?"

Duncan turned his gaze back to the east and tried but failed to wipe his mind clear again and enjoy a few serene moments.

"Wild Bill."

"Yea?"

"I screwed up with the diuretic."

"What? The Land Whale? You did all you could. He was past help. Forget it."

"Maybe if I had just given him a little less diuretic."

"You had to act. His lungs were filling with fluid. He would have drowned if you hadn't."

"I don't know."

"He was a hopeless case, Duncan. He should have died years ago. Moses couldn't have led him through his medical wilderness."

"Shukowsky won't think so," Duncan said.

Bill's conspicuous silence at his last statement only increased Duncan's doubt.

Chapter Five

At 7:05 a.m. Nurse Catherine McKane, twenty-one-year veteran of the psychiatric ward, was startled to the degree that she dropped her tray of patient's medication when the door to the housekeeping closet burst open violently and the two interns exploded into the hallway. Duncan's momentum carried him across to the opposite wall. Bill's attempt to turn caused his feet to slip, and he had to drop his hand to the floor to keep from completing his fall. Instantly they corrected themselves and converged on the elevator, both jabbing their fingers at the elevator control buttons.

"Come on," Duncan muttered. When the floor indicator above the door failed to show any progress from the elevator, he punched the buttons again.

"Dammit, Bill, I thought you were watching the time."

Bill shook his wristwatch, an old, cheap mechanical type, and held it to his ear. He gave Duncan a hard look.

"I will be glad to trade watches with you."

Duncan bit his lower lip before he spoke. "The first time I am ever late for rounds and it has to be today."

A slight tone announced the arrival of the elevator. The two young doctors bumped into each other as they tried to squeeze inside the door before it was completely open.

Dr. Briton Shukowsky, tall and gray with a crew cut cropped short enough to show a cluster of age spots above each temple, stood at attention at the nurses' desk and stared at the late arrivals. Beneath his white clinic coat he wore a white shirt starched to a cardboard stiffness and a black tie cinched in a knot the size of a nickel. The faint aroma of Old Spice aftershave drifted from his sharp jawline now clenched in displeasure. Duncan and Bill stood at the back of the small group, their faces still flush from the cold and exertion, and tried to avoid his look, a glare that had been honed and perfected by thirty years in the U. S. Army Medical Corps. Shukowsky, known among the students as Dr. Shark for his teaching methods, arrived every morning at 0630 to review records. (0730 on

Christmas day.). Rounds started at 0700. Tardiness was not to be tolerated and would be reflected in the grades of the student responsible for the delay. Shukowsky was slightly surprised to see that Duncan was late. He was one of the best Shukowsky had ever seen. It had been a real coup for their program when Duncan had surprised everyone by applying for a general medicine residency. Still, discipline had to be maintained.

"Morbidity report?" he asked the nurse standing beside him.

"One," she said as she handed him the patient's record. He looked at the intern's name on the progress notes.

"Dr. Russthorne?"

"Yes, sir."

"A forty two-year-old white male. Admitted 1/19 of this year. Cause of death?"

"Cardiac arrhythmia."

"Could you be more specific?"

Duncan cleared his throat. "He developed a ventricular fibrillation that we were unable to convert back to a normal sinus rhythm."

"No. I meant for you to explain what precipitated the arrhythmia."

This was it. Shukowsky was wasting no time; Dr. Shark moved in for the kill.

"A drug interaction," Duncan confessed. Shukowsky's eyes remained fixed on Duncan as he waited for him to continue. Duncan took a deep breath. "The patient was on several medications. One of these medications makes the heart extremely sensitive to electrolyte disturbances caused by diuretics."

"And yet you gave the patient a diuretic. Were you aware of the possible consequences of this action at the time?"

Duncan felt as if the collar on his shirt was shrinking. He cleared his throat before answering, "Yes, sir. I was."

Shukowsky looked at the chart. As he studied the pages the interns and medical students present braced themselves. They were familiar enough with Shukowsky's routine to know that he would ask the group assembled for suggestions as to how the deceased patient could have been more effectively treated, i.e., kept alive. If anyone looked interested at this time, he would call on them. No one ever spoke at this stage. Very few people could satisfy Shukowsky.

"Would anyone care to comment on this patient and his treatment?" Shukowsky asked as he looked down over the group. Duncan noticed that the other students seemed to be staring at the floor, the ceiling, or their fingernails. He didn't blame them. Shukowsky was notorious for his ability to make interns look completely incompetent. His harsh assessments of student performance were extreme and always left the victim sure in the knowledge that if he or she ever did complete their training, they would probably kill or maim every patient they touched with their blundering attempts at healing.

"The use of the diuretic contributed to the death of this patient," Shukowsky began.

Duncan's stomach tightened as he braced himself for the verbal flogging to come.

"It was a desperate attempt to resolve a desperate situation and it failed. Would anyone like to suggest a better way this patient could have been treated?" The Shark looked around the group as everyone present tried to make themselves as inconspicuous as possible. Most of the interns avoided his gaze. One, a thin, bearded intern named Hooper who stood in the middle of the group, actually tried to seem less noticeable by bending his knees and thereby reducing his height by a couple of inches.

"Dr. Hooper? Do you have any suggestions?"

Hooper scratched his beard and tried to look studious but didn't speak.

"Anyone?" he asked as he scanned the group, slowly looking at each intern as the silence continued. When no one answered he spoke, "I have to agree with your silence. In this case there does not seem to have been any correct way to treat the patient."

Duncan fought to keep his face expressionless. Bill Wammack, hidden behind a taller student, cut his eyes toward Duncan with his mouth open and his eyebrows arched high in an exaggerated look of amazement as Shukowsky continued.

"This case shows us that we are limited in our capabilities. In spite of all of our efforts, we are going to lose patients." He turned to the nurse and motioned with a quick hand signal for her to bring the cart with the patient records, did a crisp, parade-ground turn, and marched off to conduct rounds. As the students moved to follow, Bill patted Duncan on the back and grinned. Barrett turned his head and whispered, "You must really be polishing his apple."

Duncan ignored him. The sick taste he had carried in his mouth since the death of his patient began to dissipate. Maybe he HAD done all that was humanly possible for his patient. How else could he have survived the Shark's attack?

Chapter Six

Two hours later Duncan stood outside the office of the pharmacology department on the fourth floor of the research wing of the medical center, mesmerized by the white plastic letters on the office directory board as he studied the names of the professors and their room locations. Coffee cups -- the large size -- in both hands, he had almost finished one cup before he snapped out of his daze. Chew! Chew was the name he was looking for.

He wondered about his medical education. What other profession would allow life and death decisions to be made by someone who had not had any sleep in seventy two hours. Would people fly an airline where pilots had not slept the previous three days? What if jurors were forced to render verdicts after days with no rest?

He swallowed the last mouthful from the cup and threw it in the garbage can beneath the bulletin board. He started on the other cup as he walked down the hallway. Another thought crossed his mind. How long could a human being live if coffee was his only source of nutrition? Was there a toxic level of caffeine? New research indicated that coffee might be carcinogenic. If that were true, though, his body should now be carrying a tumor the size of a Thanksgiving turkey.

As he passed a service elevator, the doors opened and Barrett emerged pushing a metal laboratory cart loaded with small cages, each cage containing several large white laboratory rats.

"Dunc! Are you here to help?"

Duncan pulled one end of the cart into the hallway.

"Yea. I wanted to see what kind of evil potion you two wizards are brewing."

"Thanks, old buddy. I owe you one."

"You also owe me rent. Three months rent."

"Oh sure, Dunc. I've got the money now. I'll pay you as soon as we get home." Barrett actually sounded contrite.

"If I didn't know you so well I would think you were sincere. Where are we going with these rats?"

"Next door on the left," Barrett said.

Duncan pulled the cart through open double doors. A long laboratory table divided the room, its dark chemical-resistant surface covered with an array of technical equipment. The humming sound of a micro-centrifuge could be heard as it slowed to a halt. Next to the sink a large beaker sat on an electric stirring plate as the clear liquid inside swirled in a lazy silver vortex and a red digital number blinked below it. The left wall of the room was covered with glass-faced cabinets filled with an assortment of laboratory glassware. Against the wall to the right was a low, narrow work area with two binocular dissecting microscopes, a double sink with gooseneck faucets, and two refrigerators. In the back of the room a large oak desk was positioned next to the window. A computer screen and keyboard sat in front of a shelf filled with textbooks, with other reference texts stacked in the window. Bound folders full of papers were stacked on top of the books. A computer printer clicked as sheets of paper flowed onto the floor.

Bill Wammack sat at the keyboard as another man in a long white coat looked over his shoulder. The professor was Asian, with black rimmed glasses and a touch of gray around the temples of his otherwise coal-black hair. Dr. Chew tore a sheet from the printer and marked two spots with a felt-tipped marker.

"Very good," he nodded at the results.

When Barrett let the cart roll into the refrigerator with a clatter, the rodents squeaking in protest, Dr. Chew turned and frowned.

"Dr. Chew, this is Duncan Russthorne," Bill said as a distraction. "He has offered to help us catch up with our work today."

Duncan offered his hand. "I remember you from your lectures, Dr. Chew. Good to see you again."

Dr. Chew returned the handshake with a firm grip of his own.

"And I remember you, Duncan. You are doing well in your residency, I hear."

"Thank you, sir," Duncan said.

Chew turned to Bill. "I want all the data graphed and the records made correct by Monday." His eyes narrowed as he turned to cast a look at Barrett.

"Do you understand?" he asked.

Barrett pretended to study the rats, then picked up the clipboard and flipped through the sheets of data as Dr. Chew folded his glasses and slipped them into his shirt pocket.

"Yes sir. We will," Bill answered for them both.

Chew gave a slight nod of farewell to Bill and Duncan but ignored Barrett as he walked past him and out of the laboratory.

Bill's gaze followed the departed professor.

"He's 'very displeased' with us. We are too far behind in our work. I tried to explain to him that there are only thirty six hours in a day but he didn't seem to understand."

"Well, I'm here to help. Just show me where to start."

"You don't have to do this, Duncan," Bill said.

"But we sure could use the help," Barrett interjected from across the room.

Duncan turned to Bill. "I'm glad to help, but you need to explain to me what your research is about."

Bill motioned for Duncan to follow as he walked to the door of a storage room to one side of the refrigerator. He took a key from inside his coat pocket, unlocked the door, and stepped inside. When Duncan entered, Bill flipped a light switch and stood by a shelf that contained at least half a dozen five-gallon plastic containers that resembled oversized aspirin bottles, pointing to them in his best imitation of a game show hostess suddenly revealing the special grand prize that had been hidden behind a curtain.

"What's that?"

Bill grinned. "Opium tablets."

"Opium?"

"Opium tablets," he confirmed.

As Duncan stepped forward to inspect the label one warning seemed to stand out. "This compound not intended for use in humans. Research purposes only."

"There must be thousands of them." Duncan said.

"Enough tablets to get a large portion of the city stoned."

Duncan stared in amazement.

"What do you do with them? And why so many?"

Bill took one of the containers from the shelf, unscrewed the lid, and poured a generous portion of small white tablets into a beaker.

"Our research program is studying endorphins -- the body's natural painkillers. The brain produces these chemicals in order to control the pain that is the result of injury or even the natural day-to-day tissue death that occurs just through normal functions. But you know that, of course."

Duncan nodded. "That's what gives runners the 'high' they experience when they run."

"Right. What we don't understand, and what we are trying to learn with this research, is how the endorphins are produced, where in the brain they are produced, what areas of the brain they act upon, the mechanics by which they act to dull pain, and the method of transport of the endorphin compound from point A to point B in the brain."

Duncan raised his eyebrows to show he was impressed. "Pretty ambitious project," he said.

"It is. If we are successful, we may be able to use the information to develop better, more efficient painkillers. Or even learn how to stimulate the brain in order to make it produce more of its own painkiller. Dr. Chew thinks it may even be possible one day to eliminate entirely the need for pain medication."

Duncan pondered that concept for a moment. "But why so much opium. This must be a huge project."

"It is a very ambitious undertaking. We have hundreds of rats injected with different levels of the drug. Chew estimates it will take another year to complete the study. He purchased this many tablets in order to assure that the opium we use was produced in one batch, that the level of purity is consistent."

Barrett appeared at the door.

"OK. Cut the lecture. Let's do the work and get out of here."

While talking, Bill had filled the beaker half-full with small unmarked cream-colored tablets. He placed the large container of the drug on the shelf and locked the door as they left, then placed the beaker on the central lab table by a small mortar and pestle. Barrett rolled the cart with the rats over to the table adjacent to the sink and compared the labels on the cages with the chart on his clipboard.

"The top cages are groups 17, 18, 19, and 20, due to be sacrificed. The bottom cages are groups 24 through 32. They are to be dosed."

"Barrett, why don't you start killing them. Just do one at first so I can show Duncan how to do the dissection. Duncan has good hands; this should be a breeze for him."

Duncan studied the animals with their pink noses, white fur, and long hairless tails. They seemed agitated. Their bodies twitched and jerked as if they were connected to a low amperage electrical current, and their dull black eyes rolled in

43

spasmodic circles. The slightest motion startled them, and they increased their edgy chattering.

"They aren't feeling well. It's been twenty four hours since their last fix."

"How long have they been receiving the drug?"

Bill looked at a label on one end of the cage.

"About two months. At fairly high levels."

As they watched, one of the rodents turned on its cage mate and bit him. Long white incisors sank into the side of the victim as he squealed in pain. A red spot darkened its flank.

"Not very friendly," Duncan said.

"They are all in a pretty nasty mood. The opium we inject screws up the natural chemical regulation of endorphins and their body quits producing its own. When the opium clears out of their system, they are in pain because their own endorphin production doesn't immediately start back up. Pain," Bill repeated. "Pure pain. Severe bone-crunching pain. The kind that heroin addicts feel when they go too long without a fix. The kind of pain that can kill."

Over by the refrigerator Barrett opened up a pair of cabinet doors and pulled out a large paper cutter, the kind used in business offices to cut large batches of stationery. He sat it on the counter and tested the blade, the steel making a sharp grating sound as he raised and lowered it.

Duncan looked at Bill. "Let me guess - Royal French Rats."

Bill just shrugged. "Low-tech, huh? But it's quick and easy. For us, that is. Maybe it's not the most humane method, but we can't use other drugs to put them to sleep because it might mask some of the opium's effects and therefore invalidate the research."

Barrett reached into a cage and pulled out his first victim. The rat immediately twisted around and buried his teeth in Barrett's hand in the muscle between his thumb and forefinger.

"Shit! Son of a bitch," Barrett yelled as he slung the rat into the sink. "The little fucker bit me!"

"Family feud?" Bill asked. "I told you to use the gloves."

"Funny. Real funny," he growled as he shook his left hand. With his right hand he grabbed the offending rodent by the nape of the neck.

"I'll show you. This will be slow and painful."

He placed the rat under the blade and, with a slow, deliberate motion, lowered the sharp edge. The rodent gave a final high-pitched squeal of terror as the blade cut into its neck, its eyes bulging and its tongue protruding from its

44

mouth. The vertebrae crunched and popped as Barrett gradually crushed the life out of the rat.

Duncan winced. Bill shut his eyes and looked away in disgust.

Barrett dropped the still-quivering body of the animal into a black plastic garbage bag that lay on the floor. He scooped up the head and gave it an underhanded toss to Bill. Bill moved to his left and caught it to one side of his body as droplets of blood sprinkled the floor. He took the bloody trophy and held the snout up for inspection.

"Barrett Junior," he whispered to Duncan.

For the next few hours the three quietly worked. Bill showed Duncan how to remove the brain tissue using the dissecting microscopes. An incision across the scalp with a scalpel blade exposed the skull. A small drill was used to open a hole in the skull cap. Fine metal probes were used to remove the brain, which was then sectioned in thin slices in order to remove tissue from the designated areas.

At this stage of the procedure, Duncan passed the small gray fragments on to Bill at the central laboratory bench. Bill weighed the tissue samples on a scale, then passed the different samples from each area of the brain through a series of centrifuge vials. Duncan was too involved with his dissections to follow the entire procedure, but an hour after Bill had started his first series of tests Duncan noticed him huddled over a notebook as he documented the final results from the first batch of test animals.

Meanwhile, Barrett had finished his grisly job. Three piles of severed heads sat in metal pans, each stack from a group of rats that had been given different amounts of the test drug, each carefully labeled. With that done, Barrett had begun grinding the tablets into a fine powder. After weighing portions of the powder on a micro-scale, he mixed the drug with sterile water and drew the resulting solution into a series of syringes. Duncan grinned at Bill when Barrett donned a pair of thick cloth gloves in order to handle the rats while giving the injections.

At one o'clock Barrett peeled off his gloves. "That's it for me," he announced in a tone that suggested there would be no debate. "I'm outta here. You guys want me to get you some coffee before I leave?"

Both Bill and Duncan agreed.

"Back in a minute," Barrett said as he stepped into the hall.

When Bill was sure that Barrett could not hear him he turned to Duncan. "I'll bet you ten dollars we won't see that coffee."

"That's a sucker's bet. He's halfway to the parking lot by now. Is it my imagination or does he become more obnoxious every day?"

"It's not your imagination. Before he got his M.D. degree he would sometimes try to be halfway civil. But now he doesn't care. He knows that after his first year of residency he can get his license to practice. He is just waiting for July to roll around, biding his time until he can go into private practice and start making money."

Duncan thought about that for a moment. Barrett would make the worst kind of doctor -- arrogant and uncaring. The kind of stereotype that gave ammunition to the profession's growing number of critics.

"What about you, Bill. What are your plans?"

Bill exhaled a deep breath through his nostrils that was almost a sigh.

"I don't know, Dunc. I want to finish the full three years of residency, but you know about my financial situation. I am so deep in debt now even with the money I get from this research position and the autopsies that I do."

"You're still doing autopsies?"

"At thirty-five dollars per autopsy I can do a couple a week and make grocery money. There's a cold one waiting for me in the morgue at this very moment."

Duncan looked out the window at the sunny, cloudless day. He hesitated before he spoke.

"I can help you with that autopsy if you want."

Bill shook his head.

"Thanks, Duncan. I appreciate that, but I can't let you. You've done enough as it is. If you hadn't been here to help this would have taken all day."

"I really don't mind."

"No. Thanks, but no. Besides, I'm not going to do the autopsy until later this evening." He pointed to his notebook. "I have the data recorded. I'm going home and take a nap. I can collate and graph this tonight, then do the autopsy."

Duncan was too tired to argue. He stood and stretched, bringing his arms up high over his head. Bill put the cap back on his pen and placed it in his pocket. He gathered up the sheets of paper and stacked them inside his notebook.

"What about you, Dunc. What's on your agenda for the weekend?"

He finished his stretch and yawned. "Nothing special. Maybe a little exercise. Clean the house. Eat a decent meal. And then sleep in my own bed. Sleep *all* night. I may sleep *all* day tomorrow, too," he added with a laugh.

"I know what you mean," Bill agreed.

Duncan looked around the room. "Well, I'm gone."

"Go ahead. I just need to clean up a few things, then take the rats back to the specimen room. Thanks for the help." He offered his hand.

Duncan shook it. As he left he said, "Call me later if you want a decent supper. I plan to have a dull, peaceful evening."

Bill just nodded and gave a little wave of his hand before he turned back to his notebook.

Chapter Seven

A false spring greeted Duncan as he left the main entrance of the medical center. The sky was clear and the air was still enough to allow the warmth of the sun to soak into his clothes, but he knew better than to dismiss the winter season. The next two months would be a mix of the occasional day blessed with beautiful spring-like weather interspersed between longer periods of cold winds and chilling rains.

He stood at the edge of the parking lot, tried to remember where he had parked his car, and hoped the battery wasn't dead again. When he reached his car he ran a finger through the thin film of dust that covered it. The car started on the third attempt.

As he drove home he thought back over the last few days. Maybe it was the accumulated lack of sleep, but Duncan had an uneasy feeling that was hard to describe. Perhaps it was because he no longer felt like he was in control. There had been too many surprises recently. Strange and weird things were happening. He wasn't the type to be caught off guard by much, but lately he felt as if he were an astronaut trapped in a gravity-free environment, floating and drifting aimlessly, unable to touch the walls of his spacecraft long enough to establish an anchor.

He thought of Deena and their conversation. He thought of the cowboy and the leeches. And he thought about Gerber Frank, a.k.a. the Land Whale.

Gerber Frank first presented himself to the emergency room eight nights earlier and was an instant legend at the medical center. Actually, Gerber did not present himself. His wife backed up to the door of the emergency room in a pickup truck. A short, fat woman, weighing well over three hundred pounds, she shuffled into the E.R. wearing well-worn purple and pink bathroom slippers that matched the color of the veins in her swollen ankles. She told the receptionist that she needed help for her husband. When the orderlies rolled a wheelchair out to the truck, Mrs. Frank lowered the tailgate to reveal her husband.

He was huge - the largest human being that anyone at the hospital had ever seen.

One orderly stood and stared without speaking. The other shook his head and went back inside for help.

A crowd gathered as word quickly spread. Every nurse and doctor in the E.R., and every orderly and student not involved with a patient had left their duties and formed a circle around the truck.

When advised of the situation, Dr. Norton elbowed his way through the crowd and climbed up into the back of the truck. When he pulled back the blankets covering Gerber the confident look left his face.

Gerber lay on his back. He wore a pair of dark sweat pants with a string belt unfastened at the waist. He wore a shirt that lacked at least two more feet of cloth before it could cover the folds of flesh that quivered and undulated every time he struggled for a breath. He looked up at the doctor with unfocused eyes that seemed too small for his swollen face. When Norton asked him a question, Gerber could only mumble.

Norton sat back on the side of truck bed. Mrs. Frank stood beside the truck and rested her arms on the railing. Norton felt the truck sag slightly.

"He was having trouble breathing this morning. Breathing real hard, like he couldn't catch his breath. I knowed he must have felt bad when he didn't want to eat breakfast."

Someone stifled a laugh at the back of the crowd. Norton shot a hard look in the general direction of the laugh.

Norton turned to her and asked in a quiet voice, "Ma'am . . . how much does he weigh?"

"Well, he was up to about 570 pounds a couple of years ago, but he hadn't left the house since, so we ain't been able to get him weighed."

"Does he have any medical problems? Take any medication?"

She thought for a second.

"No. He ain't never complained about nothing. Never been sick a day since I knowed him."

Norton squatted down by the man and moved his hand from wrist to wrist to neck in a vain attempt to find an area where the patient's pulse wasn't muffled by an overabundance of flesh.

"O.K., let's get him inside. Does anyone have a suggestion as to how we do this?"

When no one moved, one orderly finally stepped forward to survey the situation as the remaining circle of spectators looked from one to another for an answer. When no suggestions came from the crowd that had gathered, Mrs. Frank finally broke the silence.

"Does this hospital have a cafeteria?"

It took over an hour for maintenance workers to weld two hospital beds together to hold Gerber Frank. As the torches flashed and sparked, nurses struggled to obtain blood and urine samples from the prostrate patient. When the preliminary tests had been completed, Norton studied the results. Gerber Frank, medically speaking, was a disaster. He was a severe diabetic although his wife claimed that she and her husband were unaware of this. His increased white blood cell count showed that serious infection, possibly a respiratory infection, raged in his body. His heart was beating irregularly, a scary arrhythmia that was possibly due to the years of strain his heart had endured pumping blood against the added resistance of such bulk. Norton suspected congestive heart failure.

Norton for once was unsure as to the best way to start treating the patient's problem, so he took the most obvious choice, a time-honored method of treatment. When in doubt -- refer.

He admitted the patient to the hospital and ordered him to be sent to the internal medicine ward on the third floor. Norton wanted Frank out of his E.R. as quickly as possible.

When the metal frame of the bed had cooled from the welding, mattresses were placed and an army of orderlies and nurses shifted Frank onto the bed. A half dozen held the bed in position against the truck. Another half dozen people in their sock feet stood in the truck and on the bed as they pulled and dragged the motionless bulk onto the mattresses.

After much sweating and cursing, they stuffed the patient onto the freight elevator. Someone reached into the elevator to push the button for the third floor to send him, unescorted due to lack of space, to materialize upstairs.

Upstairs, Dr. Shukowsky looked at the rotating assignment list to see which intern was due to accept a new patient. Not pleased with what he saw, he crossed out the name Patel and wrote the name Frank, Gerber beside the name Russthorne, Duncan. His thin, crisp lips formed his version of a smile.

Since the doors to a private room were too narrow to accommodate the bed Gerber Frank was placed at one end of the hallway, with curtains drawn around him for privacy.

Duncan cared for Frank for seven days. He began by placing the intravenous needle. This chore took more than an hour since it was difficult to find a suitable vein. His blood vessels were all hidden by a thick padding of fat. Duncan also placed the catheter after the nurses' attempts failed. He knelt on the bed between the patient's thighs while a nurse on each side leaned over to pull the thighs apart. Open friction sores oozed a pink-tinged fluid along the inner length of his upper legs. The smell, a mixture of feces and sour sweat, made one of the less experienced nurses gag.

Once the preliminary steps were accomplished, Duncan began I.V. antibiotics for the infection and insulin for the diabetes. Then Duncan could only wait for the patient to respond.

By the third day Gerber Frank showed a little improvement, although Duncan was still worried about his inability to clean the fluids from Frank's lungs. Gerber fought for each breath. The lung sounds Duncan heard through his stethoscope were scary slurping and gurgling noises as air bubbles percolated through layers of mucous.

On the forth day Frank's condition stabilized. His airways were less congested and his heart no longer gave the occasional ominous pause as it returned to a more regular rhythm.

On the fifth day Duncan removed his stethoscope from Frank's chest with a look of satisfaction and relief on his face. Frank tried to return the smile.

"Are you feeling better?"

Frank managed a nod. "A little. How long have I been here?"

"This is your fifth day."

Frank examined the tube that ran from the fluids bag into his arm. He looked around the room with unfocused eyes.

"What kind of shape am I in?"

Duncan told him the truth. "Your condition is not very good. You are a very sick fellow."

Frank was silent for a moment.

"How sick am I?" he asked.

Duncan counted off his problems on his fingers.

"First, you are a diabetic. A severe diabetic. Do you understand what that means?"

"Yea, Doc. My father was a diabetic."

"Second, you have pneumonia." Duncan paused, then continued when Frank nodded.

51

"Third, your heart isn't working too well. Right now it's being forced to work too hard because of the fluid in your lungs."

Frank was silent for a moment as he turned the information over in his mind.

"How long do you think I'll be here in the hospital?" he asked.

"A week, maybe. Maybe longer. You're a very sick man." Duncan said as he stood to leave. "And once you're home, you're going to have to change your habits some. You will have to take insulin and go on a diet. Later you will have to start some light exercise."

"A diet?" Gerber Frank shook his head and smiled. "But Doc, I enjoy eating too much."

"I agree. You like to eat too much."

"Are you talking about grapefruit and cottage cheese, Doc? I hate to tell you, but I'm not a bean sprout type of guy."

"I can tell. But look on the bright side -- you're lucky to be alive."

"I bet I won't feel that way when I see my first tray of hospital food. Wait a minute, Doc. Where are you going?"

"I have to make some notes in your record. And I also have to check on my other patients. I'll be back later," he said as he pushed the curtain aside.

"But Doc. About this diet. I enjoy eating as much as anything else in life. I mean, what if I told you that you couldn't . . . What if . . . What do you enjoy most in life? What if someone said you couldn't enjoy your life anymore?"

"Don't worry about the diet too much. We still have to get you well."

He left Gerber Frank with a worried look on the patient's face.

It would be the only conversation Duncan would ever have with Gerber Frank. That night his wife brought him a half gallon of premium vanilla ice cream concealed in a shopping bag. Frank emptied the container. Two hours later the patient's blood sugar, which Duncan had struggled to bring under control over the last four days, hit a new high. When Duncan was summoned by the night nurse after the two a. m. check, Frank had already begun to slide into a coma.

On the sixth day the situation worsened. The improvement of his lungs reversed as the air sacs continued to collect fluid and his heart struggled to pump against the extra load. His condition quickly deteriorated.

On the seventh day Duncan took the risky step of increasing the diuretic in order to drain fluid from Frank's body, decrease the burden on his heart, and prevent him from drowning in his own fluids.

On the eighth day Gerber Frank died. The diuretic, in addition to draining fluids from the body, had upset the patient's electrolyte balance which was vital to the proper contraction of the beating heart. Frank's heart, already tired and strained, quivered, seized, and then stopped. Duncan, asleep in the chair next to Gerber's bed, woke immediately when the heart monitor sounded but all attempts at resuscitation failed. Gerber Frank was dead.

Duncan left Frank's bed and went straight to the men's bathroom. He washed his face with cold water then walked across the tile floor, leaned against the wall with his eyes closed and arms folded, his chin tucked into his chest. A few minutes later he washed his face a second time, his hands quivering as he splashed the cold water around his face, the cold rivulets running down his neck to soak his collar.

When he heard footsteps outside the bathroom door, he entered one of the stalls and closed the door. As he leaned against the side of the stall he noticed a cartoon that had been scrawled on the wall. A caricature of Frank had been drawn in ink above the toilet. Across the wide expanse of stomach was written "Land Whale." A stick figure, drawn with a stove pipe hat and a beard, stood to one side holding an oversize hypodermic syringe over its head. The stick figure was also labeled. It originally read, "Duncan (call me Ishmael) Russthorne." Someone had scratched through the word "Ishmael" and replaced it with the name "Ahab."

Great, he thought, a literate toilet scribbler.

As Duncan sat in the toilet stall, his feet on the seat as he perched on the back of the toilet, two fourth-year medical students entered the restroom.

One headed for a urinal. The other stood in front of the long mirror that ran above the row of sinks and ran his fingers through his hair repeatedly in an attempt to train his hair off of his forehead.

"You hear about the Land Whale?" said the M-4 at the mirror as he preened.

"What?"

"I just heard them talking at the nurses' desk. He coded."

"Did he make it?"

"No. He's history, man."

"Gee, too bad. I never got a chance to see him. Do you think I could look at him before they take him downstairs?"

"No!" Duncan's voice thundered from the stall.

Startled, the M-4 at the urinal quickly zipped his pants.

53

"What?"

"I said No!" Duncan bellowed as he slammed open the stall door. "He wasn't some sideshow freak at the circus!"

The vain M-4 tried to speak.

"But he didn't . . ."

Duncan pointed a finger at him.

"And he had a name, dammit! His name wasn't The Land Whale! He had a name!" Duncan yelled.

The two students retreated toward the door under Duncan's angry glare, but the vain M-4 paused before leaving.

"Who do you think you are? The Avenger of the Third Floor Men's Room?"

His buddy tapped him on the chest with the back of his hand. "That's good, man. Clark Kent has a telephone booth. Dr. Do-Right here has a toilet stall!"

As their footsteps receded down the hall, Duncan stood in front of the mirror, his nostrils flaring with each breath, fists clenched. He turned to see his reflection in the mirror but did not pause for inspection, his anger having drained the last reserve of energy he could muster. He made his way to the on-call room and collapsed onto a bunk, only to be awakened a short time later by Deena's wristwatch alarm.

Chapter Eight

Duncan turned the car off State Street and onto the side street where his house was located. What had Deena said? She just wanted a life. Then he thought about Frank's question. What DID he enjoy most in life? Not much at this moment. Maybe he was like Ahab. Maybe the one thing he wanted most in life, his goal of being a doctor, was killing him, or at least a part of him.

The radio played a song by the recently murdered artist. Duncan hummed along with the tune. Strange days, indeed.

His house, the house left to him by his great aunt's estate, was set in one of the older areas of the city. The homes in the neighborhood belonged to a combination of older, well-to-do families interspersed with a sprinkling of prosperous, younger couples intent on renovation. Duncan had mixed feelings as to how this yuppie invasion would change the character of his neighborhood and had already noticed one difference. The older residents took great pride in their yards and would spend hours fussing over one hedgerow or rose arbor. The younger residents took equal pride, but it was shown in the form of a hired landscaping service that lacked originality and left the homes with a generic look and flavor. Duncan called it the credit-card-yard mentality.

His house was one of the oldest in the neighborhood. The narrow, two story brick home had been built in the late 1850's in the Greek Revivalist style popular in southern cities at that time. The two-level gallery was fronted by fluted columns. Tall windows with shutters reached to the top of each level. The acanthus leaves on the tops of the columns and the carvings on the pilaster that framed the recessed door showed the attention to detail that had been given to the construction.

Duncan parked the car at the curb and crossed the sidewalk, the hinges on the iron gatepost screeching their need for oil as he passed into the small front yard. He felt a little guilty at the amount of care he had given his own yard when he saw how the old heirloom shrubs grew unchecked around the small yard. A mixture of azaleas, gardenias, white and pink spirea, one lilac, calacanthas, crepe myrtles, and numerous other bushes hid the front porch in a riot of unchecked propagation. Maybe there would be more time for yard work during his second year of his residency, he thought. Maybe.

The mail in his box by the door overflowed; some of it had fallen on the porch. Most of it was junk mail addressed to the occupant. He noticed Barrett's mailbox had been emptied. He tried to balance his knapsack, his clinic coat, and the mail as he fumbled with the key. Unlocking the door, he stepped inside.

A long rectangle of light from the French windows fell across the hardwood floor to reach the fireplace on the opposite wall. He dropped his bundles by the hearth and sorted his mail, most of which he discarded without a second glance into the fireplace with a flip of his wrist. He placed the rest beside the antique humpbacked clock on the mantel to be opened later.

An unsealed envelope with no postage stamp had been placed on the mantel addressed to Duncan in Barrett's unmistakable scrawl. He opened it to find a stack of one hundred dollar bills. The note wrapped around the money read: *"Three months rent past due & three months rent in advance."* Duncan read the note twice. Barrett had never paid for more than a month's rent at a time, much less pay in advance. Maybe his student loan had come through and he had decided to catch up on the rent before he spent it, Duncan told himself. He placed the money back in the envelope and wondered how long it would be before Barrett would be asking him for a loan.

As the clock chimed three, Duncan looked out the window into the cloudless sky and decided that the weather was too pleasant to ignore. Changing quickly, he used the banister on the front porch for his leg stretches, then left the yard at a quick jog.

He had an established route when he ran through the neighborhood. The street dipped as he headed east, then began to rise slowly for two blocks until he reached the street that bordered the campus of a small liberal arts college. He turned to the right and tried to catch a glance of the pleasant, gray-haired lady who lived in the Tudor style home. She often sat at the upstairs window, stooped over her desk, gazing out toward the street, a portrait of the artist framed by wooden beams and stucco. Sometimes she would wave, sometimes she was lost in thought, but today the window was vacant.

He ran across the soccer field on campus and around a small pond. A young couple sat on a blanket by the water's edge, their faces etched in earnest conversation. The local duck population, trained to expect a handout, bobbed in the water and squawked as the couple ignored them.

By the third mile of his run Duncan's mind was beginning to slowly unwind; the pressures of the medical center were beginning to fade. He hit a long flat stretch and pushed himself harder as he tried to erase his mental chatter. By the fifth mile the confusion in his mind gave way to the burning sensation in his lungs. There was no room for thoughts of Kay, Gerber Frank, the Cowboy, or Shukowsky. Just a cognitive numbness as his mind shut out the world.

By the time he turned the last corner on his return, he was being chased by three dogs. One, a chocolate-colored Doberman, snapped at his heels as Duncan leaped the short iron fence into his yard. He didn't look back until he was safely through the front door.

In the kitchen he downed a glass of water, then filled the glass halfway and returned to the gallery windows at the front of the house. Duncan could see the Doberman still at the fence, its snout stuck between two of the rails, a look of canine frustration on its face. When he turned a large overstuffed chair to face the front windows, the square of sunlight from the corner window revealed a collection of gray dustballs where the chair had once stood. Another thick layer of dust could be seen underneath the plant stand he used as a bookcase. Duncan made a mental note to vacuum. He also needed to wash some clothes before he cooked dinner. Dinner presented another problem because the odds were high that his refrigerator was empty. But first he had to rest and catch his breath.

He propped his feet in the low windowsill and drained the last of the water, then rubbed the cool, ribbed surface of the glass slowly across his forehead. The silence in the house was absolute except for the ticking of the mantel clock that served only to emphasize the emptiness of the house. The pillows in the chair folded comfortably around him and the sun was warm as it fell across his legs. He closed his eyes for just a moment to rest and quickly fell asleep.

Duncan woke with a start in the dark room when he heard the disembodied voices. It took a moment for his sleep-clouded mind to realize that the voices came, filtered, through the front door. The jangling of keys soon followed as someone fumbled with the lock. The door opened and Duncan heard the sound of a hand sliding against the wall in search of the light switch.

"Yes!" Barrett exclaimed when the light came on, as if he had invented the light bulb. In one hand he held a six-pack of cheap beer. His other hand was wrapped around the waist of a very thin young girl wearing a short black dress over black leggings. They staggered into the room together but separated when she tripped over the corner of the carpet. Her laughter terminated in a squeal when she turned to see Duncan seated only a few feet away.

"Duncan, you're here." Barrett said, not trying to hide his disappointment.

Duncan, at first confused to see Barrett with someone other than Jenny, stood up to greet them.

"Hi. My name's Duncan."

"Oops. Sorry. I should introduce you. Suzie, this is my roommate, Duncan. Duncan, this is Suzie," he slurred his words as he spoke.

Duncan nodded to the girl. She had short dark hair that stuck from her head in spikes, the tips of which were dyed rose. Duncan guessed she was in high school, or maybe a freshman in college at most.

"We met down at Skid Marks," Barrett said.

"They've got the best New Wave sounds," the girl added.

"What are you doing here in the dark, roomie?"

"I fell asleep." He rubbed one eye with a finger to unglue a dry eyelid and pointed to the chair as if to explain. "What time is it, anyway?"

Barrett looked around Suzie's waist to read his watch. "9:05. You here for the evening?"

"Yea. I guess so. Guess I'll eat a bite and try to straighten up the house a little."

"Don't let us bother you. We were going to have a little party, but we'll go up to my apartment. Want a beer?" he said as he offered the six-pack.

"No thanks. I think I've got some in the fridge."

"Well, we won't bother you." He dragged the girl toward the foot of the stairway which sat adjacent to the kitchen door. She turned and gave a little wave and a giggle as she followed Barrett upstairs. In a moment he heard the door shut, followed by music from Barrett's stereo.

As Duncan moved around the house gathering up clothes to be washed, he thought of Barrett's girlfriend Jenny. Barrett and Jenny had been high school sweethearts. He was the jock and she was the cheerleader. Pretty if not beautiful, she was quiet and thoughtful. She was also devoted to Barrett in spite of the times he ignored or mistreated her, which had become more frequent. Duncan did not understand why she put up with his increasingly abusive behavior. But Duncan did not claim to understand people. Medicine was a science and an art. People were a mystery, with no textbook to explain their

58

behavior. He just hoped Jenny did not decide to call or come by the house tonight.

Duncan dumped the clothes in the washing machine in the utility closet at the back of the kitchen and scrounged through the shelves for food, then turned to the refrigerator. The only thing edible he could find was a frozen dinner. Saltillo Dinner, the label read. He placed it in the microwave and punched the button. As the appliance hummed, he opened the refrigerator and began to remove the spoiled food and place it in a plastic garbage bag. The cheese had a coat of fine green hair. The half-empty carton of milk had an expiration date two months past. He started to pour the milk down the sink but decided to drop it into the bag unopened when the congealed liquid inside failed to move when he shook the container. He peeked into a small Tupperware container and quickly discarded the whole plastic box without emptying it. He made a mental note to buy food with a longer shelf life as he twisted the garbage bag closed.

A ball of black fur shot between his legs when he opened the kitchen door. It was the neighborhood cat, owner unknown, come to beg for a meal.

"Hey, Captain Moonlight," Duncan said as he bent down to stroke its back. "Wait here. Supper will be ready in a minute." He walked out the door of the kitchen and down the steps to the back of the house. The light bulb at the corner of the house had burned out long ago, but the glow from the security lamp at the back corner of the lot cast enough light for him to find the form of the large metal garbage can tucked under the steps to the fire escape that went to the second floor.

As he opened the lid to the garbage can, the window overhead suddenly opened. Duncan stepped back against the house into deeper shadows as the sound of Barrett's voice mixed with the music filtered down to him. Duncan looked up to see Barrett sitting on the window sill, his back turned towards him as he exhaled a long plume of smoke. Barrett took a sip of beer with one hand and, with the other hand, dropped the glowing butt of his smoke out the window. As the embers fell at Duncan's feet, he recognized the strong husky smell of marijuana. Duncan crushed out the glowing roach with his heel, closed the garbage can, and went back inside to his dinner.

Chapter Nine

The dream was vague. Ill-defined forms floated through a haze around the mouth of the well in which Duncan stood, never coming close enough for him to recognize. They spoke too softly for him to understand their message, with fragments of words bouncing down the well as Duncan strained to hear. Once, in the middle of the dream, a voice became clear enough for Duncan to hear the words "Please! Please!" before it faded away. The voice was familiar but left Duncan with a sense of unease that slowly disappeared as his mind drifted deeper into the well of sleep.

Jenny burst into Duncan's room soon after midnight, sobbing and incoherent. She grabbed him by the wrist as he fumbled for his blue jeans, pulling him to the bedroom door. She pointed upstairs to Barrett's room before she sank to one knee against the door frame. He grabbed her by the shoulders as she tried to speak, but she could only choke out the name "Barrett" as she again pointed upstairs. Duncan quickly vaulted up the stairs three steps at a time and burst into Barrett's room.

The first thing Duncan saw was a pair of bare legs on the floor protruding past the foot of the bed. As Duncan moved around the bed he could see the whole body. Barrett Jeter lay sprawled and unmoving on the floor. He lay on his back with his head turned to the left, his partially closed robe showing a portion of his underwear. His eyes were closed, his right hand was curled against his cheek, and the portion of his face that Duncan could see was frozen in a grimace. Duncan's stomach gave an extra twist as he took in the ashen tone of Barrett's face.

He moved quickly to the body and knelt beside it. He tried and failed to find a pulse in the wrist that was against his cheek. As he tried to move the right arm to check for a pulse in the arteries of the neck, Duncan noticed that the hand wasn't merely resting against the cheek; one of the fingers was caught between his teeth. Barrett appeared to be biting one of his fingertips. Duncan dislodged the finger with a tug, and the hand slipped to the floor as he checked Barrett's neck for a pulse. Then he noticed a smear of blood on the floor beside the body. As he turned the head he saw that the left side of his temple had been crushed. Gelatinous clots of blood matted the hair.

When Duncan saw the extent of the sickening depression in Barrett's skull, he knew with finality that Barrett could not be revived. He stared at the body for minutes as he knelt beside the still figure, hoping that this was just another product of his sleep-deprived mind and that this bizarre dream would soon end.

But the dream did not end. Barrett Jeter was dead.

Duncan stayed by the body until a numbing ache in his knees and thighs forced him to stand. He rose stiffly and slowly, closed the door behind him, and lingered on each step as he went down the stairs to call the police.

The first policeman reached the house so quickly Duncan guessed that the patrol car was already in the vicinity. Polite and businesslike, the policeman, after seeing the body, asked a few questions, then requested that Jenny and Duncan stay in the kitchen.

The police detective arrived within twenty minutes. Duncan was surprised, not by the fact that she was black and female, but by her young age and casual appearance. Duncan guessed her age as late thirties or early forties. She wore blue jeans and tennis shoes. Beneath her jacket a maroon cardigan sweater covered a white t-shirt. Her hair was neat but slightly unconventional for what Duncan expected of the police. He noticed that her voice carried a quality of precision that lacked any hint of a Southern accent. She introduced herself as police lieutenant Alfie Storey, then left to follow a uniformed policeman upstairs.

Time passed as Duncan watched a parade of technicians carrying an assortment of equipment pass by the kitchen door on their way up the stairs. A lighter tread on the stairs preceded the police woman's entrance into the kitchen. She carried a leather-bound appointment book in her hand. Without acknowledging the presence of anyone in the room, she walked over to the coffee maker and poured herself a cup. She leaned back against the counter, book in one hand, coffee cup in the other, as she studied the names and addresses written in it.

"Is this his?" She looked at Duncan and Jenny.

Jenny sat at the table with a blanket wrapped around her shoulders as she stared into a distant space somewhere past the rim of her coffee cup.

"Yes," she said softly. "I gave it to him at Christmas a couple of years ago." She lowered her head as her eyes moistened.

"The only doctor's handwriting I've ever been able to read," the detective said to no one in particular.

The door at the back of the kitchen opened and another policeman walked in carrying a wallet he had speared with his pen. The black leather matched the leather of the appointment book. "Found this on the bottom step of the fire escape."

Alfie took a paper towel from the counter and laid it over the palm of her hand to receive the wallet. She used a fingernail to open it and carefully pulled out the driver's license. "Roger Barrett Jeter," she read. She examined the compartments of the billfold. "No money. Did your roommate have any credit cards?" she asked, directing the question to Duncan.

He thought for a moment, then looked to Jenny and touched her on her arm to bring her out of her daze. "Oh. Yes," she said softly. "A couple. He gripes all the time about being maxxed out on them." When she realized she was still talking about him in the present tense, she squeezed her eyes shut in an effort to control her tears.

"Contact the credit card companies," Alfie said to one of the policemen. "Let's see if anybody uses them." She folded the towel around the wallet. "Give this to the lab men."

Alfie walked over and put her arm on Jenny's shoulder. "I'm sorry. I know this is difficult. But I need to ask you some questions. Let's go in here," Alfie said as she motioned to the living room.

After a few minutes of soft conversation that Duncan strained to hear but couldn't understand, Alfie returned to the kitchen and sat down at the kitchen table.

"Is she O.K.?" Duncan asked.

"I think so. An officer is taking her home. She says they had an argument this afternoon. He told her he didn't want to see her for a few days, that he needed some time alone. She says she couldn't sleep so she came by to apologize. It was around one o'clock and the door was unlocked." Alfie reached into her jacket and pulled out a package of cigarettes. "Mind if I smoke?"

Duncan shook his head. He reached over to the counter by the sink, picked up a small saucer, and pushed it in front of Alfie for an ashtray.

"Are you O.K.?" she asked.

Duncan nodded. "Yes." He paused for a moment. "It hasn't really sunk in yet."

Alfie nodded, exhaled, and tapped ashes into the saucer.

"You say you were here all night."

"I went to bed around ten. Barrett came in about an hour before that and had gone upstairs. With a girl. Not Jenny."

"Who was the girl?"

Duncan thought for a moment. "I think her name was Suzie. I had never seen her before."

"Never?"

"No. I got the impression that they had just met. At a bar," he added.

"Which bar?"

Alfie took notes as Duncan answered.

"Can you describe her?"

"Short, with a slight build. Short dark hair, punk style. She said her name was Suzie but didn't give her last name."

"Were they arguing?"

Duncan shook his head. "Anything but."

"Had he been acting differently lately? Did he seem worried about anything?"

"No. No different."

"Had he any enemies?"

When Duncan hesitated, Alfie looked up from her notebook, took a long drag on her cigarette, and rested her chin on her palm as Duncan searched for the right words.

"Well, he didn't have many friends."

She exhaled a long plume of smoke. "Were you his friend, Duncan?"

"I wasn't his enemy," he said evenly as she looked into his eyes.

"Do you know of anyone who would have liked to see him dead?"

Duncan suddenly felt very uncomfortable. He was aware of her eyes as she studied the reaction to her question on his face. He dismissed the question with a shrug of his shoulders. A moment passed before she asked another question.

"Did you hear anything tonight?"

Duncan frowned. "I don't think so," he answered tentatively.

Alfie returned the frown. "What do you mean, 'I don't think so?' Does that mean you might have heard something?"

"I heard someone pleading for help. But I thought I was dreaming."

63

A clattering in the stairwell made Alfie turn. One of the attendants carrying the sheet-draped body had slipped and dumped his end of the gurney. The two attendants cursed each other as they passed the blame.

Alfie Storey closed her notebook and stood up to leave. "I'll be in touch. You will need to come downtown to my office in the next day or two. We may need to ask a few more questions."

Duncan stopped her before she moved.

"Can you tell me what happened?"

She stubbed out her cigarette in the saucer.

"His window was open. His wallet was found outside with no cash or credit cards. What do you think?"

"What? Someone breaks into his room and then kills him? You think he was killed by a burglar?"

She answered him with a question.

"Would he have been the type to confront a burglar?"

"Barrett would have probably confronted two or three burglars. He considered himself indestructible. He was that type of person."

Alfie turned to look at the silent form being carried away. "That's too bad," she said. "His room has been locked and sealed off. Be sure no one goes in." She picked up the appointment book and placed it in her coat pocket. "I'll be in touch."

From the kitchen he heard the front door shut as the last policeman left. The flashing lights from the ambulance that had flickered through the front window ceased circling across the walls of the front room. Duncan sat at the kitchen table, alone with his thoughts, as he tapped a spoon on the table top in time with the ticking of the mantel clock. The clock chimed the half hour past four before he rose and went back to bed.

Chapter Ten

Sleep never came. He rested in bed on his right side as he watched the minute dial on his digital clock blink from 0 to 9 then back again. When he closed his eyes the image of Barrett Jeter, sprawled dead on the floor of the room above him, flashed through his mind. He saw the pale color of death on his face, the hair and blood clotted together, and the finger. Odd, that. More than odd. Why did Barrett die with a finger in his mouth? Surely this was a nightmare. At 6:30 he rose and dressed. A trip up the staircase to be confronted by the yellow police tape convinced him it was all too real.

Downstairs the telephone rang. He rushed down the stairs, his sock feet slipping as he turned into the kitchen, and grabbed the receiver from its hook.

"Why didn't you call me about Barrett?" Bill's voice blurted from the telephone.

"You've heard, then. I was going to call you but . . ."

"I'm at the morgue. They called me this morning and said they had an autopsy for me to do. When I got here I pulled back the sheet and - Jesus -- I almost threw up. What the hell happened?"

Duncan proceeded to tell Bill the events of the previous night. A long silence followed before Bill responded. "Well, it's not like . . . . Aw, hell, Duncan. I disliked him as much as the next person. I'm not going to play the hypocrite now.

But this . . . to have this happen to him . . ." Finally Bill said in an almost inaudible voice, "I can't do this autopsy, Duncan."

"Why do you have to do the autopsy? What about the coroner at the State Crime Lab?"

"The Medical Center handles most of the autopsies for the SCL on weekends."

"Since when?"

"When the legislature cut this year's budget the Medical Examiner quit again. That's the third M.E. in four years. Since we are a state-supported institution, and we do the autopsy a lot cheaper anyway, the legislature dropped that responsibility on us."

"You aren't the only one doing autopsies, are you? Can't you find someone else?"

"There is a graduate student in anatomy that helps occasionally. But a physician has to be present as a witness in cases where there is a crime involved with the death and Dr. Carter is out sick today."

"Do you want me to help?"

"No, I won't make both of us go through this. Look, I'm fine. I'll be all right. It's just . . . well, this came as a shock . . ."

"Ice the body, Bill. Leave it for the grad student, or wait for Dr. Carter."

"Yea. I will. Thanks for the ear," he mumbled as he hung up.

Duncan sat by the phone and tried to think of someone else he should call, someone who might need to know that a friend had passed away. When he realized how few people would care, Duncan tried to sort through his own emotions.

Unlike others, Duncan had never really hated Barrett; he wouldn't allow Barrett that much influence and control over his life. He had viewed Barrett more as an obstacle to be avoided. But did he feel guilt because he couldn't truly mourn Barrett's passing, or was the unease he felt the sadness that comes from the realization of the wasted potential that Barrett possessed, the sad fact of a life wasted? If no man is an island, Barrett had tried his best to disprove that belief and had filled his personal landscape with barren sands and cactus.

He sat in thought for a long time, then picked up the telephone and tried to call Deena. He let the phone ring for several minutes but there was no answer.

On Monday morning Duncan's first stop was at the office of the Dean of Student Affairs, Dr. Gawain Goza. Dr. Goza was warmly regarded for his good relationship with the students. He was also highly regarded for his ability to remove a gallbladder quickly, holding the medical center record for shortest surgery time. Duncan had assisted him once in surgery and had found that his coffee cup, left in the student lounge, was still warm when he returned. A large, friendly man, he was quick to smile and did not have the total lack of humor that many professors did. He had been informed of Barrett's death but did not question Duncan on the details. He assured Duncan that it was understood that he might miss the next few days of duties.

"Take all the time you need. This was a shock to all of us, but the administration understands this must be especially difficult for you."

Duncan nodded in appreciation.

Goza rose and poured himself a cup of coffee. "Would you like some?"

"Please. Black."

Duncan took the cup and inhaled the sweet aroma. It was good coffee spoiled by the addition of a berry flavoring.

"This is such a tragedy." Dr. Goza said with a lowered head and look of regret. "He was a very good young man."

"Yes sir." Again Duncan nodded.

"And so dedicated, even in death."

Dr. Goza saw the puzzled look on Duncan's face.

"Oh, I guess you didn't know. Barrett had signed a consent form with our body bank. He left his body to the medical center to help further the education of other medical students."

Duncan fought to keep his surprise from showing. With much effort he finally managed to speak. "That was Barrett. Always thinking of others."

As he rose to shake hands, Dr. Goza fixed him with a serious look. "I hope this terrible occurrence will not affect your performance, Duncan. We are pleased with your work. You have a great future ahead of you."

Duncan assured him that he would be fine, thanked him, and left. As he stood outside the Dean's office, Duncan thought about what Goza had said. Goza had tried to be kind and considerate, but too much time had lapsed since he had been a student; the years he had spent among the bureaucrats had molded his thinking. The message had been clear. Take time off, grieve, then get back to work. Duncan shook his head. Had he really expected more?

But the fact that Barrett had donated his body to the anatomy lab disturbed him more. Duncan had never known of a student to do this. Not that it wasn't a noble cause -- it was. A medical education would be impossible without cadavers to study. But Duncan had never considered donating his own body and never would. He had signed a consent form to allow for organ donation, but that was completely different. He liked the idea that one day he might possibly help another person live. But to offer up his body for dissection, to have his naked body viewed by strangers every day as they picked and sliced him into scraps? No, he had given his soul to the medical center, they could not have his body. He hoped to find a little more solitude in his final rest.

67

Donating one's body to science was a noble thing to do, he decided. Noble was the best word. It indicated that some sacrifice was involved, a sacrifice that Duncan was not willing to make. And Barrett? Noble was not one of the words that came to mind when he thought of Barrett.

An uneasy feeling, too vague for the cause to be pinpointed, stirred in the depths of his mind. Duncan dropped his unfinished coffee into a trash can in the hallway and walked to the stairway. He took the steps two at a time on his way down to the morgue.

Dr. Carter, head of the pathology department at UMC, sat at a desk in a small office that joined the autopsy room, his head hunched down between his shoulders. When Duncan knocked on the open door, Dr. Carter lowered a pathology journal he held in his left hand and peered over his half-glasses.

"Hello, Duncan," he said as he stood and offered his hand.

On Dr. Carter's desk by the telephone a silver frame with scrolled borders held a photograph of his family. In the photograph he stood beside his wife, an attractive lady of slim but athletic build. Three smiling teenage girls stood beside them. The image of the pathologist in the photo contrasted sharply with present reality.

Dr. Carter had once been a vigorous middle-aged man but had somehow contracted hepatitis during the course of performing an autopsy. Perhaps a small, unseen tear in his latex glove had exposed his skin while he worked, or a bone drill had flung a microscopic aerosolized droplet of body fluid into the air that he had breathed. The exact mode of transmission would remain unknown, but somehow a viral particle had invaded Dr. Carter's body and taken root in his liver. The hepatitis had developed into a chronic liver disease and over the past three years the once healthy pathologist had been transformed into a caricature of one of the cadavers he routinely inspected, stark evidence to the fact that even the dead can cause harm.

Duncan shook his sallow, wrinkled hand.

"I'm sorry about Barrett. I heard that he shared a room with you." His sunken cheeks and lips revealed too much of his teeth as he tried to smile.

"Thanks, Dr. Carter. It has been a shock."

The pathologist nodded in sympathy. "You were the one to find the body?"

"His girlfriend and I did. That's why I came by this morning. Would it be possible for me to see the autopsy report?"

Dr. Carter raised an eyebrow. When Duncan saw the questioning look in his face he tried to explain.

"When I found Barrett . . . . Well, I guess it is nothing, but when I found his body he seemed to be biting his finger."

"His finger?"

"Or he had his finger in his mouth." Duncan tried to show what he had seen.

Dr. Carter thought about that for a few moments. He scratched the bald center of his head with a long fingernail.

"His right hand?"

"Yes."

Carter shuffled some of the papers on his desk. He pulled a manila folder from a stack of papers and glanced at the contents before he handed it to Duncan.

"Since the State of Mississippi has declared an autopsy or coroner's report a matter of public record, you would be able to see this eventually anyway."

Duncan took the folder and turned to the first page.

Carter continued to speak as Duncan read the report. "Cause of death appears to be due to head trauma, two or more blows to the left temporal region of the skull. The first blow was not that severe; he could have survived that one. The second blow did not follow immediately after the first, judging by the amount of bleeding into the tissue around the area of the first injury. The second blow was of such force that fragments of the temporal bone were displaced medially to a slight degree. He probably died fairly quickly. Perhaps not instantly, but quickly."

Duncan looked up from the report. "Time to reach up and place his hand to his mouth. But why?"

"Oh. The fingers were another finding." He pointed to the report. "The medial metacarpal of the index and middle fingers of his right hand were fractured."

"Fractured?" He paused. "Perhaps there was a struggle?"

"Or he was trying to ward off the blow that killed him," Carter said.

Duncan glanced through the rest of the report.

"Everything else was within normal limits?"

"WNL. Nothing unusual. Of course, the SCL hasn't had time to report on the blood and tissue samples we took from the body."

Duncan closed the folder and handed it back to the pathologist, who took and placed the record in one of the metal filing cabinets beside the desk. He considered asking Dr. Carter if he could examine the body but decided against it. He could always come back later with Bill when Dr. Carter was gone.

Dr. Carter let out a long breath of air as he sat back down at his desk. "Were you looking for something in particular, Duncan?" he asked.

"No. I just ..." Duncan shook his head. "I guess I was just trying to deal with his death, just trying to make some sense out of it."

The pathologist turned to look at the photograph of his family, studied their faces briefly, then closed his eyes in one long blink before he returned to the paperwork on his desk. "I hope you do arrive at some understanding, Duncan."

Duncan stepped towards the door then stopped, his hand resting on the doorknob as he turned to speak. "One more thing, Dr. Carter. I heard Barrett had requested that his remains be sent to the anatomy lab."

"Why, yes. I have the signed release right here." He tapped a bony finger on the document lying on his desk. "He willed it to be donated to the anatomy department . . ." He paused to adjust his glasses. ". . . and signed it last year."

"Is that very common among medical students, Dr. Carter?" He knew the answer but wanted to hear Carter confirm his suspicion.

"No, not common at all. Once they see what happens to a body in the anatomy lab ..." He paused and gave a dry chuckle. "Unusual, don't you think?"

"Yes. Very unusual," Duncan agreed.

Duncan found his road atlas in the clutter of the bookshelf in his bedroom. He would go to the funeral, he persuaded himself, because Jenny would need the support of her friends. The map showed that the directions would be relatively simple. Crockett lay in the extreme northeast part of the state. A route up the Natchez Trace - the old Indian footpath turned National Parkway - would be a straight shot.

Duncan sat with one leg draped over an arm of the chair and studied the map. The county that held Crockett was next to Bois d'Arc county - the county of Duncan's birth. He closed his eyes and tried to conjure up the memories. He couldn't remember his mother, who had died soon after his birth. Much clearer was the memory of the white frame house with its broad front porch where he had lived. He could recall the bright interior with distant ceilings and simple furnishings, and the stairway to the attic that he and his older brother would race up and down until they were told to stop. There were a few other memories -- the big loft in the barn, the dank smell of the old root cellar, the quiet love of the black lady who came to keep him and his brother every day while their father worked. His father - those few memories were the most clear. The shiny coal-black hair. The dark eyes that flashed when his temper was aroused. The way two of his fingers on his left hand were curled inward, a souvenir from the war. The habit he had of cocking his head to hear out of his good right ear, again a result of the war in the Pacific. The way he had looked at the funeral home as he lay in the coffin.

He opened his eyes and shook his head. He had left Bois d'Arc County when he was about eight years old to live with his father's sister in Birmingham. Her husband was a successful surgeon and had easily agreed to his wife's request to adopt the two boys. He remembered the day he had left Bois d'Arc County -- looking out the back window of his aunt and uncle's car at the home where he had been raised, waving good-bye to Mother Spight, their housekeeper, as she stood by the fence in the front yard. He remembered how her smile had given him courage as the car pulled away, her slight figure finally obscured by the distance and the dust from the tires of the car.

He looked at the map again. With his finger he traced a route from Crockett to Bois d'Arc County and back down to the Natchez Trace Parkway. It had been too many years since he had been to the place of his earliest memories.

He stood up, tossed the map in the chair, went back to his bedroom, and changed into his running shorts and shoes.

Duncan pushed himself hard, running at a faster pace than usual. He even added an extra few blocks to his normal route, but the mental catharsis he hoped for never came.

The fact that Barrett had donated his body bothered Duncan. Could he have misjudged a person so much? And the finger in his mouth. Was it because he was in so much pain? Does a dying person's actions have to be rational? These were questions Duncan couldn't answer. And each question seemed to raise another question. By the time he had finished jogging there was only one dog chasing him, but he entered the gate with more questions than when he had left.

Determined to put Barrett out of his mind, he proceeded to do a series of sit-ups and pushups, then rummaged through his closet for his set of exercise weights and worked with those until the sweat poured off of his body and his tendons and joints screamed for relief. When his muscles had reached their failure point, he gave in. Exhausted, he shuffled into the kitchen for a glass of water. He sat at the kitchen table, the glass trembling in his hand, as he studied the vein that ran down his left bicep. In the background the meter of the mantel clock echoed against the high ceilings and timed the seconds between the drops of sweat that rolled off the tip of his nose to splash quietly onto the hardwood floor as he waited for the pleasant quietness of an uncluttered mind that exercise always brought to him. But when the questions returned to his mind, he gave in to them. He set down his glass, mumbled a curse, and walked upstairs to Barrett's room.

"Police Line -- Do Not Cross" was printed on the yellow tape that stretched across the door to the dead man's room. Duncan hesitated. He touched the tape carefully, as if testing its effectiveness as a barrier. He moved down the hallway to another door, reached up and slid his hand along the frame until he produced a spare key, then unlocked the door and stepped into the bathroom. The same key unlocked the opposite door in the bathroom which led into Barrett's bedroom. The lock clicked; he opened the door and looked in.

Sunlight streamed through the half-closed blinds of the two windows on the west side of the room. The bed was positioned against the wall next to the bathroom. A small table beside the bed held two alarm clocks and a small reading light. Between the two windows was a wooden roll-top desk, not an antique, but a modern reproduction Barrett had found in a second-hand furniture store. On top of the desk was a bookcase half-filled with textbooks, notebooks and papers. A small dresser with a mirror stood opposite the bed. It was positioned on the north side of the room by the window which looked out over the fire escape. The door to the hallway and a closet, built into the room when the house was modernized, took up the last remaining wall.

Duncan took his first tentative step into the room. He did not remember the room being in such a state of disarray; his focus on Barrett's body had blinded him to his surroundings. The sheets of the bed trailed onto the floor and the mattress sat at an angle to the box springs. The open door to the closet revealed a tangled mound of clothes that had been pulled from the hangers with many of the pants showing their pockets turned inside-out. The drawers to the dresser had been pulled out of the slots and the contents were in a pile on the floor.

As he walked around the corner of the bed, he came to a halt when he saw the chalk outline on the floor. He shook his head; for some reason he had thought that chalk outlines were used as props on television. He stepped around the outline to the desk. Papers had been pulled out of the letter compartments and strewn on the floor. A pile of textbooks, their pages torn and covers bent, had obviously been thrown in the corner during the intruder's hasty search. A small table by the desk supported a stereo system, the only thing of quality that Barrett had owned.

He walked over to the window by the fire escape and checked to see if the latch was secured when a thought occurred to him. Where were Barrett's keys?

72

If they had been stolen with his wallet then the thief would have easy access to his house. He thought for a minute before he crossed the room to the nightstand. He opened the small drawer at the top. There were some coins, a red and white bottle of nasal spray, a short black comb, a couple of letters, and a key chain with a New Orleans Saints insignia. Duncan flipped through the keys until he found the familiar outline of the front door key. He felt a bit safer as he jangled the keys together. He turned and surveyed the room until his eyes fell on the chalk outline.

He took the stool from beside the desk, sat down, and studied the room as streaks of light from the window fell across the floor. The outline had been drawn showing where the right arm rested after Duncan had moved it. A tinge of guilt made his stomach tight. He should have told the police. No, he rationalized, it wasn't an important detail.

His thoughts returned to that night. The pain of death etched as a grimace on the dead man's face, the sickening asymmetry where his skull had caved inward, the way the hair was matted with blood. One glance at the floor showed that the dark stain of blood was still there, glowing in the sunlight like a dark ruby medallion.

He closed his eyes. Why? Why did this happen? He had asked this question so many times over the last forty-eight hours that he knew no answer would come so he didn't dwell on it. Instead he quickly changed the question to how? Or who?

Who killed Barrett? Instantly he thought of several possibilities. Good, he thought, maybe this was a question that could be answered.

Suzie was the first possibility. Suzie, the young girl with the punk haircut. What did he know about her? Nothing. Why would she want to kill him? If Barrett had tried to force himself on her, that would have been sufficient motive. Could she have done it? Possibly. But Duncan could not come up with a scenario where a tiny young girl could deliver a blow that would knock down someone as strong as Barrett. Could she have caught him off guard? Possibly. And the billfold? She could have stolen that to make it look like a robbery. She could have thrown it in the trash as she snuck down the fire escape. But why sneak away? She had already been seen by Duncan. Duncan turned this over in his mind for a moment and then filed it away.

Jenny was the next suspect. She was bigger than Suzie and a lot stronger. He remembered a time the previous summer when he had come home to find Barrett and Jenny both working out with his weights. She had explained to

73

Duncan that she didn't really enjoy lifting weights but she did it in order to make Barrett happy and to spend time with him. Could someone as devoted to Barrett kill him? Sure. Duncan saw it every day, people brought into the emergency room shot or stabbed by the wife, lover, or close friend. What if she had walked in to discover Barrett with Suzie? That would have been enough motive. She could have lost control. She would also have been trusted enough by Barrett for him to lower his guard so that she would have the opportunity to strike him. Duncan could see that happening. And she was smart enough to make the attack look like a robbery, then feign shock and surprise when she woke Duncan. Jenny as a murderer was something he didn't like to consider, but it was a distinct possibility.

The third possibility was a burglar. Perhaps Duncan was trying to make this all too complicated. Barrett might have left the window unlocked. The thief could have seen this opportunity and taken it. But why enter a room with someone in it? Perhaps Barrett had been in the bathroom at the time. Perhaps it had been dark and Barrett had tried to surprise the intruder. Duncan knew that Barrett was rash enough to tackle any stranger entering his window. But why was the expensive stereo not stolen? The murderer had not panicked and fled but instead had rifled through the room. Perhaps something had spooked him and he had fled with only the wallet.

This was the most logical explanation. And even though he felt that he had overlooked something, that something was wrong with this theory, he tried to convince himself that this was what had actually happened.

He then thought of the broken fingers. He put his arm up and tried to imagine the blow from an assailant. With his arms crossed in front of his face he could see how a blow to the left side of his head could strike his right hand.

He sat motionless as the square of sunlight from the window slowly creeped across the floor and up the wall. The sky outside was dark before he broke from his thoughts. As he left the room, he turned one more time to see the white of the chalk outline contrasted against the dark grain of the wood floor. He had come to Barrett's room with the hope of resolving some questions. As he closed the door behind him, he left with even more.

Chapter Eleven

The church building sat in a grove of majestic oaks. The simple white steeple rose up through a circle of bare branches that in the summer would shade and shelter the building. Square and plain, the chapel with its white-washed wooden boards stood out in contrast to the dark grove of trees, their trunks spackled with lichens, and the full, gray clouds. Nearby, a white picket fence enclosed a small cemetery with marble headstones that were weathered smooth and aged to a variegated gray.

Two pickup trucks, one following close behind the other, pulled into the gravel parking lot of the church and found a place to park among the other cars and trucks. Red clay was splattered and dried across the headlights, the windshields, and along the sides of the two trucks, and chunks of mud remained wedged between the cleated treads of the oversized tires.

The gravel crunched beneath a pair of polished lizard skin boots as the lone passenger of the first truck stepped out onto the parking lot. He was a bulky man with salt and pepper hair and dark bushy eyebrows that hid his eyes when he squinted. A round, fleshy nose sat slightly off-center on a weathered face that had the grain of pebbly cowhide. He checked his tie in the mirror on the door of the truck, then moved toward the church with an ease that showed that his size was more a factor of muscle and bone than fat.

The two men who exited the other truck were younger. One was clean shaven and handsome with his dark hair held back in a short ponytail. His body tapered down from his muscular chest and shoulders to his flat stomach. The other man was huge, with a jacket too small to cover his cuffs and the front of his shirt. He sported an unkempt beard, reddish-brown and patchy, that matched the color of his freckles. He had tried to manage his unwashed hair by combing water through it, but a cluster of stiff horns projected at various angles from the crown of his head.

As he walked around the back of the truck the older man inspected the two.

"Ferguson," he addressed the larger one.

75

"Yes, Mr. Jeter?"

The older man's face showed his disapproval. "You look like a cow has been slobbering on your hair."

Ferguson immediately tried to mash his hair down with the palms of his massive hands.

The older man, Erskine Jeter, turned and walked toward the church. After he had taken a few steps, the man with the ponytail turned to Ferguson and delivered his best cow imitation.

Ferguson punched him in the arm with a blow that lifted him up on one leg. "Shut up, Hubbard."

Erskine Jeter turned and silenced them with a look.

"The reverend is preaching one funeral. If you don't shut up he could be preaching three."

As they followed him up the steps to the church, Ferguson glared as Hubbard continued to pantomime his cow bellow with his lips while he rubbed his arm.

Inside the church the simple wooden pews were beginning to fill. Hubbard and Ferguson took their positions on opposite sides of the door and studied the crowd as Jeter walked down the aisle. Jeter stopped at the front and bent down over a tall woman dressed in black.

"I'm sorry about this, Sis," he said as he patted her on the back.

She nodded and wiped her eyes and nose with her handkerchief. When he was seated beside her she leaned over to him. "Erskine, I want you to do something for me."

"What's that, Sis?"

"I want you to find out who killed my son."

He glanced over his shoulder, nodded at the people sitting there, then brought his hand up to rest along the back of the pew as he leaned closer.

She continued in a whisper, 'Erskine, you know I've never asked a lot of favors of you. But I know you have ways to find out who did this to my boy."

Jeter patted her on her knee and whispered into her ear. "Don't you worry, Sis. I'll take care of things for you. Don't you worry a bit," he assured her.

Duncan looked at his watch as he drove down the winding country road. Twice he had taken a wrong turn despite the fact that he had stopped and asked directions once at Crockett and again after his second wrong turn. He realized he might have been born in the country, but he had spent most of his life in the city where directions and addresses were exact. He was not accustomed to "Go about six miles till you see a red brick home with a big willow oak in the front yard" or "You'll go around this big curve and then you take a left after the bridge."

Duncan wasn't sure he would know a willow-oak if it fell on him. Weren't a willow and an oak two different trees? And every little stream in this land of hills and creek bottoms was spanned by a bridge.

His tension eased when the church finally came into view. Not too late, he thought as he glanced at his watch. He parked the car and hurried to the door to find that the little church was almost full. Most of the people attending the funeral were older than Duncan, and he failed to find anyone his age among the crowd other than Jenny. Barrett had obviously formed his personality at a young age. Duncan sat at the back of the building just as an elderly lady with blue-gray hair sat down at an upright piano set to one side of the pulpit. The solemn strains of music filled the building. He remembered the tune from his youth but couldn't recall the words. Something about walking in the garden?

Duncan glanced around the sanctuary. A tattered hymnal stood in book-rack built into the back of the pew in front of him, its spine held together with black electrical tape. Dim gray light filtered through the windows made of pebble glass, the poor man's substitute for stained glass.

The funeral service was short and offered little comfort. The elderly preacher pounded his knuckles on the pulpit and asked in a wavering voice the same question Duncan had asked earlier - *Why?* Why had this tragedy occurred to someone with so much promise ahead in his life? And like Duncan, the preacher reached the same conclusion. There is no answer. Just acceptance, the preacher declared, and he went on to quote scripture relating to faith and trust in the Lord, his sermon interrupted occasionally by Jenny's muffled sobs.

After the service Duncan found Jenny near the front standing by Mrs. Jeter. He greeted Jenny with a hug.

"How are you making it through this, Jenny?"

She answered with a forced smile, a sniffle of her nose, and a nod.

He turned to the tall lady dressed in black. "Mrs. Jeter?"

"Oh, I'm sorry," Jenny said. "Mrs. Jeter, this is Duncan Russthorne. He was Barrett's roommate."

"We've met," she said, "at Barrett's graduation from medical school."

"Barrett was a good friend, Mrs. Jeter. I know you were very proud of him. We will all miss him very much."

77

She started to speak but then lowered her head and looked away. "Yes, we will," she said softly.

After an awkward pause, an elderly man in a ill-fitting gray suit stepped up to offer his condolences. When Mrs. Jeter turned to acknowledge him, Duncan took the opportunity to leave.

As Duncan walked down the steps, he noticed that the overcast sky had darkened during the service. The wind had risen and tiny drops of rain stung his cheek. He was almost to his car when Hubbard and Ferguson stepped in front of him.

"Mr. Jeter would like to talk to you," Ferguson said.

"Mr. Jeter? I don't think . . ."

Hubbard took one arm, Ferguson the other, and lifted him up from the ground as they led him to Jeter's truck. They opened the passenger door, pushed him in, and slammed the door shut before Duncan could react.

Jeter sat behind the steering wheel, his hands held in front of the heating vents on the dashboard as he turned them back and forth to catch the warmth. The hands were thick and rough, with darkened knuckles that were cracked open from exposure to the elements. Broad ridges of calluses ran the width of his palms. He cupped his hands in front of his face and blew on them before he rubbed them briskly together with a scraping sound.

"I'm an old man; my circulation isn't as good as it used to be," he said without looking at his guest. He offered Duncan his hand.

"Erskine Jeter," he said.

When Duncan returned the handshake, he felt as if his hand had been wrapped in coarse sandpaper. Jeter's fingers had the texture of a milled steel file.

"I'm Duncan Russthorne. I was Barrett's roommate."

Jeter gave a nod to indicate that he already knew.

"I apologize for my friends. Hubbard and Ferguson aren't real keen on manners." He gestured at the two men who had pushed Duncan into the truck. Ferguson stared through the windshield at Duncan as raindrops dripped off of his brow and nose. Hubbard stood on Jeter's side of the truck and watched the departing crowd in the parking lot.

"Barrett was my nephew. My sister-in-law's oldest child and only son. She sure is upset. This has just about killed her. Her husband ran off and left her long ago - my brother never was very dependable - so she had to raise Barrett on her own. Barrett was her pride and joy, her reason for living." He shook his head. "I don't know how she is gonna make it. She's not a strong person."

78

Duncan started to speak but stopped when Jeter turned to look at him for the first time. He sensed that the older man was the type that usually spoke while other people listened.

Jeter's thick eyebrows lowered in a frown. The creases at the corner of his eyes were chiseled deep into his temple. A muscle flexed in his jaw as he fixed Duncan with a hard stare.

"Who do you think killed my nephew?"

Duncan cleared his throat and tried to speak. He had not felt this way since the third grade when his elementary school principal had interrogated him for suspected misbehavior.

"The police think it was a botched burglary."

"Do they? I've never much cared for what the police think," Jeter said with contempt. "But I didn't ask what the police think about the murder. I asked your opinion."

"I. . . I don't know what to think about it."

"You don't know? You don't know what to think about a murder that happened in your own home?" Jeter did not attempt to hide his irritation as he talked.

Duncan opened his mouth to speak, then quickly shut it and kept silent, not knowing what the old man wanted. As Duncan sat there, Jeter silently studied him the way a wolf studies its prey for signs of weakness. After a long pause he spoke.

"I understand you were asleep when the murder occurred," Jeter said. The tone in his voice made it sound more like an accusation than a question.

"Well, I . . ."

Jeter cut him off. "I find that hard to believe."

Again Duncan didn't respond. He wondered what the two bodyguards would do if he tried to leave the vehicle. Throw him back into the truck? Or worse? A glance around the empty churchyard showed that there was no one to call for help.

Jeter reached over and tapped Duncan on the arm, a strong poke to the muscle to get his attention. "I want you to do a couple of things for me," he said in a tone that was more of a command than a request.

Duncan nodded.

"I'm going to send Hubbard and Ferguson to pick up Barrett's belongings. His mother and I would appreciate if you would help get his things packed."

"Sure. I'll be glad to," he said, relieved at the simple request. "What else?"

Jeter stared at him with a commanding sense of power. It was a look that hinted at the promise of unpleasant consequences.

"If you have any idea who killed my nephew, you let me know. You understand?"

Before Duncan could respond, Jeter tapped on the front window with the knuckles of his right fist. Ferguson immediately opened the door on Duncan's side of the truck. The interview was over.

Duncan exited quickly, half expecting to be jerked out of the truck. He turned to ask Jeter a question, but the door slammed shut just as the truck began to move in reverse. The two bodyguards moved quickly to their vehicle in order to follow, leaving Duncan to stand in the rain.

Chapter Twelve

A heavy rain followed Duncan as he drove home, the windshield wipers working at full speed to allow brief glimpses of the road. In the parking lot of the medical center he turned off the car's engine and the headlights, then reached into the back seat for his clinic coat with his identification card clipped to the pocket. He draped the coat over him and ran to the front entrance where a uniformed guard checked the laminated card that Duncan presented. The guard compared the photo to Duncan's face and pointed to the entrance log. After Duncan signed the clipboard the guard returned his identification with a polite nod.

His search for Bill Wammack led him to the research lab. His friend held a rat in a gloved hand and a syringe in the other. It was the first time he could recall that Bill had not greeted him with his trademark grin.

"I need a dose of that."

"Bad day, huh? I hate funerals. How was it?"

"How do you think it was? It was a funeral." Duncan leaned back against the refrigerator and rubbed his face with his hands as Bill silently continued his work. "Sorry. I'm just tired. Barrett's mother held up pretty well, she's probably still in shock, but Jenny lost it a couple of times. Very emotional."

"Funerals are supposed to be emotional. A 'purgative effect' I think the psychologists call it," Bill said without looking up.

"Oh, don't be so clinical," Duncan said in a way that was meant to lighten the tone of the conversation.

Wammack just shrugged his shoulders as he placed the rat back in its cage. Duncan kneaded his forehead with his fingers in an effort to forestall a headache.

"Weren't you born near Crockett County?" Duncan asked.

"Hunkatibbee."

"What?"

"Hunkatibbee. It's a Chickasaw word. Hunkatibee County is close to Crockett County."

"Did you know Barrett before medical school?"

"No. Never laid eyes on him before then. Why?"

"I was just wondering if you knew his family. I met his uncle at the funeral. A couple of his . . ."

"Erskine?" Bill interrupted.

"Yes . . ."

"Erskine Jeter?" Bill said with a mixture of awe and disbelief.

Duncan was puzzled. "You know him?"

"Everybody in that area knows Erskine Jeter."

"I don't. I grew up in Bois d'Arc County and I've never heard of him."

"That's only because you moved out of state when you were young."

"So tell me. Why should I know about him?"

Bill's grin returned to his face. "You're going to love this story," he said as he pulled a stool over to Duncan and motioned him to sit. Bill leaned back against his stool, crossed his arms, and began his story.

"Erskine Jeter is one of the last great local chiefs in a loose-knit crime organization called the Redneck Mafia."

"The Redneck Mafia?" Duncan asked.

"Just listen and I'll explain," Bill said.

"This story starts with Erskine's grandfather Ezra Jeter back in the twenties. Mississippi has always been a poor state and the northeast corner has always been the poorest. The land is nothing more than a washboard of rocky hills and ridges, more like Tennessee hills than Mississippi plantation. There are no large areas of farmland, few industries, fewer jobs, and little natural resources.

"Ezra did what every poor hillbilly in that area did to make a living and feed his family. He farmed a few acres of creek bottom and grew enough corn to raise a few hogs and cattle. He also worked at the local sawmill when they needed extra help. In the winter he ran a trap line."

"Trapline?"

"He trapped animals for their fur. And, like a lot of people up in the hills, he had a little still to make whiskey. They say he made some of the best corn liquor in the state."

"This is beginning to sound a bit too much like the Beverly Hillbillies," Duncan said.

Bill Wammack laughed and shook his head. "But it's true. Now this is where the story gets interesting. Ezra soon realized that he could make more money making whiskey than he could plowing behind a mule all summer long. He found a cool, clear spring up in one of the caves in the hills and set up a larger still and increased his production. In an area so poor that people considered themselves lucky just to make enough to live from year to year, Ezra Jeter was soon making a comfortable living. Until . . ." Wammack paused for effect.

"The 'revenooers?'" Duncan offered.

Wammack nodded.

"No! You've got to be kidding me."

"It's true. When the prohibition came along, the local sheriff decided to crack down on all the bootleggers. And since Jeter was the biggest, they started with him. I guess they wanted to make an example of him. But they made a mistake. They went to Ezra Springs while Jeter was there, didn't announce who they were, and starting shooting when they saw him.

"Well, Ezra didn't know who these people were. He only knew that they were shooting at him so he shot back. Two of the deputies were wounded before they convinced him to surrender.

"They shipped Ezra to a federal penitentiary. He was an old, old man when finally released. And that was their second mistake."

"Letting him go?"

"Yes. Because Ezra had spent his time in prison listening and learning. Ezra had never gone to school, but prison was the education that he had never had. When he returned home he took his grandson, Erskine, under his wing and set about building a small but efficient organization. Car theft, bootlegging, gambling. They perfected the art of arson and insurance fraud. They had chop shops in every isolated barn they could find and grew marijuana in small patches scattered throughout the hills. They did anything and everything to make money. By the time Ezra died in the 60's the Jeters had a part in most of the crime within a hundred-mile radius covering parts of three states."

"So now Erskine is the boss," Duncan stated. "If everyone knows this then why hasn't he been caught and arrested?"

Wammack tapped the side of his head. "He's too smart. Erskine is as shrewd a man as you will ever meet. Years ago he started shifting into legitimate businesses. On paper he looks clean, the owner of several successful small enterprises. In reality, he still controls a small but efficient band of criminals. He has everything arranged so that it would be hard to actually pin anything on him. Too many people that work for him would take the blame before the police could arrest him of a crime."

Wammack stood up and walked back over to the cart with the rats. "They say he's the last. The last of the Redneck Mafia. They say there used to be a lot of local territories, each with a head like Jeter that worked together in a sort of loose confederacy, but that no longer exists. There used to be areas like his in Arkansas, Tennessee, and the Mississippi Gulf Coast. The real Mafia -- the big boys -- have taken over now. According to the newspapers, the New Orleans mob controls the coast and southern Arkansas, and the St. Louis Mafia controls eastern Tennessee."

"So why haven't they taken over Jeter?"

Wammack shrugged his shoulders. "Maybe it's too small an area to fight over. Maybe it's too isolated, too rural. Don't you think it would be difficult for a gang of Italians to challenge a bunch of rednecks on their own territory? They couldn't drive into Crockett County unnoticed.

"Besides, it's not like Jeter is a threat to the big boys. He knows his place; he's content to be the big fish in the small pond."

Wammack snapped his notebook closed and placed it on the bookshelf. Duncan pulled the cart with the cages, the rats now high, happy, and silent, out into the hall as Wammack cut off the lights and locked the door. They walked down the hallway with Duncan deep in thought. Before Wammack entered the elevator Duncan asked, "You don't think Barrett is mixed up with his uncle? That his death is somehow related?"

"Look, Duncan. Don't try to make this into something that it isn't. A burglar didn't know anyone was home when he tried to break into Barrett's room. Barrett was arrogant enough to try to tackle him. That mistake cost him his life. A year from now some punk will be arrested for some other crime and his fingerprints will match the prints the police found in Barrett's room."

Wammack pushed the cart into the elevator, then turned to face Duncan. "I know this sounds harsh, but I didn't like him. Not many people did. And now he's dead so let's let him rest in peace. O.K.?" he said as the elevator door shut in Duncan's face.

Chapter Thirteen

Police detective Alfie Storey, a lieutenant in the homicide division of the Jackson Metropolitan Police, sat at her desk by the window on the second floor of police headquarters and watched as a slow, drizzling rain fell from low gray sculptured clouds. It should be snowing, she thought. This time of year there should be snow.

She was in her second year as a transplant from the North. A native of St. Louis, her family had moved to Chicago when she was still a child. Chicago had been a difficult change for her, but she had quickly adjusted and soon came to consider Chicago her home. It was there that she had graduated from the Police Academy with an exemplary record. It was also in Chicago that she had met her husband, an engineer in a fledgling cellular communication company.

She looked at the framed picture on her desk of her husband with her two young daughters. Her husband's career was the reason for the move south. As the field of cellular communication had expanded, he had been offered a vice-president's position in another company that was growing in Jackson. The promotion would double his salary and the stock bonuses were generous. A native of the South, her husband had also argued for the better living environment that a smaller town offered for their children.

The decision had not come easily. To her, Mississippi was a foreign country.

She had heard too many horror stories. To make matters worse, her friends had reacted with shock when she told them of the possible move. So it was with serious doubts that she consented to the move.

She had been pleasantly surprised. People smiled at her. Total strangers would give a polite wave to her as she drove around the city. Men, both white and black, opened doors for her. There was no pot-bellied gum-smacking southern cracker in charge of the police department. In fact, the chief of police was black, as was almost half of the police force.

Not that there hadn't been problems. There were still the subtle signs of racism present, faint ripples on the faces of certain people that hinted of dangerous emotions that ran deep and unseen. But when she thought about it objectively she had to admit that those signs had been present in Chicago also. People were people regardless of geography, but the people she had come to know were more relaxed and easy-going. The South was almost like California but with a lot more humidity. And better food. She found that the South suited her temperament well. After the initial adjustment, she realized that she could not go back to Chicago; it was too harsh -- both the weather and the people.

As she lit a cigarette she looked at the photograph. Her oldest daughter, who would be nine years old in May, had been asking her lately to quit smoking. Maybe if she started now she would be able to tell her daughter on her birthday that mommy had quit smoking for her. She took one drag before she extinguished the cigarette in the ashtray, then tossed the half-full pack into the trash can beside her desk.

Her thoughts shifted to the open folder in front of her. She flipped through the papers and glanced at the clock above the doorway. She wanted to go over everything one more time before Dr. Russthorne arrived for their meeting at two o'clock.

On the surface everything appeared fairly simple. In spite of all the public service announcements and articles written by the media, another life had been lost by someone trying to stop an intruder in their home. When would people learn to just run out of the house and call for help. The graveyard was full of dead heroes.

But something about this case bothered her. She believed in a woman's intuition, or, at least, her own intuitive feelings, and her inner voice was buzzing and crackling about this case. No matter how hard she looked, however, she could not find anything to give form or substance to her suspicion. Still, the investigation was not finished. More evidence could surface.

She glanced at another page. Fingerprints -- none discernible except the victim, the two girls, and the owner of the house. If there was an intruder, he wore gloves.

The girl, Suzie. She had left Barrett around 11:30. She claimed they had argued and she had called a taxi. The taxi driver confirmed picking her up at that address at that time. He also stated that a man matching Barrett's description had stood on the porch. The driver remembered because the man had shouted profanities at the girl as she fled through the yard.

The girlfriend, Jenny. She entered alone? No one to corroborate her story. Motive? Anger, jealousy, lovers' quarrel.

The roommate. Claims he was asleep during the murder. Motive? Alfie drew a large question mark.

The secretary and gopher was a temp named David who had worked at the department for three weeks. Slight of build, his efficiency at his job helped Alfie overlook the irritating habit he had of overstepping the bounds of his responsibilities as a substitute employee. He approached her desk with Duncan in tow.

"You've got company, dear."

She rose to greet him.

"Dr. Russthorne. How are you? Have a seat." David pulled a chair up next to her desk for her visitor.

"Need anything?" David asked.

"Coffee?" she asked Duncan.

"Yes. Black."

She held up two fingers to David. "Oh, and see if the lab has sent up anything."

David gave a little wave of his hand in acknowledgment as he walked away.

She pointed to his chair and they both sat. Duncan crossed his legs and propped one forearm on the corner of the desk as Alfie reached into her desk and produced Barrett's address book.

"I'm sorry I wasn't here at headquarters this morning when you came," she said.

Duncan looked down at his hands as they rested in his lap. His fingertips still carried traces of ink despite the scrubbing he had given them. He understood the necessity of being fingerprinted but, even so, it had still been a discomforting experience.

"No problem. How is your investigation progressing?"

"Like most - slowly," she said. "I need to go over a few more things with you, Doctor."

"Duncan. Just call me Duncan."

She leaned closer to Duncan and rested her arms on the edge of the desk.

"Do you know of any enemies that Barrett may have had?"

Duncan started to speak but then stopped. He hesitated, then said, "Barrett had . . ." before he stopped again. He began to speak for the third time, struggled to find the proper words, then finally said, "It's not easy to describe Barrett."

"Duncan," she said pleasantly. "You must have been his best friend."

"Why do you say that?"

"Because your reluctance to condemn Barrett is the nicest gesture anyone has made toward the deceased. Most of the people I talked with, both faculty and students, did not have any trouble describing Barrett Jeter."

"Really?"

"Really!" she said. "I tell you what let's do. I'll read some of the descriptions of Barrett that were given to me by the people that I interviewed and you tell me if you agree with them." She picked up a piece of paper from the folder and read a list of words to Duncan.

"Asshole?"

"Yes," he concurred.

"Difficult?"

"Definitely."

"Arrogant?"

"He considered himself God's first cousin."

She leaned back in her chair and spun the sheet of paper onto the desk with a flick of her wrist.

"Did this man have any friends at all?" she said with a mixture of exasperation and amazement.

"Other than his mother? Perhaps his girlfriend, Jenny."

"Perhaps? You're not sure?"

"She definitely put up with a lot of abuse from him. I think 'long-suffering' would be a good word to describe her."

"Abuse? Physical abuse?"

"Figure of speech," Duncan explained.

"Did you consider yourself his friend, Duncan?"

"I told you before, I did not consider myself an enemy," he said gravely as his eyes locked onto hers.

David interrupted their gaze as he set the cups of coffee on the desk. Under his arm he held some papers. He handed them to Alfie.

"Preliminary tox report is clean."

"Nosy," she said. "Did you tell the lab to rush their final report?"

"Yes. They laughed so hard they cried. They are probably still laughing over at the crime lab. Enjoy." He pointed to the coffee with his palms before he left.

Duncan picked up the coffee and stared down into the brown liquid, but Alfie asked another question before he could drink.

"Is there any reason why you would want to see Barrett dead?"

He looked up from his cup. He had expected this. He knew he had to be considered a suspect and had tried to prepare himself for this question, but it still caused his chest to tighten when he heard it.

"He didn't wash his share of the dishes?"

Alfie did not respond to his remark with words, but her stare reflected the serious nature of her question.

"No," Duncan answered penitently as he took a sip from his cup.

"How would you describe your relationship with Barrett."

"Strained but civil. I tried to avoid him as much as possible."

"Must be hard to do when you live in the same house and work at the same hospital," she offered.

"Not really. I'm usually pretty involved in my work."

She seemed satisfied with his answer and turned her questioning in a different direction.

"What about the night of the murder? Have you remembered anything else that might be helpful?"

He shook his head. "I've thought about that night a hundred times in the last few days. I've played it over and over in my mind. Nothing new comes up."

"Nothing unusual? Nothing at all?" she asked.

"Well. I don't know if it's relevant but . . ."

"You need to let me decide what's relevant."

Duncan proceeded to tell her about his meeting with Erskine Jeter after Barrett's funeral. He easily described Hubbard and Ferguson when asked but found it harder to describe the look on Jeter's face or the quiet air of malevolence that Duncan had sensed in the man. Duncan felt comfortable enough to finish his story with a question. "Do you think there is a connection? Other than family ties?"

"It's possible. Although he lives almost two hundred miles from here and we are seldom involved in anything directly related to him, enough information trickles down to us to know he has a lot of influence. He cooperates with the big boys in New Orleans and in return they allow him to retain control of his territory. You could say he is a pretty serious type of fellow."

"I got that impression."

Alfie lifted her coffee to her lips, took a sip, and mulled over a thought as she swallowed. She flipped the appointment book shut and handed it to Duncan. "Here, take this. We don't need it anymore. Put it with his other belongings."

"And his room?"

"You can take the tape down. We won't need to return to his room. We will contact his family and inform them that we have released his personal effects."

"Is that all?"

"Yes, I guess so. Is there nothing else you would like to add to your statement?"

Duncan thought about Barrett's corpse, the way his hand had been positioned when he first saw the body, and the fact that Barrett had donated his body to the anatomy lab but quickly decided that both were insignificant and too subjective.

"No. Nothing at all."

"Are you sure?"

"I'm sure." He hoped he sounded convincing.

As they stood she handed him a business card. "You can skip the switchboard if you use my extension. I've written it on my card. Call me if you think of anything."

Duncan slipped the card in his coat pocket as he walked past David on his way out.

"Do you think he did it?" David whispered to Alfie.

"David!"

"He looks guilty to me."

"David, I am the detective and you are a gofer. Quit being a pest and let me do my job. Now go to your computer and pull up all you can on Erskine Jeter."

"But I've done that once already," David whined. She ignored the wounded look on his face as she waved him away.

"Go! Now! I can't think with you hovering around my desk."

"But why all the fuss over a bunch of dumb rednecks?"

"David, a snake has a brain the size of an almond but it can still deliver a fatal strike. If you think a person has to be a member of Mensa to pull a trigger, you're making the same assumption that killed Buford Pusser."

"Who?"

"Buford Pusser. The movie '*Walking Tall?*'" She was answered with a blank stare. Not wishing to elaborate further, she waved David away, returned to her desk, and looked out the window as she doodled on a piece of paper. Her inner voice was buzzing again. Was it because of Duncan Russthorne? She suspected that he was holding something back. Or was it because Erskine Jeter's name had come up. Again.

She had considered the relationship between Erskine Jeter and Barrett but had failed to come up with a compelling explanation to connect the murder to the older man.

Could Barrett's death have been a retaliation against the Redneck Don? Part of a criminal feud? Perhaps New Orleans was finally making a move on Jeter's territory and Barrett's murder was the opening salvo.

Or was Erskine Jeter directly involved? It was a theory that could not be excluded. The records showed that Erskine Jeter had been the prime suspect in the disappearance of his own brother years earlier. The word on the street mentioned money embezzled from the company that Erskine had put his brother in charge of. Evidently the blood relationship carried only limited forgiveness.

The possibilities made her nervous.

She glanced around the room to see if anyone was looking before she reached into the garbage can and retrieved her pack of cigarettes.

Chapter Fourteen

At home Duncan emptied his car of the empty cardboard boxes that he had collected by making a circuit of the liquor stores in the city. Upstairs, he ripped the yellow tape off the bedroom door, unlocked it, and dropped the boxes on the floor. He started with the closet. He placed most of the clothes in two hanging travel bags he found. Shoes went into boxes. The dresser was next. Duncan made little effort to be neat with the socks and underwear. He quickly emptied the dresser. Then he stripped the bed of its sheets and blanket. The nightstand was next. The trunk at the foot of the bed Duncan left as it was.

The work progressed quickly. Barrett had collected few possessions in his short life. Within an hour Duncan had worked his way around the room as he emptied everything except the bookcase. He considered calling Barrett's mother to see if she wanted him to sell the textbooks for her. Medical textbooks were expensive and there were several hundred dollars' worth of books in the room, but the thought of talking to Barrett's mother made him uncomfortable. He decided to leave a note in the box of textbooks; if she wanted to sell them she could call.

Halfway up the bookcase Duncan came across a large photo album wedged between two large loose-leaf notebooks. It was bound in smooth black leather, perhaps another gift from Jenny, with his name embossed in gold in the lower right hand corner of the cover.

Duncan sat on the bare mattress and laid the album on the bed as he opened the front cover. Inside was the life of Roger Barrett Jeter. There were pictures of him from elementary school. Pictures of him as a child with his mother and his father, a tall dark-featured man with a stern look on his face. There were pictures of birthday parties and beaches, playing on see-saws and splashing in the bathtub.

As Duncan turned the pages the young boy grew, and soon the pages were filled with clippings from newspapers that chronicled the local team. Headlines told of many football victories and a few defeats.

Then came more photographs. There was one of him with Jenny as they posed in their high school graduation gowns and another picture with him and his mother.

A section on Barrett's college football career came next and composed the largest portion of the album. The sections of the newspaper articles that described his accomplishments on the field had been highlighted. Duncan was impressed. Barrett had not exaggerated as much as he had thought. The clippings told how Barrett and the other running back for the team, a player named Antonio Pack, had set offensive records. "Dynamic Duo Powers Backfield" read one article. "Salt and Pepper Shake-Up Opposing Defense" began another. The page of photographs that followed was devoted to Barrett and another player that Duncan supposed was Antonio. Shorter than Barrett but heavier, with muscular arms, a thick neck, and a short afro.

Some of the photos were serious football poses. The three-point-stance pose. The avoiding-a-tackle pose. Others were more playful.

The last clipping that Duncan read stated, "Star Running Back Ends Career With Injury." Duncan had started the second sentence of the article when the doorbell rang. He closed the album and placed it in a box. Before he left the room the doorbell began a series of hurried rings.

"O.K., O.K. Hold on," Duncan mumbled to himself as he headed to the stairway. Halfway down the stairs he saw two sets of work boots and blue jeans walking toward him from the entrance. He froze when their faces became visible. It was Hubbard and Ferguson.

"We didn't think nobody was here," Hubbard said as Duncan slowly finished his descent of the stairway.

"The front door was unlocked so we just came on in. We're here to get Barrett's stuff," he added. Ferguson stood silently behind Hubbard and glowered over his partner's shoulder at Duncan.

Duncan frowned. He distinctly remembered locking the front door; it was a habit he had quickly developed since the murder.

"Where's his stuff?" Hubbard demanded.

Duncan stepped away from the stairs and pointed to Barrett's room, "I'll show you."

"No." Hubbard held up his hand. "We'll get it. Just stay out of the way," he said as he walked up the stairs. Ferguson passed Duncan with a look of contempt as he followed close behind his partner.

Two hours later Duncan stood at the stove adding slices of Cajun sausage to the pot of boiling red beans when he heard the motor to the truck crank out in the street. He wiped his hands on a towel as he walked into the living room. Through the open front door he saw a street light flicker on. When Duncan reached the front porch he saw the truck, with Hubbard driving, pull away from the curb. A sense of relief filled Duncan as he watched as the red tail lights slowly move down the street. The intruders were gone; his house was again his own.

As he walked inside, the first thing Duncan noticed was Barrett's appointment book that he had placed on the table by the entrance when he had returned from the police station. He grabbed it and ran to the door but the street was empty. No big deal, he thought, I'll mail it later. Or throw it away.

He shut the door and turned on the porch light. The smell of boiling spices began to fill the house. Back in the kitchen, he took a beer from the refrigerator and opened it. Maybe he could begin to put this ordeal behind him. Tomorrow he would be back at work, back to his normal masochistic routine. He never thought he would be glad to return to the sleepless nights, blood, and pain of his internship. Tonight, though, he would enjoy one more night of rest. One last chance for a full eight hours of rest.

"Or maybe not," he thought with a grin.

He called Deena's house but hung up after several rings and called the medical center. Deena answered her page after a few moments.

"Duncan! How are you?"

"Great. I've got supper cooking on the stove. How about some red beans and rice? It's Cajun night at Café Russthorne."

"Oh, I love your cooking. But I'm on call all night."

"Any chance of you getting off?"

"I'd love to get off," she said in a sultry voice.

"Naughty, naughty. Does your mother know you talk like that?"

She laughed. "I'm sorry, Duncan. It's in-house call. I can't leave."

Duncan groaned.

"I'll make it up to you, Dunc. What about this weekend?"

"It's doubtful. Too many people have subbed for me while I've been away from the hospital. This weekend will be payback time."

"Listen, we are going to have a date," she said in a firm voice. "We are going to sit down with our schedules and see when we both have some free time."

94

"The only problem with that is finding time in our schedules in order to sit down and find time in our schedules. Right?"

Deena laughed again. "We will, I promise you."

"Great. Why don't you track me down at the hospital this weekend."

"I will. Again, I promise," Deena said. A message from the intercom echoed in the background. "Listen, I've got to go. I'm being paged."

"Wait. There is one more thing I need to ask you . . ."

"Make it quick."

"It's a medical quiz. A challenge to your expertise."

"Hit me with your best shot, big boy."

"What kind of medical condition would cause a person to bite their fingers?"

"Is this a joke?"

"No. I'm dead serious." Duncan winced at his choice of words. "No joke, Dee."

"Bite their fingers or their fingernails?"

"Both . . . or either."

There was a long silence on the telephone as she thought.

Finally she said, "A small bladder?"

"I'll pretend you didn't say that."

"Sorry, Duncan. It's really funny if you haven't had any sleep in two days. Let's see, biting fingers ... I really don't know. Other than a psychological disturbance, the only thing I can think of right off the top of my head is Lesch-Nyhan."

"But that's congenital. I'm looking for a disease or syndrome associated with otherwise normal and healthy people."

There was another pause before Deena spoke.

"I'm drawing a blank. Maybe we're approaching this from the wrong direction. Maybe you should talk to someone at the dental school."

"What was the name of the professor from the dental school that used to lecture to us?"

"I can't remember. Listen, I've got to run, I've got a stat page, but we'll talk later."

"Think about it, O.K.?"

Duncan returned to his cooking after they had said their good-byes. He took a sip of his beer, poured a little into the simmering broth in the pot, then took another sip before he set the bottle down. As he stirred he caught himself with his fingers in his mouth, as if this would inspire him into understanding why

95

Barrett had died with a fingertip clenched between his teeth. He shook his head and went back to his cooking.

An hour later Duncan finished his second plateful of food by wiping the plate with a crust of bread. He popped the crust in his mouth and washed it down with the last of his third beer. He wiped his mouth with his napkin and leaned back in the chair. During the meal he had decided that the only thing left to do in order to help put this episode behind him was to remove the chalk outline on the floor in the room above him, clean up the room, and get a new tenant. Maybe Bill Wammack would like to move back.

He lingered at the table for a few minutes to enjoy the glow from the alcohol before he rose and searched the utility closet in the kitchen for a bucket and a rag. He ran some warm water into the bucket and added a few drops of liquid soap, then proceeded upstairs.

He switched on the light to Barrett's room only to be greeted by its emptiness. Hubbard and Ferguson had been thorough in their work. The only items left in the room were a few nails in the wall where pictures had hung and an assortment of trash on the floor. Duncan picked up the papers and crumpled them together. He went downstairs and returned with a vacuum cleaner. Duncan covered every inch of the floor twice with the vacuum before the clattering of trash up the metal pipe ceased and he felt satisfied with the job.

Now for the chalk, the only visible evidence of the room's former occupant. He knelt beside the outline with the bucket and wrung the excess water from the rags. He hesitated as he stared at the tracing one last time. When his thoughts began to drift he shook his head and began to scrub.

He started where the deceased's left arm had been outstretched. The outline of the hand vanished as most of the chalk dust disappeared easily with a light swipe of the rag. Only a few streaks of chalk remained deep in the grain of the old wood. With a grunt, he worked the cloth vigorously over the spot again.

He stopped when he saw the midnight blue streak on his white rag. That was odd, he thought. Where did that come from? Not wanting to smear anything across the floor, he crept on his hands and knees over the floor until he found the origin of the stain, a pointed indentation in the wood marking the source. Duncan took the edge of his white t-shirt, stretched it out with his finger as he reclined on the floor, and rubbed it on the wood. He studied the stain it made on his shirt then rubbed the spot again with a different part of his t-shirt. Much less than the first time. It was ink, he decided. A very small drop of ink had been on the floor.

His first thought was that one of Jeter's men had stepped on a pen as they moved the furniture. But Duncan had not seen a pen when he had picked up the larger pieces of trash. And the two men weren't the type to clean up after themselves. That was evident by the amount of trash they had left.

When the implication struck, he immediately opened the canister to the vacuum cleaner, took out the collection bag, and tore it open. A cloud of lint exploded into the air as debris fell to the floor. He tore through the lint and prodded the clumps apart with his fingers until he found a fractured splinter of clear beveled plastic. Further searching revealed another one. He held them up to the light between each thumb and forefinger as if inspecting a pair of precious jewels. Prismatic light reflected from the clear, faceted fragments. Without a doubt he held pieces from a broken ink pen.

Perhaps the pen had been shattered in the struggle that claimed his roommate's life. Perhaps the police had picked it up as evidence. He shut his eyes and tried to recall the image of Barrett's body that night. He had not noticed a pen on the floor. Barrett was right handed and his right hand had been drawn up to his face. It would be easy enough to check the morgue to see if there were traces of ink on Barrett's hand.

An idea had formed in Duncan's mind -- an idea he didn't like. What if Barrett had tried to leave a message in his dying moments? Did that mean he knew his murderer?

He walked downstairs and used the kitchen telephone to call the medical center and leave a message with the paging service. Bill Wammack returned his call within a few minutes.

"What's up, Dunk?"

"Are you on call tonight?"

"All night long."

"If you get a few minutes' break would you do a favor for me?"

"Sure. What is it?"

"Go to the morgue and find Barrett's body. Check his hands for any traces of ink."

His request was met with silence.

"Bill? You there?"

"Yea. You want me to check his hands for traces of ink?"

"Yes. That's what I said."

"Do you want me to give him a manicure while I'm down there?"

"Bill. Please don't give me a hard time about this, O.K.?"

"Yea, yea. O.K. Check his hands for traces of ink. I can do that."

"Thanks."

"Uh, Duncan. Why in the hell am I doing this?"

"I'll explain later. I promise you I'm not crazy."

"Are you sure?"

"I'm sure."

"Do you want me to call you back?"

"No. I'll see you at rounds in the morning. And thanks for doing this for me."

"No problem, Dunk. As long as you don't mind when I kid you about this later," he said as he hung up the phone.

Duncan stacked a couple of pillows against the headboard of his bed and leaned back to study Barrett's appointment book. He started a month in advance and worked backwards, checking the notes and appointments for each day. Most of the squares for each day were full, with sections blocked off in black ink for clinic and on-call times. There were small notes scribbled in the margins - reminders to change the oil in his car, pay the phone bill, get a haircut - but nothing out of the ordinary.

Duncan's eyelids began to droop. He had worked back several months in the appointment book and was just about to put it aside when he came across a notation that woke him up. There, on October 11, was the simple notation -- "Dental appt."

Duncan sat up in his bed. He quickly flipped back, page after page, looking for a similar appointment. Two weeks earlier he found another. Looking further he found no appointments through the summer months but then came upon another near the end of May. The notebook revealed a cluster of appointments in April and May -- four in all. And then, as he searched further back, Duncan found what he was looking for. The notation read, "Dental appt. 10:00 - Riley Stevens." There was also a short reminder to arrive early to allow time to fill out the initial information forms. This was what Duncan had been looking for -- Barrett's first appointment. He turned down the corner of the page and set the book aside. He slipped on a pair of gray sweat pants and tightened the rope cinch before he went to the kitchen to find the phone directory.

He checked the listings twice in the business section under the heading "Dentists." There was no listing for a dentist named Riley Stevens. There was a Seagers, a Silberman, a Jonathan Stevenson, but no Stevens. He checked the date on the front of the directory to see if it was a current edition, put the directory down, thought for a second, then turned to the white pages. He quickly found what he was looking for. With a smile he said, "R. Stevens." But there was a problem; the listing did not have "Dr." printed before the name or a title such as D.D.S. printed behind it. The address listed was an apartment complex on a street adjacent to the medical center. Duncan now understood why the name had not been listed in the yellow pages. Riley Stevens wasn't a dentist. He was a dental student. Barrett had his dental work done at the dental school.

Duncan went to the bathroom and turned on the lights above the mirror. He opened his mouth for inspection and was a little surprised at what he saw. He had neglected his mouth. There was a coating of deposits on the inside of his lower front teeth, a thin build-up of tartar stained brown with coffee - the perfect excuse to visit the dental school and find out more about Riley Stevens.

Chapter Fifteen

The next morning before rounds Duncan found Bill at the nurses' desk.

"Duncan! How was your vacation?"

"Great," he said. "Can't you tell by my luxuriously deep tan?"

Wammack handed him a cup of coffee. "Here's your breakfast."

"Thanks." He took as sip. "Did I miss anything while I was gone?"

"Yes. It was amazing. Some of the patients actually improved in spite of the medical treatment they received."

Duncan leaned closer to Bill and lowered his voice. "Did you have a chance to go downstairs and check the matter we discussed?"

"Yes, but I didn't find anything."

"Are you sure?"

"Absolutely. I went over both hands twice. There was a lot of tissue discoloration from the trauma but no ink. I even scrubbed the hands with gauze to see if a stain of any kind would rub off. There was nothing."

Duncan's disappointment was evident.

"Do you mind telling me what this is all about?" Bill asked.

"Nothing. Nothing at all. My imagination flew out of control.

"Changing the subject," Duncan said, "I need your advice. I haven't been to a dentist in a while and I was thinking about going to the dental school for a check-up. What do you know about the school?"

"It's great," he responded. "I go there myself. It costs practically nothing."

"Are they competent?"

"Most of them are very good. Just be sure that you get a fourth-year student."

"Why is that?"

"Because the HODAD's are cut after the third year."

"HODAD's?"

"Hands of Death and Destruction," Bill said in an ominous tone of voice. "You see, the dental school does the work at a reduced fee, practically free in fact, in order to attract patients for the students to practice on. The D-1's and D-2's work on models mostly. The D-3's work some on live patients. By the end of the third year the faculty weeds out the HODAD's. By then they either have the skills or they don't. I had a friend from college who was in dental school. He was forced to repeat his third year of training and still couldn't produce the quality of work required. The school dismissed him."

"Dismissed him?"

"Yea. It broke him like a cheap matchstick. It shattered his confidence, and I don't think he has ever recovered. The last I heard he was a cook in a restaurant up in Yazoo City."

"That's terrible," Duncan said.

"Think about it. Four years of college plus four years of dental school all went for nothing. He spent eight years of his life and wasted tens of thousands of dollars and now he fries catfish and hush puppies every Friday and Saturday night for a living."

Bill was silent for a moment as he pondered the twists of fate.

"But to go back to your question. Yes, the D-4's do great work. The D-4's have all passed some very stiff requirements. I wish I could give you a name but the one I used graduated last summer."

"Someone recommended a student named Riley Stevens. Have you heard of him?"

"No. Is he a D-4?"

"I don't know."

"Just remember what I said about HODAD's," Bill warned.

Duncan looked up to see Dr. Shukowsky approaching.

"One more thing, Bill. I may need you to cover for me a little while this afternoon while I go to the dental school."

"No problem."

"Thanks, Bill. I know I have asked a lot of favors of you lately. I promise to pay you back."

The other interns and students gathered around the nurses desk as a nurse set a stack of records in the cart by Dr. Shukowsky. When Dr. Shukowsky cleared his throat, his indication that it was time for rounds to begin, the group fell silent.

Duncan worked at a frantic pace all morning as he moved from room to room and crisis to crisis. A fifty six-year-old woman with a history of alcohol abuse was admitted for treatment of a gastric ulcer. Just after noon Duncan was urgently summoned to her room where he found her violently vomiting blood. She sat upright in bed, a column of blood spewing from her mouth, her eyes wide in horror as she watched the bright red torrent cover her sheets. Before Duncan could reach her side she collapsed back on to the bed. He called a nurse to bring a gurney in order to get the patient to surgery. Another nurse called the O.R. to warn them of the situation. They wheeled the patient out of the room and down the hallway, the nurse cursing the slow response of the elevator to her repeated jabs on the button. Downstairs the nurses at the O.R. took over, leaving Duncan to reach for a fresh set of green hospital scrubs to replace his blood-splattered clothes.

Upon his return to the ward another of his patients was in crisis. A black man in his early thirties who had been placed in the hospital for observation following a blow to the head in a bicycle accident suddenly became unconscious. Duncan rushed him to the imaging department to scan for a probable cerebral hemorrhage. He alerted the O.R. and the neurosurgeon in case emergency surgery was needed.

Preoccupied with his patients, he ignored the growling in his stomach that indicated lunch was long past due. When he finally looked at his watch it was a few minutes before three o'clock. He finished a note in the chart he held and tossed it to a L.P.N. standing by the nurses desk.

"But what about your patients?" she asked.

"Bill Wammack will cover for me. I've got a dental appointment," he shouted back to the nurse as he ran for the elevator.

Chapter Sixteen

Duncan covered the length of the elevated crosswalk to the dental school at a fast pace, his toothbrush in his mouth. As he scrubbed his teeth briskly with a hacksaw motion, a couple of young secretaries shot him looks of disgust as he paused to spit in a clay-filled ashcan near the entrance to the library. He rinsed his mouth at the first water fountain he saw in the dental school.

Duncan tried to gather his thoughts. The appointment had come sooner than he had expected.

What did he hope to discover about Riley Stevens? What was he doing here? He shook his head, disgusted at himself. He had let his imagination take over, allowed himself to be pushed by some vague feeling, a hunch that there was some hidden story behind the death of Barrett Jeter.

He told himself again that Barrett had died as a result of an act of random violence. A tragedy, yes, but no mystery. It was time to forget about this and put it behind him, to go on with his life.

He stood in the lobby of the dental school and considered returning to the hospital and his patients. But he was already here. And he did need to have a dental check-up. If he postponed this he might not find the time to return. "What the heck," he muttered as he walked to the reception desk.

He was greeted by a middle-aged lady with a hint of Scandinavia in her voice.

"I'm Duncan Russthorne. I have a three o'clock appointment."

She checked a list, nodded, handed him a form to complete, and pointed to a waiting area.

"Excuse me," he said before she could return to her work.

"Yes?"

"Just curious, but is Riley Stevens a D-3 or a D-4?"

A knowing smile spread across her face as she held up four fingers.

"Don't worry," she whispered.

He smiled to show his appreciation and took a seat. When he was finished, the receptionist directed him through a glass door adjacent to the reception area and led him to a long desk divided at intervals with sheets of cork board to provide a small degree of privacy. There were six interview booths. On his side two of the booths were occupied by other patients. Students in short white jackets sat opposite them. The receptionist stopped at the fourth booth.

"Student Dr. Stevens will be with you in a moment."

He thanked her and took a seat. After a few minutes he leaned back in his chair to look around the partition. A group of students were clustered in a corner, engaged in earnest but muted conversation. Behind them a secretary searched through a filing cabinet.

"Hello. You're Duncan Russthorne?" a voice asked from across the desk.

Duncan turned to see a young lady standing on the opposite side of the interview booth. She was in her mid-twenties, with olive skin, and dark intelligent eyes that narrowed ever-so-slightly at the corners. Her dark shoulder-length hair was straight with a dark luster and the tips curled slightly inward over the collar of her white clinic coat. There was a hint of the exotic in the set of her eyes and the curve of her nose. Latin, perhaps, or a trace of the Near East. He rose to greet her.

"I'm Riley Stevens," she said as she extended her hand.

Duncan stared at her.

"You are Duncan Russthorne, aren't you?"

"Er . . . ah . . . yes. I am." He reached out and shook her hand.

"Nice to meet you. Have a seat." She pointed at his chair as she reached for her own.

Duncan sat, unable to think of anything to say, his face betraying his thoughts.

She smiled, a warm confident smile with steady eyes. "You weren't expecting a woman, were you?"

Duncan could feel the warmth creep up his neck and across his cheeks.

"You're blushing. That's great! I haven't seen a guy blush in such a long time!"

Duncan felt his face continue to redden.

"Don't be embarrassed. It happens all the time."

"I'm sorry. I shouldn't have assumed you were a man."

"Thank you," she said and smiled. "Apology accepted."

She glanced over the data forms that Duncan had given to the receptionist.

"The first thing we will do today is review your medical history," she said.

Duncan studied her as she made a note on a margin of the page. She kept her long, dark hair pulled back with a pair of clips, but a few strands had worked loose to frame her face as she leaned forward. Her complexion was smooth and dark, with no hint of makeup.

Duncan leaned forward and rested his elbows on the desk. He noticed that her fingernails were short and she wore no polish on them. When he inhaled he noticed a slight fragrance - light, clean, and sweet.

"Mrs. Sigurd said you requested me . . . Any reason?" She looked up at Duncan.

"Yes. Barrett Jeter gave me your name."

Duncan sensed her body stiffen slightly. The smile disappeared from her face as she quickly looked down at the record without speaking, her lower lip tucked between her teeth.

"You did know Barrett, didn't you?"

"Yes. He was a patient of mine," she replied in a clipped, professional manner.

"So you heard of his death?"

"Yes. I was sorry to hear of that," she said as she slipped the wire clasps of the manila folder through the holes punched in the information sheet.

In the space of a few seconds Riley's personality had switched from friendly and inviting to cool and distant. The sudden change in her manner puzzled Duncan. He started to speak, paused, thought for a second, then decided to gamble on his next statement.

"Barrett told me a lot about you," he said. He leaned forward to better gauge her reaction but was unprepared for what happened next.

Riley slammed her pen down so hard that it bounced across the desk and hit Duncan in the chest.

"Let me tell you something, buster. I went out with him one time. ONE time. He kept pouring drinks into me and when he thought I was too drunk to defend myself his hands were all over me. He punched me when I slapped him to make him stop and held me down on the floor. The only thing that kept me from being raped was my roommate's timely arrival and my knee in his crotch. The last thing he said when he walked out the door was that he would tell all his friends what an easy piece of ass I was."

"That's terrible," Duncan said as he squirmed uncomfortably in his chair.

"Yes. That's terrible. But you know what's worse?"

105

Duncan opened his mouth to respond but she cut him off. She pointed a finger at him and emphasized the gesture by slamming the same hand on the table.

"You are! You're disgusting. Your friend hasn't been dead a week and here you are trying to hit on every girl he said . . ."

"Whoa! Wait a minute!" He threw his hands up in a gesture of surrender. "Just calm down and give me a chance to explain."

A student peered around the corner from the adjacent booth. Riley backed him off with a look. She was calmer now, but her nostrils still flared as she took heavy breaths. After a few moments of silent truce Duncan tried to explain himself.

"I know you won't believe this, but I never heard Barrett mention your name."

She gave him a look that expressed total disbelief, a hateful sneer with eyes narrowed and lips drawn tight. "You've already said that you got my name from Barrett."

"I did."

"But you just said . . ."

"Wait. I did get it from Barrett. I found your name in his appointment book. His family asked me to pick up some of his belongings for them and I found your name in his appointment book. That's why I was so surprised to see that you were not a man."

She considered that fact for a minute. "But what about the part about us having a date? How did you know that?"

"I didn't. That was a wild guess on my part. I was just curious," he offered, his face a picture of conciliation.

They stared at each other across the desk as an uneasy calm settled in. In the background other people returned to their conversations and activities.

Duncan leaned toward her again. In as sincere a voice as he could muster he said, "I apologize. I am very, very sorry. I did not mean to upset you."

"No . . . No . . . I'm the one who should apologize," she said with her head lowered. She looked up at him with a penitent face. "I sort of blew it, didn't I?"

He shook his head. "It was my fault. I shouldn't have been so nosy. Do you think we could start over?"

"Yes. Let's do," she agreed.

After an awkward pause he said, "What do we do next?"

She looked back down at the record. "Normally, at this point, I would go over the health history questions that you answered just to be sure that you understood what all of these medical terms were and to see if you answered all of the questions correctly, but since you are a physician I don't see any reason to do that. The next step is to take you to the clinic, do an examination, and take some x-rays. Excuse me -- radiographs. I forgot that you know the correct terminology."

She stood up and walked around to his side of the booth and led him across the hallway to a clinic with several dental chairs in an open format.

The next hour went quickly. First, Riley took a series of radiographs on his teeth, eighteen or twenty small films in all, Duncan thought. Then she did a thorough exam, inspecting and probing every tooth as if it held the key to some great mystery.

When she had finished, a professor came to their dental chair and consulted with her, confirming her findings, both in the mouth and on the x-rays. "Very thorough, Ms. Stevens," was all he said.

"Do you think this class II is a proficiency-level?"

The professor pulled out a magnifying glass to study the x-rays that had been placed on a fluorescent viewing screen beside the chair. "I'll approve it," he agreed. "Get this fellow to the restorative clinic."

He made a note on a small form and handed her the bottom copy from the carbon before he moved to the next cubicle.

"Yes!" She beamed as she looked at Duncan.

"Do you get a grade for this?"

"I get graded on everything. The angle at which I took the x-rays, the charting I did of your mouth, the way I dotted my _i_'s and crossed my _t_'s when I wrote the diagnosis and treatment plan in the record."

"Is it that complicated?"

"It doesn't have to be. I sometimes wonder if the faculty doesn't sit up at night thinking up ways to make simple task into an extremely complicated procedure." She looked over her shoulder to see if any of the faculty had overheard.

"So, what's the verdict? How are my teeth?"

"You have a cavity," she said with enthusiasm.

"It bothers me that you sound so excited about it."

"That did sound a little odd, but let me explain. As students we are graded on everything that we do. The school gives us a long list of procedures to do each year -- a certain number of dentures and bridges, a certain number of extractions, a certain number of fillings of different types. After we have received passing grades on a required number of each procedure, we have a proficiency exam -- what you might call a final exam -- on that procedure. The faculty has set very strict guidelines on what type of cavity can be used for a proficiency exam, and ."

"Let me guess," Duncan interrupted. "I have the perfect cavity?"

"A perfect class II. And I need to get this done today if possible."

Duncan frowned and looked at his watch. "How long will this take?"

She pushed a button on the back of the dental chair. The chair automatically raised Duncan to a sitting position.

"About an hour."

"I don't know, Riley." He looked at his watch again. "I've been here too long as it is. I need to get back to my patients."

"Come on. One more hour. I really need to get this proficiency exam out of the way."

"But I've got to make rounds at six. Can't we do this later?"

"Oh, please, Duncan." She grabbed his sleeve. "I really need this. I'll owe you big time if you'll do this for me."

Duncan bit his lip and looked at his watch for the third time. "I don't know."

"Please," she begged.

After a moment's consideration he said, "Let me ask you one thing."

"What?"

"Do I have to get a shot?"

She rolled her eyes in disgust.

"Why do we have to go upstairs?" Duncan asked as Riley led the way toward the elevator. "Why can't we just do the work where we were?"

"That clinic is designated for initial exams and radiographs. Sort of a triage area."

They entered the empty elevator. Just before the door closed a hand was thrust into the elevator from the hallway and the automatic doors opened. A young man with a crew cut, wearing a shiny green football jersey, faded blue jeans, and muddy black tennis shoes, entered and pushed the same button that Riley had pushed. As he entered, Riley moved a step closer to Duncan to make room. Duncan noticed that she was only an inch or two shorter than himself. And that fragrance again. He filled his nostrils with it. It reminded him of the new, innocent smell of a three day old infant.

"My Lord," he thought with alarm. "I need to get a life outside of the hospital. Others might have thought of the faint fragrance of antique roses; I'm trying to compare her with a neonatology unit in the pediatric ward. If I'm not careful I'll be asking her for her blood type."

He shook the thoughts from his head as Riley watched the lights over the door blinking off and on as the elevator ascended.

"So, you don't like shots. It must be true what they say about doctors being the worst kind of patients."

"Oh, I don't mind shots in the arm or hip. I don't even mind giving blood or having an I.V. inserted in my arm. But there's something about getting a shot in the mouth. Maybe it's just bad childhood memories, maybe it's because the mouth is such a sensitive area of the body. But the thought of that big, long needle," he held his open hands about eight inches apart, "being buried in my gums until the sharp point starts to scrape against bone . . ." The young man gave a nervous glance toward Duncan. ". . . and the searing pain as the drill burrows its way into a nerve . . ."

Riley punched him in the ribs with her elbow. The elevator stopped its ascent and the doors opened. The young man in front of Duncan and Riley hesitated, then stepped back. "Go ahead," he motioned to them. "I think I've changed my mind."

Duncan and Riley stepped from the elevator and walked down the hall toward the clinic.

"If you can't stand the heat ..."

"You ought to be ashamed of yourself. That was cruel," she said as she fought back a smile.

Duncan soon found himself reclined in a dental chair again. He watched every move as Riley produced a swab with a thick cream smeared on the cotton tip. She rubbed an area on his gum for a few seconds, then she quickly picked up a syringe from a tray of instruments and approached his mouth with the hypodermic needle. When he remembered what Bill had said about HODAD's, Duncan decided to close his eyes.

"You are such a wimp," Riley chided. "This really won't hurt a bit."

Duncan felt a bit of pressure in a spot of his mouth and waited for the pain of the needle. When it did not come, he slowly opened one eye, then the other, to see the hypodermic being withdrawn from his mouth.

"Is that it? Did you give me the shot?"

"Yes, it's over," Riley said, pleased with herself. "If you have to ask then it didn't hurt."

"I didn't feel a thing."

"I told you that you wouldn't."

Duncan felt a tingling sensation flow down his face. He touched his mouth with his hand, testing the corner of his lip.

"Hey, you're good. Pretty darn good," he said incredulously.

Her response was a confident, "I know."

Duncan watched Riley as she worked, impressed by the concentration that marked her face. He noticed that her eyes were a peculiar shade of brown, lighter than most, with a few flecks of green. He noticed her fragrance again. He closed his eyes as she worked and began to relax. In a few minutes he was struggling to keep his mouth open.

"You're not trying to go to sleep on me, are you?" Riley asked.

"Nothing personal but I haven't had much sleep lately," he said.

Riley produced a small wedge of black rubber from the instrument tray and slipped it into his mouth to prop his teeth apart.

Duncan woke to find the back of the chair moving up and forward. Riley tugged on the bite block with her fingers. He stretched his mouth open to release it.

"Nice nap?"

"Pretty smooth." Duncan yawned and stretched. Riley turned to write in his chart. He stood up and stepped closer to her. "Did you pass?"

"Yes." She gave him a quick smile, then returned to her writing. "You don't know how much I appreciate this. This really helped me out a lot."

Duncan cleared his throat. "I don't suppose you would like to show your appreciation by letting me take you out to dinner this weekend?"

Riley stopped writing. Duncan couldn't be sure, but he thought he saw her frown briefly before she turned to him with a smile. "Gee, Duncan, I really appreciate the offer, but I'm leaving Saturday morning to visit my parents."

"What about Friday night then?"

He watched as her frown turned into a smile that grew broader until she burst into laughter.

"Gee, I've been turned down before, but I've never been laughed at," Duncan said.

"It's not that," Riley said as she pulled a paper towel from the dispenser and handed it to him. "You have saliva running down the left side of your chin."

He felt his cheek. "Now I can better empathize with my stroke patients." He took the towel from Riley and wiped his face.

She shook her head. "I've never had anybody drool when they ask me for a date," she said.

"See how desperate I am? So what about Friday night? Remember what you said downstairs? About how you would owe me 'big time?'"

"'Big time?' Did I say that?"

"Yes, you did. C'mon. I promise I won't attack you like Barrett did."

"I guess so."

"Great!"

"But on one condition," she added quickly.

"What's that?"

"I'm going to do a little background check on you. If I find out you're a creep and a slug I reserve the right to cancel," she said.

"Agreed." He held out his hand and they shook on it. "How does dinner sound? About 7:30?"

"Can we make it eight o'clock?"

"Fine, see you then." He gave her one more smile before he left. After he had taken two steps he turned back. "Oh. One more thing. If you need to call me, just leave a message with the paging service at the hospital. Don't call my home or my wife will find out."

She stared at him for a split second, her mouth open in disbelief, before her eyes narrowed and she squeezed her fists into knots, the fire building in her face.

"Just kidding! Just kidding! Honest!" he said as he backed away from her. "I'll call you later." He looked at his watch as he hurried from the clinic.

Riley stood by the counter as she finished the treatment notes in the patient's record.

"Riley, what have you done?" she whispered to herself.

111

Chapter Seventeen

That Friday, due to a late admission of a patient transferred from the emergency room, Duncan ran out the front door of the hospital at 7:42, jumped into his car, and made the trip from the parking lot to his house in record time, his tires squealing as he braked by the curb in front of his home. He entered the gate and ran up the steps. With one hand he worked the key in the lock, with the other he removed his mail from the letter box by the door. He noticed Barrett's box contained some envelopes, so he snatched them also before he swung the door open and hurried to the back of the house. He threw the mail on the bed, kicked off his shoes, and stripped out of his scrubs as he headed for the shower.

He emerged from the bathroom a few minutes later with a towel around his waist. He shook his hair dry with another towel as he flipped through his mail. There was a bill from the phone company, a letter from his parents, and two pieces of junk mail. He placed Barrett's mail in a separate stack and made a mental note to send a forwarding address to the post office. He took a blue denim shirt from the closet and walked back to the bed as he worked the buttons on the cuffs of his shirt. A thought struck him as he slipped on a pair of neatly pressed khaki pants.

He picked up Barrett's phone bill, quickly tore open the flap, and pulled out the short call listing. Duncan glanced over the phone bill. There were six long distance calls -- three to Crockett, one to New Orleans, and two calls to the same number in Elgin, MS. He assumed the calls to Crockett had been to his mother. But the other two? And where was Elgin?

Duncan sat down on the bed and began to pull on his socks and shoes. He cradled the receiver between his neck and shoulder as he dialed New Orleans.

A young lady answered, "Buckingham Garden Hotel. How may I help you?"

"Sorry, wrong number," Duncan said before he disconnected the call.

Of course. Barrett had called to make reservations for the trip he had planned with Jenny. But the Buckingham Garden Hotel, the hotel of choice for movie stars and rich Texas oil men? That was major bucks and way out of Barrett's league.

He dialed the number in Elgin and let the phone ring. He checked the number again on the billing record, waited three more rings, and had decided to hang up when a gruff voice finally answered.

"Yeah?"

"Hello?" Duncan said. There was music in the background, with loud guitars and a driving bass.

"Yeah," the voice said again.

Duncan fumbled for a response. "Is . . . uh . . . Samuel there?"

"Sam who?"

"Uh, . . Sam Adams?"

"Don't know no Sam Adams," the voice answered with irritation. Before Duncan could think of another question to ask, the line went dead.

He stared at the receiver for a moment before his thoughts were interrupted by the mantel clock chiming eight o'clock. He threaded his belt through the loops of his pants and checked his pockets to be sure he had his wallet and keys.

He paused before he turned off the reading lamp by the telephone. He was already late; two minutes wouldn't make any difference. He dialed the operator.

"Yes ma'am. I have a call listed on my phone bill that I don't think I made."

He was put on hold. In a moment a different voice came on the line.

"Yes ma'am. My name is, uh, Barrett Jeter and I have a call charged on my phone bill that I don't think was placed by me. Could you check that for me?"

He gave her the telephone number in question. Again he was placed on hold. It was a long minute before she answered him.

"The Club Elgin? No, I don't think so, but let me check with my roommate again. One of his friends may have placed the call. Thank you. Good-bye."

He slammed the phone down as he grabbed his jacket and ran to the front door.

Riley feigned a slight degree of aggravation at Duncan's tardiness. Duncan feigned indifference to Riley's indignation, but during the short drive to the restaurant they both dropped their attitudes and settled into a relaxed conversation.

The restaurant was located close to the river and was popular with the post-college crowd. Dark wood and brass prevailed, along with earnest young professionals wearing stylish attire. Their pretensions annoyed Duncan, but he still patronized the restaurant because of the excellent food and, especially, the music. On most weekend nights the house band was a local group with a female lead whose voice was textured and lucid -- liquid fire punctuated by an occasional burst of lightning. The band's repertoire was a mix of modern jazz and soul that forced even the most repressed to loosen up and move to the music.

Duncan requested a booth in the corner of the upper level away from the band. The waiter took their order for drinks as they settled into their seats. Duncan smiled as he noticed the waiter's gaze linger on Riley. She wore a black dress that clung smoothly to her body. A simple gold necklace rested low against her skin.

She looked around the room and studied the walls, the floor, and the decor with a puzzled look on her face.

"You've been here before, haven't you?" he asked.

"Yes, but not lately. It's not as I remember it."

"That's because this building sits in the river's flood plain. Every few years the restaurant receives a renovation, courtesy of the Pearl River."

She studied the pictures on the wall. "Is this where you bring all of your dates?" she teased.

"You should know."

"I should?"

"Your investigation, remember? You said you were going to ask around about me, check into my background, see if I had any skeletons in my closet. I assume you didn't find anything too terrible or we wouldn't be here."

"I did some checking," she confessed with a smile that hinted at some secret knowledge. "You're a very interesting fellow. I heard a lot of different comments about you, a lot of them contradictory."

"Oh, really? Do you care to tell me what everyone said?"

The waiter returned with the drinks, placed them on the table, and flipped open his order pad. Riley ordered crayfish etouffee. Duncan ordered the prime rib. The waiter was very attentive to Riley and practically ignored Duncan.

"I think he was flirting with you," Duncan said after the waiter left.

"I think he was, too. Does that bother you?"

"Not as much as it will bother him when he sees the size of his tip. But back to the investigation."

"The investigation," she said with a nod. "Let's see. First, you're a loner. Not many people know you that well. 'A riddle wrapped in a mystery inside an enigma,' one said."

114

"Ah, that would be Mr. Churchill's comment." He pointed to himself, "Russthorne, not Russia."

She smiled and continued, "Friendly, but few close friends."

"Go on," he said.

"One person said that you are supposed to be incredibly smart but that you do a good job of hiding it."

"Was that a compliment or an insult?"

"A compliment, I think. Did you really make the highest score in the history of UMC on your Surgery Board examination?"

He nodded.

"But you're not in a surgery residency, are you?"

He shook his head.

"Why?"

He looked down at his glass and gave the ice a couple of shakes to loosen it up.

"Is it hard to put into words?" she asked.

"Not really," he said. "It's easy to put into words. It's hard for people to understand. You see, I don't want to be a surgeon. All I ever wanted was to be a small town physician with a general practice of medicine."

"That goes against the grain, doesn't it? Turning down the big bucks for the demands of a rural practice, a harder way of life."

"I guess that explains why someone said I do a good job of hiding my intelligence," he said. "It sounds like you did a pretty thorough job with your investigation. I didn't have the opportunity to run a background check on you so you will have to tell me about yourself."

"Where should I start? I was born and raised in a small town in the Mississippi Delta called Indianola . . ."

As the band returned from their break, Duncan's attention was diverted when the vocalist tapped on her microphone to test it. His gaze snapped back to Riley when she mentioned the Delta.

"Is that near Elgin?" he interrupted.

"Yes. Elgin is just a few miles away."

"I've heard of Elgin. Why?"

"I would imagine you have heard of Elgin because of the college. Mississippi Delta College. The college is practically the only reason the town exists."

"Isn't that where Barrett went to college?" he asked. He regretted the question the moment he said it; he had let it escape his mouth without thinking.

115

Her chin rose as she arched her back. Duncan remembered her angry reaction when he had mentioned Barrett to her at their first meeting and braced himself for the storm to follow. Instead, she relaxed her posture.

"Do you feel you need to talk about Barrett?" she asked.

"No. Not really. Do you?"

"No, I don't. I've told you all there is to tell about my short but not so sweet relationship with Barrett. It would have been shorter but he was the only patient I could find for my gold bridge-work proficiency test. But even someone as composed as you can't be unfazed by the murder of your roommate."

"So you found out we were roommates. I guess that was unavoidable."

"Were you afraid I would think you were a creep just because you lived with a creep?"

Duncan smiled. "Do you think I'm a creep?"

"No, I don't," she said, then took a sip from her glass. "So," she continued, "do you want to talk about Barrett?"

Duncan knew it was decision time. He could continue with his questions about Barrett, continue to try to find some reason or purpose behind a senseless killing. His instincts told him there was something hidden -- a deeper level of truth beneath the facts of Barrett's murder. His instincts also told him that Riley held no secrets concerning Barrett.

Their waiter approached as she waited for his answer.

"No," he said as their food was served. "I want to talk about you."

"Dessert?" he asked when Riley pushed her empty plate to one side.

"Sure," she agreed.

"Good. I admire a healthy appetite, someone who enjoys good food."

"I enjoy it too much," she said as she patted her stomach.

"Then how do you stay so slim?"

"Good genetic factors," she answered.

"What about your temper? Who did you inherit that from?"

Riley smiled. "I'm afraid I got a liberal dose from both of my parents. My father was first generation Lebanese. He met my mother during the war when he was stationed in New England. She's Irish. They both have pretty volatile temperaments."

"I take it you got your first name from your mother."

"Exactly, although it was my father's idea. I'm the youngest of three girls. I think my father was hoping for a son when he named me. My mother says she wanted to call me 'Surprise.'"

"Surprise?"

"My mother became pregnant with me late in life," she explained.

"But what about the name Stevens. That doesn't strike me as a typical Lebanese name."

"The story goes that the immigration officials didn't know how to write my grandparents' original name but that it sounded similar to Stevens. That's what they wrote down on his immigration papers. My grandfather thought the name change was part of the process, that when you came to America they gave you an American name. He was proud of the new name, and he liked the way it sounded, so he kept it."

"That's a great story. What about your father - is he a dentist?"

"No. He owned a clothing store. He passed away last summer." Small wrinkles appeared on her brow as she pretended to concentrate on her food.

"What about you?" she changed the subject. "Tell me about yourself. You are from Birmingham, aren't you?"

"Actually I am originally from Mississippi; I was raised on a farm in Bois d'Arc county."

"You are from the hills?"

"Yes. They say people from the Delta like to look down their noses at people from the hills."

"Don't get the idea that my family belongs to the aristocracy, Duncan. My father was the son of a Lebanese immigrant. And to make matters worse he went and married a Yankee! That is almost an unpardonable sin in the Delta. No. I don't think less of you for being a hillbilly. But where did I get the idea that you are from Alabama?"

"I moved to Birmingham when I was eight years old. My father is a physician." It was not really a lie, he told himself, just not the whole truth.

"So that is where you got your desire to be a physician. Your father."

"No. I actually decided on that before I went to live with him. He's my stepfather," he explained.

"Any brothers or sisters?"

Duncan had been expecting the question. It was one that always came up during small talk, and one that always made him uncomfortable. He was spared an answer when the waiter appeared with a dessert tray and distracted Riley long enough for Duncan to steer the conservation in another direction.

The time passed quickly. Questions and answers flowed between them as they began to learn about each other. The time passed quickly as he told some of his more bizarre experiences as an intern. For every story he told, she responded with one of her own. He liked her laughter; it was strong and honest and it put Duncan at ease.

Duncan was debating ordering his third drink - on his sleep deprived schedule two drinks were usually enough to put him to sleep for eight hours - when Riley looked at her watch.

"Duncan . . ." she started her sentence as she looked at her watch.

"No. It's early yet."

"Yes, it's early -- it's early Saturday morning. I have to be at the airport in a few hours to meet my sister Elizabeth from California. She's coming home for a week to visit. My other sister, Dorothy, is driving up from New Orleans to meet us so we can make the drive home together."

"A family reunion," he said.

"Yes. This will be the first time all three daughters have been home since my father's funeral. Our schedules never seem to match."

"Sounds like a good weekend."

She hesitated before she spoke. "Yes. I'm looking forward to it."

"You don't sound convincing," he said with a questioning look.

She answered with a tired smile as she gathered her jacket and her small black leather handbag.

A comfortable silence filled the car as Duncan drove Riley home. Duncan fought off a yawn, failed, then tried to hide it by turning his head away and hoped that she wouldn't notice. The car pulled up to the curb outside her apartment complex situated across the street from the grounds of the medical center. Built in the early fifties, each two-story building housed four apartments -- two up and two down. The apartments were plain and unadorned, and were covered with a dark brown brick. A small stoop at the front opened into a hallway that ran from front to back.

Duncan paused at the door to the complex, but Riley opened the door and motioned him to follow. He followed behind her up the steps to her apartment trying hard to listen to what she was saying as he stared at the way the curves of her hips filled her dress.

She took a key ring from her jacket pocket and dropped the jacket to the floor as she turned around.

"I would invite you in, but I really do have to get up early," she said as she draped her arm over his shoulder.

He moved close and placed his hands around her waist. A smile appeared on his face as the contours of her body folded into his.

"You're smiling," she said softly.

"I smile when I'm happy."

"You're happy?"

He nodded. "Very."

"Me too," she said. She slid a hand along the back of his neck and tilted her face forward to kiss him. She leaned gently back against the door as they kissed, pulling him against her, allowing his weight to press harder against her body just as the door opened.

Duncan grabbed the frame of the door in time to keep them both from tumbling onto the floor. He looked up, startled to see a man standing in the apartment with a cardboard box under each arm.

"Sorry," the man said.

Duncan looked at Riley.

"Oh, Duncan, this is Van. He's my roommate's boyfriend." she quickly explained. Van moved away from the door to reveal a tall girl with a ponytail wearing a t-shirt that carried the likeness of a cartoon cat. She too was holding a box. "Hi," she chirped.

"Duncan, this is my roommate Jean."

"Jean. Van," he acknowledged the introduction. Van stood mute as Jean walked out of the apartment. "We were just leaving. These are the last boxes. I'll call you tomorrow," she said over her shoulder as she bounced down the stairs with Van following close behind.

Duncan peered over the banister as Van lurched down the stairs, his bulk swaying from banister to wall with each step.

"Big guy, isn't he?"

"I introduced the two last year, much to my regret," Riley whispered. "Now I've lost a roommate."

"She's moving out?"

"She's been living with Van for months, but I guess it's official now."

Duncan turned to her and grinned. "Need a new roommate?"

Riley laughed. "No. Jean has already paid her rent for the semester." She picked up her jacket and stood in the doorway. "I really had a good time. Will I get to see you again?"

"I hope so."

"I hope so too," she said as she softly closed the door.

Duncan ambled down the sidewalk to his car. The night air was crisp and stung his cheeks and the edges of his ears but he chose to linger a moment instead of seeking the warmth of his car. He leaned against the fender and gazed toward the distant buildings of the medical center. Small figures could be seen moving across the windows in the distance. A security car made its round through a parking lot. Plumes of steam rose from the vents on top of the laundry facility.

As much as he enjoyed his time off from his duties as an intern, he couldn't see staying away from the hospital for any length of time. There was still much to be learned about medicine, too much for just one individual to master. He was beginning to realize that there would always be vast areas of medicine that would remain unknown to him. Two years ago that thought would have been uncomfortable. His curiosity would not have allowed him to accept the fact that there would be so many unanswered questions, so much mystery never to be unveiled.

Barrett's death would be another riddle left unsolved, he decided. And Riley's involvement? He shook his head. That had really been a desperate attempt to try to make a connection between her and the murder. He and his blue ribbon imagination.

During the drive home he wondered if he would ever be able to tell Riley that he asked her out on a date in order to see if she had been involved in a murder. With her temper there might be a second murder -- his. Suddenly he came to a pleasant realization. For the last week his thoughts had been interrupted by the unwanted image of Barrett's body as it lay on the floor of his home the night of the murder. But now that image was beginning to fade. A new and different image had intruded itself into his mind, a much more pleasant image. It was the image of Riley's smiling face.

Chapter Eighteen

"Just like old times," Bill said as he slid his cafeteria tray onto the stainless steel ledge and into the waiting hands of one of the kitchen employees.

"C'mon, Bill," Duncan said as he followed suit.

"No. Really. It's good to have you back," Bill said as he backed through the swinging door into the hallway.

"Give me a break. I haven't been that bad."

Bill waved at a nurse pushing a cart as they passed in the hall. She grinned, then returned her attention to an older nurse that was lecturing to her.

"Yes, you have. Do you realize that in the last three weeks you've eaten lunch at the dental school almost every day. You leave the hospital every chance you get. You even faked being sick one Saturday when you were supposed to have call duty. The nurses have a new nickname for you."

"What's that?"

"The Phantom Physician. The Elvis of the Fourth Floor. Just enough sightings to keep everyone talking."

"Cute. Are you keeping score?"

"Yes."

"Are you jealous?"

"Damn right I am," Bill said.

"Look, Bill. I'm sorry. I know you've had to pick up a lot of my slack. It's not fair, and I . . . ."

Bill threw up a hand to silence him. "Don't worry about it. I'm not complaining. I'm just a little surprised that Duncan Russthorne, Super Gunner, is slacking off and stopping to smell the roses. And I don't blame you at all, considering the reason. She's a beauty."

The two interns turned into an intersecting corridor and came to an abrupt halt when they bumped into Dean Goza.

"Good morning, gentlemen. How are you today?" Goza said as he focused his attention on Duncan.

"Fine, thank you."

"Feeling better, Duncan?" he asked.

"Um, yes sir," he answered tentatively.

"Are you sure? I don't want you pushing yourself too hard."

"I'm fine, really. I appreciate your concern."

"You know you can't take care of your patients if you're not taking care of yourself. Get some rest. Don't overwork yourself. I have already talked to Dr. Shukowsky about your situation, so don't be afraid to ask for a day off if you need. And take some vitamins, too. Your body needs more during periods of stress."

His lecture finished, he gave a quick nod to both men and then continued down the hall. Duncan turned to look at him as he departed.

"What was that about? Did I miss something?"

"I just saved your hide, buddy," Bill said with a superior attitude.

"How is that?"

"I was waiting in Dr. Goza's office a couple of days ago. I wanted to talk with him concerning help with some financial aid when Dr. Shukowsky came in. He went into Dr. Goza's private office but the door wasn't completely closed. Do you know who they talked about?"

Duncan thought for a moment. "Me?"

"Correct."

"What did they say?"

"Shukowsky informed Dr. Goza of your absences. He said your work had dropped off, that he was afraid you were losing your focus on medicine."

"What did Goza say?"

"He told Shukowsky he would talk to you. But when I was called into his private office for my appointment I straightened things out for you. I had a nice long talk with Dr. Gallbladder."

"You did what?"

"After we talked about my financial aid I told him I wanted to talk to him confidentially about you. I told him I was worried about you. How Barrett's death had really struck you a pretty hard blow. I told him that you weren't sleeping well, that you were barely eating. In order to convince him of how much stress you were under I told him you had a bad case of trench mouth."

"Trench mouth?!" he blurted out. He lowered his voice when he noticed people staring. "That's the lamest excuse I've ever heard."

122

"I actually thought it was pretty good, Dunc. It's a minor illness that shows you're under a lot of stress and it also provides a good alibi for your frequent trips to the dental school."

"Yeah, but trench mouth? Couldn't you come up with something a little less. . . .disgusting?"

"Come on, admit it. I saved your butt."

"You should have been a lawyer or a politician, Bill. You lie too well to be a doctor."

"Thank you. But back to my jealousy. How is it going with Riley?"

"Good, I think. We're driving up to see her mother this weekend."

"So why the frown? Are things moving too fast for you again?"

"No. It's not that. It's Riley. One day she's very warm and open, the next day she's distant. She definitely sends mixed signals."

"But if she didn't like you, why would she invite you home with her?"

"Car problems -- hers is in the shop. I volunteered to drive her."

Bill shook his head in disappointment.

"Do you know what your problem is, Dunc?"

"I have some I don't know about?"

"You think too much. You need to relax and just let things happen, let some of the stress just roll of your back. You would live a lot longer if you did. Did you know that the average life expectancy of a physician in the state of Mississippi is around fifty eight years?"

"Because of the stress that results from the practice of medicine?"

"Because of the stress," Bill confirmed.

"Do any of them die from trench mouth?"

Chapter Nineteen

On a cool, bright Saturday afternoon the car carrying Duncan and Riley sped north from Jackson. Withered kudzu vines, their leaves curled and dry from the winter cold, covered the roadbanks and shrouded the trees and telephone poles in a tangle of runners so dense that one could only guess at the outline of the object strangled beneath their growth. The tendrils stretched from limb to limb between adjacent trees as if some mutant spider had laced a ubiquitous web of coarse gray strands across the landscape.

A road sign proclaimed the city of Yazoo City as one of the portals to the Delta. As the car came to the top a small rise, the highway dropped sharply away before them into the open bowl of the land that had once been the mouth of the ancient river. The road descended from the bluff at an angle so steep that Duncan had to keep his foot pressed lightly on the brakes as they descended. The sharp contrast from hill to Delta was so dramatic and surprising that Duncan could only utter an ineloquent, "Wow."

Riley, who had not spoken much during the ride, broke from her thoughts. She looked up to see the car rolling down the slope like the last run of a rollercoaster. "Oh, yeah. The edge of the Delta. No matter how many times I travel this road, this descent still impresses me. It's like a border to a different land."

"A land of plantations and mint juleps?"

"Not hardly. You sound like one of those journalists that periodically come here to do a story on the bad things that happened thirty years ago. They focus on the negatives instead of the majority of people, good people of all colors, trying to get along."

"Whoa, I was just kidding."

"Sorry," she said. "One of my pet peeves. Did I sound like I was preaching?"

"Not at all, Reverend Stevens."

When they reached the bottom of the steep grade they drove through the town and across the river. Soon the car was cruising across long stretches of open road bordered by wide, level fields of farmland punctuated with an occasional house. Duncan breathed the heavy smell of the rich, black soil. The clarity of the light seemed different in the Delta under the open bowl of sky. There was a sense of power in this place, a feeling that Duncan had only experienced before when he stood under the expanse of a prominent cliff prior to a climb.

"Isn't that cotton?" Duncan pointed across the road.

"Yes."

"I thought they picked cotton in the fall."

"They do."

"But it looks as if there is a lot of cotton still left on the plants."

"There is. The cotton pickers aren't as efficient as people pulling it by hand. It leaves some, but it's not worth the waste of fuel to go back in the fields to gather what little is left." She looked at Duncan. "You've never been to the Delta before?"

"No," Duncan admitted. "The only thing I know about the Delta is what I've read in Faulkner's books."

Riley smiled at his ignorance. "That is a world that no longer exists."

"No Big Woods?'

"No Big Woods," she shook her head. "This is some of the richest soil in the world. In some areas the topsoil is forty to fifty feet thick. It doesn't pay to leave a large section of land untilled."

Riley fell back into silence as the fields flew past them. Duncan's attempts at small talk brought no response. She remained distant, deep in her own world of thoughts. In a short time they were greeted by a billboard, white with wavy blue borders, that read *"Elgin - The Catfish Capitol of the World."* A smiling fish with long whiskers waved a fin as it tipped its straw hat. Soon a cluster of large buildings appeared in the distance. As they came closer, Duncan could see the rim of a small football stadium partially obscured by several featureless multi-story red brick buildings. The car slowed as he studied the campus.

"Mississippi Delta College," Riley said.

Duncan nodded.

"Do you want to drive around the campus?"

"No, not really." Once past the entrance his gaze returned to the road in front of him as the car accelerated. Riley spoke but got no response; it was Duncan's turn to be lost in his thoughts.

"I said -- 'Why the interest in MDC?'" she said louder.

"Oh nothing. Just looking."

She studied his face as he drove. Finally she asked, "You're still bothered by his death, aren't you?"

The furrows on his brows deepened. He started to speak, but stopped and simply nodded.

She reached out and gave his hand a gentle squeeze just as Duncan's attention was drawn to a building on the side of the road. He pulled his hand away from her and whipped the car off the road into a parking lot. Gravel crunched and flew as he skidded to a halt. Riley braced herself against the dashboard with both hands and stared at him.

"Look. The Club Elgin," he said as the dust settled around the car. Riley looked from him to the building and back again as she tried to understand his actions.

"It's just a juke joint," she said.

With walls made of cinder blocks and a roof composed of corrugated tin sheets, the building appeared abandoned. Flecks of light gray from the cinder blocks showed through the faded turquoise blue paint that covered the walls. A string of Christmas tree lights ran along the edge of the eaves. There was a conspicuous lack of windows; the only breaks in the wall were a metal door with a padlock and, on the other end of the front wall, a small air conditioner supported by a brace of old planks. Canary yellow paint had been used to write the name of the club in script diagonally across the front wall.

A flashing sign, the mobile kind, was chained to a concrete post in the middle of the parking lot next to the street. The plastic letters on it had been arranged to read:

From Chicago
Thu., Fri. & Sat
Albert Smith and His Band

"It's a juke joint," he stated.

"I just said that," she reminded him.

He looked around the empty parking lot. "It's closed," he said with a slight degree of disappointment.

"Yes, but we could come back tonight."

"Could we?"

"Sure, but we might be the only white spots in there. You don't have a problem with that, do you?"

"No. Not at all. But I wouldn't want to go any place where I'm not welcome."

"No problem. The kids from the college sometimes go there."

"Have you ever been?" he asked.

"It's funny, but I never came here when I lived at home. I was too young. But when I was at Ole Miss a group of my friends would sometimes go clubbing here in the Delta. The music is fantastic, especially if the band is from Chicago."

"How can a little club in Podunk, Mississippi pull a band from Chicago?"

"Because a lot of the best blues musicians alive came from podunk little towns in Mississippi. Artists like B.B. King, Albert Collins, and John Lee Hooker. When they come to Mississippi they are coming home."

"I didn't know that," he said.

She eyed him suspiciously. "If you aren't a fan of the blues, then why the sudden interest in The Club Elgin?"

"I'm always open to new experiences," he said. He avoided her gaze as he put the car in gear and pulled back onto the road.

The Stevens' home was a white two-story frame house with an open front porch that wrapped around one side. A dark green porch swing that matched the color of the shutters hung suspended by chains from the gallery ceiling. Set in a grove of pecan trees at the end of the street, the years had seen the city limits and the resulting neighborhood expand to surround the Stevens' home.

Mrs. Stevens was waiting for them behind the screen door as the car pulled into the driveway. Riley opened the car door before the car came to a complete stop and ran up the brick walk to the front porch. Both mother and daughter gave voice to small grunts of satisfaction as they hugged. As Duncan mounted the steps her mother broke away and extended her hand to him.

"You must be Dr. Russthorne?"

He noticed that her handshake was warm and firm.

"Just call me Duncan, please."

Mrs. Stevens moved in a confident manner with an air of warmth and dignity. Her hair, like Riley's, was thick and long but mostly grey. The lines of her chin and her smile confirmed Riley's heritage, but the circle of her eyes and the softer contours of her face across her cheeks and nose stood out in contrast to her daughter.

"Come in the house. I've cooked a late lunch," she said as she opened the screen door and directed them inside.

Riley's mother took great pride in her cooking. Duncan took great pride in his appetite. Lunch was a contest with no losers.

"Are you ever going to stop eating?" Riley whispered angrily when her mother stepped into the kitchen.

"I didn't want her to think I didn't like her cooking," Duncan said.

"You've more than proved your point."

"Another piece of cake, Duncan?" Mrs. Stevens asked when she returned. Duncan was tempted but saw the warning in Riley's eyes.

"No thanks. It was delicious."

"Thank you. Now why don't you go in the den while Riley and I clear the table and catch up on the news."

"But I can help with the dishes."

"Thanks, but Riley and I need to talk," she said as she took his plate.

In the den, a low fire burned in the fireplace. He stirred the coals with a poker, then added a couple of small logs from the stack of wood positioned to the side of the brick hearth. On the mantelpiece were several framed photographs. One showed three young girls dressed in their Sunday best, their hands folded in their laps and their ribboned hats perched back on their heads, seated on the front porch-swing of the house with Riley proudly displaying the gap in her smile caused by a missing front tooth. In another photograph, in sepia tones, stood a young man in uniform, his head angled to one side to show the same profile that could be seen in his daughter.

Bookcases, stretching from the floor to the high ceiling, flanked both sides of the mantel. Duncan could tell that the books that filled the shelves were not there for decoration but were reading copies, well worn and studied. He selected a copy of Emerson's *Essays* and settled into one of the leather chairs that flanked the fireplace, stretching his legs onto an ottoman.

Sounds filtered in from the kitchen -- soft conversation, the porcelain and silverware tinkling and clinking, water running in the sink. He studied the index page for a moment, then flipped through the book as the warmth from the fire soaked into his legs, the logs hissing and popping as they burned.

The fire was down and the light from the windows dim when Riley leaned over the back of his chair and kissed him on the cheek. She gently slipped onto his lap as he tried to orient himself in the darkened room.

"Hey," she said softly.

"Hey yourself," he said as he wrapped his arms around her waist.

"How was your nap?"

"Great."

"You sleep more than any person I know."

"I probably sleep less than anybody you know. I just happen to sleep when you're around."

"Am I that dull and uninteresting?"

"No. Not a bit. In fact, you happen to be the most interesting person I know.' He was tempted to kiss her but reconsidered. The kiss he wanted to give might not be appreciated by a mother that could walk into the room at any moment. He studied her face as the glow from the firelight reflected in her eyes.

"Still tired?"

"No, I'm fine."

"Do you still want to go to the Club Elgin? Do a little juking?"

"No, I don't. I want to stay here with you. I want to curl up in front of the fire and spend the evening in quiet conversation."

"What happened to the fellow who was always open to new experiences?"

"We could have a new experience here in front of the hearth."

"Duncan!" she scolded as she rose and walked across the room. "Give me a minute to change and then we'll go to the Club Elgin. You'll enjoy it." At the door she stopped and looked back at him over her shoulder. "Don't worry," she said with a smile full of promise. "The fireplace will still be here when we get back."

Chapter Twenty

A cold, misty rain fell on the cars that filled the parking lot at the Club Elgin. Duncan and Riley parked near the highway and walked quickly, their shoulders hunched and their heads down, to the front door. When Duncan opened the door, he was struck by a wave of warm air thick with the smell of sweat, strong perfume, and stale cigarette smoke. The small hallway inside the door was lined with people, mostly couples, that paid little attention to Duncan and Riley. The few that Duncan made eye contact with greeted him with warm smiles or at least a polite nod of acknowledgment. As far as he could tell they were the only white people in the bar, but no one seemed to notice or care.

The interior was composed of one huge room filled from wall to wall with an assortment of unmatched tables and chairs that appeared to have been collected over the years from various garage sales. An occasional bare light bulb hung from the ceiling and a few light fixtures were attached, without any pattern, at intervals along the walls.

The juke joint was packed to capacity. The crowd, a mix of all ages but weighted more toward the young set, made Duncan feel underdressed in his blue jeans. At one end of the building, the band played on a low, wooden platform that had been painted gold in the unmistakable splotchy pattern produced by aerosol cans of spray paint. Couples danced in the narrow space around the bandstand and in between the tables that had been pushed close to the speakers.

Duncan was beginning to think they might have to stand against the wall when Riley tugged at his arm and pointed. A single white face in a sea of ebony had surfaced nearby and was waving them over.

A middle aged woman with short brown hair and a round face stood up to greet them as they approached her table. Duncan heard her first name as she introduced herself - Ann - but missed her last name in a wave of music. She moved from a short upholstered sofa that had been pushed against the wall and took an empty metal folding chair as she motioned for them to sit down. Duncan allowed Riley to take the edge of the sofa next to the lady.

130

"Your accent -- are you from England?" Riley asked.

"Manchester," she nodded. "I'm on vacation," she yelled to be heard over the music just as the band finished their song and announced they would be taking a short break.

"There, that's better. Yes. I'm on vacation. I own a small music shop back home. I always wanted to see Graceland. Been saving up for two years for this holiday. While I was over here I thought I would take in the Blues Museum here in the Delta. One thing led to another and, well, here I am. Isn't this exciting?"

Riley and Duncan both agreed.

"You are so lucky to be able to enjoy this kind of original music here where it all actually started. I just wish I had not left my camera back at the hotel."

"Do they serve you here at the table?" Duncan interrupted.

"You have to go the bar," Ann explained. "They serve liquor in 'shots' or beer in half-liter bottles."

"Beer?" he asked Riley.

"Sure."

"Ann?"

"No, thanks. I'm fine," she said as she indicated to her half-full bottle.

Duncan weaved his way around the tables and through the clusters of people toward the U shaped bar that projected from the side of the room opposite the door. He wedged himself into the two and three deep stack of people that surrounded the bar and ordered.

The bartender, a young man with curly, gel-shined hair and a mustache that grew down along the sides of his mouth, set a quart bottle on the bar and placed a plastic cup upside down over the mouth of the bottle.

"Can I get another glass?"

The bartender slipped another cup over the first and took his money. As he waited for his change, he noticed a young white man, easily one of the largest men in the place, standing across from him on the other side of the bar. Beside him stood an equally massive black man with his head shaved in a pattern, a lightning bolt from front to back over both ears. He wore a letterman jacket that bore the markings of the Mississippi Delta college football team.

Where the bar joined the wall adjacent to where the athletes stood was an open doorway. Duncan leaned over the bar for a better view but failed to see where the opening led. He pocketed his change and carried the bottle back to his table.

131

He sat down just as the band returned from its break. The band members were all black except for the drummer, who wore his thinning hair pulled back in a short ponytail. The band leader was a tall man in a dark suit, a shiny silver shirt, and a crimson red tie, who lost no time in strapping on his acoustic guitar and ripping into a driving one-beat. His eyes opened wide and his head bobbed as he encouraged the crowd to join in the fun. The jeweled rings on his fingers made sparkling points of light as he pulled the sound from the strings and a younger man quickly joined in at the microphone with a harmonica, making it howl and crow in complement to the guitar.

The crowd responded instantly, moving and surging, clapping hands and dancing to the sound. A young man in a black silk shirt walked over to Duncan.

"Do you mind if I ask your lady to dance?"

"No problem."

"May I?" he said as he offered his her hand. She looked at Duncan.

"Go ahead. I'm not a dancer," he said. She smiled and accepted the offer.

Duncan took the opportunity to slip away while Ann was turned in her chair talking to a couple at the next table. He worked his way back to the other side of the bar, past the two football players, to the doorway he had seen. Two men turned into the doorway just as a young lady came out and put a tube of lipstick back into her purse. He stepped through the doorway. To the left down a short hallway was the men's restroom; directly ahead was the ladies restroom. To his right the hallway was longer. At that end was a door with a printed sign that said **"Private Office -- Do Not Enter."** His attention quickly focused on the pay phone on the wall next to him. He turned and pulled the receiver off of the hook. In the space where the telephone number was printed, an ink pen had been used to scratch out the numbers. He searched the front and sides for a number and found none. He hung the receiver back on its hook and walked toward the office door.

He reached for the doorknob to see if it was locked, hesitated, then raised a fist in order to knock just as the door suddenly opened. A black man who looked to be Duncan's approximate age stood facing him, surprised to find Duncan at the door. He was slightly shorter than Duncan and well built with a handsome face and short hair. He wore a white shirt with the band collar buttoned around his muscular neck, dark pleated pants, and expensive leather loafers. The look of surprise that had first appeared on his face quickly changed to displeasure. He frowned at the intrusion.

"Can't you read? This is private," he said as he pointed to the sign.

"I'm sorry. I needed to call a friend and leave a number where they could call back, but I couldn't find the number on the phone."

The man stared at him with suspicion. Duncan stared back, studying his features, a warning buzz in the back of his mind telling him there was something too familiar about the black man's face.

He looked Duncan up and down once more, then gruffly told him the number for the telephone.

"Thanks," Duncan nodded and turned away. Back at the telephone he dug a quarter out of his pocket, cradled the receiver on his shoulder, and punched in his number at home. As he listened to the recorded message telling him that the number could not be reached as dialed, Duncan glanced back over his shoulder to see the man in the office doorway still watching him carefully. Duncan waited an appropriate amount of time, then hung up and walked out of the hallway.

The man closed the office door behind him and walked down the hall to peer around the corner, head cocked to one side as he studied Duncan. He waved at one of the girls behind the bar and motioned for her to come over.

"Hey, Cuz. What's up?" She wore a short red skirt and sleeveless white top. Her hair was short with a long, tinted curl of hair plastered on each cheek.

"You've got to do a job for me, Fanita. See that white guy standing at the bar?"

"Blue jeans and tweed jacket? Standing by the ball players?"

"Yeah. That's him. I want you to card him."

"Card him? Man, he's old enough. Since when do we card anybody, anyway?"

"I don't care about his age. I want his name, address, and anything else you can find out about him." He dismissed her by pointing back to the bar.

Duncan pushed up to the bar beside the two big men. "Can I buy you fellas a drink?"

"Sure. Hell yeah," said the black man as he looked down at Duncan.

Duncan turned to the bartender. "Set them up. I'll have what they're having."

"You two play at Delta?"

They both nodded.

"What does next year's team look like?"

"Pretty good. We've got some hotshot QB from across the river in Arkansas signed. That's the only position that was weak this year. You go to M.D.?"

133

Duncan shook his head. "No, but my roommate did. Barrett Jeter? Running back? He set a school record for rushing one year."

The two looked at each other as they searched their memories.

"Four or five years ago?" one finally asked.

Duncan nodded.

"I heard about him," the bald one said. "But I didn't know him. That was before our time."

The bartender set three small shot glasses on the bar in front of them, then filled them with a clear liquid from a bottle without a label.

"This is a great place. You come here a lot?" Duncan said.

"Yeah. This is one of the few places around where we can drink whisky. The guy who runs this place played at Delta, too. He cuts us a little slack. Never checks for I.D. on any of the team members."

"As long as we don't get too rowdy," his partner added.

But Duncan didn't hear him. The familiar face haunting the edge of his memory had finally come to him. He had seen it in Barrett's scrapbook. The guy who had met him at the door of the club office was the football player in Barrett's newspaper clippings, the other running back with Barrett on the Delta football team, the pepper of salt and pepper.

"Hey, Mister," Fanita yelled through the din.

He turned to her, his thoughts still on his discovery.

"Mister, I need to see some I.D."

"What?" he shook his head as if he had not heard correctly.

"I said 'I need to see some I.D.' I need your driver's license to check your age."

Duncan grinned as he reached for his wallet. He couldn't remember the last time his age had been checked and was almost at an age when he considered it a compliment. She studied his driver's license for a moment, flipped it over, then back again, then looked some more.

"Do you have anything else?"

"Give me a break. It's a driver's license. What more could you want?"

She fixed him with a hard stare. "Do you have anything else with your photo?"

The amused look left his face and was replaced by one of puzzlement. He searched his wallet again and produced his staff I.D. from the medical center.

When she was satisfied with what she saw she handed both cards back to Duncan. "Just doing my job," she said as she pushed the shot glasses across the bar within their reach.

The football player nearest Duncan picked up two of the shot glasses. He handed one to Duncan.

"The trick," he advised, "is to take it in one gulp. Fast." The three raised their glasses in a salute then threw back their heads as they swallowed.

The pain was immediate and intense as a barrage of liquid needles hit the back of his throat. The bolus of liquid scraped the lining of his esophagus as it fell, its progress marked by the burn. He felt as if he had swallowed a pine cone, or maybe a foot and a half of radioactive barbed wire. He checked his glass to see if there might have been broken glass in the drink, then waited to see if he could hold the drink in his stomach. He prayed he could. If it hurt half as much coming back up as it did going down, Duncan was sure he would start weeping.

"What . . . what was that?" he finally asked.

"Homemade white whiskey," the white guy said.

"Pure corn likker," the other added with relish. "It's rumored that NASA once tested this stuff as a possible rocket fuel."

Duncan coughed, held up his thumb so he wouldn't have to speak again, and wiped the moisture from his eyes. He patted one of them on the back as he left.

Duncan sat down at the table and washed his throat with a swallow of beer. Searching the crowd, he found Riley and her partner dancing to a fast, funky number. Her grinding and shaking kept a smile on her partner's face as he tried to keep up with her moves. As the song closed, they both broke into laughter and returned to the table.

"You both ought to be arrested for dancing like that," Duncan told them.

The man laughed and tapped knuckles with Duncan. "Thanks, man."

"Whew." Riley sank down into the seat and swept a strand of hair back out of her face as she reached for her glass.

"Where did you learn to dance like that?" Duncan asked.

She just grinned and took a drink.

"Let me write this down before I forget it," Fanita reported to Cuz back in his office. She took a pen from the desk and scribbled on the back of a magazine. When she finished she dropped the pen with a flourish and spun the magazine around for Cuz to read.

"There. That's the name and address on the driver's license. He had another card, an I.D. from a hospital in Jackson. I think he's a doctor or something 'cause in the picture he was wearing one of those white doctor coats."

Cuz was silent as he studied the name and address.

"I listened to him talking with Arleye and Emmitt. He was asking about an old ball player at the college -- Barry or Barrett or something like that."

Antonio's eyes narrowed to a squint at the mention of Barrett's name.

Fanita glanced over to the corner of the room where the two gangsters from Chicago sat on a worn sofa, its cushions sagging under their weight. Six watched a basketball game on the television. K.L. kept his eyes fixed on Fanita.

"Thanks, girl. You done good."

"Of course," she countered but Cuz was too lost in thought to banter. When she saw that she would not receive any more attention from him, she left the room as quickly as possible, anxious to be out from under the cold gaze of K.L.

Cuz, real name Antonio Pack, leaned forward to rest his elbows on the desk while he thought. He had earned his nickname because of his relationship with Jefferson Pack, his first cousin, head of the El AZIWA gang in Chicago. He played on that relationship often, quick to let everyone know of the connection. He used his cousin's name as a weapon to intimidate enemies, as a badge of honor to recruit employees, and as a source of power and mystique when trying to bed the ladies. With Jefferson Pack himself, Cuz would often play up the family connection in the hopes that Jefferson would look on him as more than just an employee.

But in effect, that's all he was -- just another employee, although a good one. After an injury ruined his hopes for a professional football career, he had gone to work at the Club Elgin as a bartender. He had seen the potential for the club, which at that time was poorly managed. The owner concentrated more on his drinking and gambling than business. Seeing an opportunity, he went to his cousin Jefferson, who was already rising fast in the gang hierarchy. With a little money and a lot of muscle, Jefferson bought the Club Elgin and turned it over to Antonio to run. Under good management, the club quickly became very profitable. It also provided an outlet to launder money and recruit gang members from the poor youth of the area.

Antonio had hoped that his good work would impress his cousin enough to merit a promotion. He longed to move to Chicago, to be a gang lieutenant, to leave the South behind. This hope had risen when his old football buddy Barrett Jeter had approached him with a proposition. Barrett could provide large

136

quantities of pharmaceutical grade opium if Antonio, whom Barrett knew had the connections, could move the drugs in bulk.

Antonio couldn't believe his luck. A gold mine had fallen into his hands. How often does someone offer you a half a million dollars in drugs at one sixth the price. Jefferson had been impressed, too. Impressed enough for Antonio to feel brave enough to ask his cousin point-blank about the move to Chicago.

Jefferson did not say yes, but he did not say no, either. He told Antonio he would consider the request -- after they had mined this vein for all it was worth.

Antonio was pumped. He could already image Elgin receding in his rearview mirror, could see the lights of Chicago as he cruised down Michigan Avenue on a warm summer night, the windows of the store filled with expensive goods that he could at last afford.

And then disaster struck. Two days after the last buy had been made Antonio opened the newspaper to read of Barrett Jeter's death. His body had been found just a few hours after K.L. and Six had exchanged a grocery bag full of money for a large jar of opium tablets. Antonio immediately suspected the two men from Chicago and told his cousin. Jefferson was doubtful, but said he had ways of extracting the truth from them once they returned to Chicago. For now, though, nothing could be done. Antonio had to face the fact that someone had killed the goose that was going to lay him a big, fat golden egg. He was a grown man who had not cried in almost twenty years, but for three days after Barrett's death he had felt close to tears.

And now someone was snooping around. Antonio sat at his desk and wondered how something so promising could so quickly turn to shit.

He went into the hall and picked up the phone. He knew his cousin, while sometimes slow to reward good work, was swift in his punishment of sloppy work. He needed to apprise Jefferson of the situation and get advice. After the loss of Barrett, Antonio couldn't afford to screw up anything else.

Chapter Twenty One

One block off of Michigan Avenue in the heart of the business district of Chicago, the lights were still on in the law offices of Soderland and Burns. Jefferson Pack sat at the head of a large marble conference table. Expensive paintings graced the walls between tall windows that looked out over the lighted city. Pack blended into his surroundings well. With his conservative grey suit and power tie, he could easily be mistaken for a colleague of the two attorneys that were present at the table. Although the lawyers resented working so late, especially on a weekend, the money Pack paid them more than compensated for the inconvenience. Their client was eager to finish his business, and the bundle of cash wrapped in newspaper that he had brought to each of them made them more than eager to accommodate him.

Jefferson Pack, with the aid of his attorneys, was very close to reaching a whole new level of enterprise. Over the last four years he had slowly been reshaping a part of his organization in order to give it the appearance of a religious/charitable organization. This pseudo-religious branch of the El AZIWA would give Pack a powerful tool -- a legitimate entity with which to conduct business, buy property, and launder more cash, cash that he could claim came as tax-exempt donations to his "church." The extra money required to caress the lawyers during their oversight of the process would come back a hundred fold.

The three men were huddled over a stack of legal documents at one end of the conference table when the door opened and a secretary entered.

"Mr. Pack. Sorry to interrupt."

He looked up at her with some irritation.

"Your chauffeur is outside. He says he has an important message for you."

Pack continued to look at her for a moment, then he nodded. He stood up and buttoned his suit.

"Gentlemen. If you will excuse me for a moment," he said as he pushed back his chair. The secretary followed him out of the room.

Pack's chauffeur, a short rounded man with greying hair, stood by the secretary's desk. As Pack approached the chauffeur turned his back to the secretary and whispered something to his employer. Pack nodded to him and then turned back to the secretary.

"Would you please tell Mr. Burns and . . .eh . ."

"Mr. Gregg."

"Yes. Mr. Gregg. Would you tell them that I will be back in just a moment."

"Yes, sir." she said.

As they waited for the elevator, Pack turned to his man. "Did you bring the change of clothes I asked for? My dashiki?"

"Yes, sir." Earlier the chauffeur had forgotten to pick up a bag containing the traditional African garments that Pack wore when he visited the building that housed his "church."

"Good," he said as he looked at his watch. "I have another meeting later." The chauffeur hesitated before he spoke.

"Mr. Pack?"

"Yes."

"Can I ask you a question?"

Pack looked at him.

"You change clothes more than any person I know."

Pack smiled and looked back at the elevator. After a moment he asked, "Mr. Lowe, how long have you worked for me?"

"About four years," he said with pride.

The elevator door opened and they entered. Pack pressed the button marked "Lobby." When the door closed Jefferson Pack spoke.

"Mr. Lowe, what I am about to tell you will probably sound very stupid, but one of the most important things I ever learned about life, I learned at the zoo."

When Mr. Lowe didn't respond, Pack continued.

"When I was a child growing up in Mississippi our elementary school took a field trip to the zoo in Memphis. The zoo had a reptile house, a building where they kept all sorts of snakes, crocodiles and lizards. There was one lizard in particular that fascinated me. It was a chameleon. You've heard of chameleons, haven't you?"

"Sure. They change colors, don't they?"

"Exactly. They can change color to better blend in with their background in order to keep from being eaten by predators. I was impressed. But I was even more impressed when we went to the building that housed the big cats. There

139

were lions and panthers, cheetahs and jaguars. When we stopped in front of the tiger's cage there was a sign that gave information about tigers. The thing I remember most was the sentence that said 'A tiger's stripes act as camouflage, helping the tiger to blend into its environment as it stalks its prey.' I couldn't believe it. One of the largest predators on earth, not just some poor defenseless lizard, needed to blend with its surroundings."

"So that's why all the clothes."

Pack nodded. "It gives me an edge. When I'm with the suits," he pointed upstairs, "I dress and talk accordingly. When I'm on the streets, I talk the talk and walk the walk. When I need a chauffeur in town, I use you. When I drive around the hood, I use my men. There is a fancy word for that. Sociologists call it code-switching. I call it camouflage. Those lawyers upstairs are helping me with a form of camouflage. In one sense, business is camouflage. You might even say that life is the art of camouflage."

When the elevator door opened, Pack strode across the lobby to a row of pay telephones and held out his hand towards his chauffeur. Mr. Lowe reached into his pocket for a roll of quarters, having learned long ago his employer's predilection for using pay phones. When the operator informed Pack of the charges, he fed several quarters into the slot.

Antonio had grown impatient waiting. He had been standing in the hallway for over half an hour since he had first called Chicago. Twice someone had wanted to use the telephone. Twice he had held his hand across the receiver to prevent them from tying up the line. He had decided to let Six and K.L. come stand guard by the telephone when it finally rang.

"Antonio," the voice on the telephone said.

"Cuz!" he said a bit too eagerly. "How about it? Good to hear from you."

"I haven't got much time. You told Lowe that this was urgent."

"Sure, Cuz, sure. I understand." He licked his lips nervously. "We got a little problem down here."

"Wait. Are you on your office phone?"

"No way, Cuz. Pay phone," he answered.

"O.K. What's the problem?"

"You know my friend that passed? Someone's here at the club asking questions about him."

There was a moment of silence on the line. Antonio's stomach grew tighter as the silence stretched on.

140

"Police?"

"Don't think so, I think it's a doctor at the hospital where he worked. Maybe a friend of his."

"You sure?"

"We carded him. Got his name and address. We can check it out."

"Good. Do that. If the police are involved, play dumb. Don't do anything to attract any attention. If it's just someone snooping around, discourage them. Make sure they don't find out anything."

"How do you want me to do that?"

"Any way you can." The tone in his voice left little room for misunderstanding.

"Antonio?"

"Yeah, Cuz?" he said.

The last thing the head of the El AZIWA gang said to Antonio carried the tone of a threat.

"Don't mess this up."

Before Antonio could respond the receiver went dead. He wiped the sweat from his palms on his pants legs as he walked back into the office. He knew this was his last chance. If he fumbled this opportunity to show Jefferson his ability to handle tough situations he could be stuck in Elgin the rest of his life. How much did the stranger know? He obviously suspected something or he wouldn't be snooping around. Cuz chewed on the end of his thumbnail while he reached a decision. He spat out a fragment of his cuticle, walked over to the television, and turned it off. His action was met with a cold stare from each of the gangsters.

"I just talked to Cuz. He wants you to whack somebody for him," he lied. "If the hit goes smooth, if the job goes down slick, you got your ticket back home."

Chapter Twenty Two

The soft glow of early morning sunlight filtered through the curtains. When Duncan heard the door to the bedroom ease open, he turned to see Riley slip quietly through the door.

"Good morning. Sleep well?" she said as she sat on the bed.

"I couldn't have slept better," he said. When she bent down to kiss him, he slipped his hand under the side of her shirt. "Would you wake me like this every morning?"

"You prefer this to an alarm clock?" she asked as she kissed him again.

"Definitely."

"Be careful what you say. A girl might think you were serious," she said as she stood up. "Come on. Get dressed. My mother is waiting to cook breakfast for you. And I know how you like to eat." She closed the door softly as she left.

"Did you sleep well, Duncan?"

Mrs. Stevens took two soft drinks from the refrigerator and sat them beside a wicker basket on the countertop.

"Yes, ma'am."

"Care for some breakfast?"

"In a moment, perhaps. I need a cup of coffee first."

"I just made some. Help yourself." She pointed to the coffee cups that hung from hooks beneath one of the cabinets.

As he poured a full cup, he looked through the window over the sink. Outside, Riley sat on the ground dressed in blue jeans, white sneakers, and a red football jersey with white stripes that circled the shoulders, as she petted and stroked a golden retriever, its coat of hair faded with age. She threw a stick a short distance. The dog studied the stick, then slowly, with a slight limp to one side, retrieved the stick and dropped it in Riley's lap. Riley rewarded the animal with a kiss on the bridge of its nose as she scratched its ears.

"That's a pretty dog."

Mrs. Stevens stood by Duncan and looked out the window.

"Yes, and as old as I am. In dog years, that is. He also has a little arthritis just like me."

She returned to the picnic basket. "I've made a lunch for you in case you and Riley get hungry on the trip back to Jackson. Some sandwiches. Fried chicken. Corn on the cob." She took inventory of the basket to be sure she had not forgotten anything. "Some slaw, potato chips, apples, and bananas. Soft drinks. And beer. Do you drink beer?"

"Occasionally."

"Don't tell the Southern Baptists that I gave you beer to drink. Especially since it's Sunday," she said with a grin. "My husband and I are Catholics. Riley is . . . well, Riley is just Riley," she said as she filled the basket.

Riley and the dog sat in a pile of pecan leaves. She threw the stick again but the dog rolled over on his back and begged with its eyes for Riley to scratch his stomach.

Mrs. Stevens poured herself a cup of coffee and sat down at the kitchen table.

"Sit down, Duncan. I want to talk to you about my daughter."

As he walked around the table to take a seat, Duncan's face betrayed his thoughts.

"No, no," she said. "This isn't one of those 'What-are-your-intentions-toward-my-daughter' type of talks. This isn't an interrogation, but it is something that concerns you."

He pulled a chair back from the opposite end of the table and sat down.

"I hope you will keep this between us. She would kill me if she knew I was telling you these things but my daughter cares for you. I know her well enough to tell, although she won't admit it, even to herself. And I think you care for her, or at least I hope you do, so I will come to the point." She paused and took a breath before she continued.

"Riley fell in love when she was in college."

Duncan did not respond. He sat silent and waited for her to continue.

"I think it was her sophomore year of college. She had never dated much in high school. She was too much of a tomboy, more interested in athletics than boys. She loved the competition of sports. She was closer to her father than my other daughters, and I think she was the son my husband always wanted but never had."

"But anyway, in college she met someone, a young man from a prominent family in Memphis. They dated through college."

143

She lowered her voice in a conspiratorial tone. "She doesn't know that I knew this, but she moved in with him near the end of their senior year at college. She would deny it if I asked, but just because I am old doesn't mean I am stupid."

Duncan silently agreed on that point.

"Sam gave her an engagement ring on their graduation day and took a job in Jackson so they could be together while Riley continued her education. He was good at his job - bright and aggressive. Soon his company asked him to take a promotion that required a move to Dallas. Although it was difficult for her, Riley agreed that this was an opportunity that he could not afford to pass up. So he moved to Dallas but they continued to see each other. One weekend he would come to Jackson; the next weekend she would visit him."

She paused when she heard Riley whistle to the dog, the sound close to the house. Mrs. Stevens looked toward the door, waited for a moment, then continued her story.

"After a few months, Sam's trips home became less frequent. He used his job as an excuse. Sometimes he told her that he would be traveling out of town on business. Or that he had a project that required his attention at the office on the weekend. As time went by, Riley began to suspect problems, but he always assured her that he loved her, that they would be married as soon as she graduated from dental school.

"In spite of his assurances, the times when they could see each other became even less frequent. Riley has friends in Dallas and soon began to hear rumors. One day, in the middle of the week, she flew to Dallas without warning him. Can you guess what she found?"

"Another woman," he said quietly as he stared into his coffee cup.

She nodded. "Riley went to his apartment. He was still at work, but his girlfriend answered the door. That was almost a year ago."

Her story finished, she drained the last of her coffee, rose, and placed her mug in the sink. She gazed out the window at her daughter.

"I would have hated to be in Sam's shoes. What did Riley do, kill him?"

"She did nothing," she said in a soft voice. "For once in her life she was too hurt to be angry." She brushed the memory away with a shake of the head, then turned to Duncan with a forced smile. "More coffee?" she asked.

"Please."

She brought the coffee to the table and filled his mug.

"So she's been burned," Duncan said.

"Yes. Very much so."

"So that is why she acts so distant at times. She doesn't trust me?"

"Or perhaps she doesn't trust her own feelings yet. I thought you needed to know. If you care about my daughter, you will need to be patient and . . ."

Mrs. Stevens stopped when she heard the sound of footsteps running up the back steps, followed by the sound of shoes brushing against the doormat. Mrs. Stevens pressed a finger to her lips to bind their secret. Duncan nodded just as Riley opened the door and greeted Duncan with a smile.

"Good morning," she said as she sat at the table next to Duncan. He reached over and pulled a leaf from the sleeve of her football jersey.

"What are you two discussing?" she asked brightly.

"What do you think we've been discussing?" he countered.

"Me?"

"No, of course not," he said. "We've been talking about breakfast."

"I should have known."

"Speaking of which," Mrs. Stevens said as she placed a large black skillet on the stove. "The kitchen is now open. Place you order."

Duncan readily obliged.

Riley and her mother spoke to each other softly as they stood on the front porch, arm in arm, while Duncan placed the luggage in the back seat of the car. The dog joined Duncan as he walked back to the steps.

"It's a beautiful day for a drive," Mrs. Stevens said to them both as she studied the cloudless sky. "The weather is supposed to be warm today." As she stooped to pick up the basket of food, Duncan reached to help.

"Take good care of this," she said to Duncan. "And take good care of her," she said as she placed an arm around her daughter and squeezed her at the waist.

"My car should be repaired this week. I'll be back next weekend," Riley said.

"Don't feel like you have to come home on my account, young lady. I don't want to interfere with your school work."

"I will be home next weekend," Riley stated firmly.

Her mother shrugged her shoulders and looked at Duncan.

"Stubborn. Like her father."

"And my mother," Riley added, her eyes showing the love and respect she held for her mother.

"Come back to see me, Duncan, with or without my stubborn daughter."

"Thanks, Mrs. Stevens."

Duncan walked down the steps and waited in the car as Riley said her final good-byes. Her mother waved to them as the car pulled out of the driveway onto the street, a look of concern on her face as she stood at the edge of the porch. Even the dog looked sad at Riley's departure as he sat next to Mrs. Stevens, his head pressed against the length of her skirt.

Cuz watched from the back door of the Club Elgin as Six put a large brown paper bag in the back seat of the Cadillac. K.L. sat on the passenger side, shades covering his eyes, as he drummed on the windows with his knuckles.

"You sure you can find him?" Cuz asked.

Six glared at Cuz without speaking, slammed the car door shut, and cranked the engine. He answered Cuz by throwing gravel against the wall of the club as the tires spun and the car swerved around the side of the building.

Silence prevailed as the car sped down mile after mile of long level stretches and around the ever-so-slight bends in the road that crossed the wide expanses of open farm land. Riley appeared distracted, more distant than Duncan had ever seen her. She pressed against the door as if she were trying to put as much distance between her and Duncan as possible. Her eyes were narrowed in concentration, her gaze cold, with her lips pressed tight against firmly set teeth. Twice Duncan asked her if anything was wrong before she broke from her thoughts.

"I miss my father. The house feels so empty without him."

"I'm sorry," he offered. "I know what you are feeling. I know what it is like to lose someone."

Riley folded her arms and shook her head slightly as a look of anger mixed with frustration crossed her face.

When Duncan spoke again, he spoke quickly, as if any hesitation would cause him to reconsider.

"My mother died soon after I was born." He paused as he let the weight of that statement settle, then continued in a more calm and even tone.

"My mother died soon after I was born from kidney failure, from what I understand. She had a troubled pregnancy -- blood pressure problems that grew more severe as the pregnancy progressed. She had the same problems when she was pregnant with my older brother. The doctor had advised her against having any more children but she was stubborn, determined to have another child.

146

"My father died when I was eight years old. During the war he had been wounded in battle and had also contracted malaria. He was never in very good health after that, but it was his smoking that eventually killed him.

"My brother and I were adopted by my father's sister. After the funeral we moved to Birmingham to live with her and her husband. The had no children. They raised us as if we were their own. The were good parents even if they did try to spoil us."

Duncan stared at the highway as he spoke and avoided eye contact with Riley. His manner of speech was very matter-of-fact, but when he spoke of his brother, Riley detected a subtle change of tone, as if his words seemed to require more effort.

"My brother was smart but he never applied himself. He was drafted in the early seventies and sent to Vietnam. He was killed in action soon after I started college.

"I seldom talk about my family for a couple of very simple reason. One, it makes very awkward conversation, and two, I'm afraid people would think I'm looking for sympathy. I'm not. I have foster parents who love me and gave me everything I needed as a child, both emotional and material. I have a nice house. I have attained my lifelong goal of being a physician. My life has been easy compared to most, and I am constantly reminded of how lucky I am every day I walk into the hospital. So I don't complain; I have no right to complain. Lightning would come down from the sky and burn me to a crisp if I even dared to feel sorry for myself. But I wanted to tell you about my family because I want you to know I can empathize. Pain and grief are very personal emotions, but I do know what it feels like to lose someone. If you ever need to talk to someone about it, I would be glad to listen."

She said nothing. When Duncan finally looked at Riley, her face was still turned away from him, but the faint reflection in the glass of her window revealed a silent tear as it rolled down her cheek.

In the distance the horizon lifted as they approached the dark bluffs that surrounded the alluvial plain and rimmed its boundary. The monotonous drive ended abruptly when the road entered a cut in the bluff. The car dipped and rose as it followed the highway. Fields gave way to woods. Tall embankments of stratified clay, with alternating layers of blue-grey and brown, crowded the car where the road cut through the earth.

Riley took a deep breath, then pushed her arms forward against the dashboard and groaned as she stretched.

"We need to lighten the mood, don't you think?" she asked.

"We have a picnic basket full of food."

"And I know the perfect place for a picnic. Do you have to be back in Jackson early?"

"No, I'm off duty until tomorrow morning. What about you?"

"I just need to review some notes. No big deal. I can do that after we eat."

"Let's do it. Just tell me where to go."

When they reached the town of Vicksburg, Riley directed him through the military park. Stark white monuments pointed skyward at every turn. Rings of bronze cannons bordered on each side by triangular stacks of black cannon balls crowned what had once been strategically important knolls of land.

"Did you know that Vicksburg is the only city in the United States that will not celebrate the Fourth of July?" she asked.

"What do you mean they don't celebrate the Fourth? Everybody celebrates the Fourth."

"Not in Vicksburg. The Siege of Vicksburg officially ended on the Fourth of July. The city surrendered on that day."

"Don't expect me to believe that they still carry a grudge."

"Honest. They don't have a parade on the Fourth. No parade. No fireworks. Nothing."

Duncan's face expressed his disbelief.

"I'm serious," Riley said. "But if you find that hard to believe, I'll tell you something even better. The gold eagle that sits atop the dome of the state capitol building in Jackson faces south."

"So?"

"Every other eagle or ornament that adorns a capitol building in the other 49 states faces toward Washington D.C. It is a type of homage or show of respect to the federal authority."

"Except Mississippi."

"Except Mississippi. Ours faces south toward Beauvoir, Jefferson Davis' final home."

"Give me a break," Duncan groaned.

"Sad but true," she said.

The car slowed as a camper with a Minnesota license plate crept down the road ahead of them. He looked at his speedometer, then began to tap lightly on the car horn with his knuckles.

"Patience is a virtue, Duncan."

"What do you want to bet they wear black socks with their sandals?"

"You shouldn't tease. Those poor Yankees don't know any better."

"What about poor me? I'm starving. Can't we stop and eat now?"

"Not here at the park. It's too crowded. The place I have in mind is a little more solitary." She pointed to a side road. He turned, glad to be away from the camper, and soon they exited the park.

Following Riley's directions, Duncan made a series of turns onto roads that became progressively more rural.

"Are you sure we are not lost? I didn't bring my Boy Scout compass," Duncan said.

"I'm sure. The asphalt stops soon. Follow the gravel road."

Duncan turned at her directions and slowed to a crawl as the car rocked and bounced down a grassy lane bordered closely by trees. The tall grass that grew between the tire ruts made a whisking sound as it brushed underneath the car. Ahead of them, the trees thinned and the car entered an open meadow ringed by thick forests. Immediately to the left stood the Ruins of Windsor.

Duncan stopped the car and leaned over the steering wheel to get a better view of the ruins that towered before him. Two dozen huge Corinthian columns, each with a girth that rivaled the nearby ancient oaks, stood on massive brick pedestals that were as tall as a man. Thorny vines and ivy encased the base of the columns with a green wrapping. An ornamental iron balustrade still connected some of the columns at the level where the second floor gallery had been. Fifty feet above them, a small tree grew from the top of one column.

"What is this?"

"Impressive, huh?"

"Very!"

"It's the Ruins of Windsor. The mansion was built in 1861 by a wealthy plantation owner who died a few weeks after it was completed. It survived the war only to be destroyed in a fire when a house guest accidentally dropped a cigarette."

"It must have been a beautiful house in its day."

149

"No one knows what it looked like; no drawings have survived," she informed him. "It's a lonely place, isn't it? That's what I like about it, the solitude. I come here sometimes just to get away and think."

Duncan nodded in understanding as he parked the car beside a tree. He took the picnic basket from the back seat, then spread a blanket at the base of a column and stood in silent contemplation of the ruins as Riley unwrapped the food.

They ate their meal without speaking as they listened to the sound of the woods. From a distance the haunting call of a mourning dove filtered through the trees. A brown thrush flitted from bush to bush in search of twigs for its nest. Two squirrels spiralled around a tree in pursuit of each other, their claws scratching against the bark. Riley studied her notes as she ate while Duncan studied the ruins. When he finished eating, Duncan rose, wiped his hands, and walked between the columns, carefully choosing his steps as he pushed aside the tall brown weeds that filled the interior of the ruins. On the far side of the columns Duncan followed a worn path that led deeper into the woods.

Riley sat cross-legged on the blanket, her notes in her lap, her head bent down in concentration when her eyes suddenly snapped to one side. She had sensed rather than seen a flicker of a shadow among the columns. She scanned the desolate ruins but saw nothing. An unnatural, absolute stillness filled the air and made her aware of her own pulse beating strongly in her chest.

She returned to her notes and was highlighting a sentence with her yellow marker when a quail exploded into the air from the brush at the base of a nearby column, its wings churning the air in a furious burst of energy. She closed her notebook, glanced in the direction of the car, then turned back to the area where the bird had been hiding. While she was turned she heard a slight movement behind her, a whisking sound, the sound of weeds brushing against pants legs.

She whirled to her feet.

"Duncan?"

As she waited for an answer, a twig snapped behind the column where she stood. She spun around but saw nothing.

"Duncan! This is not funny. Answer me!"

In the distance a crow took flight, its rasping call a warning to others of its kind, and flew off toward the bayou. Riley eased around the column, her hand on the base of the column for support. As she leaned forward, a hand reached out from behind her and grabbed her wrist.

She wrenched her hand free as she spun around and stumbled backward onto the ground, a look of anger on her face.

"Duncan Russthorne, I am going to kill you."

"Sorry. I couldn't resist." He stepped from behind the column to offer her his hand. As she came to her feet she popped him on his arm with her fist.

"Ow!" he said in a mixture of pain and laughter.

"Not funny!" she said emphatically. Duncan turned away when she drew back her arm but he wasn't quick enough. Her fist made a deep sound as it struck the muscle in the small of his back. He arched his back in pain and stumbled away from her.

"Ow! That hurts!"

"You have a childish sense of humor."

"Thank you."

"That was not funny. You scared me to death."

"Like I said, I couldn't resist it. This place is so spooky."

They eyed each other cautiously, Duncan making the sign of a cross with his index fingers in order to ward her away, while Riley shook a fist at him. When Riley returned to the blanket, Duncan cautiously followed and sat down with his back against the brick pediment. She reached into the picnic basket and produced an apple.

"Want one?"

He shook his head, then pointed at the trees on the other side of the ruins.

"I found an old cemetery deep in the woods. It was really unusual. The ground wasn't level; it was rounded like a bowl. Some of the headstones stood out from the sides." He held his fingers at odd angles as he described it to her.

"That's because it was originally an Indian mound. Some say that the Indians buried their dead there; some say they didn't. But when Windsor was built, the original owner decided to use it for a cemetery. That is when the trouble started, according to the legend. Disturbing the Indian burial mound brought a curse upon the family. The owner died soon after and his wife lost all of the plantation land during the war. The home itself was used as a hospital -- first by the Confederates, then by the Union troops. Then the house itself burned. All of these things happened because they disturbed the mound."

"Ooh, I love ghost stories," Duncan said with a false shiver of fear.

"This place has more than its fair share. Over the years the locals have seen a lot of strange things occur here at the ruins. Some say that on a clear summer night the ghosts of confederate sentinels walk the second floor gallery looking for

151

any sign of advancing enemy troops. Others claim that the ghost of an unknown Union soldier walks the grounds, his soul unable to rest until he is returned to his home somewhere up north.

"And more than once people in town have seen what looks like a fire here at the ruins. A huge blaze reaching up into the sky as if the house itself was burning like it did over a century ago. But when the fire department arrives they never find any evidence of a fire."

Duncan twirled a stem of straw between his fingers as he listened to her.

"Isn't it funny the way the mind can play tricks on us?" he asked. "I thought I saw a ghost once."

"Really? Tell me about it."

"I once believed my brother spoke to me in a dream."

"But now you don't believe he did?"

"No. I realize now that my mind was just telling me what my brother would have said to me if he had still been alive."

"What did he say? Or what do you think he would have said?" she asked.

He concentrated on the straw as he spoke. "He told me to get my act together."

"But I thought you dropped out of the womb cool, calm, and collected?"

Duncan laughed and shook his head. In the distance a hawk slowly glided above the treeline. A smaller bird rose up from below and began to harass the predator until they both passed from view. The sound of a tugboat churning against the current as it pushed its load of empty barges upstream carried over the trees.

"Is that the river I see in the distance?"

Riley looked up from her notes to see where he was pointing. "No. That's the bayou that branches away from it. Listen, Duncan. I hate to be rude but I really need to study." She emphasized the point by tapping her notebook with a yellow marker.

Duncan pulled off his sweater, rolled it into a pillow, and reclined on his side. A high stratum of thin clouds crossed a hazy blue sky as the sound of the tugboat faded into the distance. He closed his eyes and noticed the first faint promising scents of spring as the sun warmed his body.

Chapter Twenty Three

The streetlights were beginning to flicker on as they approached the city of Jackson. Duncan turned on his headlights as they pulled onto the interstate that looped around the city.

"Did your brother talk to you again?" Riley asked.

"What?"

"You had a dream while you were napping. You were mumbling and twitching just before you woke up."

Duncan shook his head.

"I've been having some weird dreams lately. I think it's because my sleep patterns are so scrambled; I either get too much sleep or not enough. And all the caffeine I drink just makes it worse." He looked in the rearview mirror as he changed lanes.

"Did you finish your studies?" he asked.

"Almost. Another hour and I can wrap it up. I can do that while I'm at the laundry."

"You need to wash clothes?"

"Just the essentials. Enough to get me through the next couple of days."

"You could use my house. It's a lot better place to study than a public laundry."

"You don't mind?"

"Not at all," he said as he veered onto the exit ramp that led to her apartment. "I'll even cook dinner for you."

The burgundy Cadillac reached Jackson at dusk. Six and K.L. drove by Duncan's house once, not too slowly, careful not to draw attention to themselves, then left the neighborhood. They waited half an hour before they repeated their reconnaissance.

Duncan carried the laundry basket up the steps and unlocked the door for Riley. In the laundry room at the back of the kitchen he found the laundry detergent for her and returned to the car. On their second trip past Duncan's house, Six recognized the car that was parked at the curb. It was the same car they had seen depart the Club Elgin the night before. As they drew nearer, Duncan stepped out of the house and down the sidewalk toward the street. K.L. slumped down into his seat. Six raised his hand to his temple in order to hide his face. Duncan paid little attention to the car and its occupants as he removed his overnight bag from the back seat and returned to the house. At the end of the street the brake lights on the burgundy Cadillac flickered on.

Six looked at his watch. There were several hours to kill yet. They would find a bar, drink a few beers, let everyone in the neighborhood go to sleep. Then it would be time to do business. He looked over at K.L., and noted the sinister smile on his partners face.

"Good to back in action," K.L. said.

"Even better to be going back to Chicago," Six bobbed his head as he spoke, his body rocking in anticipation.

"Got that right," K.L. agreed as the car accelerated away from the intersection.

Duncan heated the black iron skillet on the stove. A stick of butter melted in the skillet while he chopped mushrooms into thin slices. He cooked them in the butter until they darkened, then added the crabmeat and the sliced artichoke hearts. He sprinkled a pinch of seasoning from between his thumb and forefinger as he stirred the mixture with an oversized wooden spoon.

Riley filled the glasses and sliced thick slabs of bread from the loaf she found in the refrigerator.

"It's done," he said. He wrapped a potholder around the skillet handle and carried it to the table. He used the cooking spoon to fill their plates.

Riley inhaled the aroma of the steaming food. She carefully nibbled a steaming hot chunk of crab meat, then took a bigger bite.

"This is good!" she said.

"Thanks."

"I mean it. This is really good."

"I know."

"I'm surprised somebody hasn't already snapped you up for a wife." she said between mouthfuls.

"I play hard to get," he said as he matched her bite for bite.

After supper, Riley slipped away to a quiet part of the house to finish her studies while Duncan stayed in the kitchen to clean up. He picked the few lumps of crabmeat left from the skillet and placed them in a small bowl he kept on the back porch for Captain Midnight. As he finished washing the dishes the buzzer on the clothes dryer sounded. Duncan pulled her clothes from the dryer and attempted to fold them. This was a new experience for him. He never folded his own clothes, choosing to leave them in the dryer where he would withdraw them as needed. The few times he did take his clothes to the bedroom he would drop them unfolded into the drawers.

He folded a towel and a pair of khaki shorts, then matched a pair of socks. Then came a bra. After a moment's thought he fitted the cups together. No problem. Then came the puzzler. He held up some sheer satin panties that looked more like a deficient jock strap than underwear. Except for a small patch of cloth, the rest was merely strings. He tried to fold it but failed, the results looking like a drunkard's attempt to play cat-in-the-cradle. He finally dumped it and the rest of the clothes back into the laundry basket.

As he walked into the den a faint glow of light reflected down the hallway from his bedroom. He tread softly down the hall to find Riley resting on his bed, her eyes closed, with one arm folded beneath her head, the other resting on an open textbook. When he turned off the lamp, the bed was illuminated with a faint silver glow from the security light at the back corner of the lot. He eased onto the edge of the bed, deftly slid the book out from under her hand, and set it on the nightstand. As he rose to leave, Riley stirred and halfway opened her eyes.

"Sorry. I thought you were asleep," he said as he sat back down on the bed.

"I was. I was having the most wonderful dream," she smiled. She stared into his eyes for a moment, then raised up on one elbow. With her other hand she drew his head forward and kissed him. He responded, gently at first, then with increasing passion, kissing her neck, her chin, her mouth. Her hands slipped under his sweatshirt, kneading the muscles of his side and back, then she grabbed the border of his sweatshirt and pulled it off over his head. Their clothes fell to the floor one by one as they kissed, their lips in constant contact, until she rolled to one side of the bed in order to pull the cover back and slip under the sheets. As Duncan fumbled with his shoes, Riley arched her back to unfasten her bra, then she took his arm and pulled him into the bed.

155

He took her in his arms and squeezed her body next to his. Her hands caressed his neck, his shoulders, the muscles across his back. As the intensity of their kisses increased, she pushed him over onto his back and sat on him, straddling his groin. He propped his arms behind him as he lifted his head forward to kiss her, gently kissing her neck and her breasts, then pulled her down over him, her hair falling over her shoulder to softly brush against his face. His hands followed the curvature of her back down, around, and forward to gently squeeze the folds of her thighs as the first tear splashed down onto his cheek. The second and third tears soon followed to drop gently onto his chest before the sensation penetrated his instinct-driven brain. The realization jerked him to a halt.

He touched the drops of moisture on his chest, then ran a thumb across her cheek.

"You're crying?" he said as she sniffed slightly and tried to smile.

"It's O.K. It's alright," she said softly as she bent forward to kiss him again.

"No, you're crying," he said as he studied her face for an explanation.

"I cry sometimes when I am happy," she said weakly.

When he tried to look into her eyes she turned her head away from the window, her face hidden in shadows as she composed herself. She wiped her cheek with the back of her hand, squeezed her eyes shut for a brief moment, then turned back to him and brought her lips toward his. He pulled back with a puzzled look on his face. After a long moment of silence she slid to one side and lay down, her back to him.

"I'm sorry. I don't know what to say," she offered.

Duncan remained silent, his teeth clenched, wanting to speak but unsure of what to say. He took a deep breath and slowly released it in an effort to relax the knotted muscles at the base of his neck and along his shoulders.

In a moment she spoke again, still not facing him.

"I wanted this. I did," she said as if to convince herself.

She slowly faced him, then in a still softer voice she said, "I didn't mean to . . I didn't expect this night to turn out this way. I'm sorry."

Moments passed as Duncan struggled to understand, the silence growing longer, filling the room with its awkward weight. Finally, with a long, soft sigh, Riley sat up, swung her legs off the side of the bed, bent down to pick Duncan's sweatshirt from the floor, and quickly slipped it on.

"Would you take me home?" she asked as she sat with her back to him.

Duncan reached out to her and placed a hand on her shoulder, let it linger there a moment, then traced a fingertip down her spine.

"You don't have to go," he said.

She tugged on her lower lip with her teeth as she stared at a blank space on the wall.

"I wish you would sleep here with me tonight," he said.

"Are you sure?"

"I'm sure, as long as you're finished crying. I hate to sleep on soggy pillows."

A trace of a smile appeared on her face. She slid back into bed and backed up to him. He cupped his body against her contours and draped an arm over her side.

"I'm really sorry, Duncan."

"Is this my punishment for sneaking up and scaring you today?" he asked, careful with the tone of his voice to let her know he wasn't serious.

She rolled over to face him and placed the palm of her hand on his chest. "You've snuck up on me, alright. And I guess I am scared. More than I'd like to admit. I just have a few things I need to sort out in my mind." She ran her hand up to his chin and outlined the angle of his jaw with her thumb.

"Take your time, Riley. I'm not going anywhere."

"You promise?"

He took her hand and squeezed it. "I promise."

She kept his hand as she turned away from him and looped his arm between her neck and the pillow as she nestled her back against his side.

"Riley?"

"Yes?"

"I really had a lovely time this evening?"

He laughed when she poked him with her elbow, their unspoken apology to each other. "Good night," he said gently.

She snuggled closer. "Good night," she answered in a soft, dreamy voice.

157

Chapter Twenty Four

K.L. drove as Six worked on the bomb. He held the five gallon can full of gasoline between his feet on the floor of the car as he wrapped duct tape around the four sticks of dynamite he held in his hand. When these were bound together, he strapped the explosive to the side of the can with more of the silver tape. He repeated the action several times until the dynamite, held firmly in place, would not move when he tested it. When the fuse was in place the bomb was complete. Crude but efficient, the blast would be devastating. The resulting fireball from the gasoline would assure the death of anyone knocked unconscious by the shock of the explosion.

K.L. stopped the car close to Duncan's house in an area of shadows where the streetlights failed to reach. Six slipped the bomb into a large brown paper bag, eased out of the car and quietly closed the car door without a word as K.L. left to circle the block.

Six glanced quickly around the empty street. Head down in a casual walk, he stayed close to the hedge that bordered the sidewalk. When he reached the alley adjacent to Duncan's house he silently disappeared into the shadows.

Once behind the house he squatted between two large shrubs. He was familiar with the yard. The two gang members had tailed Barrett after their first meeting. Barrett, never suspecting that he was being followed, had led them straight to this house. Six had then watched to see which lights had come on. From this he knew that Barrett slept in the upstairs back room of the house. And that Duncan's room was on the first floor. He took the can of gasoline with the dynamite from the sack and slinked forward from the bushes. He crept up the steps of the fire escape just as stealthily as the old black tom cat raced down. Careful not to be seen, he positioned the bomb by the glass window where the blast would spew the liquid flames inward, lit the fuse and ran.

For once in his life sleep did not come easily for Duncan. His mind focused on every noise that came from deep in the timbers of the old house. When

Riley's breathing lengthened into the soft regular rhythm of sleep, he carefully extracted his arm from beneath her and rolled away. His eyes on the ceiling, he counted each square of the stamped-tin ceiling until he arrived at a total for the room. His eyes shifted to the plaster medallion that centered the light fixture. In the dim illumination from the window he studied the grooves and patterns in an attempt to distract his mind. A stranger to insomnia, he had never played the sheep game.

A motion in the window caught his attention. A feline silhouette passed across the window sill several times before it curled up into a ball in the corner of the window frame, its fluorescent yellow-green eyes blinking drowsily. Duncan closed his eyes and floated into a shallow and uneasy sleep.

In his dream he was at Windsor in a bedroom on the top floor. The oil lamps positioned around the room emitted a soft amber glow. He stood in front of a mahogany framed cheval mirror and admired the large four-poster bed with a red velvet canopy in the reflection. The strange clothes he wore gave him the look of a riverboat gambler. He turned to one side, tugged on the border of his satin vest to straighten it, then raised one arm to admire the lace ruffles on the cuffs of his shirt. He was adjusting his black silk tie when there came a knock on the door.

He smiled. That would be Riley, dressed in a hoop skirt, her hair held up with an ivory comb and long formal gloves that reached past her elbows. As he crossed the room the heavy wooden door glided open effortlessly. He was disappointed to see the Cowboy from the E.R. standing there. Duncan fought the urge to look down but was relieved to see that the Cowboy was fully dressed. He wore a red shirt printed with dancing carousel ponies that held lariats clenched between grinning teeth. Shaggy fur chaps covered a worn pair of denim dungarees. From the top of his ten gallon hat to the silver spurs on his boots, he looked as if he had just walked off some comic version of the Ponderosa.

"How are you?" Duncan inquired.

The Cowboy held out his hand and waffled it from side to side.

"So-so," he said.

"What are you doing here?"

"No time for that. We've got to get out of here." He threw his thumb up over his shoulder in a they-went-that-a-way type pose. "The house is on fire."

"Again?"

"Hey, it's not my dream," the Cowboy shot back at him.

Duncan stuck his head out of the room. Down the hallway puffs of smoke rose from the stairway as shadows and firelight shimmered on the walls from flames unseen.

Duncan followed the cowboy as he sauntered down the hall toward the stairs. "Is there another staircase?" he asked his guide.

"No."

"What about a window?"

"We are too high to jump," the Cowboy answered.

As they neared the banister, Duncan saw flames ascending the steps. The bottom half of the stairwell appeared to be completely engulfed in fire.

Duncan turned to the Cowboy. "This is impossible. We can't make it through that." He coughed as the first wave of smoke hit his face.

"We have to. It's our only hope." As the Cowboy spoke his face suddenly froze, then filled with terror as the color drained from his cheeks. "Oh, no. Not again!" he screamed.

Duncan turned to see the object of his fear.

It was a leech. Not a small, medicinal leech but a monstrous nightmare of a leech, longer than a python, and as thick as a man's leg. The leech slithered up the stairs unharmed by the flames and coiled itself at the top step, blocking their escape. The leech drew its sightless head up as if to strike. Its mouth, a round orifice the size of a saucer, was opened to expose its jaws -- a radial row of glistening blades.

Duncan pointed at his companion's holster.

"Can't you shoot it?" he asked.

"You know that my pistol doesn't work anymore," the Cowboy said angrily.

"Then what do we do?"

"We're in trouble, Doc. It doesn't look like the cavalry is going to make it in time."

"Forget the cavalry, cowboy. With a dream like this I need Sigmund Freud."

The leech loomed larger above them. From the pit of the creature's throat a high sibilant hiss emerged as it prepared to strike.

Duncan's eyes snapped open. The nightmare ended but the sound did not. He turned to the window to see a tiny comet, a hissing spark slowly traveling in an arc as the fuse burned toward the explosive.

He recognized the danger a split second before he threw back the bedsheets. With a terrified yell he rolled over Riley and landed on the floor. She rose up

160

from her pillow, but before she could utter a sound Duncan grabbed her by the arm.

"Bomb!" he screamed as he anchored his foot against the bed and dragged her to her feet. He took another step backward, then slung her around and through the bedroom door in a life or death game of crack-the-whip.

As their momentum spun him around and toward the door the bomb exploded just as his body crossed the threshold into the hallway. The force of the blast came as a wave of pain that picked them up and slammed them down the hallway as a hundred splinters of glass from the broken window clawed his back and the flames singed his exposed skin. Riley, farther down the hallway and partially protected by Duncan's body, escaped the slicing wave of shattered glass but she frantically slapped at a corner of her hair as it began to burn. Duncan crawled forward to help crush the flames between his palms.

"Are you O.K.?" He gasped between breaths.

"Yeah, I think so."

They looked back to see flames filling the end of the hallway. Riley's face showed a mixture of fear and befuddlement. "What happened?"

Duncan helped her to her feet and pulled her away from the advancing heat. In the kitchen he picked up the telephone and just as quickly hung up.

"It's dead."

When Riley turned on the light, Duncan quickly slapped the switch off.

"Hey, what's going on?"

Without answering, Duncan left the kitchen and moved to the front of the house. He cautiously looked through the front window to see lights beginning to blink on in houses throughout the neighborhood.

Billows of smoke boiled out of the hallway and moved up the stairwell. The crackling and popping of the fire that had gradually grown louder was now being replaced by the dull roar of convection. Riley instinctively moved toward the front door but jerked to a halt when Duncan grabbed her by the wrist.

"Wait! We've got to wait," he said as he peered around the curtain.

She looked at him in confusion and anger.

"What the hell is wrong with you? We've got to get out of here."

He took her by her shoulders and looked her in the eyes.

"Someone just tried to kill us. That was a bomb planted outside the window that exploded. I woke up just in time to see the fuse burning in the window. Just in time to get us out of there."

"A bomb?!"

"Yes. We need to wait until some people come out on the street or the firemen or police arrive. We're not going out there alone," Duncan said.

"You think whoever did this is still out there?"

"No. I think whoever did this is probably trying to get as far away from here as possible but I don't want to take any chances."

As the smoke thickened, they squatted by the front window and lowered their heads as they tried to find a layer of breathable air. The roar of the fire increased and the planks of the floor seemed to vibrate as the fire quickly spread through the old timbers of the house. Duncan watched as the inferno advanced along the hallway toward the stairway and the kitchen, moving at a rate Duncan would not have believed possible. The heat and smoke reached a critical level just as a faint wail in the distance announced the arrival of a fire truck.

"Come on." He took her hand and ran to the front door. Duncan snatched their jackets from the coat rack as Riley turned the dead bolt lock. She jerked the door open and they darted down the steps just as the fire truck pulled up to the front of the house.

Within minutes the house was engulfed in a solid pillar of flames as a tight, twisting jet of fire roared up into the black night sky. The firemen quickly realized the futility of saving Duncan's house and switched their efforts to the containment of the flames by spraying water on the roofs of the adjacent houses.

Duncan sat in the back of the ambulance, his feet dangling out of the rear. One of the neighbors, an elderly man with thick horn-rimmed glasses, had been kind enough to find him a pair of shoes and some pants. Duncan held a blanket wrapped around his legs and waist as an emergency medical technician tried to pick slivers of glass out of his back with a pair of hemostats. His upper back and shoulders were peppered with shrapnel from the shattered window, the larger fragments of glass projecting from his back like transparent fins on a fish.

Duncan let out a deep grunt as he tried to hide the pain.

"That's it, man," the med tech said as he threw down the hemostats. "I ain't doing no more. You're gonna have to go to the hospital to get the rest out. They can treat your burns afterwards."

Another neighbor appeared with cups of coffee for Riley and Duncan. Duncan accepted the cup in silence. For several minutes he sat and stared as the fire continued unabated and the pyramid of flames towered up into the night. Where the tongues of flame tapered off, high in the dark night, sparks danced like manic fireflies. Riley took the blanket and gently pulled it up over his bloody back. She sat beside him quietly, her hand resting on his leg, as they watched his house and all of his possessions consumed by the blaze.

Police detective Storey conferred with the fire chief for several minutes before she walked over to the ambulance.

"Doctor," she greeted him.

"Hello, lieutenant. Bring your marshmallows?"

"Not very original tonight are we?"

"Sorry. It's hard to be clever when you've just been fire-bombed."

The med tech had cleaned much of the blood from Duncan's face and neck, but his hair was still gooey and matted. The police woman inspected his wounds.

"Are you going to be all right?" she asked.

Duncan dropped the blanket and bent forward to show her his back. "It looks worse than it actually is," he said.

She turned to Riley.

"Riley Stevens, meet Police detective Alfie Storey," he introduced them. Alfie gave a polite nod.

"Duncan, you told the officers on the scene that you didn't see anyone."

"Not a soul. Just a fuse burning toward what looked like a gasoline can."

Alfie nodded. This confirmed what the firemen had said. Some kind of accelerant was necessary to explain the rapid progress of the fire.

"Did you see anyone?" she asked Riley.

"No. I was asleep until Duncan woke me just in time to drag me out of the room."

"So you can't confirm his story?"

"Well, no. I didn't see the bomb, if that's what you're asking. But I can confirm the blast."

"That's very lucky, isn't it?" she asked Duncan. "You woke up just in time to see the blast."

Duncan's reaction was immediate. He stood up and dropped the blanket. "What do you mean by that?" he barked. Alfie took a step back, startled at his intensity, then regained her composure and stepped forward to confront him nose to nose.

"Cool off, Doc. It's my job to ask questions."

"Poor choice of words, lieutenant. I'm not in the mood for oblique accusations."

163

They stared at each other until Riley took Duncan by the arm and sat him down in the ambulance. The reflection of the blaze flickered across his face, a face seething with anger.

Alfie stood and waited.

"O.K." Duncan finally said. "So ask questions."

As she began to speak, the roof succumbed to the fire and collapsed inward with a slow, sickening groan. The firemen closest to the house backed away to escape the surge of flames and flying embers as the timbers crashed to the ground.

As he watched his house crumble into the flames, Alfie studied Duncan's face. His features had softened some but traces of anger were still there.

The emergency medical technician emerged from the back of the ambulance.

"Can we go?" he asked the policewoman

Duncan looked at Alfie. She nodded to the attendant. "Come by headquarters tomorrow. We need to talk," she said softly to Duncan as the med tech helped him up into the vehicle. The attendant closed the door to the ambulance as the flashing red lights came on, their brilliance muted by the intensity of the blaze.

Alfie turned to gaze at the ruins of Duncan's house, her eyes hypnotized by the flickering lights. One question kept circling through her mind - why would someone want to kill Duncan Russthorne? Her mind occupied, she paid little attention to the crowd of curious onlookers and failed to notice the tall black man who watched with interest as the ambulance disappeared down the street.

In the darkened bedroom of Erskine Jeter, his light snoring was interrupted when the ringing telephone finally roused him from his sleep. But, once awake, he was instantly alert. He reached over to turn on a lamp before he picked up the phone.

"Yeah," he answered.

The caller spoke for a full two minutes. As Jeter listened his face took on an expression of deep interest that increased in intensity as the message unfolded.

"When?" he asked, then looked at his wrist watch on the nightstand by the bed. After a moment he said, "No, it wasn't me. But I'll find out." He swung his legs out of bed as he hung up the telephone.

Jeter's wife, his third and twenty-two years his junior, rose groggily from her pillow. "Is anything wrong?"

"No," he scratched his chest. "Some cattle have busted down a fence and gotten loose. I got to find somebody to round them up."

He stood up and put on his robe. "I'll use the phone in the kitchen. You go back to sleep."

She mumbled a reply and rolled over as he shuffled out of the room.

In the kitchen he flipped on the fluorescent light recessed in the cabinet above the bar, propped himself on a barstool, and lit a cigarette. He took a couple of drags, his eyes squinted against the smoke. When he reached his decision, he picked up the telephone and punched in a number.

"Hubbard, wake up," he said. "Get Ferguson. I want you to leave for Jackson immediately and find a fellow for me. I want to talk to him." After a pause he said, "I don't care, just as long as he can still talk. I suspect he knows something about Barrett's death. Something he ain't telling."

Dr. Norton walked over to the garbage can, snapped off his blood-smeared gloves, flipped up the lid by depressing a foot pedal, and dropped them into the garbage. As he scrubbed his hands in the sink, the nurse opened a small blue jar of salve.

"How many sutures?" Duncan asked the nurse.

"Thirty, thirty-five maybe, in groups of two's and three's. Except for the scalp wound," she said. "That required ten."

"As good as any plastics man could do," Norton bragged. "Shouldn't be much scar tissue development, except for the scalp, and that won't show. That was the worst one, a pretty nasty laceration. There was a little bit of bone exposed in one spot."

"And the burn?" Duncan asked.

"Nothing serious. The topical cream should take care of it."

Duncan involuntarily jerked when the nurse applied the cream to an especially tender area.

"Sorry, Duncan," the nurse grimaced in sympathy. "I'm trying to be gentle."

"No problem," he looked over his shoulder at the area. "It's just cold," he lied as he tried to smile.

"What did you say happened?"

"I really don't know. It must have been the hot water heater that blew up. Or maybe the gas line in the house."

"You're lucky to be alive," the nurse said.

Duncan remembered the image of the bomb in the window.

"You can't imagine. You really can't imagine," he said as he stood up and took the green scrub-suit that the nurse had found for him to wear. He eased the scrub top over the sutures. "How's Riley?" he asked.

"She's fine. Slight burn on her left ear lobe and left side of her neck where her hair caught fire, but other than that, *nada*."

Riley was seated outside the cubicle on a gurney she had pushed against the wall. She smiled when she saw Duncan and dropped down from her perch.

"Are you O.K.?" they asked in unison.

"Let's see," Riley said.

Duncan turned to show her the shaved area of his scalp.

"Nice hairdo. How bad does it hurt?"

"Not too bad. My back is worse, feels like I've had forty lashes." He turned back to inspect her damage.

"You've got a nice 'do yourself," he said as he reached out to touch the crisped ends of hair over her left ear. "Sort of a punk look? Short on one side, long on the other?"

"Looks bad, huh? People will think I left the beauty parlor halfway through my hair cut." She pulled some frazzled ends toward her face to assess the damage.

She dropped her hands and stuck them in the pockets of the white clinic coat she had borrowed. Her face took on a serious aspect as she stepped up to him and looked him in the eye. "Duncan, I want you to tell me what's going on here. Why do you think someone tried to kill us?"

He gave a quick glance around the E.R., then thought for a second.

"Not here. Come on," he said pulling her along by the arm. They turned down the hallway, past the central desk, toward the elevator.

"Where are we going?"

"To find some answers."

Once the elevator doors closed Duncan told Riley what he suspected. "This is all somehow related to Barrett's death. I think Barrett knew his killer. And now the killer thinks I know something."

Riley tried to comprehend what Duncan was saying. "You're saying that Barrett's death wasn't just a random crime. Why do you think that?"

"I think Barrett was trying to write something before he died, perhaps a name or something. And Barrett wasn't the type to leave his body to the medical center. That's something he wouldn't do."

166

"Is that it? Is that all you have? No proof? No evidence of any kind?" she said angrily.

Duncan turned to look at her in silence. She stuck out her lower lip and sent up a puff of air to blow a strand of hair out of her face.

"Sorry," she said. "I guess I have a pretty strong case of denial. I just don't want to believe someone tried to kill us. I expected something a little more concrete."

He rubbed his forehead with his finger. "I know it's frustrating. I wish I could offer you something more substantial. Right now it's just a feeling I have," he said.

"Your 'women's intuition?'" she asked.

"Let me try to explain. You've taken tests before. Have you ever had a question on a test where you *know* that you have the answer hidden in some little pit or fold of your brain but something in your gray matter just doesn't click so that you can spit it out. The answer is right there on the tip of your tongue, begging to come out, but it can't, so you skip over that question and come back to it later. You're sitting there, looking at the clock, kicking yourself because you know if you don't run out of time, if the professor doesn't collect the test papers, you'll finally have that flash of inspiration and you can write the correct answer."

He turned to look up at the elevator lights. "That's the way I feel about Barrett's death. I've had this uncomfortable nagging in the back of my mind all along that something isn't right." He looked her in the eyes. "And now somebody else thinks I know something, too. Something serious enough to warrant trying to blow me up in my sleep." A tone of anger had crept into his voice.

"So where are we going?" She moved next to him and linked her arm with his.

"The Anatomy Lab."

Chapter Twenty Five

A wave of cool air flowed past them as they walked through the large double doors of the anatomy laboratory. The air temperature of the room, maintained at a constant 68 degrees, prevented the putrefication of the cadavers kept there for the education of medical, dental and nursing students. The room, large and open, was designed for the efficient long term storage and study of the human body. Over three dozen study areas were arranged in an equidistant fashion throughout the laboratory. The centerpiece of each study area was a stainless steel box, approximately the same dimension as a coffin, supported by thick tubular metal legs. The manufacturer called them cadaver containment tables; the students called them body boxes. Each one contained the partially dissected remains of a human body.

The signature characteristic of the anatomy laboratory was the strangely sweet, thick chemical smell of formalin preservative mixed with the unmistakable odor of grease, grease that came from the cadavers themselves as the body fat slowly dissolved into the liquid preservative. The two mixed together and produced a strong scent that permeated anything that came in contact with the cadavers to the degree that first year medical students could be distinguished by their aroma as they walked down the hallways of the medical center. Clinic coats and scrub suits worn during dissection were, of necessity, discarded after the students finished the course in human anatomy. Even years after he had used them during his time in the anatomy lab, Duncan's anatomy textbooks still held that distinctive smell and oily feel. He kept them in his locker outside the anatomy lab, the only textbooks he did not keep in his book case at home.

"We have the place to ourselves," Duncan stated as he looked around the room.

"Are you surprised? It's 3 o'clock on a Monday morning."

"Makes no difference," he said. "Students are usually here at work day and night." He checked the bulletin board next to the door. "But this explains it. They just had an exam Friday. Everyone is probably still home nursing their hangovers. That's good. We won't have to try to explain what we are doing here."

Duncan found a box of long latex gloves, put on a pair and snapped the cuffs into place, then handed her a pair.

"What are we looking for?" Riley asked.

"Anything that might be the earthly remains of Barrett Jeter." he answered as he moved into the cone of light that projected from the incandescent bulb that hung suspended three feet above the top of each tank.

"What do you hope to find? A clue as to why Barrett was killed?"

"Yes. It may be a long shot, but it's all we have." As he pulled on the handles, the shiny metal doors of the body box hinged open to reveal a murky chocolate brown liquid. When he put his weight on the metal lever at one end, the surface of the liquid parted as a partially dissected cadaver slowly levitated from the depths of the preservative bath, gurgling and dripping as it rose on a mesh tray elevated by the pulley mechanism.

Duncan locked the bar into place and moved closer. The head had been stripped of skin and hair to expose the whorls and fans of muscles that wrapped the face. The teeth were exposed, long and fang-like with the absence of lips, and the eyeballs were missing; empty sockets directed their dark, hollow glare toward the ceiling. The formalin had turned the flesh a purple-brown color.

"Right height, but a little too much fat." He pointed to a layer of adipose tissue, yellow and curdlike, that had been exposed by the incision that opened the abdomen. "Barrett was an athlete. This fellow was probably older." He slowly lowered the body back into the fixative, accompanied by a bubbling and gurgling sound as the cadaver settled back into its resting place. He closed the lid and moved to the next body box.

Although the double doors to the anatomy laboratory each had a small square window set at eye level, the instructors in the anatomy department kept the windows papered in order to keep out the prying eyes of the curious. As Riley and Duncan worked, the hinges on one door gave a whispered creak as the door opened slightly. Riley and Duncan moved from one cadaver to another, unaware that they were being watched. After a few moments the door silently closed.

For the next hour the pair moved from body to body performing the same reverse baptism, a macabre ritual for the dead. Some of the cadavers were rejected at a glance. Others required more study, only being eliminated after a thorough inspection. The effect of the formalin solution hampered their efforts by

169

rendering the color of the hair and skin a common neutral tone which made it difficult to determine the race of the cadaver, especially if the body had been soaking in the preservative for a long time and on most of the cadavers the defining facial features, the key to identification, had been removed by the dissection process.

As they worked the last row of bins, a corpse came up out of the fluid that promised to be Barrett's; it was the correct sex, height, and body size. The face, peeled of its skin, was roughly the correct form. Duncan's heart beat stronger when he saw the trauma to the left side of the young man's head. The torn muscles of the temple, darkened by hemorrhage, covered a tell-tale depression in the skull. Duncan bent forward to inspect the damage.

"Uh, oh," Riley warned.

"What?"

She pointed to the left arm of the body. It lay folded in an unusual angle. Duncan pulled on the arm and found that it moved without the usual stiffness.

"Broken," he pronounced. "Multiple fractures." He pulled back the chest wall flap to reveal the rib cage. Riley pointed to the broken ribs.

"It's not him."

"MVA?" Riley suggested.

Duncan shrugged. "Damn," he muttered as he leaned against a low bookcase. Behind him on the wall hung a variety of charts that illustrated the pattern of blood vessels, muscle groups, nerves and internal organs of the human body. The shelves were filled with plastic models: bleached skulls, the inner ear, giant eyeballs, a life-size brain which unhinged, clamlike, to allow inspection of its gray inner areas.

Riley stood with her feet apart and her hands on her hips as she stared at the body. She turned when she heard a sudden clatter behind her and came face to face with the open-jawed grin of a skeleton. Her sudden look of surprise quickly turned into an expression of barely constrained tolerance.

"Quit that," she said.

Duncan manipulated the bony arms stood of a human skeleton that hung suspended in mid-air from its display stand.

"But I have a confession to make, Riley." Duncan said in a low ghostlike moan. "I have a feeling about you. A feeling in my bones!" He waved the fleshless appendages in the air, the loosely hinged hands flopping back and forth as he spoke.

"How original," she said with a smirk. "And how old did you say you are?"

170

Duncan laughed and stepped out from behind the skeleton.

"Seven years old. But I'll be eight next month."

"I thought so. Well, now that we are baring our souls, I have a confession to make also. There is no one I would rather examine corpses with in the middle of the night than you."

He slapped his hand over his heart.

"I'm touched. Thank you."

"You're welcome. Now let's finish up. There's only one left."

"It has to be Barrett."

It wasn't. The last cadaver was the frail body of an elderly female. Duncan returned the body to its watery grave after only a quick glance.

As they sat down on a table and surveyed their work, Riley snapped off her gloves and threw them in the wastebasket.

"Did we miss anything?"

Duncan slowly peeled off his gloves as he shook his head. "No ... no," he said. "I don't have any doubts. We were very thorough. Barrett isn't here."

"Is he still in the morgue? Maybe they're holding his body downstairs."

"No. I checked on that three weeks ago. His body was transferred here."

"Would they have sent him back to the morgue for any reason?"

"No reason to. His body had been released by the coroner and the police department."

"Well, he couldn't have been completely dissected in this short a time. There would have to be something left. Is this the only place he would be?"

"You don't do any dissection over at the dental school?"

She shook her head. "We do all our dissections here," she said as she pointed to the floor. "So do the nursing students."

Riley studied the floor in silence. Duncan stared at the ceiling as he scratched the stubble on his chin with the clawlike tips of the skeleton's fingers.

Finally Riley spoke. "So where is the body?"

When he didn't answer she turned to face him.

"And what do we do now?"

Duncan slowly stood up and stretched, wincing when his back reminded him of his injuries.

"Now we go to see the Owl."

Their thin scrub suits were little defense against the cold wind as Duncan and Riley hurried along the sidewalk with their clinic coats clutched close around them. They left the campus, crossed a deserted street, and walked along a neatly sculpted hedge until Duncan stopped beside an ornate brick pillar. He turned up the steps that led from the sidewalk to an apartment complex.

The apartments were nicely kept, imitation New Orleans style, with scrolled iron-work columns and balconies. Carriage lamps mounted on the iron-work cast a flickering light across the inner courtyard and pool area that was surrounded by brick walls.

Duncan turned a corner into a hallway and entered the brightly lit laundry room. Riley quickly shut the door behind her. They both stood there shivering and rubbing their arms for warmth.

"Why are we in the laundry room?" Riley asked.

"I need to warn you about the Owl before you meet him. He's a little different."

"Different?"

"Actually, eccentric would be a better way to describe him."

"You mean he's strange."

"Strange would be a good word," Duncan nodded. "First, don't call him Owl. His name is Francis Nystrom, and he's probably the biggest albino you will ever meet in your life. And a true albino. Not just fair skinned, but the whole bit -- pink skin, white hair, no pigment in his irises. Everyone calls him the Owl, either as a short version of albino, or because of his habits. He is seldom seen on campus, especially during the daylight hours. It hurts his eyes so he pays people to record lectures for him. I warn you only so you won't be thrown by his appearance and stare at him."

"I can handle that."

"Good, because his looks are the least strange thing about him. He's brilliant -- a genius, actually. And I don't use that term lightly. That's his problem; he is so smart he has trouble communicating with people. He would have graduated at the top of our class if he had been graded just on the didactic part. When he hit the clinics, though, people were either afraid of him or couldn't understand him. He just can't converse with the average patient. They can't relate to him."

"No people skills."

"Exactly. He's headed for a research position somewhere. He won't have a private practice."

Riley thought for a moment. "How did he pass the interview panel? He can't be that unusual or he wouldn't have gained admission."

Duncan grinned. "I asked him that one day. He didn't interview. He is from North Dakota. Went to college there, too. His first interview was rescheduled because a blizzard hit, snowed in the airports, and he couldn't fly out. His second interview was canceled due to a death in his family. By then the admission committee had filled almost all the slots in the class. He looked great on paper, one of the best records of any of the applicants. Perfect grades in college. High score on the MCAT. So they waived the admissions interview. He is the only person ever admitted to UMC without a personal interview. And probably the last, considering."

"So why are we here? How can he help us?"

"Because the owl knows everything that occurs at the med center."

"What do you mean knows everything?"

"Which students are in trouble academically, which students are having affairs with faculty members, things like that."

"Gossip," she said.

"Gossip . . . and more. He has an uncanny knack of knowing what is fact and what is just rumor."

"But how does he happen to know these things if he stays in his apartment most of the time?"

"It's just a theory, but I think he tutors some of the freshmen and sophomores in exchange for any information they can gather for him. That and his computer skills. He's a real information freak," Duncan said.

Duncan led the way up the stairs to a second floor apartment that faced the courtyard. He approached a door of an apartment that, to Riley, appeared completely dark. Upon closer inspection she noted a very faint glow of lights from a gap in the curtains.

"Shouldn't we have called first?" she asked.

"Don't worry. He's awake," he said as he tapped on the door. A moment passed and he knocked again. Duncan had raised his knuckles to tap for the third time when a voice on the other side of the door spoke.

"Duncan?" a muted voice asked.

"Frank! Let me in. We're freezing out here."

The chain lock rattled and a bolt turned before the door opened. Riley followed Duncan into the dark apartment and, as they moved to the center of the room, she turned to see the large outline of a figure slowly setting the latches on the door. A single reading lamp with a dim bulb cast a small circle of light from its position next to a large overstuffed chair. As her eyes adjusted to the light she saw books stacked and scattered throughout the room. A nearby bookcase overflowed with volumes of magazines, paperback books, and sheaves of paper bundled loosely with strings. In one corner of the room the books were two and three deep in stacks that reached to the knees. Framed photographs and shadow boxes with specimens of leaves, fossils, seashells, and minerals competed for space along the walls. A framed insect collection was overlapped by pages from medical journals and pieces of scribbled notes were pinned at odd locations. One page of notes had been stuck to the wall with a fork. The apartment, with its nineteenth century air of bookishness, looked more like the storage room of a Victorian museum than a residence.

On the coffee table was a personal computer with a video display terminal facing the sofa, its cables stretched out in a tangled maze. Riley stepped over them, careful to keep Duncan between her and their host. Beside the computer display was a coffee machine with a glass carafe full of coffee. A small red light showed that the heating element was on.

"You've brought a guest, Duncan," he said, still standing in the corner by the door.

"Riley Stevens, this is Frank Nystrom. Frank, this is Riley."

Frank made no move to shake hands. Instead, he slowly shuffled around the perimeter of the room, still in shadows, until he reached the end of the sofa opposite the lamp.

"It is a pleasure to meet you, Ms. Stevens," he said as he gave a stiff half-bow from the waist. "Both of you, please, be seated." He gestured to two wingback chairs opposite the sofa.

"Thanks, Frank," Duncan said. He turned to Riley and nodded as he cleared the clutter from his chair. Riley's chair held two cardboard shoe boxes. When she picked them up to move them Frank stepped forward and put out his hand in warning.

"Please don't open those boxes," he said urgently. As he spoke one of the boxes began to vibrate gently, followed by a soft rustling sound. She quickly and carefully placed them on the floor and pushed them away from her chair with her foot. As she sat down she shifted uncomfortably to one hip, produced a meerschaum pipe from under her thigh, and placed it on the coffee table.

Frank created a space for himself at the end of the sofa. As he lowered his bulk onto the cushion he finally entered the cone of light cast by the lamp.

He was big, as Duncan had said. Not only tall, but fleshy, with the bulk of someone who never exercised anything but his mind. He wore dark pants, a pair

174

of navy corduroy houseshoes, and a red velvet smoking jacket that Riley, prior to this encounter, did not believe actually existed outside of British television dramas. His hair was thin and almost transparent, making it hard to distinguish where his hairline started. Parted in the middle, it swept back in a crest. A pair of fragile half-glasses perched on his nose. He sat with his pudgy fingers interlocked and resting on his protruding belly. If not for the eerie lack of color to his eyes, Riley thought, he might pass for a young Santa Claus during the off season.

Francis Nystrom turned his attention to Riley.

"I understand you are a very good dental student, Ms. Stevens."

"Please call me Riley."

"Very well, Riley," he said.

"I'm sure Duncan's opinion of me is not very objective," she said as she looked toward Duncan and smiled.

"Oh, I haven't heard Duncan talk of you," he stated. "In fact, I haven't spoken to Duncan in several weeks. But I understand why he prefers your company to mine," he said with a grin. "I trust your injuries from the explosion aren't too serious."

"I'm fine, thanks," she said, uncomfortable with his apparent familiarity of her. She was thankful when he finally turned his milky gaze toward Duncan.

"And you, Duncan? A lot of sutures, I understand?" he said.

"Minor damage, Frank. News travels quickly, doesn't it."

Nystrom smiled, pleased at the recognition of his talent.

"I was very disturbed when I heard that your home had been destroyed and you were injured," he said. His voice was soft and almost too concerned to sound sincere.

"I'm fine, really. It's nothing that a little time won't heal."

The Owl nodded. "So what can I do for you? You have come to ask my opinion of something?"

Duncan leaned forward to rest his forearms on his knees.

"Who killed Barrett?"

"Ah," the Owl exclaimed. He brought his hands together as if in prayer and touched them to the tip of his nose. "I knew you wouldn't let me down, Duncan. I knew you would see." He turned to Riley. "That is what I admire about Duncan. Not just his intelligence, which is great, but something else, something more. This is the perfect example. He doesn't ask 'Who attempted to kill me?' He has already seen beyond that, seen the greater pattern involved." He moved his hand in a swirling motion, his eyes turned up toward the ceiling. "He has a translucent awareness of all the possibilities."

He turned back to Duncan, covered his mouth with his pudgy pale fingers as he cleared his throat, then shook his head. "I can't answer your question, Duncan, it pains me to say; I haven't really thought much about Barrett's death. But now that the problem has progressed to a higher level, now that you are involved, I promise to direct my attention to your dilemma."

"You weren't very upset by Barrett's death, were you?" Duncan asked.

The albino gave a cold, emotionless chuckle. "Upset? My dear Duncan, I was delighted! I *loathed* Barrett Jeter. He tormented me from the first day of class when we were freshmen, made cruel statements concerning my physical appearance, bullied me, and laughed at my obvious lack of athletic ability. He even struck me one day."

Duncan related the incident to Riley. "Frank bumped into Barrett one night at the anatomy lab while Barrett was using a scalpel on one of the cadavers. Barrett erupted. He screamed at Frank, some nonsense about how Frank had almost made Barrett cut himself. Then he slapped the glasses from Frank's face, shattering the lens as they struck the floor."

"The left lens," Nystrom corrected. His face twitched with anger momentarily, a spastic grimace as his eyes narrowed to slits, before he brought his emotions under control. "Yes, I hated him," he continued. "So did a multitude of other people. But I didn't kill him. You know that."

"Yes, I know," Duncan agreed. "But I have a problem. I want to inspect Barrett's body again and I can't find it. I think it may hold a clue as to why he was murdered."

"Why, it's in the anatomy lab. You know he donated his body to the med center?" Frank said, incredulous that Duncan had not heard.

"It's not there, Frank."

"Yes, it is." Frank answered with certainty.

"Riley and I just spent the last hour examining every cadaver in the anatomy lab, Frank. The body is not there."

For the first time that night, Frank appeared uncertain. His look of initial surprise quickly transformed into a look of deep puzzlement.

"I saw the body in the morgue," Duncan explained. "I went back to check it again and they said it was due to be sent to the anatomy laboratory. Obviously it never made it upstairs, but where did it go?"

176

"But it did reach the anatomy laboratory," Frank said. "I know that for a fact."

"For a fact?" Duncan asked.

Frank hesitated. He first looked at Duncan, then at Riley as his face showed his hesitation. Finally he nodded, his decision made. He pushed himself to his feet and walked around Duncan's chair to a walnut apothecary cabinet situated against the wall. He opened one of the glass doors and selected a small glass jar from among several that sat on the shelf. He returned to his seat and placed the specimen jar on the coffee table. Duncan picked it up and, after a quick glance, set it back down.

"A trophy, Frank?"

"I will be the first to admit that I have a strange sense of revenge."

Riley picked up the jar and held it up to the light. An elliptical object that resembled a small pickled egg floated in a liquid, bobbing suspended in a slow orbit until the iris and pupil came into view. She caught her breath when she realized it was a human eyeball and quickly set the jar on the table.

"Is that . . ." she paused.

"That is Barrett Jeter's left eye. I took it from his body, which was in the anatomy lab, a week after he died."

"One week?" Duncan asked.

"Exactly," Frank answered. "So it is an established and proven fact that the body of Barrett Jeter was at one time in the anatomy laboratory."

"But it is not there now," Duncan said. "None of the cadavers we inspected tonight could have been his body. I'm sure of it. And there hasn't been enough time for it to be completely dissected."

"Correct," Frank agreed. "That process takes two complete quarters of the school year. It has been slightly more than a month since Barrett was murdered. A substantial amount of the corpse should remain."

Duncan rested his elbow on the arm of the chair as he rubbed his chin with the back of his hand. Riley noticed Frank staring at her. He peered at her over the top of his glasses and smiled. The skin on the back of her neck began to tingle as she fought the urge to leave the apartment.

Suddenly Duncan spoke.

"The Diener!" he exclaimed.

"Yes!" The Owl clapped his hands together. "I knew you would see the next step to take. The Diener!"

"The Dean?" Riley asked.

"Shall I explain?" Frank asked Duncan.

"Go ahead," he said.

"The Diener is a caretaker for the dead," the albino man informed her. "Diener is from the German. In its original sense the word translates literally as 'a personal servant' but the word has taken on a different meaning in medical schools here in the United States. In American medical centers it is the title or position of the person responsible for the cadavers. The Diener sees to the transportation of the cadavers from one place to another. He monitors the preservatives in the tanks to see that the cadavers do not putrefy. His duty is to assure that the cadavers are not mutilated, desecrated, or removed. And, when the dissection process is over, he is charged with the disposal of the remains. He is an overseer responsible for the care of the cadavers. A caretaker for the dead."

"I've never heard of this before," Riley said.

"But you have probably seen him. You may have mistaken him for a janitor or other employee of the medical center. It is very easy to hide in plain sight," Frank observed.

"Hide in plain sight," Duncan repeated the words softly, his gaze lost in the pattern of the oriental carpet on the floor, before he abruptly stood up. Riley quickly followed, glad to be leaving. Frank rose and reached out to shake Duncan's hand.

"Back to the anatomy lab?" the albino asked.

"Yes. There and the morgue. There has to be a record of disposal or some trace of the body."

Riley did not wait to say her farewells. She opened the apartment door, stepped out onto the gallery, and turned, propping the door open with her foot as she waited for Duncan to follow.

Duncan pointed to the jar on the table.

"He always was afraid you would cut him."

"I'm afraid it was a very sloppy job of dissection, although it did give me immense satisfaction," he said as a sickening grin spread across his colorless face.

Riley shivered, more from the effect of Nystrom's smile than the cold, and hurried down the stairs ahead of Duncan.

The sky was beginning to lighten in the east as they walked back to the campus.

"'A translucent awareness of all possibilities?' I didn't know you were the Buddha."

"Even better, I'm Doctor Buddha. But you can call me Bud."

"I didn't realize you were so deep."

"I hope someday to have enough time for the luxury of a philosophy. Interns are usually more concerned with the simple matter of sleep and food."

"You sure have him fooled."

"I have a lot of people fooled," he said "but if I were as smart as Nystom thinks I am, I would know what's going on around here. How are you holding up?"

"Fine, but I was glad to leave Frank's apartment. You were wrong. He is more than odd and eccentric. He is just plain creepy. And sick."

"He definitely bears watching."

"Did you see the way he looked at me?"

"Yes. I can tell that he likes you."

"Yuk," she said as a shiver shook her body.

"You're not interested in Frank? I thought after what happened tonight you might like someone a little more sedate."

She laughed and paused for a moment, then laughed again.

"What?" he asked.

"I was just thinking. When my friends ask about our relationship I can say, 'Well, the earth doesn't move for me but the bedroom has burst into flames.'" She smiled as she slipped her arm around his waist. He reciprocated as they walked up the sidewalk with the wind to their backs.

"Do you think he is involved?" she asked.

"Frank? No, I don't think so. In his own mind he may have had reason to kill Barrett but he wouldn't have any reason to kill me. I think the trick with the eyeball was sufficient revenge for him. And he was genuinely surprised to hear that the body was missing. He prides himself in knowing things like that."

"So what's our next move?"

"Are you tired?"

"A little. It's been an eventful night. You?"

"I'm getting my second wind. Do you feel up to a little more snooping?"

"Not back to the anatomy lab," she looked at him with disgust.

"Yes, I'm afraid so. I want to get a list of names of the cadavers from the lab to compare with the morgue list. Then I want to go to the morgue and check the

179

paperwork on Barrett's body. There may be a record of the cadaver's removal from the lab."

"I'll go along for that. But then you have to buy me breakfast. A big one, with eggs, bacon, waffles . . ."

"Hey, wait a minute. I'm the one that's destitute and homeless, remember?"

"How could I forget. O.K., breakfast is on me. Then we'll go back to my place for a nap."

"Oh, no!" Duncan shook his head. "The last time I got in bed with you I almost got blown up."

"I promise you there won't be any fireworks, just some good restful sleep. You need it."

Duncan agreed. Serious fatigue had set in. He hated to miss another day of clinic. He had already missed too many this year, more days than students were officially allowed to miss, but he had to find Barrett's body. And he had the perfect excuse. Who would fault him for missing clinic the day after his house had burned to the ground? He would worry about that later. Now he would focus on one thing, finding Barrett's body. That was the key to the mystery.

The double doors to the anatomy laboratory slammed open as Duncan barged into the room. Riley followed, narrowly avoiding the rebound of the doors as they swung shut. He strode to the corner of the room where a desk was pushed against the wall. Searching through the tubular pen holder on top, he produced a pair of scissors. He quickly squatted down under the knee hole of the desk.

"What are you doing?"

"There's . . . a small . . . hole," he grunted, "beneath the middle drawer on most desks like this. If you pry against the bar in this hole, the drawer will . . ."

The drawer sprang open.

"Where did you learn how to do that? Your misspent youth?"

"College," he said.

He searched through the drawer until he found a small key ring and jingled the keys as he held them up to Riley with a smile.

"The office secretary leaves the key to the record room in this drawer."

The door to the record room opened on the second try. Inside, on top of a filing cabinet by the door, Duncan ran his finger from one large loose leaf binder to the next until he found what he wanted. He opened it and flipped through the pages. He pressed the tabs, the rings popped open, and he removed several pages.

"Records of the last two months." He said as he folded them into his pocket and tossed her the keys. He quickly shut the door to the office behind him as she returned the key to the desk.

From the hallway outside a hand pushed against the door to the laboratory. Through the crack in the door an eye watched Duncan and Riley as they moved toward the exit. Duncan froze when the door opened in front of him and Kate stepped into the room.

"Oh, hi, Kate. You surprised me."

Kate looked at Riley for a long moment before she turned to Duncan and spoke. "I've been looking for you, Duncan. We need to talk."

When Kate looked at Riley again, Riley responded with a confident smile. Duncan could sense the instant dislike between the two. Kate had the guarded look of the family canine when a strange dog invades its territory. She studied Riley for a moment, her eyes ranging from Riley's face to her shoes, then back again. Riley smiled politely when Duncan introduced the two, but Kate continued to stare at her. Riley returned the look in a calm, self-assured manner. When it became obvious that Riley was going to hold her ground and not leave, Kate turned to Duncan again with a look of concern.

"Are you O.K.? I heard about the fire."

"I'm fine, thanks. Just a few cuts and bruises."

"Thank God it's nothing serious. I've been so worried. Is there anything I can do for you?"

"No, I'm fine."

"Are you sure?" she asked, her voice was full of concern.

"Really. I'm fine," he assured her. "I'm going to take the day off and rest but I'll be back at work tomorrow."

She stepped closer to him and tugged gently on the collar of his clinic coat. "If there's anything I can do for you, please call me. Any time."

Duncan could feel a blush warming his face. "Thanks, Kate. I appreciate it."

Kate stepped back and turned to leave. "Oh, by the way, Duncan, I need to pick up a uniform I left in your locker. Is the key still where it always is?"

"Uh. Yeah . . . sure." Duncan said.

Kate paused to give Riley a knowing smile before she slipped out the door.

"Gosh, that went well, don't you think?" Duncan said. "I can tell that you two are going to be close friends."

Riley stepped forward and grabbed the collar of his clinic coat.

"*Ooh, Duncan,*" she cooed. "If there is *anything* I can do for you, *please* call me. *Anytime,*" she breathed heavily as she spoke.

Duncan rolled his eyes.

"I didn't know you had a fan club, Duncan. Am I the flavor of the month? Cherry vanilla? Kate the nurse? Rocky Road or Riley Stevens?"

"O.K. Cut it out. I don't need this."

"Just trying to keep you humble."

"I've been humbled enough for one night, thank you. I wonder how she knew we were here in the anatomy lab?"

"She keeps a close eye on you, doesn't she? Perhaps a little too close, a little too much concern?"

"What? Blow me up so she can nurse me back to health? I don't think she's capable of that. Still, I guess everybody is a suspect," he said as he pushed through the double doors.

Down the hall Kate stood by Duncan's locker, stretched up onto her tiptoes, and felt around on top of the locker until she found the key. As she turned the key in the lock she noticed Duncan and Riley approaching. She stepped back to open the door to the locker with a flourish, an act of pique that probably saved her life since it took her to one side of the locker and away from the main force of the explosion that next occurred. The blast picked her up, spun her around, and slammed her against the metal lockers on the opposite side of the hall.

Duncan and Riley watched in shock as Kate's body slowly slumped on the floor on her knees, head bowed as if in prayer. A second later they rushed to her side. A cloud of acrid smoke burned Duncan's eyes as he knelt beside Kate, her face a smear of blood.

"Unconscious, but a good pulse. Find a gurney. We're taking her to the E.R."

Chapter Twenty Six

Less than an hour later the two were approached by Police Lieutenant Storey as they sat in the staff lounge across from the surgical suites. Riley was curled into a ball on the sofa. Duncan was bent forward, his cheeks on his hands, his elbows on his knees as he stared at the floor. He looked up when he heard footsteps.

"Hello, Doctor."

"Duncan," he corrected her.

"Duncan. Hello, Riley."

Riley sat up and rubbed the sleep from her face.

Alfie looked at her watch. "Two bombings in twelve hours. That's a new record. And you survived both."

Duncan stood up and began to stretch his arms but flinched when the sutures in his back began to pull against the edges of his wounds.

"How is the nurse?" Alfie asked.

"Not too bad. Her right eye is damaged; the edge of the locker's metal door struck it as it blew open. She's in surgery now."

"How are you? You look pretty washed out."

"A little tired," he conceded.

"I know you need to rest but I want you to come downtown with me. You and I need to talk."

Duncan shook his head. "I've told you all I know."

"I don't think so," Storey said. When he started to respond, she raised a hand to cut him off.

"Listen to me, Doctor Russthorne," she said firmly. "There are three possibilities. One, you are not telling me everything you know about Barrett Jeter's death." She again silenced him when he tried to protest. "Wait. Hear me out." When she saw that she had his attention, she proceeded. "Two, you know something about Barrett Jeter's death that you aren't aware of. In other words, you may have seen or heard something that is very important in this case but you don't realize the importance of the clue. The third possibility is that you really don't know anything but someone thinks that you do. Anyway I look at it I think you hold the answer to all that has occurred. And that is why we need to talk."

"Now?" he asked.

"Now."

"How long will this take?"

"I don't know. A good part of the day, probably. We need to start at the beginning and go over every detail. I'll need to hear your version, too," the policewoman said to Riley.

"Me?" Riley said.

"Don't worry. You probably won't have to stay as long as Duncan. Come on. Let's go." She stood to one side and motioned for them to lead the way.

As they stepped from the elevator on the ground floor, Storey walked beside Duncan.

"I want to suggest something to you, Doctor. I want you to think about police protection."

"Protective custody? As in jail?"

"That might be best. Someone *is* trying to kill you. They've tried twice."

"And the third time's the charm? No. I'll take my chances on the outside."

"Just think about it," she urged him. "For your own safety."

As the three walked out of the building into the bright sunlight, Duncan and Riley lagged behind.

"I'm sorry I got you involved in all of this."

"Don't be. Duncan?"

"Yes?"

"How long will they keep you?"

He shrugged. "I don't know. I don't think they can keep me in jail for too long unless they charge me with a crime."

"Charge you? For what?"

"I don't know. Suspicion of something or other? I haven't read enough legal thrillers to know the terminology. And I don't know enough about the law to even guess what the police can do."

"Do you think they could do that? Charge you with a crime?"

"You heard the Lieutenant. She sounded pretty determined to keep me out of trouble."

Alfie did not see the gunman; for once her sixth sense failed her. Alfie had stopped to wait for the couple to catch up when she saw Riley's mouth drop open. The police woman spun to her left in time to see Six pull the trigger of his .45 semi-automatic pistol.

Duncan had been lost in thought as he walked. When Riley paused he stopped also and looked up to see the expression of shock and disbelief on her face. He jerked his head around to find the lanky gang member standing twenty yards away in a shooting stance - feet apart, shoulders squared, eyes lined up over the barrel of a gun held straight in front of him with both hands.

The blast from the gun was amplified under the pavilion that covered the walkway. It was the deafening roar that kicked Duncan and Riley into action. Riley tried to push Duncan aside just as he turned. Their legs tangled as Duncan twisted around and dropped to one knee, his hands down on the ground to stop his fall. He turned his head up and to his left to see Six advance, the barrel of the pistol growing larger with each step.

Alfie hurried to pull her pistol from her shoulder bag as the gunman lowered his aim and squeezed off another shot at his victims. She did not take the time to check on Riley and Duncan but from the angle of the gunman's stance she knew one of his targets was down.

Six fired his second shot, another ear splitting blast that echoed off the building. Duncan flinched when the bullet whipped through his clinic coat as it hung down below his chest, the projectile tugging at the fabric as it barely missed his body. The bullet glanced off the concrete behind him and spun into the distance with a whine. In a split second Riley reached down, grabbed the collar of Duncan's clinic coat, and jerked him to his feet. Together they leaped through a gap in the landscaping that bordered the walkway and vaulted a hedge. As they ducked behind the corner of a building a flurry of shots erupted behind them.

Alfie rushed her first shot, pulling the trigger at almost the same instant that Six fired his third shot. In her haste her aim was slightly off center. The bullet passed under Six's right arm, struck him in the side, and blew out part of a rib as it exited his back. The force spun him around and staggered him, his face a look of puzzled surprise. He swept his gun around as he instinctively sought the source of his pain. A second before he targeted Alfie, she fired again, her shot striking deep into his chest. He collapsed onto his back between two shrubs as the pistol slowly dropped from his left hand onto the ground. His fist reflexively clenched and opened twice, as if he was trying to grasp the breath of life that was escaping from the wound in his chest, before a shudder ran through his body and he lay still.

K.L. watched the shoot-out from the passenger side of the front seat of the car. The spare, hard grin on his face disappeared when he saw the woman draw her pistol. From his position in the parking lot he was unable to warn his partner, but his face remained expressionless, blank even after Six's body hit the ground. He calmly drew his pistol and reached for the door. "I can pop the bitch while her back is turned," he thought aloud.

K.L. froze when he heard footsteps behind him in the parking lot. Out of the corner of his eye he caught the blue uniform of a security guard as it flashed by his window. He slumped down into his seat, gun tucked between his legs. The medical center was suddenly a swarm of activity as security converged on the scene. The guard from the security booth at the entrance to the parking lot appeared with his gun drawn, then two more guards burst from the main entrance with pistols and walkie-talkies in hand.

Without hesitation, K.L. slid over to the driver's side, started the car, and calmly backed out of the parking space. He drove past the now empty security booth, slowly veered out of the parking lot, and merged into traffic as a police car, blue lights flashing, roared past him on its way up the hill to the medical center. Without a backward glance K.L. headed north.

Riley and Duncan did not stop running. They ran down the sidewalk, across a parking lot, and past the Alumni Association building. A group of nursing students on their way to class stopped to stare at the couple as they dodged and weaved their way through the parked vehicles. On the lawn at the perimeter of the medical center a groundskeeper, using a stick with a nail on the end to pick up scraps of paper, paused when he heard footsteps. He turned to see Riley and Duncan fly past him, the tails of their long white clinic coats sailing behind them. Tires squealed as they crossed the street without slowing their flight.

K.L. turned east when he reached the north corner of the medical center grounds. He planned to hit the interstate and head back to the Delta. It was time to put some distance between himself and all the heat. A police car, crossing the intersection as it responded to the call, suddenly flipped on its siren. Startled, K.L. was checking to see the direction of the police car in his rearview mirror when the brake lights of the car ahead of him suddenly flashed on. He slammed on his brakes, his tires squealing hard as his car stopped short of the other car's bumper by inches. He cursed under his breath. That had been close. He didn't need the attention that a car accident would bring. His eyes narrowed to slits when he saw the reason for the delay. Riley and Duncan bounded across the street ahead of him. He sat frozen as he watched them cross the median. When he saw them enter the apartment complex, he whipped into the left lane, crossed the median, and pulled in the driveway that looped around the cluster of apartment buildings.

K.L. parked and quickly scanned the streets for witnesses. Seeing none, he opened the car door but then stopped and held perfectly still when a flicker of movement caught his eye. As he crouched behind the car door he looked across the patio behind Riley's apartment to the opposite side of the drive to see Hubbard and Ferguson emerge from a late model black Ford pickup truck.

"Rednecks," K.L. thought. "Big, dumb, gobby-assed rednecks." But something different about these two made him pause. Both were huge but one was double large. His jacket fit so close that the pistol holster on his left side was perfectly outlined. K.L. checked the other one, the one with the ponytail. He was packing, too. Not as obvious as the double large redneck, but the fullness of the jacket told K.L. that both of the guys strolling toward the apartment were carrying weapons.

They did not look like the police. But if they weren't cops, why were they heading to Riley's apartment? K.L. closed the car door and settled into his seat. He would wait and see.

Riley burst into her apartment with such force that the door bounced back into Duncan's face. He caught the door with his forearm and slammed it shut behind him. With the same motion he quickly snapped the deadbolt lock closed and slumped against the door.

As they both gasped for air, Riley tried to speak but couldn't find the breath. Duncan dropped his head against his chest as he sucked in long draws of air, pausing only when he saw the damage the bullet had done to his clinic coat He pushed a finger through the ragged hole in the cloth and wiggled it.

"Thanks," he said.

"Tit for tat," she said between gasps. "We're even now."

Duncan moved to the window as the phone rang from where it sat on the baker's rack against the wall, the sudden sound making them both jump.

Duncan looked at Riley.

She shook her head. "I'm still out of breath. You answer it."

187

He stepped past the dinette table and picked up the telephone, pausing for a moment before he put the receiver to his ear.

"Hello?"

"Duncan! It's Lt. Storey. Are either of you hurt?"

"How did you know we would be here?"

"I'm a detective. It's my job to know things like that," she said. She wanted to add the word "stupid" but she held her tongue. "Are you both O.K.?"

"Yeah. We're fine. Just a little shook up at the moment. Who was that trying to shoot us?"

"I'm not sure but from his colors on his jacket I would say El AZIWA."

"El who?"

"El AZIWA. It's Swahili. It means 'The Important Ones.' Listen, Duncan. Have you ever spent any time in Chicago?"

"No."

"Are you sure?"

"Never been there, I don't even know anyone from Chicago."

"Well they sure know you. Because if I'm not wrong, one of the biggest gangs in Chicago is trying to take you out."

Duncan held the phone away from his ear, his mouth a perfect circle of surprise.

"Duncan? Are you still there?"

"Yes. Yes. What did you say about a Chicago street gang?" His voice trailed off as he leaned against the wall and gazed out the window.

"I want you to listen to me. Stay where you are. Don't even think about leaving the apartment. Keep the doors locked and stay away from the windows. I'm sending a patrol car over."

"They had better hurry." Duncan pulled the curtains slightly to one side to get a better look at the two men slowly advancing toward the building. Hubbard was motioning for Ferguson to circle to the front. Hubbard unzipped his jacket and placed his hand inside as he moved to the back door.

"An officer will be there in ten minutes."

"That won't be soon enough."

"Don't worry. Everything is under control. You're not in any danger now," she assured him.

"I've got news for you, lieutenant. Jeter's men are outside the apartment and heading this way. And they have guns."

"Jeter's men!" the policewoman yelped. "Duncan? Duncan!" she barked into the dead receiver as she snapped her fingers to get the attention of the policeman standing nearby. "Let's go. Lights and siren," she said as she climbed into the black and white.

"Jeter's men?" Riley asked as she ran to the window in time to see the two men, one big and redheaded, the other clean-shaven with his hair pulled back, walk up the sidewalk that led to her apartment.

Duncan moved from room to room inspecting the windows.

"No fire escape," he observed. He opened the window and cautiously peered along the side of the building.

"What are you doing?" she demanded.

"Looking for a way out. Jeter's men are coming up the steps and they are armed. We'll have to jump." He nodded toward the window.

She pulled away from him. "Get the police back on the phone."

"But they're already on the way."

"Can't we push the bookcase or the sofa against the door to buy us a little time."

Duncan shook his head and took her by the hand again. "It's too late. We'll be dead by the time the police arrive if we stay here. You're not afraid of heights, are you?"

"No, just tired of running. I say we stay and fight."

"Fight? Riley, these people have guns. What do we have? Kitchen knives? Discretion is the better part . . ."

"Don't lecture me! You're really annoying when you lecture, did you know that?"

He looped one leg out of the window as he straddled the window sill.

"Come on," he motioned impatiently. "I'll hold onto the window sill. You climb over my back and slide down until you are close enough to drop to the ground."

"What about you?"

"Don't worry about me. Just do it! Hurry!"

Downstairs Hubbard and Ferguson checked the name on the mailbox.

"Number 4," Hubbard said as he pointed to Riley's box. He checked the hallway before he headed up the stairs. Ferguson followed closely behind.

Upstairs in the apartment Riley stuck her head out to survey the drop as Duncan hung from the window. When she glanced back through the bedroom to the front door to see the doorknob slowly turn, she scurried onto the window ledge and crawled out.

The rednecks weren't police after all, K.L. decided as he propped the butt of his pistol on the car door. But whoever they were, they had flushed his quarry. The doctor and his girlfriend stood out like big white and green targets against the red brick wall as they hung from the second floor window, the girl trying to use his body as a rope. This is almost too easy, he thought as he lined up his sights and squeezed the trigger.

The wood splintered with a crack as Ferguson kicked the door open with such force that the door frame pulled away from the wall. Hubbard drew his pistol and entered the room with Ferguson following close behind. Before they could move to the bedroom two gun shots sounded through the open window followed by a police siren gradually growing louder in the distance. Ferguson moved toward the sound of the gun fire but Hubbard grabbed his shoulder and stopped him. With a quick shake of the head and a wave of his gun, he led a hasty retreat from the apartment.

K.L. was pumped. Two for two! He had fired two shots and two bodies were on the ground. He was oblivious to the blue lights that flashed in his rearview mirror as the police squealed to a halt in front of the apartment complex he had just left. Ahead of him the black Ford pickup with the two rednecks veered onto the interstate. They too were headed north. He hated rednecks but he was tempted to pull along side them and wave. After all, he thought with a grin, they had been partners in this hit. Rednecks for partners! K.L. had been the hunter, they had been the bird dogs. And the two birds had fallen, crumpled, to the ground.

Chapter Twenty Seven

Riley fought to breathe. She could not force the air to enter her lungs through the bands of pain that constricted her chest. She felt as if she were drowning - drowning on dry land. When her breath finally came to her with a gasp, she sucked in the cold air too quickly. The pain was not sharp, just constant and pervasive. She found that short breaths were easier, tiny nibbles of air that caused the least amount of movement in her ribs. She lay still for a moment, staring at the blue sky, the overlapping eaves of the building, and the red brick wall that rose up beside her. When the pain subsided she raised her hand to her chest and slowly moved her fingers around from shoulder to navel and back to the opposite shoulder. There were no holes and no blood. She could move her feet so she wasn't paralyzed. Her inventory completed, she decided that she had only had the wind knocked from her by the fall and tried to roll by slow degrees onto her side.

She stopped breathing again when she saw Duncan. He lay on his side, blood streaming down his face, his eyes swirled in their sockets as his eyelids fluttered. An almost inaudible groan escaped from deep in his chest.

"Oh my God! Duncan!"

She crawled over to him and examined his injuries. A flap of scalp was peeled forward above his ear. She gingerly repositioned the skin and applied pressure to stop the bleeding. "Oh my God," she repeated softly. The pain caused Duncan to jerk away from her. His eyes focused, slowly at first, to a spot in the distance.

"Lie still. You've been shot," she cautioned him.

When he tried to sit up the world began to spin. He shut his eyes when the vertigo hit. A snowstorm of multicolored lights spun crazily against the background of his closed eyelids.

"We've got to get out of here," he croaked.

"Duncan, you need a doctor. You've been shot."

He slowly opened his eyes to find that the world was almost stationary. The spinning had stopped, only a slight jiggling of objects here and there. He touched his temple lightly where the pain originated.

"I don't think so. When the first bullet struck the brick next to my head, I flinched and lost my grip. I think I struck my head during the fall." He looked up at the brick ledge that protruded beneath the first floor window.

"Give me a little help," he said as he extended his arm.

She planted her feet as she pulled him up. He wobbled a little at first, then leaned against the brick wall. When he gained his balance he scanned the parking lot. "Where is your car?"

"The police are on the way," she said as she pointed in the direction of the siren sound. "They'll call an ambulance for you."

"No," he said firmly. "No police. No ambulance." He wiped the blood away from his eye with a trembling hand. "There is no time to talk. Where is your car?"

When she tried to protest he cut her off. "Where is the car?" he asked, his voice steadier.

The sharp wailing of the police car grew louder. She stood with her fists clenched, her head turning from Duncan to the direction of the siren, then back to Duncan. She made her decision, one she knew she would regret, and shook her head in resignation.

"Over by the cafeteria," she said.

Duncan immediately headed in the direction she had pointed. She watched as he walked away with a weaving shuffle to his feet. After several unsteady steps he paused and turned. "Are you coming?"

The sirens were almost upon them. She looked toward the street, then back at Duncan.

"This is the wrong thing to do," she said and cursed silently as she ran to catch him.

Duncan and Riley slipped through a gap in the hedges that separated the apartment complex from the adjacent shopping center as a tour bus with a charter sign over the front window that read "Silver Sojourners" disgorged a group of elderly tourists in the parking lot. As the bus riders headed toward the entrance to the cafeteria they stared and whispered among themselves as they saw Duncan stride past. On one side his white clinic coat was streaked with dirt. The other side was sprinkled with drops of crimson. By the time they reached Riley's car the entire group of retired vacationers had halted their progress into the cafeteria and stood transfixed as they stared at Riley and Duncan. One elderly gentleman adjusted his glasses on his nose to a better focus, his mouth gaped open, and pointed as the rest murmured their surprise at the sight.

As he slipped into the passenger side he turned to Riley.

"Do you think anyone saw us?"

"No. No way. We slid by them completely unnoticed," she returned his sarcasm. "By the way, have you thought of where we are going?"

"Yes. Head north. Up the Natchez Trace."

She hesitated before she put the car in gear. "We could still go to the police. It's not too late."

He started to shake his head emphatically but stopped when the dizziness began.

"No. Let's get out of here," he said as he pointed north.

The outskirts of the city were behind them when she spoke again. "You need to be at a hospital," she said as she adjusted the rearview mirror. When she looked at Duncan, he was slumped against the door with his eyes shut.

Was there a bumblebee in the car, he thought? Or maybe three? No. They were inside his head. Three large bumblebees buzzed loudly as they did a series of barrel rolls around his brain.

"A little rest and I'll be fine," he answered.

"Do you feel like talking?"

"Sure," he said, but his eyes remained closed.

"On the telephone you said something about a Chicago street gang. Is that who took a shot at us at the med center?"

"I think so."

"And the two rednecks that chased us out of my apartment. They were Jeter's men?"

"Uh-huh. I saw them at Barrett's funeral."

"Are they the ones that shot at us as I crawled out the window?"

"I couldn't tell. It happened too quickly."

"Help me with this. I don't see the connection between a Chicago street gang and a couple of good ole boys from the hill country.

"I'm an equal opportunity victim," he said.

Riley shot him a look.

"I'm glad to see you can find humor in all of this."

"I'm wounded, not dead. It's a defense mechanism," he said as he opened his eyes to inspect their progress. "Turn east when we get to highway 16."

"Where are we going?"

"To a friend's house."

"Not another friend like the Owl, is it?"

"The Owl is not a friend, more like an acquaintance. Jay is a friend, a close friend, from college."

"Before we go any further I want to know more about him."

Duncan thought for a moment. "He's laconic."

Riley looked at Duncan and waited. "And? And what? Laconic? Is that all? That's not a lot of information."

"You'll meet him soon enough," said Duncan.

"Tell me more."

"Why?"

"I want to know what to expect. I don't want to be caught off guard like I was at Nystrom's apartment," she said, her impatience escalating.

Duncan grinned. "O.K. Fair enough. In college he reminded me of what a gospel preacher would probably act like if he were on a powerful acid trip. But that was a long time ago. He's a lot calmer today -- quiet but brooding. Is that enough?"

"A gospel preacher on acid?" She grimaced. "Do you have any normal friends?"

"Normal is dull," he said as he curled his knees up onto the seat and rested against the door. "Don't forget to turn east on Highway 16." He shut his eyes and left her alone with her thoughts.

Riley roused Duncan when she saw the highway sign.

"Where next?"

"Stay on this road for the next few miles. I'll tell you when to turn." He tilted the rearview mirror toward him to check his scalp wound. Blood continued to ooze through his hair. He folded his coat to find an area not already stained with blood and gently pressed the clean white area against his head.

"Duncan?"

"What?"

"Why are we running? Why didn't we stay at the apartment? The police were almost there. They would have protected us."

He turned the mirror back over to Riley.

194

"Do you read the newspaper?" he asked.

"Usually."

"A few months ago there was a story in the paper concerning a young man from Louisiana, from New Orleans. He was arrested at a routine traffic stop in Jackson when the narcotics dog singled out his car from a line of vehicles."

"I don't recall . . ."

"He was found dead in his cell the next day?" Duncan said to jog her memory.

Riley shook her head. "Sorry. I missed that story. What does that have to do with us?"

"The car contained several kilos of cocaine. Carefully packaged and hidden in specially constructed compartments in the doors and body of the car. The police couldn't find anything in their search of the car and started to let the driver go but the dog acted crazy every time they let him near the car. So they impounded the car, took it to a garage, and dismantled it to find the concealed drugs. It was a very professional job."

"Professional? As in 'Mafia?'"

"Exactly. The poor driver as surprised as anyone. He was just a mule; he didn't know the car had been loaded with cocaine. When the police confronted him with the evidence he tried to cut a deal. He told the police who had paid him to drive the car, where it was to be delivered. He told them everything."

"And?"

"He took a shoelace, tied it to a bar in his cell, and then twisted it around his neck. When he slumped to the floor it slowly strangled him until he passed out. When the guard found him he was dead."

"That's terrible," Riley said. She shook her head in sympathy.

"It is terrible," Duncan agreed. "But here is the odd part of the story. The dead guy was wearing loafers."

"Fashion police?" Riley said immediately but made the connection before Duncan could say anything. "The shoelace!"

"Exactly," he said. "The jail system in this state is notoriously understaffed. Just ask the Justice Department."

"And you think . . ."

"I think that if someone wants to kill me, police custody won't protect me. Understand?"

"Yes," she said soberly. "I do understand."

"The next right."

"Huh?"

"Take the next right."

A small break in the line of trees marked the gravel road that cut through a bank of red clay as it disappeared into the trees. Riley drove for several miles, a plume of orange dust trailing behind the car. When they approached a dented and rock pocked mailbox that sat askew atop an old fence post, Duncan motioned her to turn.

Riley turned into a driveway that was little more than a grassy path. She clenched the steering wheel as the car crept down a sharp grade and across a narrow plank bridge that spanned a small stream. The wheels of the car thumped over the loose boards as a house came into view.

Jay's cabin sat on a small knoll hidden in a grove of tupelo gum trees overlooking the river. Cedar planks, weathered to a grayish-brown, covered the sides. The top of a rock chimney projected from the tarnished tin roof which sloped out over a broad front porch. On the porch were two wooden chairs, their backs and seats made of woven cane strips. The steps to the porch were made of loosely stacked concrete blocks. A jeep was parked by the steps, its red paint covered with a layer of mud and grime.

A smaller plank building stood to one side of the cabin. Riley eased the car into the shed, parked, and they swung the wooden doors of the shed closed to hide the car.

At the cabin the only sound that greeted them was the rattling of the leaves as a breeze blew them scuttling across the wooden porch. Duncan walked up the steps to the front door, knocked, waited, then rapped on the door harder a second time with no result. When he tried the door, it opened and he stepped inside.

At the south edge of the porch, the ground fell away at a sharp pitch toward the river. A well worn path led from the cabin through the trees to a small wooden dock at the edge of the water.

"No one's home," Duncan said as he rejoined Riley. "I'm going to rest on the couch."

"Go ahead. I'll be just a minute."

Riley needed time to collect her thoughts. After Duncan closed the door, she pulled one of the chairs against the front wall of the cabin and leaned back in it. As the adrenaline surge that had carried her through the night and that morning came to an end, the knotted muscles in her shoulders and neck began to gradually relax. She rested her head against the boards of the cabin wall behind her as her brain, numb from the onslaught of stimulation over the last twenty four hours, shut down. Soon she was falling asleep to the sounds of the Pearl River as it flowed through the woods.

Chapter Twenty Eight

She woke to find the sun low in the sky. Her neck was stiff and her legs tingled; the angle of the chair had cut off the circulation. She leaned forward to massage the calves of her legs. In the distance the hum of an outboard motor grew louder.

Riley forced herself up and hobbled to the edge of the porch. The image of a small aluminum fishing boat with its lone occupant flickered, kinetoscope-like, through the trees. The sound of the engine disappeared and the boat slowed as it glided to a halt by the dock. Riley went inside the cabin and roused Duncan from the sofa. When they returned to the porch they could see the figure of a man walking through the woods towards the cabin.

He was of above average height and moved with a slow confident gait. He wore a pair of faded blue jeans and a navy blue flannel shirt, tail out, underneath a brown corduroy jacket. His face was plain and featureless except for his mouth which was a thin line drawn across his face. A prominent chin was counterbalanced by an abundance of hair, a shock of wiry tight hair resembling an untamed hedge that seemed to grow straight up. As he approached the cabin a faint smile appeared when he recognized Duncan.

Duncan grunted as he stood up from the edge of the porch and extended his hand. Jay took it and raised his other arm to clasp him on his shoulder but stopped when Duncan quickly raised his hand in a warning.

"What's wrong? You look like hell," he said as he studied Duncan's pale and bloody face.

"I feel like hell. We'll talk in a minute but I want to introduce you to somebody first." He turned to Riley as she took a step forward. "Riley. This is a good friend of mine, J.A.O. Falkner. Jay, this is Riley Stevens."

Jay extended a long thin hand; Riley was surprised by the warmth and gentleness of his grip.

"Faulkner?" Riley asked. "As in 'William?'"

"Different spelling. There's no 'u' in my name."

"But the original name . . ."

"No relation," he said firmly.

With a nod he motioned them both into the cabin.

"He's a little sensitive about his name," Duncan whispered as they followed behind.

"Now you tell me."

The inside of the cabin contrasted strongly with its primitive exterior. Warm, well-lit, comfortably furnished, Riley thought, but definitely no woman's touch in the decor. The front room stretched the entire length of the cabin which made the interior appear larger than it actually was. To the right of the entrance was a small table and a kitchen area. To the left a couple of chairs and a large leather sofa covered with a Navajo blanket were arranged around a stone hearth. Jay stepped forward to stir the coals and add some logs.

"Are you a physician, too?" he asked Riley.

"No. I'm in dental school. My last year."

He nodded approval.

"What about you?" she asked.

"Assistant Professor of Biology at Magnolia State University."

"You're a little far from the University, aren't you?" she asked.

"I'm on sabbatical this semester. Field research," he said without elaboration.

"Do you have any bandages, alcohol, disinfectant?" Duncan interrupted.

Jay disappeared into the back room and emerged a few minutes later with his arms full of first aid gear and a small shaving mirror. He dumped them onto the sofa beside Duncan. Duncan took the mirror, moistened a cotton ball with the alcohol, and tried to clean the crusted blood from his hair.

When he bent over, the low collar on his scrub suit revealed some of the stitches on his back.

"You always were good at finding trouble," Jay said.

"Well, I found some serious trouble this time." Duncan informed him.

"I want to hear all the details. But first ..." He picked up a large black skillet from the stove and deftly spun it around by its handle. "I haven't eaten since breakfast."

Over dinner, Duncan told the story as he picked at his food. The throbbing in his head grew as the story progressed and he shifted around in his chair to find a position that would ease the pain from his back and his shoulders. By the time he reached the point of the story where he met Riley, she had already finished her plate of the pan-blackened catfish.

"He thought I was the murderer," she told Jay.

"I hope you've changed your mind," Jay said.

Duncan managed a faint smile and waved off an offer of more food from Jay. "I was just asking questions. And she was one of the questions." He continued with the story, a detailed chronology of events, as if reciting them over would help clear the confusion.

Jay cleared some of the dishes from the table and placed them beside the sink. The compressor in the old refrigerator rattled to a stop as Jay opened the door. He removed a beer and wiped the top of the can with the tail of his flannel shirt before he popped it open. He took a long swig of beer, swallowed, then turned to Duncan.

"Well, you can't stay here because it wouldn't be safe. Jeter's men run trap lines all along the river. They stop here routinely."

"How long do you think we have?"

"It's hard to say," Jay said. "They check their lines at least every third day and they usually stop by here just to talk and borrow a beer from me on their way through. We have an uneasy truce now but at least we're on talking terms."

Duncan looked at him. "You've had problems with them too?"

"When I first came here a few years back, I didn't know about the Jeters. I set out some traps, live capture traps for my research, but the traps kept disappearing. Then one day I met a couple of Jeter's men out running their trap lines. They told me to back off and quit putting my traps out, said the river was their line. I told them I wasn't going to quit, that I had permits from the property owners.

"That was before I built my cabin. I was living in a little camper that I had pulled down here in the woods, just me and my dog, a Rhodesian Ridgeback named Spenser. The day after they warned me I came home from running my traplines to find my camper turned upside-down. There was a note on the door warning me not to put my traps out any more. To emphasize the point they had killed Spenser, skinned him, and nailed his hide to a tree."

"That's sickening," Riley said as she pushed her plate away. "But I don't get it. What's the big deal about a few animal traps?"

Jay took another sip of his beer. "Well, it's a very big deal to these people. Most of the people who run trap lines are just trying to make ends meet -- small farmers, factory workers, etc. A trapper who pays attention to his traps and knows what he is doing can make $8,000, maybe $10,000 a year doing that. And for some of these people, that's a whole lot of money."

"So how does Jeter come in? What's his role in this?"

"Jeter controls all the trapping in Northeast Mississippi and Northwest Alabama and some of Tennessee. The people who run the trap lines take the animals to Jeter, who acts as a broker. Jeter's men skin the animals at his barn then he sells the hides to the tanneries and other fur markets. Best of all, he pays them in cash. They can just stick it in their pockets and they don't have to report it as income.

"Jeter pays them a lot less than what the skins are worth, but they accept it because they're getting paid in cash and also they know that they can always call on Jeter if they need any favors done or get in any trouble. Most people think it's just penny-ante stuff, but if he's got twenty-five or thirty people running trap lines, and he's making a good $5,000 or $10,000 profit off each trapper, then Jeter clears a nice little bundle each year just by acting as broker. Perhaps even more, if he pays them off with whiskey he has made or dope that he's grown. Then his profit margin is even greater."

"How do you know all of this?" Riley asked.

"The fellows that run the line along this section of the river like to brag. Especially after they have had a few beers."

"So Jeter's men come through here every two or three days?" Duncan asked.

"Yes. They were here . . . mm . . . day before yesterday. Late. They might come down the river again tomorrow."

"So we need to find another place?"

"My cabin is not safe. They watch me all the time. I routinely find footprints outside the windows."

"I don't guess I should try to go home?" Riley asked.

Both Duncan and Jay shook their heads. "That's the first place they would look."

"My sisters?"

"Probably just as bad," Duncan said.

"We could travel. Move from hotel to hotel."

"Riley, I think it would be safer for you if we weren't together," Duncan said softly.

Riley protested immediately. "I appreciate your concern, Duncan, but this is no time for macho posturing. You're not in any condition to travel by yourself. You need rest and I can help." She looked to Jay for agreement but found none.

"But they expect you to be traveling together. It might be better for you to split up." Jay said.

"I think I know a place where they won't find me." Duncan said. "Do you think you could keep Riley here for a few days, pretend she's your girlfriend?"

Jay thought for a moment. "Can we assume that they don't know what she looks like?"

"Do you think they do?" she asked.

"They came to your apartment looking for me," Duncan answered. "They may have been watching you for some time. We can't take that chance."

"What about a disguise?" she asked. "I could cut my hair and dye it. Or maybe a wig."

The two men shook their head in unison.

They sat around the table staring at a common spot on the tablecloth, their thoughts focused on a solution. After a moment Duncan grinned and laughed.

"What?" Riley asked.

He shook his head. "A stupid idea."

"What?" she asked again.

"Maybe it's the concussion. It's a crazy idea. But I was thinking ... weren't you in a sorority at Ole Miss?" Duncan asked.

"Oh, come on, I'm disappointed in you."

"What do you think, Jay?" Duncan turned to his friend.

Jay studied his plate as he considered the idea. He was quiet for so long that Riley though he had not heard the question. He raised his head, then raised an eyebrow.

"It might work," he said with a note of caution in his voice.

"Oh, come on," Riley groaned in disbelief.

"No. Think about it," Duncan said. "The sorority houses at Ole Miss have the tightest security on campus. When all of those Oklahoma oil tycoons and Kentucky horse breeders send their darling little daughters to college, they expect them to be safe. The campus police watch the sorority houses like a hawk."

"I think it might work," Jay repeated.

"She would fit in perfectly in that setting," Duncan continued. "A black gang member snooping around a sorority house at Ole Miss would definitely attract too much attention. So would someone from the Redneck Mafia. In fact, any male trying to get near a sorority house uninvited would probably be shot on the spot. Your meals would be provided at the house. You wouldn't even have to step outside. It's the "Hide In Plain Sight" theory."

"You're right," Riley said.

"You like the idea?"

"No. You're right about it being a crazy idea. The concussion has affected your ability to think straight. It sounds more like the "Sitting Duck" theory to me."

"It is a crazy idea. That's the beauty of it. Who else would think to look there?"

"Can't you think of a better option?" she asked.

Duncan sat at the table in silence as he pushed his half-eaten food around the plate with a fork, his left arm resting on the table as he supported his chin, his face blank with fatigue.

"I'm open to suggestion. But I can't think on the problem anymore tonight. I've got to rest." He dropped his napkin onto the table as he stood and left the room.

Riley turned to Jay as Duncan disappeared behind the bedroom door.

"He's hurt, worse than he wants to show."

"I know," Jay agreed.

"Don't you think we need to get him some help, some medical attention? Don't you think we should turn this over to the police?"

Jay stood up and offered to take her plate with a gesture of his hand. She pushed it toward him. He stacked the dishes on one arm, moved to the sink, turned on the faucet and squirted detergent out of a plastic squeeze bottle into the hot water.

She watched his adam's apple bob as he took another swallow of beer.

"No," he said.

"Why not?"

He took a plate and scrubbed it with a tattered washcloth.

"Because he is smart enough to know if he needs to be seen by a physician. He'll let us know if it's necessary."

"And the police?" she asked.

"I have seen him in difficult situations before."

"You have?"

"Yes."

"Worse than this?"

203

Jay paused as he thought, his gaze focused out the dark window above the sink.

"Duncan has been through a lot in the past, some very tough times. He has been knocked down before but he always gets back up," he assured her. "Always," he said with a small laugh.

"I wish you would tell me what you find so humorous about our situation," Riley snapped.

He fished a piece of silverware from the water in the sink, inspected the tines of a fork as he scrubbed it with the washcloth. He finished with the fork and picked up a knife. "You shouldn't underestimate him."

Riley stared at him in disbelief. "This must be a male thing," she said. "Testosterone poisoning, or some macho hormone, that makes you men feel like you can handle your problems without any help and fly into the face of danger with the odds stacked against you. "The General Custer Syndrome." 'We can handle these Indians, General Custer,'" she mumbled to herself. "'We're only outnumbered twenty to one.'"

Jay rinsed a plate under the faucet and dried it with a towel in a slow circular motion before he placed it on the shelf. He repeated this action twice without any response before Riley gave up on the conversation and moved across the room to the fireplace. She took the blanket from the sofa and wrapped herself in it, reclined on the pillows, and gazed into the fire. The flames reflected on a tired face lined with worry and doubt. As tired as she was, she knew she would not rest easily that night.

In the bedroom, Duncan carefully lowered himself onto the bed and was immediately hit by a wave of vertigo. He clutched the sheets and squeezed his eyes tightly shut as the room whipped around. After his eyeballs had quit spinning, he rose and staggered his way to the bathroom. The bumblebees had returned, but they were bigger now and more dense. Steel bumblebees, like winged ball bearings, were bouncing off the inner wall of his skull. He stood in front of the mirror, eyes shut, arms extended and tried to touch the tip of his nose with the tip of his index fingers. After each try he opened his eyes. Close enough, he thought. He returned to stand by the bed. Putting all his weight on the foot nearest the bed, he had shut his eyes and leaned his upper body toward the bed. He had no problem leaning over to his left and then returning upright. He turned and repeated the procedure to his right. Again, no problem. But when he tried leaning backwards over the bed another wave of vertigo kicked his feet out from under him and he crashed onto the mattress, the impact pulling at his sutures in his back.

So much for his neurological self-examination. After the sickening whirlwind stopped he slowly opened his eyes and raised his trembling hands. Without a doubt he had sustained a concussion in the fall from the window. His brain was bruised from slamming into the skull and then bouncing back to slam against the inside of the skull at a point opposite from the blow -- coup and contra-coup, as the neurologists called it. Like the yolk of an egg can be damaged by shaking the egg too hard, Duncan knew he had scrambled some neurological wiring, as attested by the vertigo and the tremors in his extremities. And when he shut his eyes sparks of light showered the dark screen of his eyelids. At any other time he would have checked himself into the hospital, ordered a CAT scan of his head, and hooked himself up to a respiration monitor.

At any other time. As it was he had no idea of the extent of the damage. One of the thousands of tiny capillaries in his brain could be torn, slowly leaking into the fluid filled bag of tissue surrounding his brain, leaking ever so slightly as the pressure in his skull gradually increased. The respiration center of the brain would gradually be compressed so that his breathing would become more shallow, his respirations would come farther and farther apart until his brain would eventually quit sending out a signal to his lungs. He imagined it would be a gentle way to die. The last thing he needed to do was to go to sleep.

But he was so tired. So very, very tired.

The door to the bedroom opened. Jay walked in with a stack of magazines in one hand and a large cup of coffee in the other. He pulled a chair next to the bed and adjusted the shade on the lamp so the light would be directed toward him and away from Duncan as he sat down.

"Sparky is in the front room preaching your funeral," Jay said.

"She does have a temper."

"That's alright. I like a person with a little sand and grit."

"Then you'll love her."

"But can she stand up under real pressure?"

"She's sturdy."

"She had better be. She had better have a backbone set in bedrock, Dunc. I don't know about this gang from Chicago, but Erskine Jeter is another story. If his men can't kill you then he has the connections to the big boys in New

Orleans, he'll bring in some outside talent. If they can get to the president of the United States, they can get to you."

"That's why I want her out of the way."

"Which brings up another topic. This sorority house plan ..."

"Is it that bad?"

"It's okay, I see your point. But you can't hide forever. Jeter will be waiting for you as soon as you surface."

"All I need is a few days rest and a little time to think."

"And you think Barrett Jeter is the key?"

"Bodies just don't disappear without a reason," Duncan said.

Jay took a sip of coffee, leaned forward in the rocker to set the mug on the floor, then stood and walked to the closet. He took a coat hanger from the rack and bent the curve out of the hook then reshaped it at a right angle. He dropped to one knee, found a groove between the planks of the pine floor, inserted the hook as easily as slipping a key into a lock, twisted the hanger, then pulled up a short section of one board. His arm disappeared into the hole up to his elbow as he searched for something. When he stood up he held a dark, stained, oilcloth. He unfolded one corner of the bundle and removed a large black semi-automatic pistol by its checkered grip.

"9 mm," Jay said.

"Do you have anything smaller?"

Jay replaced the pistol in the oilcloth and produced another pistol. "A .38. Not as much firepower but much easier to conceal."

Jay checked to be sure the gun was loaded then let the hammer down on an empty chamber. He returned the oilcloth to its hiding place before he returned to his chair and placed the .38 on the table by the bed.

"Jay?"

"Yea?"

"Do you think we're doing the right thing? Not going to the police?"

Jay picked up his mug. "Nothing against the police, but the fewer people who know your where-abouts, the better. But don't try to sort it out now. Get some rest, see if things look different in the morning."

Duncan closed his eyes and tried to ignore the firestorm in his head. The bees were in a slower orbit, the starbursts smaller. He slowly turned away from the lamp light, tucked a pillow beneath his head, and another between his knees.

When he woke the next morning, Duncan found Jay in the same chair, a cup of coffee in one hand, the light from the east streaming through the window at a low angle over his shoulder, as he read from a magazine he held in his other hand.

Chapter Twenty Nine

Nina Ratliff, a secretary in the registrar's office at the medical center, pulled into the staff parking lot at ten minutes before seven the following morning. In her sixteen years on the job she had never arrived early at work. She had her morning routine practiced to such a degree that, barring traffic, she walked into her office, placed her purse under her desk, and poured her first cup of coffee in time to see the hands of the office clock touch eight o'clock.

Today was different, thanks to Robert Earl. In the three years she had known him, she had never been happier. At the moment, though, she couldn't decide whether she loved him or hated him. Robert Earl was always in trouble -- trouble with the police, trouble at work to the degree that he had difficulty in holding a job for any length of time, trouble with money. And now he was in serious trouble. Since the gambling casino had opened on the Gulf Coast six months earlier, Robert Earl had somehow managed to lose several thousand dollars, money borrowed from questionable sources he knew from up in the hills. And now they were calling their loans in. He either had to pay them or face the consequences. Or do a favor for them.

Robert Earl had broken down and begged Nina the night before. If she could get certain information from the files at the medical center, they would forgive his debts. If not, well . . . He had not spelled out what actions would be taken against him but the consequences, although vague, were definitely serious.

She had no illusions about herself. Six foot one and, as her mother used to describe, "big boned," she knew she was no beauty. She should have left Robert Earl a long time ago, but she was approaching forty with few prospects as far as other men were concerned. Robert Earl had been her first and only lover. Robert Earl, with all his faults, was all that she had.

With this in mind, she hurried across the parking lot towards the administration building, the cool air tingling against the sweat that had formed tiny beads across the crease in her chin. She smiled nervously at the security guard at the entrance without making eye contact. Some of her tension eased when she saw the unlit office. Just as she had hoped, it was too early for anyone else to be at work at the registrar's office. Unlocking the door, she flipped on the lights and went straight to the filing cabinets. She pulled a piece of paper from her purse with the two names on it and found the folder she wanted -- one was of an intern, the other a dental student. She quickly carried the records to the copying machine, turned it on, and, when the indicator lights showed the machine was ready, began copying the contents of each. She had never before noticed the sound of the copier but now the noise seemed to fill the room. In twenty minutes she had finished her task and returned the files to the cabinets. As she sat down at her desk, the copies hidden in her oversized purse, she noticed how cold and sweaty her hands were. She looked up at the clock - twenty until eight. Time enough, she hoped, to calm down before any one else arrived.

"We have to stop for gas," Duncan frowned as he looked at the dashboard. "I had hoped to make it to Oxford."

"Does it make any difference?" Riley asked.

"I guess not. But in a college town it would be easier to go unnoticed. There are always new faces around, so we wouldn't attract attention." They had followed the back roads since leaving Jay's cabin around noon, Duncan taking direction from Riley who sat with the road map in front of her, carefully navigating a route that would take them through the fewest number of towns as possible. She consulted the map.

"I think we have twenty or thirty more miles."

Duncan spotted a small country store in the distance with a solitary gasoline pump in front. He was debating whether to stop or not when he heard Riley stifle a giggle.

"What?"

"I'm sorry," she apologized, then laughed outright.

"What? What is it?" He glanced back and forth between her and the road as she stared at his clothes. Duncan had exchanged his surgical green for some of Jay's clothes. The long sleeves of his flannel work shirt and the oversized legs of his blue jeans folded up like an accordion around his hands and ankles. On his head sat an old leather cap with padded earflaps.

"You look like a retarded lumberjack," she laughed.

"Thanks. Thanks a lot. I feel like a lumberjack who just stood under the wrong side of the tree."

"I'm sorry. I thought you were feeling better."

209

"I am. Just a slight headache," he said. He was reluctant to tell her how bad he really felt.

"Do you want me to drive?" she asked.

"After we fill up."

He pulled off the road and onto the gravel parking lot of the one-room country store and stopped in front of the pump. A young boy, his hair neatly parted and greased, ran out to help. As Duncan walked to the building, the boy inserted the nozzle in the tank, then ran to the windshield and began washing it.

The country store was a small white frame structure with a tin snuff sign nailed on the outside wall next to a larger sign advertising a long defunct brand of motor oil. A Coca Cola thermometer was tacked next to the screen door. The wooden steps sagged in the middle as he stepped up on the porch. When Duncan stepped through the screen door, a wave of buried memories carried him back to the small country store near his father's farm. Homemade wooden shelves filled the small room, mostly stacked with canned goods. A counter near the cash register held small individual packages of crackers, a stack of Vienna sausage cans, and a large hoop of cheese with the black wax coating cut open to reveal the orange cheddar inside -- the essentials of the working man's lunch in the South. On the wall behind this were displays of work gloves, fishhooks, cigarettes, and headache powders.

A big, red-faced man with oil-stained hands, his hair neatly parted and greased just like the boy's, took Duncan's money for the gasoline.

When Duncan returned to the car, Riley was behind the wheel. As they drove off the man and his son watched through the screen door.

"Did you get the license number like I told you to?"

"Yes, sir." The boy held up his hand with the number written in ink on his palm.

The father walked behind the counter to the telephone, looked at a number scribbled on a wall calendar, and began to dial.

As they approached the town of Oxford from the south, the courthouse rose like a castle to dominate the center of the town square. The massive three story building contrasted bright and glistening against the dense gray low-lying clouds. The white of the walls was emphasized by the dark green color of the long window shutters. Atop the building was clock tower, a clock face to each of the four sides of square. Below, concrete steps led from the street to the elevated grounds around the courthouse. Oak trees, huge in themselves but dwarfed by the presence of the courthouse, ringed the grounds. Cast iron ornamental lamp posts mounted with white globes alternated between the trees. Wooden benches awaited fair weather when the old men of the town would congregate to swap impossible, incredible lies, trade knives that had already been traded at least a dozen times, spit tobacco at the foot of the confederate memorial statue, and whittle their sticks of cedar as the shavings piled up around their feet.

"Tall as a cloud . . ." Duncan said.

"Solid as a rock . . ." Riley added.

"You recognize the quote?" Duncan asked.

"You can't live in a haunted house for years and not recognize the ghost," she answered.

Rows of brick buildings fronted the street that circled the courthouse. Duncan inspected the stores that defined the life of the small town. A small cafe, a shoe store, and a pharmacy. A clothing store, a bank, and the corner book store. Many of the buildings had second floor balconies bordered with ornate wrought-iron metalwork.

Riley eased into the flow of traffic around the square and exited on the northwest corner.

"Have you ever been to Ole Miss?" she asked.

"No, I haven't."

"It's a beautiful campus."

Duncan agreed. A grove of trees formed the heart of the campus and provided a park like setting. Between the trees Duncan glimpsed the rust-red bricks of the buildings. He studied the students as they moved from building to building. A young man with long blond hair and wire rim glasses wore an assortment of bead necklaces over a sweatshirt bearing the likeness of Jimi Hendrix, a young black man teased a young girl who was trying to hide a grin behind a mask of disinterest, and a bevy of fraternity clones, each wearing a button down Oxford cloth shirt with pressed khaki pants and boat shoes, walked solemnly toward class under the leaden sky.

"Do you miss this?" Duncan asked.

"What? College?"

"Yeah."

"It was fun. I made a lot of close friends. But I wouldn't want to go back. Do you?"

"Go back to college? No. But I miss the diversity. And the atmosphere that encourages people to challenge ideas and ask questions. Medical school frowns on any behavior that deviates too far from the norm."

They approached a row of large Greek Revival buildings and turned into the parking lot of one that appeared larger than the others. Massive white columns across the deep porch gave the building an epic proportion.

"The Greek system is alive and well at Ole Miss," he noted.

"That's an understatement."

As they walked up the sidewalk toward the sorority house, Riley reached out, slipped her hand into his, interlocked their fingers with a squeeze, and rubbed her thumb against his grasp.

A young co-ed bounced down the steps of the sorority house with a notebook clutched to her chest. She stopped when she recognized Riley.

"Riley! It's good to see you again! Have you come back to visit? I'm late for class but I hope you'll stay long enough for us to talk."

"I plan to be here for awhile."

"Good."

She turned to introduce herself to Duncan, took him in at a glance, her eyes coming to a halt when she saw the cap resting on his head, the earflaps at an angle poised for take-off, then quickly turned back to Riley.

"Well, I'm really late. Gotta run! Bye!"

"Are you coming in?" Riley asked Duncan as they watched the young girl leave, each carefully avoiding the other's eyes.

"No, I need to be going," he said slowly.

"Are you sure you'll be safe?"

"Yes, and you will be too if you stay inside."

"But what if I need to talk to you?"

"I'll be in touch," he said, trying to sound reassuring.

"How long are you going to be gone?" she asked, but Duncan had no answer for her.

There was an awkward silence until he asked, "Does someone know you're coming?" He knew the answer; he had asked the question before.

"I called Debbie from Jay's house. I didn't use my name like you said. She recognized my voice. I told her to expect me. She's smart. She didn't ask a lot of questions but she could tell something was wrong."

"Well, I guess I should be going." He paused for second before he turned to go.

"Duncan," she said quickly.

He stopped. "Yes?"

"Duncan. I . . . uh . . . I want you to be careful. Take care of yourself."

"I will." He smiled.

"Duncan?" She stepped down and quickly pressed her lips to his. His arm folded around her as he drew her close.

A chorus of cheers erupted from the second story windows. The two looked up to see four sorority sisters staring down at them, clapping and laughing.

"About time," one commented.

"Goofy cap," another said. "But cute dimples."

"And a nice butt," a third added.

Duncan's face turned red. He pulled off his cap and made a long sweeping bow. He straightened himself, donned his cap, pecked Riley on the cheek, and left in a quick walk.

He exited the parking lot and drove past the house. Riley waved good-bye as she leaned against a column, a look of concern on her face. When he reached the highway, he turned the car east toward his destination in the hill country of his youth.

Chapter Thirty

Erskine Jeter managed his small criminal empire and various businesses from an office in his home. The room was sparsely furnished and plainly functional. The bookshelves held very few books; Jeter did not read a book unless it was directly related to one of his business ventures. Instead the shelves were stacked with information related to his various corporations -- accounting audits from his trucking fleet, sales figures from his three small manufacturing facilities, deeds, duplicates of bids made by his construction company -- all the information of his legitimate business transactions were within reach. No records were kept of his illegal activities. Erskine Jeter kept a careful accounting of that in his head.

In a series of round hole safes set in concrete in the floor under his desk were several hundred thousand dollars in twenties and tens. He was not concerned about burglars or thieves. His reputation alone served to protect his house and properties. No one with sound judgment would be tempted to take anything that belonged to Erskine Jeter.

Two leather chairs faced the desk. The only other piece of furniture in the room was a walnut gun cabinet in the corner. Custom made shotguns and rifles stood upright in the cabinet, their engraved walnut stocks a warm brown and oiled metal barrels glowing midnight blue in the beam of a small recessed spotlight.

The lone picture on the wall was a black and white photograph of Ezra Jeter sitting on a moss encrusted rock outside the entrance to the cave where he first distilled his corn whiskey. The picture had been taken when Ezra was an old man, and, although he appeared gaunt and feeble, the photograph showed that his eyes still blazed with an intensity that his grandson Erskine had inherited.

The only other decoration that adorned the room, if it could be called a decoration, was a clear Lucite sphere that rested on Jeter's desk. Embedded inside was the severed head of a rattlesnake with jaws open and fangs exposed. He had found the snake one morning inside the barn where he skinned the animals the trappers brought to him. Seeking warmth, it lay coiled between the legs of the wood burning stove. Jeter had calmly stepped on the rattler's broad head and severed it from the writhing body with his pocket knife. The body he threw in the hog pen outside the barn for disposal. The head he kept for a totem and as an example of what would happen to any creature, animal or human, that dared to invade his territory.

Erskine Jeter sat at his desk as he studied the files he had just received from the medical center on Duncan and Riley. He closed the file on Duncan for the second time and was turning to the other file when the phone rang. Without looking away from the papers he picked up the receiver.

"Yeah?" he said. As he listened, he picked up his pen and wrote down a license plate number, a satisfied look spreading over his face.

"Heading north," he repeated into the phone with a nod of his head. He listened for a moment, then spoke.

"You done good," he said. "Real good. Why don't you come visit with me soon. I'll have something for you. And bring that boy of yours. He can do a little fishing on my private lake. Does he like to ride horses? Yeah? Good . . . good. Just give me a call when you're heading this way. Thanks, my friend," he said as he hung up the phone.

He opened Riley's file for the second time.

"South of Oxford heading north," he said to himself. He remembered something from Riley's file, searched her record for a moment, then produced a page from the manila folder and set it down on the desk in front of him. He adjusted his reading glasses and placed a thick finger on one particular section.

A light knock came from the door to his study. The door opened and his wife, lean and graceful with a refined face, stepped halfway into the room. From the doorway she said, "I'm going shopping. Do you need anything?"

"Annette, come here a second," he said as he motioned her over with a finger. "You went to Ole Miss, didn't you?" It was more of a statement of fact than a question.

"For one year," she said as she approached the desk. She seldom entered her husband's study. She especially disliked the disembodied head of the snake on his desk. She circled the desk on the side opposite from where it sat.

"What is this?" he asked.

She looked where he held his finger.

"That's Tri Omega. A sorority."

"That's a girl's club?"

"Sort of, except they live together and do things as a group."

"What does a sorority do? Why would someone join?"

"It's purely social, Erskine. Sort of like a country club for girls."

He thought for a minute. "Did you say they live together?"

"The sororities have their own private houses, huge *Gone With the Wind* type mansions, that the girls live in. Once you are admitted to the sorority you get to live in the house. They have their own kitchen and serve meals there. Some even have their own swimming pools and tennis courts," she said with a smile. She knew Erskine would look down on anything that sounded of pretention and pampering.

Erskine fell silent. When his wife saw that she was no longer required, she moved to the door. "I'll be back in a couple of hours, maybe longer."

"Nette?" he called after her.

"Yes?"

"If you see Hubbard or Ferguson, send them in. I need to talk with them."

When she left, Erskine rose and walked over to the French doors that opened out onto a small veranda. He gazed down the hill and across the pastures that stretched along the banks of the wide creek below. He fondly studied the thoroughbred horses that grazed on the rich, green winter grass.

His horses were a source of special pride to him. Some of the best bloodlines in the country ran through their veins. Unfortunately, the horses could never be registered or their ancestry acknowledged because of the manner in which the stud services had been obtained.

Erskine Jeter had a monopoly on the horse disposal business in the Southeast. Horse breeders in Tennessee and Kentucky that needed a horse "stolen" would contact Jeter. The horse would disappear mysteriously, the owner would contact the police, and eventually the owner would collect a check from the insurance company, a check that would reflect the over-inflated value of the horse.

Jeter had the means to dispose of the horses without a trace. He would collect a percentage of the insurance, and, without the owners' knowledge, keep some of the better stallions alive just long enough to breed with his mares.

He watched as a foal played in the pasture. The young chestnut-colored colt stopped to peer over the edge of the bank along the creek, then bolted as a covey of quail erupted from cover.

The woods started on the opposite side of the creek that meandered through the bottom land. Barely discernible in the distance was the reflection of sunlight on the tin roof of his skinning barn.

He knew that the medical student and his girlfriend were headed to Oxford. She would try to hide at the girl's boarding house, that sorority he had read about. And the young doctor? Where was he going?

He couldn't guess. But if he could get his hands on either one of them, he would take them to the skinning barn. And then he would have some answers about the death of his nephew.

Not that he cared about Barrett's death. He didn't. But he could not afford to give the impression that he was softening in his old age. Although he had a working relationship with New Orleans, he knew that the Louisiana Mafia kept an ever-watchful eye on him. They would leap at the chance to annex his territory at the first sign of weakness on his part.

As his eyes once again caught the light glinting off the tin roof of the skinning barn, Erskine Jeter almost smiled as he considered what he had planned for the two fugitives.

The sun was setting behind the low hills as the car moved along the dusty road and crossed the plank bridge that traversed Hell Creek. It was the land of Duncan's forefather's, first settled one hundred and fifty years before by a wiry and determined Scottish ancestor who had settled here when the land was covered with dense hardwoods. Today the creek had been straightened from its original path and the trees were gone. Fallow fields stretched along the creek awaiting the promise of activity that would come in the spring. He drove past the large whitewashed house that had once been his home without much of a glance. His was the first generation of his family not to occupy the house which had grown out of the log cabin of the original settler. At any other time he would have stopped, knocked on the door, and introduced himself. There would be time for that later -- he hoped. Instead he drove on. As the road began to rise out of the rich bottom land, he turned from one dirt road onto another, narrower road that ran parallel to the creek, a road less traveled to judge by its condition. The car drifted around a curve to reveal a small white frame house tucked against the backdrop of a sloping hill. Duncan turned off the headlights and stepped out of the car. For a long moment he stood, hands in his pockets, as his thoughts traveled back in time.

In this modest house lived the lady who had raised him, the first real mother he had known. Mother Spight had been at his father's house, waiting on the front steps, when his father brought Duncan home from the hospital, three days old and two days after his mother had died. Every day for almost eight years she would be at their house before daylight, when he would awake to the smells of bacon and breads rising from the kitchen. Every evening at dusk she would climb up into his father's truck to be transported back across the bridge to her home. She was the one who fed and clothed him, scrubbed his face and ears, and spanked him when he deserved punishment. She arbitrated fights between him and his brother, taught him about life and people, and read to him from her large leather-bound Bible, the sides of the Book spilling over from her narrow lap.

No one knew more about the world than Mother Spight, except perhaps his father. He remembered the fright and uncertainty the day of his father's death. Mother Spight had stayed with him and his brother that night at their home, the first night she had ever done so. The next day his aunt and uncle had arrived from Birmingham. Two days after his father's funeral he sat in their car and stared out the back window as they drove away. He remembered the look of loss in her eyes as she stood, erect and proud, and tried to present a brave face for him as her form receded in the distance.

Another memory crossed his mind. In college he had met a girl, a sociology major from Pennsylvania. They had dated some, enough for him to eventually share with her the true history of his childhood. When he told her about Mother Spight she had chastised him, said that his father's employment of a "Black nanny" was degrading to the African-American race, that here was another disgraceful example of the South's vestigial slave society, stereotypical to the point of being cliché. In a long lecture in which she had implied there were no decent white people in the south, she tried to enlighten Duncan, to explain why Mother Spight had worked for them out of fear. Duncan calmly told her that she had read too much and experienced too little and had never seen her again. He didn't need anyone to explain his relationship to Mother Spight; a child knows when he is truly loved.

Two wooden steps led up to the covered porch. A light inside the window gave a warm orange glow in the twilight. The spring on the screen door creaked as he opened it to knock on the wooden door. In a moment the bare light bulb beside the door came on. The door slowly opened to reveal a brown face wrinkled from three generations of laughter and pain.

"Who's that?" she asked as she peered up at him through thick glasses with silver frames that matched, unintentionally, the small silver pins that held her gray hair bundled in place. She wore a dark blue sweater over a long white cotton dress printed with small purple flowers.

"It's me, Mother Spight. It's Duncan. Duncan Russthorne."

Immediately a smile erupted on her face as she opened the door wide and stepped forward to greet him, her delicate hand held up in surprise.

"Oh, Lord. It's my child come to see me." She held up two fragile hands to enclose his cheeks as he bent down to hug her and kiss her forehead. When his arms closed around her, he was struck by the frailty of her slight form, as if he were grasping a sheet supported by a broom handle.

"Come on in, son. I got supper cooking. You hungry? You like vegetables any more than you did?" She did not wait for a response as she turned toward the kitchen.

"Wait a minute, Mother Spight, we need to talk."

She turned back to him. "Is something wrong?"

"I'm in a little trouble."

"What's wrong. Tell me about it, son."

"Well, it's a long story, but I need a place to stay for a couple of days and . he paused, unsure of the right words, "you may be in danger if I stay."

The frail figure stepped closer to Duncan, put a hand up to his chest, and tried to adjust her glasses so she could see his face better.

"Son," she began, "I'm an eighty-one year old black woman who's lived in Mis'sippi all her life. You don't think I've seen trouble in my times? Ain't nothing gonna scare this old woman." She shook her head at the thought. "Now, you got some clothes or a suitcase you need to bring inside? Go get it. I'll be in the kitchen." She turned and walked away, chuckling to herself.

After Duncan hid his car behind the house, he returned to find Mother Spight had set a place for him at the small wooden kitchen table. She served his plate from the stainless steel pots that steamed on the stove.

During the meal Duncan told his story, changing certain parts slightly to downplay the close escapes from death. When he told of the explosion that destroyed his house, he told the story as if he had not been at the house when the fire started. He deleted the parts about the gunman so she would not be too alarmed. He simply said that someone had tried to shoot him. Mother Spight listened intently as she moved back and forth between the table, the stove, and the refrigerator. She made no comment, just gave an occasional shake of the head, until he finished his narrative.

"Why, Duncan? Why is someone doing these things to you?" she asked.

Duncan had no answer and told her so.

He studied her as she ate her scant portions of food. She was old when he was a child but now she seemed impossibly old, with a face as wrinkled as crumpled paper. She had always been small and wiry; now her body seemed a fragile frame with skin drawn over it. She talked throughout the meal, asking questions about his life and work, beaming with joy as he told her of his duties as a physician.

He eventually worked the conversation back around to her. He asked about her son, and about her health.

"My doctor says I'm fine. Says the only problem I got is my sugar."

"Your blood sugar?"

"Yeah. He says that's the reason my eyes aren't as good as they used to be."

"Are you taking insulin?"

"My shots?" she asked. "Yes, twice a day. But I feel fine. My son comes and checks on me a couple times a week. Takes me into town when I need it."

She carried a pot from the stove, dipped a ladle into the contents, and filled his plate again until he could eat no more, then moved to the cupboard and produced a chocolate cake. She cut a large piece for Duncan and placed it in a bowl. She topped it with two scoops of ice cream and repeated this using much smaller portions in a second bowl. She sat one bowl in front of Duncan; the other was hers. Sitting at the small metal table, he watched as she delighted in her dessert. She loaded her spoon with a large chunk of the ice cream, then slowly swirled her tongue around it. He was fighting the urge to warn her about her diet when she stopped and waved her spoon at him.

"I know what you're thinking, but don't fuss at me, son. I know this ain't supposed to be good for me," she said as she snipped off a piece of cake with her spoon. "But it's only a little bit and this is a special occasion. You come to visit only once every ten years," she chastised, then smiled as she slipped the spoon to her mouth. "Now eat your cake."

He obeyed her just as he had twenty years earlier.

During the night a cold front pushed the clouds to the south. Across the campus at the University of Mississippi, students, accustomed to the wild swings in the weather during early spring, trundled to their morning classes under the cold bright skies, wrapped tightly in heavy coats and thick scarves. On the third floor of the south side of the Tri Omega house a glass enclosed sunroom ran the length of the sorority house. Inside, Riley stood by the window in shorts and a T-shirt as condensation collected on the glass. She cupped a mug of steaming coffee in her hands. She was glad to be in the warmth and coziness of the sunroom as she watched the frosted breaths of the students below as they traveled the sidewalk. She took a sip from her mug and rubbed the dust from the leaf of a fig tree that grew in the corner of the room.

"This is really nice, Debbie."

"What?" asked Deborah. On a large towel spread out on the floor of the sunroom was Deborah Vuncannon. She lay on her stomach with the string to her bikini top undone as she studied a large textbook propped up by a pillow in front of her.

"I wish this sunroom had been completed when I was in college."

"Yeah. It really helps us get a head start on our tans," she said as she ran a series of numbers through a calculator that rested on her notebook.

"So you will be graduating in the spring. It seems just like yesterday when we first met. You were a freshman, I was a senior," Riley reminisced.

Debbie closed her book and set her pen down, then reached back to tie her swimsuit top tight before she sat up.

"It's hard to imagine you studying for your MBA at Princeton next fall," Riley said. "It's a little early for them to be selecting the next class, isn't it?"

"They know a good thing when they see it," she laughed.

"I take it that you didn't pull your dumb blond routine during your interview."

Debbie immediately opened her eyes wide in a dumbfounded manner. She smacked her gum and raised her voice an octave.

"Like, uh, what do you mean by, uh, dumb blond?" Debbie asked, then lowered her voice to its natural tone. "But I don't have the opportunity to do that routine much any more. After four years of college people around here know me too well."

"You used the role enough when you were a freshman."

"Only with the assholes, Riley. Only with the guys who expected me to be an airhead because of my looks. I just gave them what they wanted to see."

"You made them look like fools."

"Only when they deserved it. If a man is a pig, who am I to try and change him?" Debbie asked as she folded up her towel and dropped it on a chaise lounge with her books.

Riley returned her gaze to the campus below. The stream of students rushing back and forth between buildings slowed to a trickle as the top of the hour passed. Directly below her, Riley watched as a delivery truck with the logo of a food supply company pulled up to the service door at the rear of the sorority house. The truck stopped and the driver, tall and handsome with his hair pulled back in a ponytail, stepped down from the open door with a clipboard in his hand.

When she heard Riley gasp, Debbie turned to see Riley's coffee cup slip from her grasp and shatter on the floor. When Debbie reached her side, gingerly stepping around shards of porcelain with her bare feet, Riley was pointing to the source of her surprise.

A second man had emerged from the truck.

"It's them," Riley said.

"Who?"

"The two thugs that chased Duncan and me from my apartment in Jackson. How could they have found me so quickly?"

"I'll call security. They will be here within minutes," Debbie said as she turned to go.

Riley stopped her. "No, wait. I can't be here when security comes. We have to sit tight for a minute."

They watched as the two rednecks walked toward the kitchen door and disappeared from view.

Riley took Debbie by the arm. "Come with me. I've got a plan."

Chapter Thirty One

Rose O'Hanlon managed the kitchen at the Tri Omega sorority house. She had been the head cook for twenty-two years and had developed a routine that never varied. She arrived dressed in her white uniform dress, white shoes, and white stockings every weekday at 9:45 in the morning. As soon as she walked into the kitchen at the sorority house she would proceed to the coat closet where she would remove her sweater or coat. She would then produce a pint bottle of gin from her purse, unscrew the cap, and take a long swallow. She would then hide the bottle in the bottom of her purse where it would stay until her afternoon break.

On this morning, after her ritual with the bottle was finished, she took her customary place on a stool by the sink where she planned the day's meals before her two kitchen assistants arrived at 10:30.

Short and plump, she kept her hair dyed jet black and always wore it pulled up in a net while she worked. Her pale skin came close to matching the color of her uniform except for a slight flush of pink across her cheeks and nose.

She sat on her stool, staring down at her swollen ankles as she pondered the menu, when she heard the food service truck arrive at the kitchen door.

Outside the house, Hubbard killed the engine and stepped down from the truck. Ferguson checked the driver again to be sure he was still unconscious and nodded to Hubbard.

Rose was biting her cuticle when Hubbard knocked at the back door. With effort she climbed down from the stool, walked over to the door, and opened it. "What?" she barked.

"I'm here from food service, ma'am."

"Who are you?" she asked. "Where's the other boy that usually comes by?"

"He's sick, ma'am. I think he's got the flu. I'm working his route just a few days until he gets to feeling better."

"Humph, well, do you have my order?"

"Well, ma'am, I'm new at this and the orders got shuffled. I'm not really sure which one is yours. What was it you wanted again?"

"I was waiting on the chicken breasts. I've got to have those for my lunch."

"Ma'am, I know this is inconvenient, but could you come out to the truck and help me pick out exactly what your order was so I'll get it right?"

"I ain't coming out to the truck. That's not my job. Now you go get my food and bring it in here. I've got to start lunch now or it won't be ready to serve come 12 o'clock," she fussed as she turned away.

Hubbard tapped her on her shoulder with his finger. When she turned around, Hubbard pointed his gun at her nose.

"Ma'am, please come to the truck," he said as he motioned her out the door. Holding his gun inside his jacket where it couldn't be seen, he followed behind her as she walked, trembling and wheezing, as she struggled to make sense of what was happening. When they reached the truck, Ferguson opened the back door and helped her inside where he forced her to sit on a box beside the driver who lay sprawled on the floor.

"He's locked Rose in the back of the truck. He's coming back inside. You had better hurry," Riley said as she peeked through a slit in the curtain from Debbie's room on the second floor. Debbie stood by the closet as she quickly slipped a short tennis skirt over her bikini bottom.

"Don't worry. Just wait for your cue," Debbie assured her. She dropped her bikini top and slipped a white knit shirt over her head.

Riley took her hand from the curtain.

"You warned everyone downstairs?"

"Yeah. The ground floor is clear. It's up to our visitor now. You had better take your position while we wait for him to make his move."

Hubbard regretted hitting the old lady, especially after the way she squealed in pain when the butt of the pistol struck her the second time, but he had to be sure she was telling truth. Rose had admitted to knowing Riley Stevens, but swore that the girl had not lived in the sorority house for years.

Hubbard eased open the door to the dining room to find it empty of people. He walked past the rows of tables to the hallway, his sneakers silent on the marble floor. He softly tread down the hall, its walls covered with composite pictures of past graduates from the sorority, until a doorway to the left opened into a small formal sitting area. Hubbard looked inside to again find no one

224

present. The opposite doorway in the hall opened into a larger den. In the corner the television spoke to an empty room. On the tube a talk show host stood in the audience and questioned a serious looking gentleman in a coat and tie but there was no one in the sorority house to listen to the debate. Hubbard began to feel uneasy at the conspicuous absence of activity in the house. Maybe the girls who lived here were at class? Maybe they were all upstairs asleep. He smiled at the thought. It reminded him of a movie he had seen once when he was in high school. He and his buddies had climbed the fence at the local drive-in; they were too young to be admitted at the entrance. The movie was about a maintenance man who worked at a women's college dormitory. Hubbard and his friends did not have the benefit of a speaker, but it was the kind of movie that did not require dialogue.

Hubbard now stood by the stairs at the front of the sorority house. Upstairs the sound of a door slamming shut broke into his daydream. Somebody was home! He took the carpet covered steps two at a time. At the top of the steps the second floor landing branched into three separate hallways. Again there was a dead silence. He stood debating which direction to take when down the hall to his left he heard the sound of a door opening and the soft shuffle of footsteps.

Debbie turned the corner with a bouncing gait and came to an abrupt halt when she saw Hubbard.

"Well, hello!" She beamed her brightest smile at him as she advanced.

Hubbard was caught off guard by her friendliness. He had expected anyone he met to scream or run. Or at least question what he was doing there.

Instead she took a step closer. Hubbard was hypnotized by her bright, inviting eyes and long tan legs.

"Aren't you going to say hello?" she said as she moved closer and looked up into his eyes.

"Uh, . . . hello. Hello!" A sappy grin covered his face.

She dropped her tennis racket from in front of her body and locked her arms behind her back as her breasts pointed up toward the intruder. The fragrance of her perfume filled his nostrils and his eyes locked onto her shirt as his brain registered the fact that she wasn't wearing a bra.

Hot damn, he thought, just like in that movie!

"What's your name?" she asked sweetly as she rocked back and forth in her tennis shoes.

Hubbard noticed that his mouth was suddenly dry. He cleared his throat and spoke.

"Hubbard. My name is Hubbard."

"Hubbard! she said with delight. "I think that's a great name! I've heard of you. How's your mother and her poor old dog? I think you're a very good looking fella."

She reached out and placed a hand on his chest as she rattled on. "I like your hair. The way you pull it back in a pony tail. That's very chic but not many men around here have the courage to make a fashion statement like that. I bet you got the idea from one of those men's magazines, didn't you? Aren't you going to ask me my name?"

Hubbard forced himself to break eye contact with the front of her shirt and look her in the face.

"It's Debbie," she said before he could ask. She slid her hand across his chest to his biceps.

"Boy, what big muscles you have!" She giggled as she squeezed his arm. "Are you a professional athlete? I bet you could be. Would you like to play some tennis?"

Hubbard finally found his voice. "It's a little cold outside for tennis, ain't it? I bet you and me could find something to do inside that would keep us warm," he said in a smooth voice. If the talk didn't work, he told himself, he could always use his gun.

"That sounds like fun. But I don't want to play tennis with you. She does." Debbie pointed over his right shoulder.

Hubbard turned to look behind him just in time to see Riley shift her weight onto her forward foot as she began a vicious two-handed backswing. The racket head was turned sideways as it swept up from the floor to strike him across the face, breaking his nose and crushing his left cheekbone.

He stumbled back against the wall and wobbled unsteadily on his legs as he struggled to keep his knees from buckling. A sharp, bloody angle in the flesh under his left eye marked where the bone over the sinus had collapsed inward. Debbie placed the sole of her tennis shoe into the side of his hip and pushed him down the stairway. He rolled halfway down the steps before his left arm hung in the banister and brought him to a stop.

"I've heard of right-brained and left-brained people but I think he belongs in the below-the-belt brained category," Riley said as she peered over the banister to look at the silent crumpled form on the stairway.

"Nice stroke, sister," Debbie said.

"Thanks, but I broke your racquet," she said as she held it up for inspection.

"Don't worry about it. What do we do now?"

"I'm not sure but I know I can't stay here any more. And I've got to get out of here quick, before lover-boy here wakes up."

"Go to the Pike house and ask for Sperry. He'll take care of you, give you time to plan your next move."

"Thanks, Deb," she hugged her friend quickly. "Give me a couple of minutes, then call security."

Riley used the railings to vault over the unconscious body blocking the stairs. At the bottom of the steps she turned to smile at Debbie once more before she disappeared out the front door.

Chapter Thirty Two

Duncan's head began to ease after the first night spent at Mother Spight's. On the second full day in hiding with his old nanny Duncan sensed his body healing. The sutures in his back itched and tingled but no longer hurt; the burning sensation was gone. His scalp was still sore and tender, but he could sleep at night without waking if he happened to turn his head the wrong way. Best of all, his mind began to clear. He could concentrate without the distraction of the pain and vertigo.

After lunch on the third day, Duncan excused himself from the table and wandered into the den. From the window he looked out across the fields. In another month the tractors would plow the ground and plant the crops, but for now the land around Mother Spight's house remained undisturbed. The isolation and stillness of the countryside invited a sense of lethargy.

Duncan stretched out on the sofa, pulled a crochet Afghan from the back of the sofa, and wrapped himself in it. One more nap, he told himself, then it would be time to work.

When Duncan awoke the room was silent except for the slight hissing of the gas heater that stood against the opposite wall of the small room. Mother Spight sat in an overstuffed armchair beside the heater, her legs turned to catch the warmth of the low blue and orange flames, her hands folded in her lap, head back with lips parted slightly as she napped.

Duncan swung his legs from the sofa to the floor. He rubbed his face with his hands, stood, and crossed the room to the kitchen without waking Mother Spight. He sat at the table, tore several sheets of paper from the notebook, and began to reconstruct the life of his dead roommate. Everything he knew about Barrett, every fact he could recall, every rumor Duncan had heard about him, he wrote on the long yellow sheets of paper.

At the top of a second sheet of paper he drew a large question mark. This page filled quickly with a list of unanswered questions that presented themselves as Duncan outlined Barrett's biography. Forty-five minutes later he pushed the stack of papers aside as he stood up and stretched, then searched the kitchen for some form of caffeine.

After brewing a cup of instant coffee he returned to his work. He began an outline, a flow chart of events, that started with the week prior to Barrett's death. Slowly, he patiently detailed each day in chronological order, skipping every other line of the page in order to have room for additions that he might remember later.

Every line seemed to give rise to a new question. Duncan added each to the question list, no matter how insignificant it seemed. He knew from his medical training that the diagnosis of a disease often comes from the unveiling of the most trivial fact. He also knew that finding the correct answer required asking the correct questions.

Time passed slowly as he filled the pages. He tried to recall each incident in detail, the specific words used in every conversation. He felt as if he were drowning in minutia, but he forced himself to be patient. He could not err in this diagnosis; he might not get a second chance.

He took the last sip of coffee from his cup and stopped to gauge his progress. In the outline he was at the police station and his interrogation by Lieutenant Storey. Halfway finished, perhaps? In the den he heard a slight rustling noise that indicated Mother Spight was waking from her nap.

He looked into his empty cup, rose from the table, and stretched. At the sink he filled the small pot with water and placed it on the stove. From the cabinet above the stove he took out the small jar of instant coffee crystals. He preferred drip brewed coffee but any kind would do. Just as long as he had his caffeine fix.

As he leaned back against the counter and waited for the water to boil, a new question formed in his mind. The answer followed immediately, striking him hard as a wave of nausea swept through his body and a bitter, metallic taste filled his mouth. His hands, damp and cold, began to tremble. He squeezed them tight and struggled to take a deep breath. The knowledge of Barrett Jeter's murderer came to him with a sudden insight that flooded his mind, not in a golden epiphanous moment, but with the feeling of sickening disbelief.

Suddenly the room was too small and confining. The house seemed to be shrinking around him, and the mustiness of the gas heater turned foul in his nostrils and clogged his chest. He had to get out of the house in order to breathe. He stalked out of the kitchen toward the front door and fresh air.

"What's wrong, son? You look shook up." Mother Spight called from the corner of the room as he hurried past.

Duncan stopped and turned to see her sitting in her corner chair with her reading lamp on. The light fell over her shoulder to illuminate her Bible as it lay open in her lap.

"Are you alright?" she asked.

"Fine. I'm fine, Mother Spight," he said as he took a step toward the door. He stopped and dropped his head. 'No," he said softly. "I'm not alright."

"Is it anything I can help you with, son?"

He paused for a moment. "No, Mother Spight. I don't think anyone can help me now. I'm past helping."

"There is always someone who can help you, Duncan," she said as she placed a delicate hand on the Book she held in her lap.

He felt a twinge of guilt as he thought back on a path he had left a long time ago, before he had accepted the twin gods of knowledge and logic. The last several years of his life had been filled with too much science and not enough faith.

"I remember a story you used to read to me, a story about a valley full of dead people."

Mother Spight nodded her head. "That was Ezekiel and the miracle of the dry bones. The Lord brought bone to bone, added sinews and muscles and skin, and brought the dead back to life. He wanted to show the prophet His power, His ability to resurrect and restore even the most hopeless."

Duncan thought about what lay ahead for him. He faced an impossible task, the task of exposing Barrett's murderer and pointing the police in the right direction. Hopeless was an accurate description of his plight.

"Pray for me, Mother Spight. I need that kind of a miracle," he said as he opened the door. "I'm going for a walk."

He stepped from the porch and walked up the field road at a brisk pace, lost in thought, toward the dark green cedar trees in the distance.

Chapter Thirty Three

Alfie Storey scratched her forehead with the thumb of the hand that held her cigarette. With her other hand she made a note in the margin of the report on her desk. She lay down the pen, took a deep drag from her cigarette, blew out the smoke and watched it roll across the desk as David approached. Without a word he deftly snatched the pack of cigarettes from her desktop and dropped it into the garbage can.

"I'll tell your children what a nice person you were," he said.

"I plan to be around to show them myself. You concentrate on your own children." She smiled to soften the insult.

His eyes narrowed to slits.

"You are so cruel. I'm tempted not to give you this." He waved a sheet of paper in front of her face.

"David. I would love to arrest you for interfering with police business."

He let her snatch it from his hand.

"I'll save you the trouble," he said. "It matches the description of one of the guys that the young doctor described before he disappeared."

"How did you know that?"

"Just me being 'nosy,'" he said in a wounded voice.

"O.K. I'm sorry. You did well."

"Do you mean that?" he said. "Well, thank you. I was thinking that this . . ."

"David."

"What?"

"Don't push your luck," she warned as she continued to read the report.

"Ole Miss?" she asked herself.

"A sorority house?" Her brow furrowed deeply as she leaned back in her chair. David started to speak but she raised a hand to silence him. Several moments passed before she stood up, nodding to herself.

"David, I'm gone for the rest of the day."

"What should I say if someone asks for you?"

231

She took her jacket from the back of her chair and put it on, then opened her desk to retrieve her badge and her pistol.

"Tell them I've gone back to school."

"Elementary or junior high?"

She gave her best imitation of a southern belle. "Ahm a goin' to Ole Miss. Ahm a goin' to join a sorority," she drawled.

David laughed, a short, crisp snort. "You have no chance whatsoever of being admitted to a sorority at Ole Miss."

"Are you saying I'm the wrong color?" She feigned indignation and placed a hand over her wounded heart.

"No. Much worse." He leaned forward and lowered his voice. "You're a damn Yankee."

Alfie made the drive from Jackson to Oxford in a little over four hours. The closer she came to her destination the slower she drove. She now realized why she had never ventured out of Jackson; small towns and rural settings were unfamiliar. For some reason the cluster of tall buildings and the firmness of the concrete sidewalks gave her a sense of control. She knew the streets, but anything past suburbia was a blank spot on her map.

When she reached the town square she was amazed at what she saw -- a postcard perfect small southern town. She felt as if she had stepped onto the back lot of a Hollywood movie studio.

Her scalp began to tingle as one hundred thousand hairs tried to stand at attention in unison. This was the kind of place her friends in Chicago had warned her about. All this needs to be complete, she thought, is for Atticus Finch to walk out of the courthouse.

She parked her car and walked down the sidewalk as she inspected the town. The wood statuettes in the window of the art gallery were amusing. The rich smells that wafted from the door of the adjacent restaurant were tempting.

She scanned the streets, looking for the source of her discomfort. It wasn't the people she met on the sidewalk. They acted as if they barely noticed her but were friendly in the casual way she had come to realize was the southern habit -- a polite smile or a cursory nod of recognition, all done with eye contact. No staring at the sidewalk, none of those looking-through-you-but-not-seeing-you type stares. But if she felt out of place here in this small town, the people she met did not seem to recognize the fact.

She entered the book store on the corner. Near the front door, a young lady with a stack of books in her left arm arranged the display on one of the many tables scattered throughout the store. She wore a ribbed tunic and blue jeans. Her long straight brown hair revealed enough of her face to show her light complexion and warm eyes.

"Can I help you?" she asked.

"Yes. Could you give me directions to the campus? I'm looking for the University police department."

"Sure. Where are you parked?"

"In front of the art gallery."

"O.K. Just circle the square." She made a sweeping motion with her arm as she faced the front window that looked out across the Courthouse yard. "Then take the street that exits off the northwest corner. There," she pointed with the book she held in her hand. "Follow that street until you see the arches on your left."

"Thanks."

"No problem. Is there anything else I can help you with?"

Alfie hesitated. She was here on business but books were her weakness and book stores were her sanctuary.

"Do you have a section on African-American literature?"

"Yes," the young lady smiled. "A very extensive one. It's upstairs. I'll show you."

She put the books down and moved toward the staircase. "We also have a small cafe upstairs. Would you like some coffee, or maybe some herbal tea?"

"Coffee would be nice."

"I'll get you a cup. How do you like it?"

"Black. No sugar."

Alfie browsed through the shelves, pleased with the decisions that faced her. She measured a bookstore by its ability to present the dilemma of too many selections, a pleasant confusion that required careful deliberation in order not to destroy her personal budget.

She sipped her coffee as she studied the many autographed photographs on the wall, a pantheon of the state's literary deities. How could a state with a reputation of being one of the more illiterate seem to produce the greatest writers?

She strolled out onto the balcony and gazed onto the sidewalks below. There was something about the town she couldn't describe. Quaint? Not exactly. Comfortable? Yes. That was the word for it. It was a comfortable town that imparted a sense of familiarity. Her inner voice confirmed her feelings; there was no inordinate amount of danger here. This was a far cry from what she'd expected.

What a kick, she thought. She had been prejudiced about a town being prejudiced.

Alfie showed her credentials to the chief of security, a trim man with gray hair and blue eyes, who's last name was Harrison. When she explained the purpose of her visit, Captain Harrison produced a typewritten report from a stack of papers on his desk pertaining to the incident at the Tri Omega sorority house.

The report was brief and not very helpful. The driver of the delivery truck had never seen who hit him. The cook, an older lady named Rose O'Hanlon, had been too distraught to remember much of the details. The only member of the sorority to see the intruders, Deborah Vuncannon, had seemed so confused during questioning by the chief that he had given up on taking a statement after only a modest attempt at interrogating her. With little to go on, Chief Security Officer Harrison had informed the local police department of the incident and doubled the patrols along sorority row.

Alfie sat in his office as she flipped the pages of the report. "What is your impression of this, Chief Harrison?" It was her habit to maintain formalities unless told otherwise. She was, after all, an uninvited guest in his jurisdiction.

"Hard to pigeonhole." He spoke in a chopped manner as he sat behind his desk with his fingers interlocked in front of his face and slowly swiveled the seat of his chair from side to side. "A little too serious to be your average fraternity prank. The assault on the driver. The hijacking of the truck. The forced constraint of the cook in the back of the truck could be construed as kidnapping. But what was the purpose? Both were released. Nothing was stolen from the sorority house. An elaborate attempt was made to gain entry into the house. It succeeded but then the perpetrator stops and leaves. It doesn't make sense. The city police, the sheriff's department and the Highway Patrol are investigating. There is some talk about asking for the FBI for assistance considering the possible kidnapping charges, but I'm not sure the University wants that much publicity about the incident.

"This Deborah Vuncannon. She's the student that saw the intruder?"

"Yes. She said she saw him on the second floor. When she screamed, he turned and ran. She couldn't give a good description."

"Would you mind if I spoke with her?"

234

"Not at all." He reached forward on his desk and pushed a button on his intercom.

"I would like to ask one more favor," she said as a secretary appeared at the door.

"What is that?"

"Would you contact the Registrar's office and see if you can arrange for me to look at a couple of student records before I go to the sorority house?"

"Records? Have I missed something?"

"No. It's just a hunch."

A puzzled look crossed his face for a moment but then disappeared. "I can have that approved. No problem. They will be expecting you by the time you arrive." He nodded to the secretary. "I'll have one of my officers escort you."

"That won't be necessary," she said.

"Are you sure?"

"I appreciate the offer but I don't think I'll have any problem."

He shrugged his shoulders. "Let me know if you find anything."

"I will." She stood and thanked him as she left.

Alfie hesitated at the door of the Tri Omega house. Should she knock or just walk in? Wasn't it just like a dormitory? She had decided to open it herself when the door pulled back and a young coed stepped from the house. She froze when she saw the policewoman.

"Oh. Can I help you?"

Alfie showed her badge. "Is Rose O'Hanlon here? I would like to speak with her."

"I'm sorry. She's taken a couple of weeks vacation. She's gone to see her sister in Texas, I think."

"What about Deborah Vuncannon? Is she here?"

The girl hesitated for a moment then opened the door further.

"Upstairs" she pointed. "You'll find her in the sunroom. Third floor at the back of the house. Good luck," she said with a grin.

Alfie moved past her and up the stairs as she wondered about the girl's last comment.

Deborah sat in a lounge chair wrapped in a long pale yellow terry cloth robe. She held a textbook propped on her knees and used a yellow felt tip marker to underline a paragraph. She jumped when she realized Alfie was standing beside her.

"Hello, Deborah. Can I call you Debbie?" Alfie tried to give her most sincere smile.

Debbie removed her glasses and slipped them into the pocket of her robe.

"Hi," she drawled in a high voice. She didn't know who this stranger was but she wasn't taking any chances. Her uncertainty vanished quickly when Alfie flashed open her badge case. "My name is Alfrieda Storey. You can call me Alfie. I would like to ask you some questions, if you don't mind me interrupting your studies."

"What, this?" Debbie said as she let the book drop to the floor beside her. "It's not mine. Somebody left it here. I was just glancing through it. Can you believe how hard some of these courses are? It makes me glad I'm just a home economics major. I would be lost if I had to . . ."

"Cut the crap, sister," Alfie snapped.

"What?" The harshness of the policewoman's words brought Debbie's voice down to it's natural tone.

"Don't try to shine me. I know all about you. You are a straight A student. You're going to graduate with honors this spring with a bachelor's degree in economics."

Their eyes locked for a moment. When Debbie finally looked away, Alfie smiled and walked over to the edge of the sun room to gaze out across the campus. Between two buildings she could see the wind whip the flag on a distant flag pole. A few drops of rain began to fall against the glass.

"I hate this weather. Sunny one day, rainy the next. Warm, then cold, then warm again. I never know how to dress."

"You want to talk about the weather?"

"No, I want to talk to you about Riley," she said.

"Who?"

Alfie remained at the glass with her back to Debbie as she surveyed the buildings. Something caught her eye, distracted her as she said, "Riley Stevens, the girl you roomed with when you were a freshman."

Debbie lowered her head in defeat.

"It's important that I talk with her, Debbie. I can help her. She doesn't need to be out there without police protection. They've tried once. They will try again. This isn't a game for amateurs. You need to tell me where she is."

"She's not here. You can search the house if you want."

236

"I'm sure she isn't here. She's too smart to stay in one place. But you need to tell me where . . ." Alfie's voice trailed off. She broke into a smile and turned to leave the room.

"Thanks, Debbie. I appreciate your time," she said.

Before Debbie could move, the policewoman was gone. Debbie stood up and looked out the window from the spot where Alfie had stood. When she realized what Alfie had seen, she ran to her room to call Riley. She had to warn her before the policewoman reached her.

Alfie Storey ran down the stairwell two steps at a time and exited the sorority house from the same service entrance Hubbard had once entered. Outside, she glanced up at the sunroom to orient herself, then looked for the building she had seen from the third floor. Her view was obscured by the limbs of two large oak trees and a low, ivy-covered brick wall at the edge of the backyard.

She rushed up the slope, cursing as her feet slipped on the wet grass. She circled the brick wall and stopped at the edge of the parking lot to catch her breath.

A small red sports car pulled up to the curb and parked. Alfie walked over as the driver, a slim brunette with perfect hair and a perfect smile, emerged from the car and fumbled with an umbrella as she tried to hold a text and two notebooks under her elbow.

Alfie reached her just in time to catch the books before they slipped to the ground.

"Thanks," the girl said. "Terrible weather, isn't it."

"Yes. Could you help me?" Alfie asked. "This is my first time on campus and I don't know my way around. What is that building?"

The girl looked where Alfie pointed.

"The large one with the whitewashed brick?" she asked.

"No. The smaller one just behind it."

"Oh. That's the Pike house," the girl answered.

"Is that a sorority?"

"No. A fraternity."

"Fraternity?" Alfie said. "Thanks," she added as she headed to the Pike house. As she approached the fraternity house her suspicions were confirmed. From the advantage of the sunroom she had seen someone on the roof of the building. A lone figure walked from corner to corner on the flat decking, occasionally stopping to peer over the side of the guard rail along the edge.

237

Alfie's attention had focused on the young man when she first saw him while casually scanning the campus from the warmth and security of the sunroom. Why in the world was someone on the roof on a cold, windy day? Why didn't he go inside when the rain started? The answer came to Alfie immediately.

Because he was a lookout, a sentry to warn against unwanted visitors.

Because Riley Stevens was inside.

As she stepped into the yard of the Pike house she saw a young man tilted back on a stool by the front door. A blue and red toboggan was pulled down to his eyebrows. He wore a thick orange insulated hunting jacket and matching gloves. He sat propped against the wall as he blew streams of frost up into the air with his breath, trying to blow smoke rings without the benefit of a cigarette.

"Hello," Alfie announced herself as she stood on the steps.

Startled, the young man brought the front legs of the stool down with a clatter.

"Uh, hello," he said. He looked around to see if anyone else was present.

"Are you bored with guard duty," the policewoman asked pleasantly.

The young man fumbled for a response. "I'm, uh, just sitting here. That's all."

Alfie smiled at the lie and walked up the steps onto the porch. She reached into her jacket for her badge and showed it to him.

"It's alright," she said. "I'm here to help. Debbie told me where to find Riley. I need to speak with her now."

The confusion brought a slight grimace to the young man's face. "I don't know. I'm just a pledge. Let me let you speak to Lord Jim." He darted to the door and slipped inside, slamming the door shut behind him.

"Lord Jim?" Alfie asked herself.

The door opened and a young man stepped out. He looked to be older than the other college students she had seen on campus. He had a full build and a business-like attitude with strong hazel eyes full of confidence that looked out from beneath the brim of a baseball cap.

"Hello. I'm Jim," he said.

"Lord Jim?"

"Just a nickname. Can I help you?"

She held up her badge. "I'm Lieutenant Alfreida Storey, Jackson Police Department. I would like to talk with Riley Stevens."

"What makes you think she's here?"

"A sentry on the roof? A sentry at the front door? Come on, who do you think you're fooling?"

He maintained a carefully neutral expression on his face as he spoke. "Oh, them? That's just something they do as pledges. It's part of their initiation."

"I don't buy that," she said.

"And I don't buy that," he pointed to her ID.

"My shield?"

"You could have bought that badge anywhere. You could be an imposter. Why, just the other day someone posing as a delivery man forced his way into one of the sorority houses."

Alfie struggled not to lose her patience. She paused before she spoke and took a deep breath. In a calm voice she said, "I hope you realize how serious this matter is. I could arrest you for interfering with a police investigation."

"Lady, just because you speak Latin, it doesn't mean you're the Pope. This is private property, under the supervision of the university. I don't care who or what you are. You can't come in unless I invite you, or you have an official of the University approve your inspection of the premises."

He reached behind him and pounded on the door with his fist. Immediately a group of five men filed out of the house, lined up on each side of their leader, and presented Alfie with a wall of muscles and frowns.

"Are you threatening me?"

"No," he said. "I'm refusing you permission to enter our house." He folded his arms across his chest in an exaggerated manner for emphasis.

"I could have the chief of campus security here with me in fifteen minutes," she threatened.

"And by the time you returned this house would be empty," Jim shot back at her.

Alfie grunted in frustration. She knew that Riley Stevens was inside. And possibly Duncan. She also knew that the minute she stepped away from the fraternity house that they would both vanish, spirited away by the fraternity members to disappear in any number of directions. She wanted to scream.

Lord Jim had won the standoff and both he and the policewoman knew it. They were both surprised when a voice called down from a second floor window.

"It's alright, Jim. Let her in."

Alfie looked up to see Riley leaning from the window, her hair hidden beneath a baseball cap that sat low on her forehead.

"Are you sure?" Jim asked.

"Yes. Let her in. We need to talk."

Without a glance at the policewoman, Jim turned and walked into the house, leaving the door open behind him for Alfie to follow.

Chapter Thirty Four

Centuries ago, long before native Americans arrived to settle in the southeastern part of the country, the eastern wood buffalo migrated along a path that ran diagonally across what is now the states of Mississippi and Tennessee. Generations of the animals followed this course from the Mississippi River to the rich summer feeding grounds of Kentucky and points farther north. The trough their hooves cut in the earth was already deep when the first moccasin tread upon the dusty path. The Europeans soon followed and named the pathway the Natchez Trace after the trading post at its southern terminus.

In its time, the Natchez Trace was a major trade route to the frontier. Boatmen from the Ohio and the Mississippi floated down the river, sold their wares, then followed the Natchez Trace north to their houses, careful to travel in groups to discourage the highwaymen and robbers that hid along the way. Adventurous Tennesseans used the Trace on their way to Texas and the Alamo. Meriweather Lewis, of Lewis and Clark fame, had survived the dangers of his expedition in the Northwest territories only to find an end to his wanderings when he was mysteriously murdered along the Natchez Trace.

Lined with bandits and highwaymen, crime flourished along the isolated stretches of the frontier roadway. The danger involved with travel along the Natchez Trace earned the old Indian path a new title -- The Devil's Backbone.

That thought crossed Duncan's mind as he drove south on the Natchez Trace shortly before midnight. He had used the same roadway a few weeks earlier to reach Barrett's funeral without a second thought, the same route that tonight took on an air of menace.

A narrow grass right of way on each side of the road was delineated by an abrupt, high wall of trees, vines, and brush that gave a tight, closed feeling. The thick canopy of limbs that stretched above him blocked out the dark night sky and formed a low roof to the tunnel of trees.

The reflected eyes of a predator stared out of the darkness as the headlights swept around a curve. Orange-red eyes blinked and shadows flickered between the knobby projection of the bald cypress trees that rose up out of the dark, stagnant water of the bayous that Duncan passed.

But the sense of isolation also gave Duncan a sense of safety. The Natchez Trace Parkway was not used much by the locals because, as a National Parkway, access roads were restricted and low speed limits were strictly enforced. The limited access made short trips difficult for people who lived in the communities along the Trace, forcing most of the local residents to use other roads. The Trace was a highway designed for the leisurely pace of sightseers and tourists and not one to be regularly traveled by Jeter's men. Duncan took great care not to exceed the speed limit. He just hoped that the Park Rangers did not have Riley's tag number on their lookout sheets.

Soon a sign appeared in the distance that said "River Overlook - 1 mile." He checked his watch as he turned into the rest area and held his breath as he scanned the parking lot for other cars. There were none. Maybe his luck was changing.

The car rolled to a stop at the edge of the parking lot that was set on a bluff of the Pearl River. The thick brown water filled the banks of the river as it approached the overlook where it then turned south at a right angle. A counter-current split off from the main stream to swirl back to the north and feed a bayou filled with cypress and lily pads.

He switched off the lights and waited for his eyes to adjust to the dark. After a few minutes he stepped out of the car and surveyed the parking lot. A light mist began to fall that dampened the fecund smell of fish, rotting vegetation, and mud churned up from the river bottom by the currents swollen with the heavy winter rains. Satisfied that he was alone, he returned to the car and flicked the headlights on and off in a quick series of flashes.

The high beams reached the opposite bank of the river in a soft glow diffused by the thickening mist. He paused, then flicked the lights several more times before cutting them off. There was no response. He reached down to send the code again when he saw the flashlight. A small strip of white sand had been deposited in the bend of the river. From the woods above came a slight flickering that mimicked the car's headlights. A moment later he heard the coughing sound of an outboard motor being cranked.

Jay was coming in his boat.

Duncan moved quickly. He stripped off his coat and rolled his left sleeve up above his elbow. He took his belt and fashioned it around his biceps as a tourniquet, pulling it tight and holding it with his teeth. From the coat pocket he

242

produced two insulin syringes that he had taken from Mother Spight's medicine cabinet.

He paused to check the parking lot one more time before he turned on the car's inner lights. As he pumped his fist, the veins in his arm began to bulge. In the dim glow he found the vein he wanted in the fold of his arm. With a twinge of pain, he slipped the needle into the distended blood vessel. Next came the tricky part. Drawing blood with a syringe using only one hand was difficult. It was made worse by the fact that the small bore needle of an insulin syringe wasn't designed for this purpose; the blood did not flow freely into the syringe. Duncan kept the body of the syringe gripped tight with his outside three fingers while trying to inch the plunger out with his thumb and forefinger. The burgundy fluid, almost black in the dim light, spurted into the syringe. When it was filled he repeated the procedure with the other syringe.

Through the open window of the car the sound of the boat grew louder. Duncan opened the door of the car. Taking the syringes, he squirted his fingers and hands with fresh blood. With careful thought, he then placed his blood-stained handprints around the car -- one on the dashboard, the steering wheel, and several along the door. He used the seat cushion to rub off the excess blood from his hands. This accomplished, he stepped out of the car and donned his jacket. He retrieved the revolver from under the car seat, put it in his pocket, and eased down the slope to the river.

He no longer heard the boat's motor. The only sound that greeted him was the rhythmic lapping of the water against the shore. He scanned the water as he strained to hear evidence of Jay's presence.

Suddenly a thought struck him. What if Jeter's men had followed Jay? Or had come across Jay as he waited for Duncan? What if the signal had not come from Jay but from Jeter's men? They could have already landed and be sneaking up on him in the gloom.

Duncan tried to control his edginess. He turned on the small flashlight he held in his hand and swept the area with it, but the weak beam illuminated little but the thick mist. He quickly extinguished it when he realized the flashlight only served as a target.

Beads of sweat appeared on his lips.

"Jay?" he whispered.

"Jay!" he hissed louder and waited for a response. When none came he pulled the pistol from his coat and eased the hammer back.

A faint sound came from the water, the sound of water slapping against the metal hull of a boat. A voice in his head told him to run back to the car. Instead, he flipped the flashlight on again and pointed the beam in the direction of the sound.

"Jay. Is that you?"

The bow of a boat emerged from the gloom, a dark figure crouched in the front, as the mist divided to reveal the familiar outline of Jay Falkner drifting toward the shore.

"My dog is missing. Have you seen it? It has three heads," Jay said.

"Country boys aren't supposed to be literate."

"I like playing against type."

"I could have shot you," Duncan said as he slipped the pistol into his coat pocket.

"Good to see you too, old buddy," Jay answered as the boat crunched into the soil on the side of the river and he stepped onto shore.

Duncan shook his head and gave Jay a hard look that was lost in the darkness. He tossed the empty syringes into the current, then squatted down by the water's edge. By the beam of Jay's lights he scrubbed the remaining blood from his hands.

"Do you have the gloves?"

Jay produced two pair and gave one to Duncan.

"Put yours on and follow me," he said as he turned and scurried up the embankment.

Duncan started the engine and eased the car up to the edge of the parking lot. After several tries, and with Jay's added weight on the trunk of the car to improve traction, the front wheels of the car jumped over the concrete lip of the parking area onto the grass. When the back tires followed with a bounce, Duncan jumped out. The car rolled down the slope and splashed into the river, coming to rest halfway submerged. Without pausing to admire their work, the two ran to the boat and pushed out onto the water as the abandoned car hissed and gurgled in the background. The mist quickly enveloped them as they floated downstream.

Chapter Thirty Five

Police lieutenant Alfrieda Storey projected a dark mood that permeated the squad room. She bristled and glared at anyone who dared approach her desk. Even David, who loved to provoke her when she was in a foul temper, kept his distance.

She sat with a shoe in one hand and a wad of tissue paper in the other as she scraped mud from her shoe into the wastebasket, a souvenir from the morning spent on the river waiting for the wrecker to pull Riley Steven's car from the water. She knew Duncan Russthorne had been in possession of the car. Blood had been found throughout the vehicle but no body had been found. The newspaper would report the next day that foul play was suspected in the young doctor's disappearance.

It had been her duty to break the news to Riley. Alfie had driven to Riley's apartment adjacent to the medical center where Riley was kept under watch -- one policeman on guard at her front door and a police car on duty at the curb outside. She hated this part of her job. She always felt inadequate when she had to deliver bad news.

So now, mumbling and cursing, she sat at her desk as she attacked the dried clay that had engulfed her shoe when she had slipped into a soggy hole at the river's edge.

She hated that she had ruined another pair of good leather shoes. She hated to be the bearer of bad tidings. And she hated to be taken for a fool.

There had been something in the way Riley had responded to the news. Alfie had seen a true reaction too many times in the past, more times than she cared to remember. It was almost always the same: the look of disbelief followed by the struggle to comprehend, the tears and sobs of pain and loss, and, finally, Alfie's futile search for words of consolation.

Riley's performance had been superb. She had the part down pat but for one detail -- her hands. Her hands had betrayed her. Alfie had seen fists clenched in frustration and knuckles stretched white in rage and shock. Riley's hands had been too relaxed, too loose and graceful as she dabbed her eyes with a tissue.

Alfie suspected the truth. Riley had not been surprised; she had known what to expect when Alfie called. Duncan had planned his disappearance and had informed her, perhaps just before Alfie's appearance at the fraternity house. Why else had she come out of hiding so easily?

As she labored with her shoes, Alfie attacked a new problem. What was Duncan Russthorne's next move?

That afternoon a bank of fog hung suspended between the dark marble-smooth surface of the river and the ghostly outline of the trees that loomed over the water on the opposite side of the Pearl River. A great blue heron unfolded its wings and slowly launched itself into the air from where it stood in a cluster of lily pads. The bird glided in a wide arc over the leaden water and into a black, wet grove of cypress trees.

The two men walked up and down the path from the cabin as they loaded the boat.

"A cold front is coming. A real polar bear, supposed to reach record lows," Jay said as he studied the sky.

Jay stuffed a thick sleeping bag beside a styrofoam cooler and stepped back to take an inventory of the boat. Satisfied that they had thought of everything, he turned to inspect Duncan. Duncan wore an old khaki work shirt beneath a camouflage jacket. His jeans were stained with grease and had a small tear in the left knee that showed the white ribbed cloth of long insulated underwear. His work boots were scuffed and dirty.

Jay pointed at Duncan's hands. "Too clean," he observed.

Duncan looked at his fingernails. He stooped and dug his fingers into the clay of the river bank and rubbed the dirt into his hands.

"Do you have a fishing license?"

"No. I haven't needed one since I entered medical school."

Jay took one of the fishing rods out of the boat.

"I would hate for you to be arrested by a game warden after all you've been through," he said as he placed an extra gas canister in the boat.

"Ready?"

"Let's go."

Jay stepped into the stern of the boat. Duncan used a wooden oar to push out into the stream. When he had the boat pointed downstream, Jay started the motor smoothly with the first pull of the rope. The nose of the boat rose as the prop churned the water, and the boat began to pick up speed.

Just before sundown they reached an area where the river broadened as it opened into the reservoir. The boat glided down a narrow channel surrounded on both sides by the skeletons of half-submerged trees, their trunks stripped of their bark by the elements. Woodpecker holes pocked the bleached shafts of timber, and broken limbs projected from the gray water like the grasping fingers of a drowning man. To the west, the clouds broke and a band of sky glowed fiery orange. The temperature had dropped perceptibly in the last two hours. Duncan reached under his seat and removed a thermos. He first poured a cup of steaming coffee for Jay and handed it to him; then poured one for himself and turned to look at the distant shore. On the horizon, lights began to appear as the daylight faded. Jay spoke but the words were lost between the sound of the motor and the rush of wind in his ears. As Duncan turned to look at him, Jay pointed across the lake to a cluster of lights by the spillway that was their destination. Duncan nodded that he understood.

The sky had been dark for more than an hour when Jay cut the motor and let the boat glide to a halt at the boat ramp by the spillway. Now came the hard part -- the portage of the boat. The two men dragged the boat up the concrete ramp until they were clear of the water. Jay went to work unbolting the outboard motor from the frame. When he was finished, they each grabbed one end of the motor, thankful that traffic was light along the road that ran along the crest of the spillway.

They scuttled across the road with the heavy metal motor between them, their backs bent under the weight. They returned to do the same with the boat. Duncan welcomed the exercise. His legs were stiff from the hours spent in the boat, and the chill factor from the wind had cut through his clothes and left him shivering. A tingle of warmth returned to his fingers and toes as they worked, but he still stamped his feet and beat his arms as Jay finished bolting the motor into place.

"Lucky there is no one fishing the spillway tonight," Duncan said through chattering teeth.

"Not in this weather," Jay said. When he was finished tightening the bolts, he pulled the stainless steel thermos from his knapsack and poured another cup of coffee for them both. He handed Duncan a cup, set his on a rock, and opened the cooler with the food.

"I think the outside temperature is colder than inside the cooler."

He offered a sandwich to Duncan but he refused.

"Eat it," Jay commanded. "You'll need the energy later. You've a long night ahead of you."

As Duncan took the sandwich and began to unwrap the cellophane, they sat on one of the large granite boulders used for erosion control along the spillway.

"The river is high," Duncan observed.

"There has been a lot of rain this spring," Jay said, "but that's good. The river hasn't been dredged and cleared below the spillway lately. If the water was low we would have to drag the boat over a lot of fallen trees. With the river high, we should make good time."

Duncan took another bite of his sandwich and listened to the roar of the water churning down the spillway. Jay devoured his food in four huge bites, wadded up the wrapper, and threw it into the boat. He downed his coffee in two big gulps before turning to his friend.

"So. What's the plan? Or don't you trust me?"

Duncan gave his friend a look of irritation.

"Okay. I know you trust me. It's just that you are so damn tight-lipped."

"I didn't want to bore you with my problems."

"Your problems aren't boring."

"I should have said 'involve' instead of 'bore.' I didn't want to involve you in my problems."

Jay let out a deep laugh, stood up, shook his head, and laughed again.

"That was a stupid thing to say, wasn't it?" Duncan admitted.

"Yes, considering the degree to which I am already involved."

Duncan used the flashlight to read his wristwatch. "We had better go."

"Are you going to tell me the whole story?" Jay asked.

"Sure, Jay. I'll tell you everything," he said as he bent down to grab hold of the boat. "But let's get back on the water first. We can talk on the way downriver."

With a grunt, the two men dragged the boat and motor the short remaining distance to the river.

Riley tightened the laces to her running shoes before she stood up from the sofa and checked her watch again. It was ten minutes after nine. Most of the students would be gone from the dental school by now. The time had come for her to act.

She crossed over to the door and peered through the spy-hole. The policeman was still there, leaning against the wall to one side of the door. In his hand he held a paperback book opened halfway and folded back cover to cover. When he heard a door open downstairs, he lowered the book and looked over the banister down into the stairwell. Satisfied with what he saw, he returned to his book. She hoped that the book was a good sign. Maybe her guard would be flexible enough to grant the favor she was about to request. She offered up a quick prayer and opened the door.

He lowered the book upon hearing her door open. He was young and quick to smile with deep dimples that marked his cheeks. His sharp chin had a smaller dimple in the center.

"Hello, officer . . ." she crooked her neck to one side as she tried to read his name tag.

"Lipford. Just call me Don."

"Thanks, Don. I'm Riley," she said as she offered her hand. He accepted it with a quick, hard shake.

"I need a favor. I really need the notebooks that I left at school."

"I'm sorry, ma'am, but I can't let you leave."

"No. I'm not asking you to let me go alone. Or for you to go for me. I was wondering if you could perhaps escort me to the school."

"Can't you call someone, a friend, maybe? Have them bring your notes to you?"

"I've tried. I can't reach anyone that I trust with the combination to my locker."

"It might not be safe for you to leave your apartment."

"Couldn't you take me to the school in the police car you have outside. You would be there to guard me and it's only a block away. It wouldn't take ten minutes and I really need those notes," she pleaded.

A look of indecision covered his face. "Couldn't you try calling your friends again?"

She looked at her watch. "I've tried all evening. Security will lock everything down at the school in a few minutes and then no one will be able to gain entrance until the morning."

He struggled with the decision.

"Please," she implored.

He studied her face for a moment and then gave in.

"I hate it when people beg," he said. "I'm a sucker for begging."

"Oh, thank you . . ."

"But stay close." He pointed his finger at her. "At the first sign of trouble you do exactly what I say. Got it?"

"Got it!" She saluted.

He shook his head and motioned for her to follow as he walked down the stairs.

The river below the spillway was a series of narrow curves. Duncan kneeled in the front of the boat with the flashlight and used the beam of light to point out submerged logs as Jay steered. After the boat passed under a bridge, the river took a sharp turn to the west. A few minutes later Jay killed the motor and handed Duncan an oar. Soon they began to hear the distant noise of traffic punctuated by the unmistakable rumble of an occasional heavy truck. Jay steered the boat toward a small sandy patch of shore below a tree-covered embankment.

"We are now approximately one hundred yards from the seventh tee of Riverside Golf Club. If it were July and we had a baseball glove, we could shag golf balls hit by the golfers who have a bad slice in their swing," he said.

Jay pointed to a thicket on the opposite shore. "I'll wait across the river. There is a place I can hide the boat and make a fire without being seen. I'll be here when you get back."

Duncan tested the firmness of the ground before he stepped out of the boat.

"Give me until midnight tomorrow. If I'm not back by then . . ." his voice trailed off, then he ended the sentence with a shrug.

"That means you're in police custody."

"If I'm lucky. If I'm unlucky, then either the El AZIWA or the Redneck Mafia got to me first."

"Should I go to the police? Tell them the story you just told me? Or should I pay a visit to Barrett's murderer?"

"Go to the police, Jay. Just to put the record straight."

"And if the police can't do anything?"

"Does it matter what I say?" he asked.

Jay broke into a grin. "No," he said firmly.

Duncan studied the embankment. When he turned to clasp his friend's hand, Jay had pushed off into the current with his oar.

"Good luck," Jay's voice came floating towards him through the darkness.

Duncan used the roots and branches that projected from the steep river bank as handholds as he scrambled and pulled himself up to the edge of the golf course. He lay in the weeds and surveyed the area. On the far side of the golf course ran four lanes of interstate highway. On the other side of the highway began the grounds for the medical center. He could hear the soft distant swish of tires on asphalt, but the glow of street lights from the highway was too weak to cast shadows across the fairways. Closer still was the golf course clubhouse. The cluster of lights around the building and the adjacent parking area painted the grassy lanes with a faint silver glow. Duncan struck out across the golf course in a cautious lope.

He crossed the golf course without incident, went up and over an access road, and found cover in the drainage ditch that ran parallel to the interstate. Breathing hard, he listened to the flow of vehicles above him; periods of quiet alternated with the occasional rush of cars. When the traffic eased, he rose and confidently walked up to the shoulder of the road. He pulled his cap down lower upon his brow in the glare of the oncoming headlights and waited for a break in the northbound traffic. When it came, he calmly walked across the asphalt, trying to act as if it were normal for him to spend his nights walking across interstate highways. He crossed the median and the southbound lanes and crouched in the grass near the drainage ditch on the west side of the highway.

His back to the highway, he studied his next obstacle. The highway skirted the base of the plateau that formed the grounds of the medical center. Ahead of him was an eighty yard slope of hill that rose before him at a forty five degree angle, resembling the inside bowl of a football stadium without the steps. At the top was a high wire mesh fence. At regular intervals along the fence hung large white signs with bold lettering. They read:

NO TRESPASSING
RESTRICTED ACCESS
PROPERTY OF THE UNIVERSITY OF MISSISSIPPI
MEDICAL CENTER

He waited patiently for a pause in the traffic. Minutes passed before no headlights appeared in the distance and the road was again dark.

Duncan darted up the hill in a surge of energy, the sides of his boots biting into the wet turf as his legs pumped and churned. He slipped, twice, where erosion had exposed the slick clay, but he dug his fingers and toes into the ground and pulled himself up, spurred by the sound of approaching traffic in the distance. He pushed himself hard, careful not to let his momentum waver as he neared the top of the slope. His thighs burned and the cold air cut his lungs as he gasped for breath. He hit the fence at full speed, threw himself onto the wire mesh with a leap, and scrambled up the fence. With a twist, he swung his feet over the top rail and allowed his momentum to pull his body across. He fell to the ground and rolled against the fence to look down as the approaching traffic sped past into the dark night without slowing.

"The side door is the only entrance that is open after six p.m." From her position in the back seat, Riley instructed the officer driving as Lipford rode shotgun. Riley waited for the officer to unlock the door after the car glided to a halt.

"I'll be right back."

"Unh - unh," Lipford warned. "I have to go with you."

"It's really not necessary," she protested. "The building has security guards."

"I'm going with you," he said firmly. "Wait right here," he instructed his partner before he turned and walked in front of Riley to the ground floor entrance of the Dental school.

The security guard had seen the pair approaching and opened the door.

"Is there a problem?" the guard asked.

Officer Lipford tilted his head toward Riley. "She's had threats against her. My partner and I are on her watch detail for a few days. She needs to retrieve a notebook from her locker."

Riley produced her student I.D. The guard inspected it and pointed to the check-in sheet. Riley wrote down her name and the time of admission.

"Are there many people here?" the policeman asked.

"None, except for myself and the other security guard. He's making his rounds of the building now. Oh, I almost forgot. One of the oral surgeons is working late. He's in his office on the second floor."

"Nobody's here?" Riley asked. "None of the students are in the tech lab?"

"Nope," the guard answered. "We've cleared the lab already. It's time for the ten o'clock lockdown. You had better hurry."

The guard turned to the officer. "No students are allowed in the building after ten p.m.," he explained as Riley started down the hallway.

"Wait up," the policeman called after her.

She wheeled about, hands on her hips, a look of disgust on her face.

"Are you planning to follow me into the women's locker room?"

Lipford stopped, torn between duty and propriety.

"Don't worry about her. No one is here. The building is secured," the security officer assured him.

"Go." The policeman waved her on. "Five minutes!" he yelled after her as she turned the corner.

"No one can get in?" he asked the guard again.

"No way. All the doors have been checked. No one can enter the building and there are only two ways to exit, this door and the second floor exit into the medical school."

The policeman reacted with alarm. "I thought you said all doors were secured."

"Relax. The second floor exit has a press bar release that can only be activated from inside. You can walk out but you can't enter."

"Does she know about that exit?"

"I'm sure she does as long as she has been a student here. But if she does try to skip out on us we will know it." He tapped a lighted electronic panel on the wall with a knuckle. "She will break the door circuit, and this panel will light up. We can catch her before she reaches the other end of the skywalk." He pointed out the door to the elevated walkway that spanned the distance between the dental school, the library, and the medical school. "If she tries to use the skywalk, I can call the guard stationed at the other end and he can stop her."

The police officer looked at his watch as he leaned back against the wall by the entrance to wait, then looked at his watch again. "Five minutes," he told the guard. "Five minutes is all I will give her; ladies room or not."

As soon as Riley turned the corner, she broke into a run and sailed down the hall past the elevator to the wooden door marked "Women." She ran through the small restroom area, past a row of sinks, and opened the door to the locker area. She took a sharp left and ran past two rows of tall metal lockers painted orange and brown. At the corner of the room, she veered right and ran the length of the

253

lockers, the colors of the lockers blurring as she ran. She slid to an halt when she reached the back entrance to the locker area.

She had to exercise caution. If the security guard that was making his rounds caught her during her run up to the roof, Duncan would be stranded, and .... She pushed the thought from her mind and concentrated on her task.

She eased open the door, listened for a moment, slipped across to the stairwell door, opened it, and listened again for footsteps as she counted to ten. When her ear failed to detect any movement, she planted her right foot on the bottom step and peered upward into the dimly lit stairwell. Ahead of her rose five floors plus the stairs to the roof. She took a deep breath and lunged up the steps.

The woods that covered the eastern, undeveloped half of the medical center property were dense and pristine. Grandfather oaks spread their moss-covered limbs low to the ground. Hickory and walnut trees provided forage for the fat orange-gray fox squirrels that dwelled there. A deer was rumored to have found refuge in the park-like setting.

Officially, these woods were off limits to everyone, including students. Unofficially, school officials had asked security to turn a blind eye toward students who used the woods during the day as a peaceful retreat from the stress of their studies. The students and the security guards had an understanding; if the students didn't go out of the way to advertise their presence in the woods, security would not go out of it's way to enforce the restricted access rule. Students often strolled through the woods, enjoying the tranquillity of the grove. Some worked out their frustrations with jogging on several footpaths that had been worn in the forest floor. In the summer, the woods were a favorite retreat for picnics. Young couples had been known to conceal themselves behind the still-visible earthworks that had been constructed during the Civil War.

The policy changed at night. The security force had strict orders to allow no one in the woods after dark. Students caught breaking this ordinance were only given one warning. Those not associated with the medical center were immediately arrested for trespassing if caught on the grounds, night or day.

A luminous moon glowed through the bare limbs of the trees as Duncan made his way to the Dental school, following a path that coursed through the dark middle of the property. He silently crept from tree to tree, stooped to avoid a low-hanging branch, then stopped to listen. The woods were full of noise. The trees creaked, popped, and crackled as the grain of the wood sounded a protest to the freezing assault the ancient hardwoods experienced only once every generation.

Ahead of him the darkness thinned as the trunks of the trees were outlined by the lights from the dental school. To his right, a dark hump rose from the ground. It was the Crater, the name given to the largest of the dirt ramparts built over a century ago by Confederate soldiers. He climbed over the lips of the bowl and slid down into the center of the Crater. Duncan checked the luminous dial on his watch. It was almost ten o'clock. Riley had told him that the building closed down at ten. He would give the security guards another half hour to make their final rounds before he would make his move.

The security alarm system for the dental school was simple. If a door was opened after it had been secured for the night, a contact switch was broken and a corresponding light for that entrance would light up on the panel by the guard station on the ground floor. It was a simple but effective way to monitor the exits of the building. The system had a built-in oversight. No contact switch had been placed on the service exit to the roof.

Riley did not slow down when she reached the top floor. She continued up the stairway to the roof, reached the door, and hit the press bar release with her left hand. The cold night air poured in around her. She removed the number two lead pencil that she had tucked through her hair over her right ear and wedged it between the door and the door frame as she closed the door; the weight of the door snapped the wood with a crunch. She carefully checked her work. The door appeared to be shut but was not closed completely, the pencil creating enough of a space to keep the bolt mechanism from falling into a fully closed and locked position. When she was sure of her work, she turned and started her run downstairs.

"Five minutes," the policeman grumbled as he looked at his watch. "I told her five minutes."

"Maybe she had to use the john," the security guard said distractedly from his chair, his feet propped up on his desk by the entrance.

Lipford studied the security panel. "Are you sure this thing works?"

The guard gave him a hard look before he returned to his magazine.

"Where is the locker room?"

"Round the corner to the right." The guard pointed down the hallway. "The door is marked."

Chapter Thirty Six

Over a century earlier, men in tattered gray and butternut-brown uniforms had stood watch through the night in the same earthen fort where Duncan now lay hidden. The soldiers had waited and watched in vain. The area would be bypassed as the Union generals focused on more strategic centers. The grand defensive strategy of the South had failed against the invasion of numerically superior and better equipped forces.

Duncan knew that if he waited he would also fail. He had to act before all traces of Barrett's body disappeared, before all the evidence was destroyed. He hoped he wasn't too late.

Duncan had chosen the School of Dentistry as his point of entrance to the medical center because he knew it afforded the best chance of entering the complex undetected. The University Medical Center security force was the fourth largest police force in the state. Well-paid and well-trained, they took their job seriously. Access into the various buildings on campus was tightly controlled. But the School of Dentistry offered a way to enter without the required ID check. He would use the same entrance that the students used when they took their cigarette breaks -- the roof. Once inside, he hoped to blend in with the dozens of other people that roamed the halls in scrubs and white coats. He based his entire plan on one premise -- the mindset of the security guards was toward the prevention of unauthorized entry, not toward the scrutiny of personnel that were already in the medical center.

He looked over the edge of the Crater and studied the Dental School with a rock climber's eye. There was a feature to the building that had caught his attention before.

The building, built with a light yellow brick that had darkened with time, was of a Modernist design. The architect had sought to distinguish some of the basic components of the construction. From above, the School of Dentistry was a large square with two smaller squares on the east and west sides. The smaller squares were extensions that held enclosed stairways. To accentuate the stairway extensions, the architect had used a reveal, a recess of narrow glass windows where the smaller squares joined the main building. This groove ran from the ground to the roof. Duncan estimated it was two to three feet wide. It was almost like the Hoser, except the brick would provide a better surface for traction.

He rose from the Crater and crept to the edge of the woods, the border of which came to within twenty yards of the stairway extension. To the right of the extension was an emergency exit. A covered light above the door cast a circle of light across the sidewalk but left the end of the stairwell extension still hidden in shadows.

Duncan crouched behind the base of a large sycamore tree as he scanned the dark windows of the building for signs of movement. Riley had told him of the two security guards. He hoped they were at their post at the entrance on the other side of the building and not roaming the building. If one happened to be looking out the window . . .

He shrugged off the thought and darted across the open ground to the hedges at the base of the brick wall.

"Ms. Stevens," Officer Lipford called through the door of the ladies room. He paused for a moment before he called again. When there was no answer, he raised his knuckles to knock on the door. He struck the door once before it flew open and Riley ran out.

"Oh!" she blurted in surprise as she tried to stop.

"What's wrong? You're out of breath."

"Nothing," she said as she took in a deep breath. "Nothing's wrong. I was in the back of the locker room when I heard you call and I thought something might be wrong. That scared me," she gasped.

"Are you okay?"

"Yeah, sure. I found my notes." She held a spiralbound notebook up for him to see as she walked down the hallway toward the exit. She wanted to put some space between them until her breathing slowed to a more normal rate.

Duncan slipped into the recess on the dark side of the extension. He tested the traction of his boots against the wall. The mortar was not flush with the surface of brick -- a deep groove ran between each brick that allowed the toe end of his boot soles to grab the wall. He pushed against the opposing wall with his back, testing to see how well his healing wounds would take the pressure. He would have preferred a little more depth to work with, but it still felt good. He looked up to the top once more, then pressed his back and feet against the opposing brick surface and began his climb.

Progress was slow. The climb could not be rushed. He brought his feet up a brick at a time. With his hands behind his buttocks, he pressed hard against the brick as he scooted his body higher. He repeated the process over and over, using slow, precise movements. Plant the toes, press hard with the hands, and push the body higher as the knees unbent slightly while still maintaining pressure to keep the body wedged in the slot. He developed a steady rhythm and ascended at a careful pace. The window in the slot allowed him to check his progress as a band of concrete at regular intervals told him when he had reached another floor.

The first two floors passed without problem, but then Duncan's rate of ascent began to drop rapidly as the energy drained from his body. He quickly realized that he was not in the best shape for climbing. How long had it been since he had done any climbing? Ten months? A year? He chided himself. He should have known that jogging and weights would not maintain his climbing skills; different muscles were involved. His legs were beginning to burn and tremble, and his head began to pound; his injuries did not make the climb any easier.

He was tempted to hurry his climb. The fourth floor was approaching, and if he could scramble up the last two floors, move his legs just a little faster, he would not have to keep his muscles tensed as much. This would burn less energy and lessen the chance of a cramp, but to rush his movements would increase the chance of a slip. He had to remind himself that he was climbing free; there was no rope to stop his fall if he lost his grip.

He chose to go slowly. His legs were tired but still steady enough to go the distance to the top. He assured himself that he could last that long as he pushed himself up another six inches.

A concrete strip appeared in the corner of his field of vision. He had reached the fifth floor! A surge of energy swept through his body when he realized he was only one floor away from the top.

He pushed himself up past the floor of the fifth level. Almost immediately the elation he had felt gave way to a similar, but harsher, surge of fear. Out of the corner of his eyes he detected a movement in the stairwell! He instantly froze his position. Slowly, he turned his eyes toward the glass and strained to see through the dark window. He waited, but saw nothing. Just when he began to feel it was safe to continue his climb, something inside the stairwell moved again. A dim form took shape as it moved closer to the glass. Through the window, Duncan stared at a pair of shoes less than twelve inches away from his face.

Above the shoes were a pair of trouser cuffs. He slowly tilted his head as he followed the pants legs upward. He could not see a face, but he could see the dull glint of a large square metal buckle on a thick leather belt. Duncan suddenly realized that the silver points around the belt were not decorations but the tips of pistol cartridges. A security guard stood at the window in the stairwell only inches away from where Duncan, hidden in the shadows of the slot, clung to the side of the building.

Duncan's heart, already beating fast from the exertion, quickened its pace. He knew he couldn't advance, but he didn't know how long he could stay frozen in his present position. He could already detect a slight quiver in his legs as fatigue set in. He gently eased the pressure off of one leg as he increased it on the other. He alternated this action between his legs in an effort to keep both from locking into cramps.

"Move, dammit," he whispered to the guard. "You're supposed to be making rounds."

As if to answer him, the guard slowly raised his cup of coffee to his lips and took a drink, then lowered the cup and began to rock back and forth on his feet.

Duncan waited, his pulse pounding in his brain, and squeezed his eyes shut. When he opened them the guard was still there. He watched as the policeman leaned toward the glass to stare across the campus towards the Veterans' Administration Hospital in the distance. If the guard were to look down from where he stood, Duncan knew he would be discovered.

The frigid conditions had not bothered Duncan while he had been climbing, but now that he was immobile the cold began to soak into his body. Already his fingers and hands were numb from the exertion and his shoulders were beginning to weaken. His legs began to shake, both from the cold and from fatigue, a tightening sensation that Duncan knew was a prelude to cramps.

There was no way he could move up and not be seen. His only option was to return to the ground, but in his weakened condition Duncan doubted he had the strength to make it back down.

An image flashed through his mind, the image of a young man who had committed suicide by leaping from a highway overpass. The ambulance had brought the patient to the ER during Duncan's shift. He was D.O.A. At the time, Duncan had been surprised at the amount of damage that can occur from a fall of only thirty feet, and now Duncan was a lot higher up the wall than that. With luck, he might make it back to the third, or perhaps the second floor, before his legs gave out and he fell.

He peered down over his left shoulder as he tried to remember the locations of the hedges at the base of the building. There was a large holly to one side of the groove. If he felt himself slipping, if he had enough time, he could try to direct his fall. Landing in a holly bush would not be fun, but it would beat striking hard earth.

He took one last hopeful look at the guard before he began his descent. The interior of the stairwell was suddenly lighter. At first, Duncan thought he had been detected, that the guard had seen the shadow in the groove and had turned on his flashlight to inspect the unusual dark form below him. But the light came from the open stairwell door. Duncan caught a glimpse of the guard's back as he disappeared from view, the light decreasing as the door slowly swung shut.

The guard gone, Duncan slowly tested his arms and legs, then continued his climb to the top. He mumbled a prayer of thanks as he climbed. It was a deeply sincere prayer. The old saying was right, he thought, there are no atheists in foxholes; they can't be found clinging to the sides of tall buildings, either.

The sky opened up above him as he reached the roof. He hooked his right elbow over the parapet that crowned the roof and pushed himself out of the slot and over the top bricks with a final, painful push of his legs to land on the roof with a thud.

It had been close. His left leg had begun to cramp the last few feet of the climb. He was aware of traces of the nausea and dizziness that had accompanied his earlier bouts of vertigo. His legs ached and his body trembled. When he closed his eyes, the sky did not disappear, but was replaced by a different, pulsing, set of stars that spun into action against the backdrop of his eyelids. He lay lifeless on the roof of the building, the minutes passing before he did anything more than breathe. When the sweat on his face had cooled to a frosty rime, he rolled over onto his knees and stumbled to his feet. He trudged to the roof's access door and stepped inside as a blast of warm air rose up to greet him.

Chapter Thirty Seven

Deena rose from the bench in the short hall that connected the library to the crosswalk to peek around the corner. The crosswalk was empty. She was not surprised at the lack of activity. The School of Dentistry at one end of the crosswalk had closed at ten o'clock. The library had closed at the same hour. Now, fifteen minutes later, the staff exited the library building. The night watchman prepared to lock himself in as the last employee hurried out the door. Deena heard the tumbler click as the lock set.

She quickly returned to her bench and removed a notebook from her knapsack. Pulling a pen from the pocket of her scrub top, she made a deliberate effort to give the security guard the impression that she was a student who had finally found a quiet spot in which to study.

She occupied her time by writing Duncan's name over and over across the page.

On the ground floor of the School of Dentistry, Duncan eased open the door of the stairwell. Hearing no sound, he slipped across the hall to the men's locker room, eased open the door, and disappeared inside.

The men's locker room, a mirror image of the women's locker room, held four rows of metal lockers alternately painted orange and brown.

Duncan opened the first locker. It was empty. He quietly closed it and moved down several lockers to the next one that was unsecured. Inside were some small cardboard boxes, two thick textbooks on a narrow shelf, and a white clinic coat. He removed his thick hunting jacket and dropped it on the floor of the locker. When he tried on the clinic coat, he found the sleeves were a little short, but there was no time to worry about fashion. He removed his cap and placed it on the hook inside the locker door. He closed the locker door and then quickly reopened it. He had almost forgotten something very important. He retrieved a small brown paper bag from the right hand pocket of the discarded jacket and slipped it into his clinic coat.

261

As he closed the locker, he heard a toilet flush. Duncan turned and looked down the row of lockers to the restroom door. Almost immediately the door began to open. Duncan caught a glimpse of a blue uniform before he pressed himself against the end of the lockers and listened carefully for sounds of the guard's location. The tread of shoes could be heard as the guard strolled down the middle aisle between the lockers, heading toward the spot where Duncan stood. As soon as Duncan determined the guard's movements, he moved stealthily in the opposite direction, toward the restroom door, one soft step at a time, as he kept a row of lockers between himself and the guard.

His timing was perfect. He reached the corner just in time to see the officer turn toward the exit that Duncan had entered only moments before. When he heard the slight creak of the door hinge, Duncan gently opened the restroom door and slipped inside.

He ran past the sinks and into the hallway. Across from the elevator was the door to the central stairwell. He ran up the steps to the second floor. He didn't know the routine the guard followed during his rounds, but he knew he had little time in which to act. The longer he stayed in the dental school, the greater his chance of being detected.

He scanned the hallway on the second floor. To his left were the four glass double doors of the main entrance. He turned to his right toward the exit to the crosswalk. As he walked, he pulled the paper bag from his pocket and removed a spool of fishing monofilament and a two foot length of insulated electrical cord with alligator clips on each end.

He held one of the alligator clips in his mouth as he tied the fishing line to the middle of the electrical wire with a double knot. He tested the knot with a couple of firm tugs, then he began to strip several feet of fishing line from the spool.

The security system, in addition to the lack of a monitor switch on the access door to the roof, held another flaw that Duncan had realized in his telephone conversations with Riley. The system was designed to prevent unauthorized entrance, not unauthorized exits, from the crosswalk to the Medical Center. The metal contacts of the door's security system were not built into the wall but were mounted on the inner side of the door frame. This allowed Duncan to attach an alligator clip to the contact on the door frame. He clipped the other end of the wire to the small metal contact box on the door. He tested both with a slight pull on the wire. Satisfied that they would hold, he held his breath and opened the door just enough to allow him room to slide through. As he did, he carefully watched the wire to be sure that he did not open the door too wide and dislodge the clips.

Once through, he slipped the fishing line under the door and closed it. With his foot against the door, he pulled on the fishing line with a slowly increasing force. The alligator clips popped loose from the contacts and fell to the floor as Duncan continued to pull on the line.

The bottom of the door was sealed with a strip of grey rubber matting that had been secured to the floor. When the electric cord met the rubber strip it stopped. On the other side of the door, Duncan wound the monofilament around his hand several times for a better grip. As he pulled harder, a portion of the wire squeezed through the door seal until enough protruded for Duncan to bend down and grab the wire itself. By slowly twisting and pulling on the wire, one end popped through. He doubled his efforts, but the alligator clip on the other end of the wire was caught at an angle and jammed under the door so tightly that Duncan could not retrieve it. With one final effort, he pulled on the cord with all of his strength only to have the wire snap at the junction with the clip.

Duncan inspected the bare end of the copper wire. He hated to leave the clip behind, but he hoped he would be far away when it was discovered. He hastily rolled the fishing line onto the spool as he started down the crosswalk.

The glass walls of the crosswalk, supported by diagonal steel crossbeams, and the bright fluorescent lights above revealed his movement like an actor on a stage. He walked deliberately and with confidence. He could no longer hide; he would have to act calm and try to blend in to his surroundings.

The crosswalk was eerily quiet except for his padded footsteps. The sound from his shoes seemed amplified as the slight echoes reverberated down the tunnel. He checked his watch; he was almost an hour late.

His heart rose when he turned into the library hallway and saw her. She was bent over, head propped in her hands, her eyes halfway closed, but when she saw him she was instantly awake.

"Duncan!" She jumped when she saw him, then quickly turned to check the entrance of the library annex.

"Quick," she said as she picked up her knapsack and opened it. "Before the library guard comes back from his rounds." She handed him a surgical mask and head cap. Duncan quickly donned them. After he finished tying on the mask, he pulled it down to give the appearance of someone who had forgotten its presence following surgery; to wear it in place would have only attracted attention.

"You don't know how glad I was to hear your voice when you called the other night. I thought you were dead."

"Sorry for the scare, but I wanted people to think I was dead. I needed some breathing room."

She pulled a pair of scrub pants from the knapsack and handed them to Duncan. As he slipped them on over his pants, she removed her surgical foot coverings and offered them also.

"You'll need these to hide those ugly, Paul Bunyan boots you're wearing."

When he held her shoulder for balance, she took the opportunity to move closer to him.

"Deena," he said, a slight grimace flickering across his face. "Can we talk about this later?"

"No. No we can't," she said firmly. "That's been my problem; I've put things off for too long. I moan and groan about not having a life when all along it's been my fault. It's been *MY* fault. But when I heard you were missing, presumed dead, I realized how good I've become at delaying gratification. How I . . ."

"Deena," he interrupted, "I need to tell you something."

She waved him off with a hand.

"Oh, I know. I know you are seeing someone, that you're involved with that dental student. I just wanted to say . . . I just wanted to say . . ." Her eyes glistened with moisture.

"You're glad I'm not dead?" he offered.

"Yes." She sniffed and leaned in to give him a hug. "Can you teach me to be that eloquent with words?" she said with a soft laugh.

He squeezed her gently. "I'm glad I'm not dead, too, but I may not be able to say that for very long if we don't move it."

"Right," she agreed. She bent down to pick up her notes while Duncan peered around the corner to see if anyone was in the crosswalk.

"All clear. Let's go."

"Where? The morgue?"

"The morgue."

A guard making rounds nodded a perfunctory greeting to the pair as they reached the end of the crosswalk to the medical center. Duncan kept his head buried in an open notebook. Deena gave a polite smile. They both held their breath until they were safely around a corner.

The pair zigzagged through a series of turns until they reached the elevator. Deena pushed the button, but Duncan tugged at her sleeve without a word and walked past her to the stairway. Duncan hurried down the steps with Deena following close behind.

On the ground floor, Deena took the lead until they reached a corner where two hallways intersected.

He pointed to their left.

"Check out the E.R. We may be able to exit from there unnoticed if there's a lot of traffic."

"Are you sure you don't need any help?"

"I might. Meet me back here as soon as you can."

"How long will this take?"

"Until I find where Barrett's body is located."

"Good luck," she said as they separated.

At the morgue, the door to the autopsy room was ajar, the light from within casting a line across the dark hallway. Duncan approached the opening and looked inside. Cold air, heavy with the scent of ammonium sterilizing solution, flowed from within. A variety of stainless steel instruments, knives, retractors, drills, and bone saws, laid out in a precise and orderly fashion on the white counter-tops, glistened under the cool, antiseptic glow of the fluorescent lights. A scale used for weighing the various organs removed during the post-mortem hung to one side of the stainless steel autopsy table.

Duncan could hear movement on the other side of the door, a slight shuffling, the low humming of a deep voice that paused occasionally. Duncan gently pushed on the door. Through the opening he saw a dark hand at the end of a white shirt sleeve as it used a rag to polish the gutter that ran the length of the autopsy table. Another hand appeared holding a spray bottle that squirted a fine mist along the gutter as the other hand continued cleaning.

Duncan relaxed, took a deep breath, pushed open the door, and entered the room.

"Good morning," he gave a swift hello and a nod.

The man cleaning the autopsy table straightened himself. He was a big man with a broad nose that dominated his face, thick puffy eyelids, and short, salt-and-pepper hair. He nodded to Duncan and bent back down to his work. Duncan crossed the room to the inner office and tried the doorknob but the door was locked. He paused a moment, stepped back, then made an exaggerated show of searching his pockets.

"Damn," he muttered audibly as he turned to the janitor. "I came all this way and forgot my keys. Must have left them at home. Do you have a key to the office?"

The janitor slowly looked at Duncan. "Yes."

"Great! Could you unlock this for me?"

"No," he said and returned to his work.

Duncan thought for a moment before he spoke.

"Look, I've got to get some papers from the office. You said you had the key, didn't you?"

"Yes."

"Then open the door."

The janitor did not look up from his work. "No," he repeated. He looked closely at an area on the table, then worked the cloth with his thumb over the spot with a slow, deliberate motion.

"I am a physician on the staff here at the hospital," Duncan stressed as he pointed emphatically to his I.D. badge clipped to his clinic coat.

"I know. I've seen you around, but I'm not supposed to unlock the morgue office for anyone, anymore."

A chill ran through Duncan when the janitor recognized him. That shouldn't be too surprising, he assured himself. After all, he had been here at the Medical Center for five years. But was he just as a familiar face, or did the janitor really know who he was?

"Why? Since when?" he asked.

"Dr. Carter sent out a letter last week. Said if you don't have a key, only security can open the morgue office for you after hours."

"You mean I am going to have to go all the way to my car, drive back to my home, and get my keys, when all you have to do is unlock the door for me?"

"You don't have to do that. Just get security down here. They have the master key; they'll unlock it for you."

"Sure. I'll do that," Duncan said.

The janitor moved to the other side of the autopsy table and began work on the opposite gutter. He squirted the cleaner onto the shiny steel and slowly rubbed the spot with his rag. Duncan watched as he repeated the action the length of the table. When he finished, he set the rag and bottle on the table and wiped his brow with the back of his hand.

Duncan stood transfixed to the spot. He had come so close. Only one door separated him from the answers he needed, one plain wooden door with a single lock, but it might as well be a reinforced steel bank vault. If he couldn't think of a way to gain entrance, he was finished.

He suddenly felt very tired. The climb had exhausted him and his head was throbbing; the pain in his temples was so severe that it affected his vision. If he could get rid of the pain, maybe he could think of a way out of his predicament.

He slumped onto a nearby stool and began to massage his temples, pressing his thumbs hard into the tense muscles on each side of his head where a pounding pressure behind his eyes threatened to explode and force the bony plates of his skull to buckle outward. He considered again the possibility of an aneurysm. People with concussions needed to rest, not climb buildings.

"Headache?" the black man asked.

Duncan grimaced as he rubbed his head. "A killer."

"I know the feeling." The janitor searched his shirt pocket for a small blue and white package of folded paper. "Here, take this. These powders are the only thing that will touch the headaches I get."

Duncan took the paper from the janitor's outstretched arm.

"Thanks. I'll take it on the way out," he said as he stuffed it into his clinic coat.

The older man considered Duncan for a long moment before he spoke.

"You know, you got a lot of guts to show back up around here when everybody and his brother is looking for you."

Duncan stopped rubbing his head. The janitor had crossed the room to a cadaver storage tray. He opened the drawer and checked the toe tag on the cadaver as he consulted a list on a clip board. Satisfied that the names matched, he shut the drawer.

"You're not a janitor. You're the Diener," Duncan gave voice to his thoughts.

"Uh-huh. I'm the Diener."

"You know who I am?"

"Yep. You're the young doctor that everyone is looking for. Some people here think you killed that Jeter boy."

"They do?"

"Why else would everybody be looking for you?"

"I had hoped that people would think I was dead."

267

The Diener nodded. "Well, most people do. But you haven't got everyone fooled."

"No?"

"No. That's how I knew who you were. That Dr. Nystrom said for me to expect you. Said you would show up here eventually."

"Nystrom? He said that?"

"He said you wasn't dead, that you would have to come here to the morgue office."

The Diener leaned back against the counter and folded his arms. "I don't know about him. He's an awfully smart feller -- that's what people say, at least -- but he sure is different. I don't think he's the kind of doctor I would want looking at me if I were sick."

Duncan closed his eyes again. The pain inside his head had not eased. An artery had burst, he was convinced. The pressure inside his skull would increase until he collapsed. He hoped he would be unconscious before the pain became too severe.

"Are you going to call security?"

"Son, I'm the Diener; I ain't the police. What did you do, anyway, to get in this deep kind of trouble?"

"Deep kind of trouble. I like that. I am definitely in the deep kind." Duncan smiled in spite of the pain. He thought back on the last few weeks of his life. It had taken an incredible accumulation of small, almost insignificant coincidences for him to arrive at this degree of peril, like the proverbial butterfly that can affect the weather by the flapping of its wings.

"What did I do?" he asked aloud and promptly answered his own question. "Hell if I know."

The Diener clapped his hands together and let out a short, deep bark of a laugh.

"Now that's an honest answer if ever I heard one," he chuckled. "I had a brother-in-law. He stayed in trouble. Every time he got caught, he said he was innocent. A victim of mistaken identity, he claimed. Even if he was caught red-handed, he always claimed he wasn't guilty.

"Now the innocent ones, the ones who really get screwed by the system, the ones who get hit by the train when they ain't looking, they say what you just said, 'Hell if I know.'"

Duncan looked at the Diener. The old man's face told of a hard-earned wisdom that comes from experience. Duncan looked deep into his eyes and saw a life spent trying not to be screwed by the system, a lifetime of being hit from the blind side, only to get back up, dust himself off, and continue with the lot that fate had designated.

"You know what's been going on in the anatomy lab, don't you?" Duncan asked.

"I have my suspicions. But there's a big gap between knowing it and proving it."

Duncan slowly pushed himself up from the stool.

"That's why I need your help," he said softly. "This could be my last chance to find the proof I need."

The Diener stared at Duncan as he studied his face, then slowly shifted his gaze to the floor. He studied his shoes, scuffed at a stain on the floor with his toe, then he began to shake his head before he shuffled over to where Duncan stood and pointed his finger in Duncan's face.

"I didn't see you tonight and you didn't see me," he said. "You understand?"

Duncan nodded.

The Diener hesitated, scratched his chin, then pulled a set of keys from the ring on his belt.

"Do you know why this door wasn't locked?" he asked as he stepped past him to insert the key in the office door. He paused as he waited for an answer.

"One of the staff must have forgotten to lock it when they left," Duncan answered.

The old man nodded approval. He turned the key and the door clicked open. Without looking at Duncan he turned and headed toward the door.

"Thanks."

"Good luck, son," he said as he turned off the light and shut the door behind him.

Chapter Thirty Eight

Duncan steered through the dark room by memory. When he reached Dr. Carter's desk he felt for the reading lamp and found the switch. From the low perimeter of light he read the labels on the filing cabinet until he found the correct drawer, opened it, and searched the files until he came to the manila folder labeled "Jeter, R. Barrett." He pulled the folder from the file cabinet and spread the contents on the desk.

He read every page of the autopsy twice. He held the consent form up to the light to study the signature and did the same with the autopsy report. He then studied the entire contents of the file for a third time, poring over every word.

One page bothered him more than the others. The final disposition form, the document that was completed when the Diener removed the remains of a body from the anatomy lab and took them to the incinerator, had been signed and dated. If authentic, there was no body to exhume because Barrett Jeter no longer existed. The proof that Duncan needed was gone.

The plan had been brilliant. Flawless, actually. Duncan almost admired the skill required to fake the documents so thoroughly. He knew who killed Barrett and why, but he could not prove it. He doubted that anyone could.

He collected the papers together and replaced them in the folder. There was nothing more to do. He had exhausted this avenue of evidence. He would have to return to the river in the hope that Jay could hide him for a few days. He needed time to think, to find a new direction from which to attack the problem.

A sense of unease filled him. His inner voice, a voice deep within his mind, told him there was more to do. But what? Had he missed something?

He placed the folder back on the desk and started through the papers again when he heard the outer door to the morgue open. From beneath the door he saw the lights flicker on in the other room. Was the Diener returning to finish his work? Or worse, had he cooperated with Duncan as a ruse to keep him there while he informed security of Duncan's presence in the morgue?

A set of keys jangled, then he heard the metal-on-metal sound of a key being inserted into the slot. The door swung open and a white-clad figure turned on the overhead light.

Bill Wammack stood at the door. In his right hand he held a set of keys. In the left hand he held a cup of coffee. A second cup of coffee was nestled in the crook of his arm as he held it against his body to negotiate the doorway.

"Hey, Duncan! I brought you some breakfast. Extra sugar for extra energy."

He sat the cup down on the desk in front of Duncan.

"It's good to see you! I knew you couldn't be dead! I just knew it!"

"Disappointed?"

Bill gave Duncan an odd look.

"Aren't you glad to see me?"

Duncan did not respond. He carefully placed the papers back in Barrett's file, pushed it to one side, and with his other hand pushed the coffee away from him.

"Don't you want your coffee? It's not poisoned. I'll swap with you if it will make you feel any better."

Bill took the cup from the desk and replaced it with his own.

Duncan ignored the gesture. A full minute passed as he stared at Wammack. Finally he spoke, "You were expecting me, weren't you?"

Wammack nodded as he sat down in a chair on the opposite side of the desk. "Yes, I did expect you to show up sooner or later. When they couldn't find your body in the river, I began to have my doubts that you were dead." He peeled the plastic lid from his cup and took a sip of his coffee.

"Find anything?" Bill asked as he pointed to the file of papers on the desk.

"You know that I didn't. You did your job well; you were very thorough."

Silence settled into the room as the two interns stared at each other; neither one moved or spoke. Finally Duncan leaned forward and rested his forearms on the desk.

"Why, Bill?" he asked in a soft voice, "why did you kill Barrett?"

The perpetual smile disappeared as all the expression drained from Bill's face. He shook his head a couple of times, then averted his eyes from the glare of his accuser.

"C'mon Bill," Duncan said impatiently. "The room isn't bugged. I don't have a hidden microphone on me. No police detectives are hiding under the desk waiting to hear your confession. If I'm the person that has to bear the

271

consequences of his murder, I think I have the right to hear it from you personally."

Bill acted as if Duncan had not spoken; he just looked at Duncan with lifeless eyes. There was another silent pause before he finally shook his head.

"Why do you think I had anything to do with this? What makes you so sure that I would have anything to do with the murder of a friend?"

Duncan gave a derisive snort. "Friend?" He picked up the reports from the desk. "I'll tell you why I think that you killed him. First, Barrett would never have signed a release for his body to be used for dissection. No way. He wasn't the type."

"That's completely subjective," Bill countered. "One man's opinion."

"True. But this toxicology report isn't a matter of opinion. It was falsified."

"Why do you say that?"

Duncan held up a sheet of paper.

"Because this report says there were no traces of any drug found in Barrett's body. When I was at police headquarters I overheard them mention that the preliminary tox report was clean. It didn't register at the time, and I had forgotten that important fact until I thought back over everything that had happened."

"So?"

"That's really odd, because the night he died I saw him smoking a joint with a girl he picked up at a bar. I saw him with my own eyes, but this report say he was clean. The SCL found no traces of marijuana whatsoever."

"So?" Bill said again, still refusing to concede the point.

"So that means it was falsified."

"Again, completely subjective. It's just your word against the post mortem signed by Dr. Carter and myself. Is that all?" Wammack almost smiled as he spoke.

"No, there's more. Barrett tried to write a message after he was attacked but before he died. I think he was trying to write the name of his murderer."

Wammack's half smile disappeared as a look of surprise flickered across his eyes.

"So let's put this all together. Who could forge Barrett's consent form to allow his body to be dissected? Someone who had his signature or copies of his handwriting, perhaps an old roommate.

"Who could switch tissue samples to make it appear that Barrett did not take drugs? Perhaps the person who did the autopsy. Someone who could get blood and urine from other patients, patients of which he knew the medical history, so he could guarantee the samples were drug free.

"Who could have forged his signature? Who did his autopsy? And was that person someone that Barrett knew?"

Wammack did not yield. "You can't prove any of that, Duncan. You can't prove a thing."

Duncan nodded. "I know." He took a deep breath. "The perfect crime -- and I can't prove a thing. So tell me. Why? Why did you kill him?"

"What do you think, Duncan?"

"Opium," he said as he reached for the cup of coffee. "It has to be something to do with the opium. That's the only thing that can explain why you wanted the body disposed that way, why you switched Barrett's tissue samples."

Bill's face slowly filled with rage, his composure dissolving in a series of twitches. When he erupted, it was with a violence that shocked Duncan. He sprang to his feet, his eyes full of rage, and slung his coffee onto the desk, the hot liquid splashing into Duncan's face and eyes. Momentarily blinded, Duncan dropped his own cup and pushed his chair back as he stumbled to his feet. He tried to wipe the coffee from his face, expecting Bill to circle the desk and attack him.

But Bill was still across the desk from him when his vision cleared, pacing from side to side across the room in frustration. As he passed his chair, he placed his foot against it and kicked. The chair flew across the floor and slammed against the wall with enough force to shake the framed photograph of Dr. Carter's family from its hook, the glass shattering on the floor.

"Dammit, Duncan! Who made you the Diener? Who made you Barrett Jeter's very own personal Diener? You didn't even like the son-of-bitch. Why didn't you just let him stay dead?"

Duncan watched solemnly as Bill regained his composure and his pacing slowed. His arms, locked tight around his chest as if to hold himself together, loosened and dropped to his side. Eventually he retrieved the chair, uprighted it, and sat down, his energy spent. His face, a mask of frenzied emotion just a moment earlier, suddenly looked haggard. His eyes fixed on a spot on the desk where the coffee dripped onto the floor. He watched each drop, hypnotized, his eyes locked in a daze.

"It wasn't my fault, Duncan. You've got to believe me, it wasn't my fault. I didn't mean to kill him." He turned to face Duncan. "You're right; it was the opium. Barrett wanted to try the opium. We both got high in college, smoked a little dope, you know? I smoked dope a couple of times with Barrett when he shared rooms with me; he talked me into trying it -- bullied me into trying it, really. After he joined the research program, he stole a couple of the opium tablets and took them. The way he described it . . ." Wammack shook his head. He smiled, a dreamy smile of ecstasy. "It was smooth. Really smooth. Not a worry in the world, wrapped in a blanket of tranquillity, floating from one peaceful dream to another. Now I know how easy it is for someone to become a junkie."

The blissful smile left his face as quickly as it had appeared. "And then he came up with this plan. A plan to make money. You know how hard it's been for me, Duncan," he pleaded his case. "I had to work my way through college, hold down two and three jobs at a time to put myself through medical school. I've been dirt poor all my life. And Barrett's plan sounded so simple. He would take a thousand opium tablets from the lab. He said he knew someone who would buy them, someone who would pay ten dollars apiece. That was $10,000 - half for him, half for me. Five thousand dollars," he said in disbelief. "It doesn't sound like much, but it was more money than I had ever seen in my life. And the one hundred tablets, we could hide the fact that they were missing very easily, considering the number of tablets we used each week in our research."

Wammack squeezed his eyes shut, as if trying to forget the memory, and said softly, "So we did it. He sold the tablets and gave me half the money."

"But it didn't stop there, did it?" Duncan asked.

"No, it didn't. A few days later I was checking the inventory and discovered, to my horror, that a container had been tampered with. You won't believe what he had done, Duncan. He had gone to a drug store and bought all the baby aspirin he could find; they resemble the opium tablets we use. He had replaced ten thousand opium tablets with baby aspirin. Ten thousand tablets! He had pushed the container to the back of the shelf in hopes that it wouldn't be detected. I couldn't believe it! What was he thinking?"

"So you came to my house to confront him."

Wammack used his fingertips to wipe off the beads of sweat that had formed on his brow. "Yeah, I came up the fire escape so no one could see me. I tapped on the window when I saw he was alone. It took forever to wake him. I could tell by the look on his face, the way his eyes were glazed and dreary, the way he stumbled to the window, that he had been hitting the opium. I really just wanted to talk to him, to try to persuade him to return the tablets. But it was too late; he had already sold them. I told him we would be put in jail if we were caught. At the very least I would be kicked out of medical school as an accomplice. That's when he got nasty. He said if I told anyone, or if he was caught, that he would swear that I was just as involved with the theft as he was, even claim that I had stolen the drugs.

"He was crazy, Duncan. I don't know whether he had been on the opium for too long or whether his natural arrogance made him think we could pull it off without getting caught. Either way, he was crazy."

He shut his eyes again. A look of pain crossed his face as if the painful memory was too tormenting to recall with his eyes open.

"That's when I lost my composure. I started babbling. He tried to calm me down, saying we wouldn't get caught, how Dr. Chew never checked the inventory, how he trusted us too much. Barrett said he had already thought of a way to fake the data for a series of experiments to hide the fact that the drugs weren't used. It would be easy, he said.

"The argument got worse. I was begging him, 'Please, please, my whole life depends on this, everything I've worked so hard for.' I don't know why you didn't hear us, why you didn't wake up.

"Finally, he had had enough. He grabbed me, picked me up, and slammed me against the wall. My glasses flew off, pens fell out of my pocket. He picked me up again, held me against the wall, his forearm against my throat, his eyes full of hate as he pushed his face up to mine. As we struggled my hand fell upon one of his athletic trophies. He tried to block me with his arm, but I guess his reaction time was slow because of the drug. I don't think I really meant to hurt him; I just didn't want him to hurt me. The next thing I knew Barrett was lying on the floor."

Duncan could not find any trace of emotion on Wammack's flushed face. Bill sat, stonelike, and continued to stare into some distant space as he talked, a close imitation of the cadavers that were held in cold storage in the next room.

"I thought he was dead. He should have been dead. His temple was crushed. I stood there for a long time, shaking so hard that I couldn't think, trying not to vomit. Eventually I calmed down enough to search the room. After I found the money ...."

"The money?" Duncan interrupted.

"Yeah. Almost $120,000 in hundred dollar bills. It was hidden inside the box springs of his bed. After I gathered it all together, I turned to see that Barrett was still alive." Wammack had regained his composure. "He was trying to write something on the floor with one of the pens that had fallen from my pocket. I kicked it out of his hand . . ."

"Breaking the pen and his finger," Duncan added.

"I stomped on his hand pretty hard," he agreed. "I wanted to stop him before he scratched a message into the floor.

"Then I hit him again a couple of times to be sure he would die," he said matter-of-factly. "I left his empty wallet outside where it would be found to make it look like a burglary."

"And the autopsy report? The donor consent form?"

"The consent form was easy. Like you said, I just traced his name from his endorsement of an old check that I had written to him. The autopsy report required more effort.

"I made sure that I would be on autopsy duty following Barrett's death. Dr. Carter has not been working much lately. His illness is progressing, and he has turned a lot of his responsibilities over to me. He left the morgue before we finished Barrett's post mortem and signed the report the next day after it was typed. He trusted me; that made it possible for me to pull this off. I took some blood and tissue samples from other patients and cadavers here in the hospital and substituted them for Barrett's samples. I knew that if the opium was discovered in Barrett's body, an investigation of the research project would follow. I couldn't let that happen.

"I thought the consent form was a stroke of genius. Once his body was stripped into a thousand bits and pieces and these pieces were disposed, there would be no way new tissue samples could be obtained to test for traces of opium if questions arose later."

"But where is the body now? It's not in the anatomy lab."

"I began to worry. The dissection process is too slow, so each day I would sneak into the anatomy lab when no one was present and dilute the preservative in the tank. The Diener couldn't understand why one body had begun to putrefy when all the others were fine. Soon the body was past use and had to be removed before it stunk up the whole floor. The day your house burned, the Diener wheeled the body to the incinerator. And now he's gone. Not a single cell that can be identified as Barrett Jeter," he said, confident in the thought.

"But what if I went to the police, or Dr. Chew?" Duncan asked. "What if I told them what really happened. There would be an investigation. Dr. Chew would check the opium inventory and your theft would be discovered."

Bill Wammack dismissed the threat with a flick of his hand. "It's too late. Over a month has passed since Barrett's death and I've really immersed myself in the endorphin project. In that time, I've run more experiments and collected more data than in the previous three months. Dr. Chew is very impressed with my work. He says he has never had a research assistant so motivated. Of course, a lot of data has been faked. I extrapolated the results from other tissue series. It's not perfect, but it's close enough to withstand inspection.

"The bottom line? If an inventory were to be run on the stock, all the opium used could be explained by the amount of research that's been done. As for myself, I would be glad to take a screening test to verify that I am not taking drugs. Enough time has passed for all traces of the opium to have cleared my body."

Duncan's mind churned as he searched for some mistake, some flaw in Bill's strategy. He was thinking out loud when he asked, "What about fingerprints? The murder weapon?"

"The football trophy? It's in as many pieces as Barrett. I scattered the fragments along roads and across the city. That is, what was left of it after it sat burning in my fireplace for two days.

"And fingerprints? That can be explained easily. I used to live there, didn't I?

"No, Duncan, it won't help to go to the police and accuse me of anything. That would only appear as a desperate attempt to divert the blame from yourself."

Duncan leaned forward and rested his arms on his knees. "But what about me, Bill? How do I get out of this?"

Bill looked at his friend with a look of sincere regret.

"I'm sorry, Duncan. I really am. The day after the murder I struggled with the idea of going to the police and confessing. I could have claimed self defense. Everyone knows how Barrett was; no one would have doubted me. But it's too late now. There is no way I could come out of an investigation and still be allowed to practice medicine after I tried to cover up things like I did.

"And I think about you and that bothers me. It really does. But your involvement is not my fault. You should have left things alone, just accepted his death and let it be. The police would have eventually dropped the case. In a few months, life would have returned to normal and . . ."

"Except for Barrett," Duncan said.

Bill ignored the comment as he rose to leave. "The perfect crime, yes?" he said to Duncan, his face a puzzled mix of pride and regret. "You know, Duncan, you're smart. But not as smart as some people give you credit. If you were, you wouldn't be in this situation." He closed the door behind him as he left.

"I can't argue with that," Duncan said to the empty room.

Chapter Thirty Nine

Minutes passed. Duncan sat at the desk, his face buried in his hands, as he slowly kneaded his forehead, then suddenly froze, afraid that any motion might cause him to lose the thought that had just popped into his head. He started to smile, a smile that grew into a broad grin. Something Bill Wammack had said had given Duncan a small measure of hope that there might be a way out of this yet.

He stood up and quickly left the office, a spring of excitement in his stride. He felt better than he had in days.

Duncan met Deena in the hallway outside of the E.R.

"We can't go through there. They've brought in two suspects wounded in a convenience store holdup. A policeman was also wounded. Cops are all over the place."

"I can't wait. Bill Wammack knows I am here. I've got to get out before he decides to tell security that I am in the building."

"Wild Bill? But why would he turn you in?"

Duncan stopped and looked her in the eye.

"Because Bill Wammack murdered Barrett Jeter."

"What? No, you're wrong!"

"I wish I was, but I'm not. Who's in charge of the E.R. tonight?"

"Norton," she said as he pulled his surgical cap out of his pocket and adjusted it low on his forehead.

"But everyone is busy, right?"

"Right. We might be able to slip out in the confusion, as long as no one asks us to help with patients. It has been a zoo tonight in the E.R., but I think things are beginning to calm down."

He took a deep breath. "Okay, let's go. Just walk slowly, don't look around, and don't stop."

They turned the corner and headed to the E.R. As they entered the treatment area nurses, doctors, aides, and orderlies crossed the room in a flurry of activity,

279

each one too focused on their respective duties to notice the two doctors as they walked through the room, and the couple did not look up to see if they were recognized as they slowly marched across the linoleum.

"We're not going to make it. We're not going to make it," Deena whispered in a soft mantra.

Duncan took a small appointment book from her white coat pocket. "Keep walking. We're doing fine. Look at this book and pretend that we're talking about it."

"My appointment book?"

"Yes."

An orderly pushed a patient on a gurney out of a treatment cubicle in front of them with another orderly holding the I. V. bag aloft, forcing Duncan and Deena to pause as it passed. When they resumed walking, Duncan flipped through the pages of the appointment book.

"What will we do if they recognize you?"

"Create a diversion while I run for the door."

"Like what? Scream? Fall on the floor and fake a seizure?"

"A doctor walking away from a patient in distress? That could backfire, make my actions appear too obvious."

"Then walk on ahead of me. If I see the guards eyeing you, I'll go into my act."

He buried his head in her appointment book as an orderly and a nurse walked past.

"How did you manage this? Four days off in a row."

"It's Easter, remember? Do you have any plans for the holiday?" she said as her eyes darted from side to side.

"I don't know. I'm not sure what the activity schedule will be at Parchman Penitentiary."

At the corner of his vision, Duncan noticed a familiar small figure stroll calmly into the center of the hallway. He looked up to see Dr. Norton directly in his path, his side turned to them, as he rocked up and down on his heels. He had not seen Duncan, but it was apparent that Duncan and Deena would have to walk past him. He stood less than twenty feet from the automatic doors that represented freedom.

Deena hesitated when she saw him.

"Keep walking," he whispered as he took her by the arm.

As they approached, Dr. Norton slowly turned. He looked up at Duncan just as he passed. Duncan did not pause but quickened his pace.

Duncan kept his eyes fixed on a security officer and a police officer that were engaged in conversation as they leaned against the wall next to the automatic doors. Just a few more steps and he would be past them; just a few more steps and he would be out of the hospital.

"Security!" Dr. Norton's voice call out behind him. The security guard and the policeman turned instantly, alert to the sound of urgency in his voice.

Duncan gauged the distance to the exit. Should he run, attempt to brush past the police? A curious sense of calm filled him when he realized he was too far away for any attempt to succeed. He stopped and slowly turned to face his betrayer.

Dr. Norton waved his hand at the police. "Security," he called again.

Duncan closed his eyes as the policeman walked past, exhaled, and accepted his fate. There was no further reserve of adrenaline, no last hidden amount of energy left to carry him past this last hurdle. But when Deena punched his arm, he turned to see Dr. Norton pointing toward the back of the E.R. "We need your help back here. We're having trouble with one of the patients." Deena grabbed Duncan's arm, turned, and walked him past the security guard, out the door and into the winter air.

As the automatic glass door glided to a close behind him, Duncan turned to look back into the E.R. Dr. Norton rocked back and forth, his head cocking upward with each apogee, a look of smug achievement on his face. Duncan gave him a wave of thanks. Dr. Norton, an ex-Navy man, returned a quick salute.

The security officer at the door turned in the direction where Norton had gestured but the light from the E.R. cast a glow across an empty parking lot.

"I'll finish with rounds about eight," Deena said as she unlocked her apartment and pushed the door open with her shoulder.

"I'll be long gone by then."

"You're pushing yourself too hard, Duncan. You'll be safe here. Stay and rest."

Duncan kicked off his boots and stretched his aching legs upon the sofa.

"Thanks, Deena. But it's too risky for you. Just a quick nap, then I have some things to do."

"Things?"

Duncan adjusted a pillow under his head and cocked his surgical cap forward over his eyes.

"Could you call me around six?" he said as he settled into the cushions of the sofa. "Before daylight?"

"Sure," she said as she paused at the door.

"Duncan?"

"Huh?" he said wearily.

"Tell your friend not to make any mistakes."

"My friend?" Puzzled, he tilted his head and peered out from under the cap with one eye.

"Your girlfriend. Tell her not to make any mistakes concerning you. I'll be waiting if she does," she said, then slipped through the door before he could respond.

Duncan closed his eyes and fell asleep with a smile on his face.

Chapter Forty

The sky was still dark as the lone figure emerged from the apartment building to walk down the steps to the sidewalk. At the street, Duncan turned right and walked one block west to the convenience store, the collar of his coat turned up in a futile attempt to protect his neck from the piercing cold.

Outside the convenience store, a man wearing a yellow construction hard-hat stood by the telephone. He wore a gray knit parka over brown coveralls, with several layers of shirts evident at the collar of the parka. The skin of his face and neck was rough and chapped by the weather.

Duncan kept his distance as the workman finished his conversation and placed the phone on the hook. As he turned and walked to his truck, Duncan stepped up to the phone.

In his right hand he clutched a couple of quarters he had taken from a small basket in Deena's apartment where she kept her spare change. In the palm of his left hand, written in ink on his skin, was a phone number.

Before he could place the first quarter into the phone he heard footsteps, the crunch of boots against gravel, behind him. He looked over his shoulder to see the construction worker behind him as the workman's large, gloved hand reached out for Duncan.

Duncan dropped the phone and spun to his right as he stumbled back against the wall.

"Whoa! Easy, fella," the workman said.

"I forgot my coffee." He pointed to the telephone, carefully stepped around Duncan, and retrieved a large styrofoam cup that sat on top of the telephone box, then backed away from Duncan a couple of steps before he turned. Duncan watched him carefully as he returned to his truck, laughing as he slammed the door, and drove away.

Duncan straightened himself and tried to shrug off his jitters. He took a couple of deep breaths then, with his heart still pounding, turned once again to the phone.

Erskine Jeter walked across his kitchen, his slippers making shuffling noise on the tile floor, and poured a cup of fresh-brewed coffee. He eased his bulk carefully onto one of the stools by the breakfast bar and lit a cigarette, turned to squint at the thermostat on the wall, adjusted it, and pulled his robe closer around him. Through the frost on the window across the room he could see the first glow of sunlight on the horizon. He brought his coffee cup to his lips just as the telephone rang.

He listened as he put his receiver to his ear. A smile slowly spread across his face. "Yes, I'll accept." A pause. "Hello?"

"Hello, Mr. Jeter? This is Duncan Russthorne."

"Well, well. I have to admit that not many people catch me off guard, but you surprise me, Mr. . . . excuse me, Dr. Russthorne."

"Call me Duncan," he said as his heart pounded in his chest. "I hope you don't mind me calling collect; I'm a little short on change."

"No, not at all."

"And the early hour. I hope I didn't wake you up."

"Doctor, you should know how us old men are. I don't sleep well. But why are you acting so all-fired polite?"

There was a slight pause before Duncan continued.

"I need to talk to you," he said.

"Good," Jeter said as he took a drag on his cigarette. "I guess you know I've been trying to find you so we could talk."

"Yes, sir."

"Why don't you tell me where you are so we can get together. There are a lot of questions I would like to ask."

Duncan responded with a nervous laugh. "Mr. Jeter, I really don't think that would be a good move on my part, do you?"

Jeter agreed, "You're a very smart man, Doctor, but you are also in a lot of trouble from what I understand."

Duncan's heart beat even faster.

"That is why I called. I want to talk to you about the death of your nephew, Barrett."

There was a silence from Jeter's end of the line.

"I know who killed your nephew and why," Duncan continued.

"I think I know who killed Barrett too," he said in a voice filled with venom. Duncan remembered the look on Jeter's face in the truck at Barrett's funeral. Duncan took a deep breath.

284

"I've heard a lot about you lately, Mr. Jeter. Everyone says you are a very clever man, a shrewd businessman. I have a proposition for you. It's a proposition that could help both of us."

"I really don't think you can help me in any way," Jeter sniffed.

"Yes, I can," Duncan said in a firm voice. "I know who killed your nephew. I know for a fact, no doubt at all. And if I have figured this out, don't you think the police will too? What if you acted on the wrong information? Took retribution against the wrong person? Wouldn't that be embarrassing when the truth finally comes out? It might appear that you weren't on top of things if you were to make a serious mistake like that, wouldn't it?"

"If I were to 'take retribution,' as you say, it might also send the message that I don't discriminate between people who work against me or people who even appear to work against me. That might be a good message to send."

"But why take the chance of Barrett's murderer going unpunished?"

Duncan hoped the silence that followed was a good sign, that Jeter was thinking things over. Duncan noticed that his hands were sweaty in spite of the cold. Finally, Jeter's voice returned.

"What is your offer?"

"Simple. I tell you all I know. You get the murderer to clear me. We both benefit."

"Why don't you just go to the police?"

"You'll understand once I tell you."

At his home, Jeter leaned his elbows forward onto the table, took a long drag off his cigarette, exhaled, and used his thumbnail to scrape a speck of tobacco off the tip of his tongue. He squinted as the smoke curled up around his face.

At the convenience store in Jackson, Duncan stood motionless with head bent and eyes closed as he waited for a response.

Finally, Jeter spoke. "Okay. If I like what I hear you got a deal. Doctor Russthorne?"

"Yes."

"You had better do some slick talking. You understand?"

"I understand."

Duncan leaned against the brick wall and began his story.

Chapter Forty One

At the regional airport in Tupelo, Mississippi, the small turbo-prop jet rolled to a stop outside the terminal. Antonio Pack watched from a window as the ground crew wheeled the mobile stairway out to the plane. The door opened and the third passenger to disembark on the morning flight from Chicago to Tupelo via Memphis was Jefferson Pack.

The head of the EL AZIWA paused at the door of the plane. He was dressed in a indigo plaid denim, brown corduroy pants, and work boots. A red wool vest stood out from beneath a hooded hunting parka. Cuz had to look twice before he recognized the gang leader.

As Jefferson Pack walked into the terminal, Antonio greeted him.

"Hey, Cuz. You look like you stepped out of a *Field and Stream* magazine."

The gang leader did not attempt to explain. He knew the subtleties would be lost on his cousin.

"Hello, Tony. Did you get the truck?"

"I sure did, Cuz. It wasn't easy, though. The rental car companies here don't rent trucks, only cars, so I had to borrow one. We could still rent a nice luxury ride if you want to change your mind."

The look that Jefferson Pack gave to his cousin made it plain that the gang leader was not going to change his mind.

"I'll go get the pickup truck. I'll meet you out front," Cuz said as he hurried ahead, anxious to get away from the disapproving look of his cousin.

Cuz was frightened and worried that Jefferson Pack had decided it important enough to leave Chicago to conduct his business personally. Something important was happening. Cuz only hoped that his failure to silence the medical student wasn't a big part of the reason Jefferson Pack was here.

His uneasiness was made worse by the location. Why hadn't Pack flown into the Delta regional airport in Greenville instead of here in the hills. This was redneck country, serious paleskin territory. There were a lot of things that

286

puzzled him, but he knew not to ask questions. He was in trouble; better to just obey orders and hope that blood still meant something to his cousin.

On the west side of Tonchie Creek, a small country store sits at the intersection of County Road 913 and a narrow gravel road that winds up into the hills, away from the sandy bottomland of the creek. The dirt road has no official name, but the residents of the area call it Ezra Springs Road. As it tracks north, the gravel road dips and winds through the hills. Less than two miles north of the store, another, smaller, gravel road branches off to the west. The locals have no name for this road, but they know not to travel it unless they have business at Erskine Jeter's skinning barn.

"I ain't never been this cold, Hubbard. Ain't you cold?" Ferguson asked as the two stood outside the door of the barn where Erskine Jeter ran his fur trade. They stamped their feet on the frozen ground and waved their arms from side to side in order to keep warm.

"Of course I'm cold," Hubbard answered. He no longer wore the bandages on his face, but his nose and one cheek were still swollen. Half of his face bore a deep purple bruise that had begun to turn a greenish-yellow around the edges.

"I gotta go inside and stand by the wood stove for a few minutes," Ferguson said.

"You can't. Mr. Jeter said to stay out here and wait for a fellow he's expecting. He's got some business with that doctor we brought from Jackson, and he don't want us inside."

"Then what's Mr. Benjamin doing in there?"

"He's got animals to skin."

"I thought trapping season was over."

"It is, but it's been such cold weather this spring that the pelts are still good. People are still bringing 'em in," Hubbard answered.

Behind them, one side of the barn door opened and a black man emerged wearing worn green coveralls; wine-dark splotches stained the front of both legs. A circle of grizzled silver hair showed beneath a green and yellow cap that bore the logo of a tractor company. He moved his legs in a stiff, forced manner, the arthritis in his joints making each step require effort. From each hand hung the pink carcass of a freshly skinned fox.

"What's so important about this nigger from Chicago?" Ferguson grumbled.

"Watch your mouth, boy," the black man said.

Ferguson turned as the black man walked past.

"Gosh, Mr. Benjamin, I wasn't talking about you. Honest I wasn't."

Mr. Benjamin continued down the hill toward the hog pen to one side of the barn.

"You nice to my face but call me nigger behind my back?"

Ferguson hurried to catch up with the man and explain. If there was one person he feared other than Erskine Jeter, it was Mr. Benjamin. Mr. Benjamin was hot-tempered and skilled with a knife, both for skinning furs and carving up people. In addition, he enjoyed Erskine Jeter's total confidence and protection.

"Not at all, Mr. Benjamin. You now I wouldn't do that. I was talking about those fellers from Chicago that're supposed to be here today."

"Don't use that word around me, understand?"

"Yes sir, Mr. Benjamin. It's just the way my folks used to talk. I'm trying to get over it. Here, let me help you." He reached out and took one of the dead animals from him.

Mr. Benjamin stopped at the net wire fence that enclosed the pig yard. A long low plank structure with small doors at regular intervals stood a few yards inside the fence. The black man pulled the carcass back and flung it over the fence. It spun through the air and smacked into the side of the wooden hog shed with a dull wet thud.

The response was immediate. A chorus of squeals and grunts erupted as a stream of russet-colored sows and pigs emerged from the shed. They jostled and fought for position as they converged on the carcass and began to tear it apart.

"When I was growing up we fed ours corn," Ferguson said.

"If you keep 'em hungry enough, they'll eat anything," said the old man.

"I know. It's enough to make a person give up sausage and ham."

Ferguson rocked back on his legs in order to throw the second carcass into the pen.

"Wait." Mr. Benjamin stopped him. "Throw that one over here."

The old man took a few steps along the fence to a separate pen closer to the barn. In the center of the pen was another hog shed, but with a single large opening. Alerted by the sounds of the other hogs, a huge boar, weighing well over a quarter of a ton, stood at the fence and worked his broad leathery snout in the air.

Mr. Benjamin nodded and Ferguson threw the carcass to the boar. The men watched as the boar descended on the carcass with a speed that belied its bulk.

"Mr. Benjamin, why does Hoffer get special treatment?"

"It's 'Hoffa,' son. And you don't want to know. You really would give up your sausage and ham," the old man said with a chuckle as he headed back to the barn, leaving Ferguson with a look of puzzlement on his face.

Chapter Forty Two

Bill Wammack's senses quickly returned to him as he regained consciousness. The twin stimulants of pain and fear snapped his mind into sharp focus.

He remembered the two men who had abducted him as he stepped from his apartment, the long quiet ride in the pickup truck up the Natchez Trace, and the fear that turned to panic when he realized where he was being taken. His nose, lips, and chin were swollen and crusted with blood from the beating he received when he tried to escape from his abductors as they stopped for gas at the small country store. He had yelled for help, but the man pumping the gas had only turned his head. It was the last thing he remembered.

Now he woke to a nightmare. His face throbbed; his nose must be broken. The pain in his face was matched by the aching pain of his arms and shoulders as he hung suspended in the air. He looked up to see the thick hemp rope that tied his wrists together and held him hanging a few inches from the plank boards at his bare feet. All of his clothes except for his underwear had been removed, but the cold was not the reason the he shivered. He had heard of this place. He was in Erskine Jeter's skinning barn.

Pelts of animals, scraped of their fat and ready for delivery to the tanner, hung from every wall and rafter of the building. Above him, stretched on frames for drying, row after row of fur-bearing hides hung suspended from massive wooden crossbeams. The timbers were dark from age and roughly hewn, the fins in the wood showing where the workman's adz had bitten into the grain. He saw dozens of small bright furs from the red fox and the silver-grey fur of its larger cousin. One row of small brown lustrous mink stretched from wall to wall. Beaver, bobcat, raccoon, and other assorted skins filled the barn. The heavy odor of stale blood mixed with a feral pungency hung in the air.

To the left of the door, between the wood stove and the door, was a stack of dead animals, untouched and skin intact. To the right of the door, away from the stove, was a mound of sawdust. The hide of a brown bear covered the wall beside the door.

He lowered his head and feigned unconsciousness when he heard the footsteps behind him. As the steps moved past him, he opened one eye to see a short black man in green coveralls open the grate to the wood stove and add two logs. He picked up a small metal shovel and moved to an area close to Bill. Two ropes, smaller than the one that bound him, hung from a rafter at a spot beside the suspended captive. Directly below the ropes, the man bent to scoop up the sawdust that was stained and clotted with dark brown clumps. He emptied the scoop into the stove and shut the grate as a burst of sparks tried to emerge.

Bill watched as the old man crossed over to the mound of fresh sawdust, filled the shovel with the wood shavings and brought it to dump on the floor where he had just cleaned. He selected a gray fox from the pile of dead animals, its teeth bared in a frozen grimace of death, and returned to the area where he had prepared the fresh sawdust. He quickly tied one of the hind legs of the fox to each rope. From his left pocket he pulled a whet stone, from his right pocket a knife.

It was a small but wicked knife, a miniature version of a Bowie knife. The shiny blade flashed in the light of the incandescent bulbs that hung suspended on bare cords between the rows of furs. He sharpened the knife on the stone, pushing the blade away from him, each stroke sounding an abrasive chord. His fingers wrapped around the handle at an odd angle, his knuckles swollen and twisted from arthritis.

He stepped up to the animal and circled each hind leg with the blade just below the rope. A quick incision was made down the inside of each leg, then one down the belly all the way to the chin. This done, he moved back up to the hind legs. He freed the hide from the underlying fascia with quick, short flicks of the knife until a few inches of fur hung loose on each leg.

Mr. Benjamin dropped the knife into the sawdust and grabbed each of the leg flaps and pulled down. The hide peeled from the flesh with a faint tearing sound, leaving the exposed muscles covered with a translucent silver membrane, as the whole body was slowly uncovered. With one final jerk, the hide separated from the body at its snout and the task was complete.

"There," he said. He tossed the hide to the floor and turned to the back of the barn.

"Mr. Jeter, he's awake now. He's up here playing possum," he said without looking at Bill.

At this, Bill dropped his pretense and strained to see behind him. He heard the sound of a chair as it scraped across the wood floor. Heavy footsteps followed. The planks groaned and creaked under the slow, deliberate stride of the unseen Erskine Jeter.

"You know who I am, boy?" Jeter asked as he stepped in front of the terrified young doctor.

"Y-Yes, sir," Wammack said when he finally found his voice.

"You know why you're here?" he asked more loudly.

"No, I . . ."

Jeter slammed a fist into Wammack's rib cage. The force of the blow set his body swaying back and forth.

Jeter stopped the human pendulum when he seized Wammack by the neck, his massive fist blanching as he squeezed the young man's throat shut.

"You're here because you killed my nephew Barrett," he said as he stepped close to his victim's bloody face.

The veins in Wammack's forehead bulged as his face turned grey. A sharp croaking sound escaped from his cracked lips as he struggled for air.

"You're here so I can kill you!" Jeter said as he stared into Wammack's bulging eyes.

"But first . . ." he stepped back and released his grip. As Wammack gasped to catch his breath, Jeter motioned to Mr. Benjamin who immediately tossed the knife over to his boss. Jeter deftly plucked the knife out of the air and wiped the blade of the knife on his coat sleeve. His eyes narrowed to slits as he spoke.

"But first I'm going to make you regret killing him." Jeter said as he held the blade up for Wammack's inspection.

"Have you been watching Mr. Benjamin skin those animals?"

Before Wammack could answer, the head of the Redneck Mafia reached out, grabbed a fistful of his captive's hair, and placed the edge of the blade at the hairline. Wammack shut his eyes when he felt the steel bite into his scalp. As the first drop of blood popped out of the skin, a fist pounded against the door from outside the barn.

A look of annoyance crossed Erskine Jeter's face as he paused, then ordered Mr. Benjamin toward the door with a nod of his head. The old man walked to the door and opened it slightly, spoke to someone standing outside, then turned back to Jeter.

"That fella you're expecting. He's here," Mr. Benjamin said.

Jeter turned back to Bill Wammack.

"Hold that thought."

He bent down to pick up the freshly skinned hide. He worked quickly, cutting two long strips of fur. He tied one piece across Wammack's mouth as a gag. The taste of rancid fat filled Wammack's mouth as the raw, inner surface of the skin was wedged between his teeth, and the corners of his mouth split when Jeter tightened the knot with a jerk. Jeter then used the other strip as a blindfold for his captive. When he finished with the knot, he turned to Mr. Benjamin and nodded for him to open the door.

Hubbard stepped into the barn, followed by Jefferson and Antonio Pack. Ferguson entered last and shut the door behind him. He lowered a wooden board into place across the door to secure it.

Cuz took one look around the barn and came to an abrupt halt when he saw the bloody form of Bill Wammack hanging by a rope from the rafters. That, combined with the stench of blood and death, convinced him that he had to get out of the barn, regardless of how it would reflect upon his cousin. He would take his chances with Jefferson later. He would rather sit out in the cold truck than stay in a barn in this remote area with a bunch of crazy huckleberries who hang people up for torture.

He turned to leave but saw the big man behind him bar the exit. He was trapped! He instinctively reached for the pistol he had tucked in his belt but stopped when he felt the cold muzzle of Hubbard's gun pressed against his cheek.

"Hubbard, what-the-hell-are-you-doing? These fellas are my guests!" Jeter erupted.

"He was reaching for a gun, Mr. Jeter," Hubbard said defensively.

"I saw him," Ferguson agreed.

Erskine Jeter looked to Jefferson Pack.

"I'm sorry, Erskine. My man here sometimes acts without thinking." Jefferson said as he turned to Antonio with a hard stare. "He won't do that again," he said, directing his last statement as more of a warning to his cousin than an assurance to Jeter.

Cuz felt all eyes focused on him. He nodded, managed a weak smile, and lowered his eyes to the floor. Hubbard returned his gun to his coat pocket as the tension in the room eased.

"Well, Jefferson." Erskine said as he stepped forward and extended his hand. "It's good to see you again. I appreciate you traveling all this distance."

293

"No problem," the head of the EL AZIWA said as he returned Jeter's handshake. "My business interests bring me back to Mississippi occasionally. I was past due for a visit."

"Why don't we step to the back where we can talk?" Jeter pointed the way for his guest. "You boys stay here and help Mr. Benjamin," he said to Hubbard and Ferguson as he turned to follow.

The two men walked a path between tall stacks of cured skins, through a poorly lit section of the barn, toward a closed door. Jeter opened it for Jefferson Pack as they stepped up into the warmth of the back office, well-lit by a stream of light through the frosted panes of the four-square windows set high along the south wall.

A crude plank table, used as a desk, set against the wall. On it, a gooseneck lamp shone on an open record book with a small pocket calculator to one side. A smaller but equally rough-hewn table stood in the middle of the room flanked by cane chairs on three sides and a wood burning stove on the fourth.

Jeter pointed to one of the chairs. Jefferson Pack sat and studied the room but kept one eye on his host. Jeter circled the table to add fuel to the pot bellied stove.

"I had forgotten how much heat they throw off," the black man said.

"When you were young?"

"Yes."

"You still have family down here?"

"No. No one close. Most left Mississippi long ago for greener pastures."

"Did they find them?"

"Some did, some didn't. The big cities can be just as bad."

Jeter took two glasses from the shelf above his desk.

"Whisky?" he asked.

"Yes."

"Bonded or white?"

"Is the white clean?"

"My own special stock. I made this batch myself. No bugs. No radiators. It's pure and clear."

"White, then."

Jeter poured a portion of the bright liquid into each glass from an unlabeled bottle. He sat the bottle between them as he eased his bulk into the cane-bottomed chair. They raised their glasses to each other and quickly downed their drinks.

The whiskey burned as it dropped. Pack had never developed a fondness for corn whiskey -- there was no taste, only pain -- but it did provide a false sense of warmth. He reached for the bottle and poured them both another drink.

Jeter almost grinned. He approved of anyone who could drink his special stock without gasping and choking and then ask for more.

"So let's get down to business," Jeter said.

Pack nodded. He waited for Jeter to open the discussion but the man took his time. Jeter slid his chair closer to the stove and opened his hands to catch the warmth.

"This is the second month in a row that you have bought only half of the usual marijuana from us."

"I've got a new source that can deliver product with a higher potency. Much higher."

"Domestic?"

"No."

"But at a higher cost, then."

"Yes. But it's worth it." Pack countered.

Jeter paused as he mulled the information over in his mind.

"Are you going to drop us completely?"

"No. I have no plans to do that," Pack assured him. "I can still use your product, too. And, in the future, I may even need more if my plans for expansion go well."

"But in the meantime?" Jeter lit a cigarette and blew the smoke up toward the light that streamed in from the small window.

Pack shrugged his shoulder as he watched the loops and swirls of smoke disperse. "Sorry. Frankly, Erskine, some of the stuff you have sent me in the past has been marginal at best."

"But if we upgrade the product?"

Pack nodded. "I would reconsider."

"And lowered the price?"

Pack grinned. "That always helps."

"What about the bootleg whiskey? Any problems with that?"

"No. No complaints at all. In fact, I could use more. But you will have to help out with the shipping."

Pack saw Jeter smile for the first time as the last Don of the Redneck Mafia poured another drink for them both.

He threw his head back and swallowed the whiskey in one gulp as the smoke from his cigarette curled around his face.

"Good," said Jeter. "Then let's get down to the details," he said as he produced a stub of a pencil from his shirt pocket and began to write numbers on the wooden top of the table.

Chapter Forty Three

Antonio "Cuz" Pack spent the time waiting for Jefferson by trying to think of a worse place to be than the barn where he now stood, but his imagination failed him. He crowded the stove and tried to soak in as much heat as possible, careful to keep his hands in plain sight in spite of the fact that Hubbard had relieved him of his gun.

He watched, fascinated, as Mr. Benjamin continued his work. Cuz had always known where fur came from but had never given any thought to the actual process of skinning an animal. It was similar to the revelation he had at the age of eight when he finally made the connection between the milk in his glass and a cow's udder. He watched the old man work with both awe and a sickening dread.

He was convinced of one thing -- if they started peeling the hide off of that skinny white boy in his presence, he was leaving. It would take more than two overgrown, unwashed country boys with guns and a barn door to keep him there.

He was relieved when he saw Jeter and his boss emerge from the back. Erskine Jeter patted his business partner on the shoulder as they walked, saying "Good deal. Good deal."

As they reached the spot where Wammack hung suspended, Jeter stopped, reminded of a promise he had made.

"Oh, just one more thing. That young doctor down in Jackson, the one your men took some shots at the other day, he doesn't know anything. He's not a threat to you."

Pack frowned, surprised at the extent of Jeter's knowledge about his affairs.

"How can you be sure?"

"Because," Jeter pointed to Wammack, "this fellow here is the cause of all the problems. As you can see, I'm taking care of that."

Pack stood and considered Wammack for a long moment. He finally nodded, satisfied that the situation was under control. He shook Jeter's hand and moved toward the door. Jeter nodded at his men and Hubbard moved quickly to unlock the door for them.

Jefferson Pack left without a word. His cousin followed as closely as possible without actually stepping on his boss's heels.

"Hubbard, you go with them to the county line. See that they don't have any problems. Ferguson, you stay here and help us. We got work to do."

As soon as the door closed, Erskine Jeter turned his attention to Bill Wammack. He stood silent as he stared at the pale body of the young doctor. His eyes were almost closed, just narrow slits, as he considered what to do with his prisoner.

He removed his hat, pulled a folded handkerchief from his hip pocket, wiped his forehead, and slowly turned his hat in his hand as he wiped the moisture from the inside band of the hat.

"Want me to crack the door?" Mr. Benjamin asked.

"It's just the whiskey. Leave it closed."

He dropped his hat onto one of the cane bottomed chairs by the stove, then removed his coat and hung it on an oversized peg on the wall by the bear skin.

As he passed by Mr. Benjamin at work on the bright red hide of a fox, he reached over his shoulder and took the knife from him. At Wammack's head, he made two quick slices with the blade that allowed the strips of hide to fall from Wammack's ashen face.

"What . . ."

Jeter slapped the broad side of the knife blade up to Wammack's lips.

"I didn't take that off so you could ask questions. I am going to ask the questions and you are going to answer. Understand?"

Bill Wammack was quick to nod.

"Why did you kill my nephew?"

Wammack's lips were moving but no sound emerged.

Jeter pressed the blade up on nostril until blood emerged. Wammack's body writhed as he tried to twist his head up above the point of the blade, but Jeter held the blade firmly in place.

Tears flowed down Wammack's face. He whispered through his pain, "It was an accident, I swear. I didn't mean to kill him. Please . . ."

Jeter withdrew the blade and slapped it against his lips again.

He brought his face up nose to nose with Wammack as he slid the blade down Wammack's chin to his breastbone and applied pressure until the edge of the blade sank through the tissue to the bone.

Wammack gasped, squeezing his eyes shut. Jeter released the pressure on the blade, stepped back, and grinned when he saw Wammack open his eyes to

298

inspect the blood oozing from the slit in his skin. Bill's chin and lower lip began to quiver uncontrollably.

Jeter put his hands behind his back, with one hand gripping the wrist of the hand that held the knife, and began to pace from side to side, all the time keeping his eyes locked onto Bill Wammack's bloody face in a cold squint.

"Maybe I believe you, Doctor. Maybe it was an accident. But, accident or not, he's still dead, and you have to pay the price for your mistake," he said in a tone as sharp as the knife blade he had just used.

Jeter paused and shook his head.

"That's wrong. Calling you 'Doctor' is wrong. Doctor's give life, they don't take it, like you did my nephew's. But since you ain't going to be a doctor for very much longer, I guess it's alright."

Jeter continued his pacing, his head down as he studied the plank floor.

Things used to be much simpler, he thought. Ten years ago the young doctor would have been dead by now. And, given a week, there would be no trace left of his body.

But he had better help in those days. Mr. Benjamin was younger then and could handle all the dirty work. Hubbard and Ferguson were a different story. Not that they weren't loyal; they would do anything Jeter told them. They just didn't think too well on their own.

The foul-up at the college had been one of their worst mistakes. Hubbard and Ferguson had let too many people see them. Now his sources told him that there was a chance that the FBI might be asked to join the investigation. If that happened, the trail could lead back to Jeter.

No, he couldn't afford to have the FBI snooping around before all the body was destroyed. Yet he couldn't appear to be lenient in this matter. New Orleans would see it as a weakness, that he was getting soft, and take it as an invitation to start trouble.

He turned to Mr. Benjamin.

"Mr. Ben."

"Yes sir?"

"How do you think the young doctor would be received down at Parchman?"

The old man let out a deep, wicked laugh and shook his head in amusement at the thought.

"Mr. Jeter, there are a lot of fellows down there that would fight over that sweet young boy."

"Then we might just arrange for the young doctor to spend a little time down there."

Ferguson's confusion was evident. "You mean you're going to let him go? Just like that? Without any kind of punishment?"

"Ferguson! Do I have to explain everything for you?" He shook his head in disgust. "Tell him, Mr. Benjamin."

"Remember this, boy!" the old black man said. "If you got the choice of doing a job yourself or letting someone else do it, always let the other person do the dirty work. Besides, we ain't getting paid for this."

Mr. Benjamin quit talking when he saw Jeter give him a slight shake of the head as a warning. Ferguson knew about the horse disposal business but had been kept in the dark about the other aspects of Jeter's disposal service.

Ferguson's brow was furrowed with wrinkles as his small brain tried to absorb and understand what had been said.

"Don't worry," Jeter assured him. "He's not getting away scott free. Now go outside and start the truck; be getting it warm for me."

Erskine Jeter turned his attention to Bill Wammack. He took a deep breath and shook his head, forced to make a decision that was against his instinct. He stepped close to Wammack's face.

"You should consider yourself very lucky, Doc, because I usually don't give people a second chance or a choice but I'm giving you both. I'm going to let you go."

Wammack stared in disbelief. He started to speak but Jeter silenced him.

"Listen carefully."

He held up two thick fingers.

"You have two ways to go. One - you go to the police and confess to Barrett's murder.

"Or . . ." he paused for emphasis, "or you can leave here and not go to the police. You can deny your guilt, perhaps try to run and hide, or try to assume another identity.

"That won't work, I promise you. If you don't confess to the police, anywhere you go, I'll find you. I'll have my boys bring you back to this barn. And you'll never leave.

"Do you understand?"

Wammack nodded.

Jeter rubbed his chin with the back of the hand that held the knife as he looked to the ceiling with a thoughtful gaze.

300

"You're a smart fellow, aren't you? You never could have made a doctor if you weren't. I bet you're thinking that you're a lot smarter than me. Me, Erskine Jeter, just an old country boy with no formal education. Given enough time, you're thinking, you might be able to figure a way out of this predicament, so I had better convince you otherwise."

He reached down, slit the sides of Wammack's underwear, and used the point of the blade to strip the last piece of clothing from his body.

Jeter looked down at Wammack and grinned.

"Well, hell, son. You ain't never been circumcised!"

Jeter reached into the pocket to his coat and pulled out a pair of work gloves. He put them on and walked over to the stove.

"I'm pretty good with a knife, ain't I, Mr. Benjamin?"

"You sure are. You can skin an animal quicker than anyone I know, except maybe me."

"I bet I coulda been a doctor if I'd had the chance. A surgeon, maybe."

"I bet you coulda."

Jeter opened the metal door to the stove. He grasped the knife by the extreme end of the hilt as he held the blade into the flames, slowly rotating the knife until the heat forced him to withdraw. A wisp of smoke curled up from the metal as he inspected it.

"A good surgeon always sterilizes his instruments. We wouldn't want any nasty infections setting up, would we?"

"No, sir," Mr. Benjamin agreed.

Jeter moved quickly before the knife could cool. He advanced on Wammack, a look of vengeance on his face.

Outside the barn, the pigs squealed and ran when they heard the scream.

Chapter Forty Four

The morning sun was bright as Alfie pulled her car into the parking lot of the donut shop near the intersection of Lakeland Drive and Old Canton Road. She killed the engine and glanced at her watch. She was early, as usual, but something told her that Duncan would be waiting.

She tried to distinguish his outline among the patrons inside but the frost on the windows was too thick. Another record cold day had begun. It was a brittle, shattering cold, even by Chicago standards.

Alfie spied Duncan in the corner booth as she entered. At the counter, she picked up a cup of coffee and walked over to him. As she sat down, his gaze never left the window.

She looked him over.

The morning sun streamed across a face that showed a week's worth of stubble. The purple-black shade of fatigue around his eyes looked almost like a pair of thin bruises. His jacket was soiled, a fragment of a leaf clung to the collar of his shirt, and his boots were wet and caked with mud. A few strands of matted hair stuck out at an angle from under his cap.

"You look like hell," she said.

Duncan took a long drag of his cigarette, coughed, and blew a plume of smoke from his nostrils.

He spoke deliberately, as if he were practicing his elocution. "I have been under a little stress lately."

Alfie noticed his awkwardness with the cigarette.

"You haven't been smoking long, have you?"

He tapped his ashes into his empty coffee cup.

"About a week," he said.

She fought back the urge to bum one from him.

"A little bit of advice -- quit now while it's still easy."

Duncan used his sleeve to wipe off the needles of ice that had formed from the condensation on the window.

302

"Like I said, I've been under some stress."

"It's not that I'm entirely unsympathetic about what you've been through, Doc, but you could have saved yourself a lot of grief by coming to me with your suspicions instead of taking this on yourself. This was a real-life murder investigation, not some television detective show. I'm a professional, like you, and I'm good at what I do. You should have talked to me."

Duncan's eyes squinted in anger. He began to speak, but stopped and shook his head. He took a final drag on his cigarette, dropped it into the empty cup, then tipped the cup in his hand until the butt extinguished with a hiss.

"You know as well as I do that the police have certain limits as to what they can do," he said as smoke flared from his mouth and nostrils.

Alfie backed off, realizing that she was pushing Duncan a little too hard. She tried to deflect the anger she sensed in his voice by changing the subject.

"So. Where have you been hiding?"

He took another cigarette from his pack and lit it.

"On the river, less than a mile from here. We pitched a tent . . ."

"We?"

"A friend. We pitched a tent in a grove of trees on the bank of the river. My friend came into town everyday for food and a newspaper to see if Wammack had turned himself in."

"What made you think he would?"

"Because I called Erskine Jeter and told him why Wammack had killed his nephew. Erskine had his men bring Wammack to him." After a pause he added, "I'm just glad they didn't kill him."

The policewoman could not hide the look of surprise on her face.

"Well, that explains a lot. I've never seen anyone as anxious to confess as Bill Wammack. He practically knocked people down trying to get into the police station. What made you suspect him?"

"I didn't suspect anyone at first. Questions kept popping into my mind that left me with an uneasy feeling. The more I tried to answer those questions, the more uneasy I felt about Barrett's death. Then people started trying to kill me."

"And one of the things that made you uneasy was the position of Barrett's hand when you found him?"

"Yes. Did you ask Bill about that?"

She nodded. "Yes, but he refused to comment. We did some checking, though, and found the answer at a pawn shop down the street from where Bill

303

lived. The pawn shop owner identified a picture of Bill, said he came in regularly to sell gold teeth.

"We think Barrett somehow learned that Wammack had become so desperate for money that he was stealing the gold teeth from the cadavers in the morgue, then selling the gold at the pawn shop. Barrett tried to indicate that fact by clenching a finger with his teeth, a section of his mouth which, according to his dental records, had gold bridgework in it."

"Pretty weak clue, huh?" Duncan said.

"Not really, considering he was dying. I've seen stranger things," she said. "Besides, it did accomplish what he intended. It made you curious enough to keep asking questions."

"That was only a small part of it. The fact that he donated his body to the anatomy lab bothered me more. But a couple of things still puzzle me."

Alfie drained the last of her coffee.

"What?"

"The bomb in the locker. Was that Wammack?"

"We think so, but he won't admit it. It was a simple chemical bomb. Amateurish. The pros would have used something more efficient. Wammack has a degree in chemistry. He could have easily scrounged the material from the laboratories at the medical school."

"And the money?"

"Wammack denies he found it. Claims it must have been destroyed when your house burned."

"What do you think?"

"Don't worry," she said. "We'll find it."

Alfie motioned to a passing waitress for a refill. Duncan placed his hand over his cup and shook his head when the waitress turned to him. Instead, he took another cigarette from the pack and tapped the end of it on the table.

"You said you had something for me when you called," Alfie said.

Duncan laid the unlit cigarette on top of the pack and reached into his pocket to produce a small glass jar.

"I don't know if this will help in your case against Wammack, but I thought you might need it."

She took the jar and inspected its contents. Puzzled, she turned the jar at different angles.

"Jesus, Doc, is this an eyeball?"

He nodded.

304

She quickly sat the jar on the table. As she stared at it, she automatically reached for the unlit cigarette that rested in front of her.

"Surprised?"

"Yes."

"A tough cop like you?"

"Doc, I have seen eyeballs in and out of their socket, but I don't usually expect people to carry them in their pocket and pass them around the breakfast table over coffee and donuts."

Duncan grinned as she fumbled in her purse for her cigarette lighter.

"A human eyeball in 10% formalin." Duncan explained. "The last remaining vestige of the recently deceased Barrett Jeter. If the state crime lab will test the fatty tissue connected to it they will find traces of opium in the cells. This will corroborate the fact that Barrett was using the opium that he had access to as part of his research at the medical center."

He reached into his other pocket and pulled out a folded envelope.

"This is a notarized statement from the physician, Dr. Nystrom, who removed the tissue sample. In it he states that the specimen was, indeed, removed from the body of Barrett Jeter."

As Alfie examined the statement, Duncan stood up and began to button his coat. He dug into his jeans, removed a couple of wadded dollar bills, and dropped them onto the table.

"Are you okay?" Alfie asked.

"I just need a warm shower and a little rest."

"Is there anything I can do for you?"

He thought for a moment. "The Dean may have some questions. It wouldn't hurt if you talked to him, in case he had some doubts about my role in all of this."

"Sure. I'll call him today. Anything else?"

His gaze met the frost on the window. "How about a ride?"

"Where?"

"Riley's apartment."

As the car pulled to a stop at the curb by the apartment, Alfie put the gear shift in park and turned to Duncan.

"Good luck in your profession, Doc. You'll make a good one."

"Thanks, lieutenant. If you ever need my help with a case, don't call me. I'm hanging up my deerstalker and magnifying glass."

"You know, Sherlock had an opium addiction. Or was it cocaine?"

305

"He was also fictional. Good-bye, lieutenant," he added as he stepped out of the car.

"Hey!" Alfie called after him.

He caught the door before it shut.

"You forgot your cigarettes," she said as she waved the pack in the air.

He shook his head. "You're right. Those things can kill you. I'll stick with coffee. One addiction at a time is enough."

Alfie wedged the pack between her coat and the jar that sat on the seat beside her and watched as Duncan crossed in front of the car and walked across the lawn.

As Duncan neared the front door, Riley emerged and walked down to stand on the bottom step.

They embraced without a word. He grasped her with both arms and buried his face into her sweater. Her right hand clutched the short, tangled hair at the back of his neck as she squeezed him close. She kissed him gently on the temple and whispered in his ear, then took him by the hand and led him inside.